"Watase has a gift for involving characterization. Though she sometimes uses Miaka for laughs, she also lets us see her heroine's compassion and courage. The Emperor Hotohori is not quite as noble as he seems, nor is the wily Tamahome as self-centered as he would have others believe him to be. Even treacherous empress-candidate Nuriko has many levels. Watase's storytelling is an engaging one. She paces her story well and knows when to pump up the energy."

—Tony Isabella

"One of the best manga ever, it can be enjoyed by female and male readers alike."

—Protoculture Addicts

"There are two points in Fushigi Yûgi's favor. The first is Watase herself, who has written margin notes for the compilation. Unlike many creators who rabbit on about trivia, she wants to talk about her craft, and has interesting points to make about research and the creative process. The second is that the strip succeeds in being quite charming; in spite of its derivative storyline—at one point a character admits the similarities to an RPG! But any comic that leaves me wanting to know what happens next definitely delivers value for money."

—Manga Max

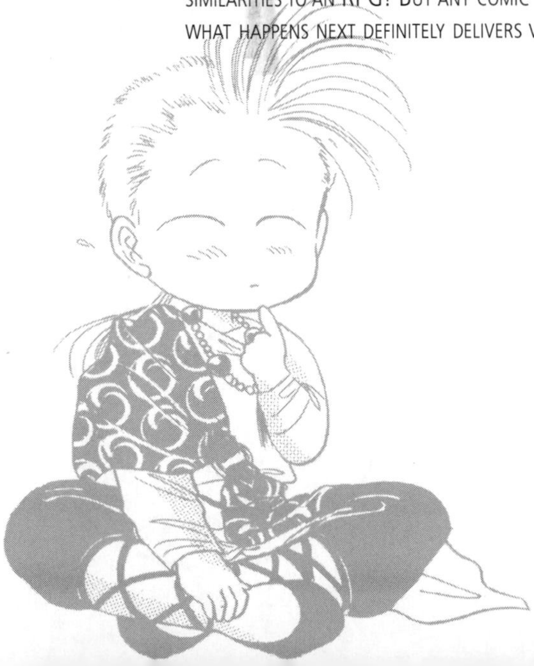

ANIMERICA EXTRA GRAPHIC NOVEL

# fushigi yûgi™

*The Mysterious Play*
*VOL. 7: CASTAWAY*

# Fushigi Yûgi™
## The Mysterious Play
### VOL. 7: CASTAWAY

This volume contains the FUSHIGI YÛGI installments from ANIMERICA EXTRA
Vol. 4, No. 12 through Vol. 5, No. 6 in their entirety.

## STORY & ART BY YÛ WATASE

English Adaptation/Yuji Oniki
Touch-Up Art & Lettering/Bill Spicer
Cover Design/Hidemi Sahara
Layout & Graphics/Carolina Ugalde
Editor/William Flanagan

Managing Editor/Annette Roman
VP of Sales & Marketing/Rick Bauer
Editor-in-Chief/Hyoe Narita
Publisher/Seiji Horibuchi

Printed in Canada

Published by Viz Communications, Inc.
P.O. Box 77010, San Francisco, CA 94107

10 9 8 7 6 5 4 3 2 1
First printing, October 2002

ANIMERICA EXTRA GRAPHIC NOVEL

# fushigi yûgi™

*The Mysterious Play*
*VOL. 7: CASTAWAY*

*Story & Art By*
**YÛ WATASE**

# CONTENTS

# STORY THUS FAR

Chipper junior-high-school girl Miaka and her best friend Yui are physically drawn into the world of a strange book—*The Universe of the Four Gods*. Miaka is offered the role of the lead character, the Priestess of the god Suzaku, and is charged with gathering the seven Celestial Warriors of Suzaku who will help her complete a quest to save the nation of Hong-Nan, and in the process grant her any wish she wants.

Yui's fate is much crueler than Miaka's. Upon entering the book, Yui suffers rape and manipulation which drives her to attempt suicide. Now, Yui has become the Priestess of the god Seiryu, the enemy of Suzaku and Miaka.

The only way for Miaka to gain back the trust of her former best friend is to summon the god Suzaku and wish to be reconciled with Yui. But after a desperate struggle to gather her seven warriors, one warrior turns out to be a Seiryu spy, and the summoning ceremony is spoiled. With the summoning ceremony ruined, the oracle, Tai Yi-Jun, has suggested a new quest to summon the god.

*THE UNIVERSE OF THE FOUR GODS is based on ancient China, but Japanese pronunciation of Chinese names differs slightly from their Chinese equivalents. Here is a short glossary of the Japanese pronunciation of the Chinese names in this graphic novel:*

| CHINESE | JAPANESE | PERSON OR PLACE | MEANING |
| --- | --- | --- | --- |
| Hong-Nan | Konan | Southern Kingdom | Crimson South |
| Qu-Dong | Kutô | Eastern Kingdom | Gathered East |
| Bei-Jia | Hokkan | Northern Kingdom | Armored North |
| Tai Yi-Jun | Tai Itsukun | An Oracle | Preeminent Person |
| Shentso-Pao | Shinzahô | A Treasure | God's Seat Jewel |
| Ming-Ho | Meiga | A Canal | Signature Stream |
| Zhong-Rong | Chûei | Second Son | Loyalty & Honor |
| Chun-Jing | Shunkei | Third Son | Spring & Respect |
| Yu-Lun | Gyokuran | Eldest Daughter | Jewel & Orchid |
| Jie-Lian | Yuiren | Youngest Daughter | Connection & Lotus |
| Kang-Lin | Kôrin | A lady of Hong-Nan | Peaceful Jewel |
| Liu-Chuan | Ryûen | Nuriko's given name | Willowy Beauty |

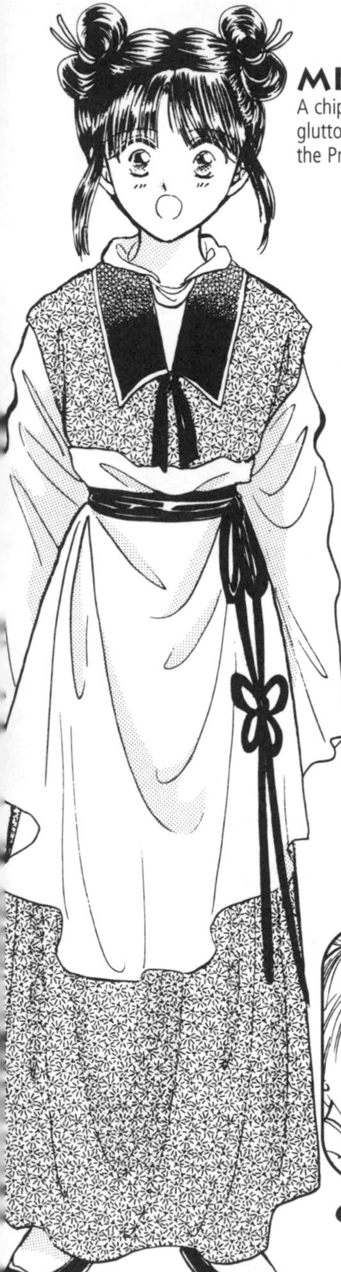

**MIAKA**
A chipper junior-high-school glutton who has become the Priestess of Suzaku.

THE CELESTIAL WARRIORS OF SUZAKU

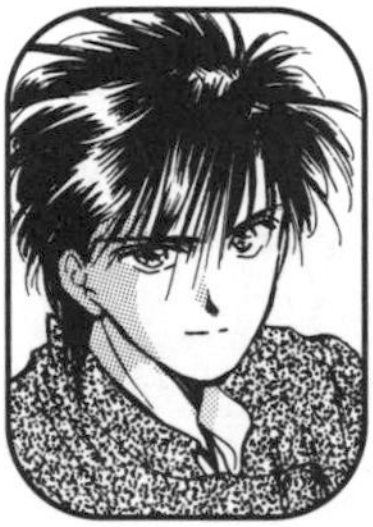

**TAMAHOME**
A dashing miser.

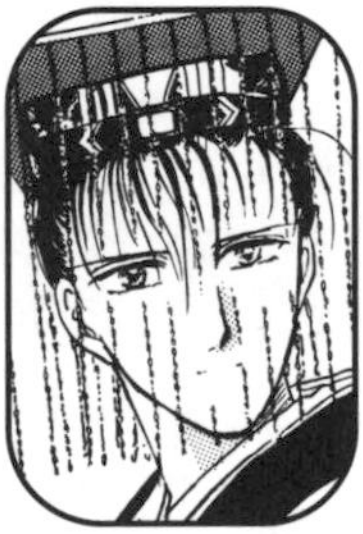

**HOTOHORI**
The beautiful emperor of Hong-Nan.

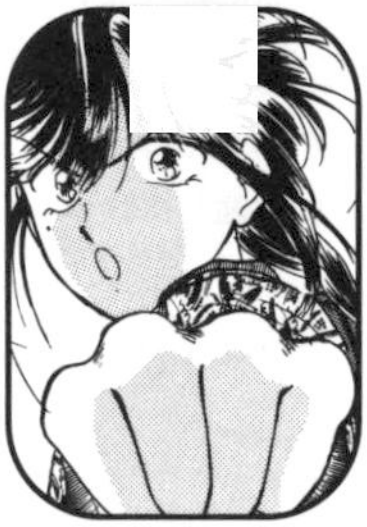

**NURIKO**
An amazingly strong cross-dresser.

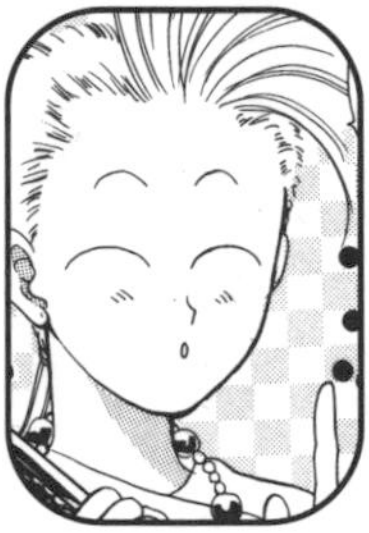

**CHICHIRI**
Former disciple of the oracle.

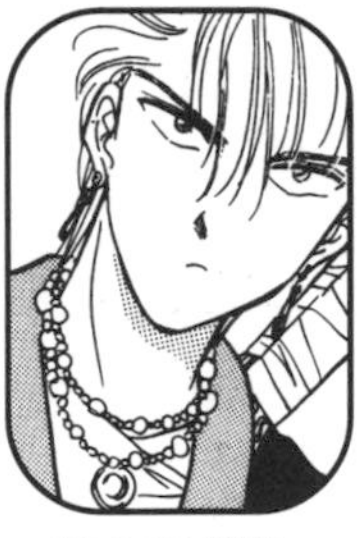

**TASUKI**
An ornery ex-bandit.

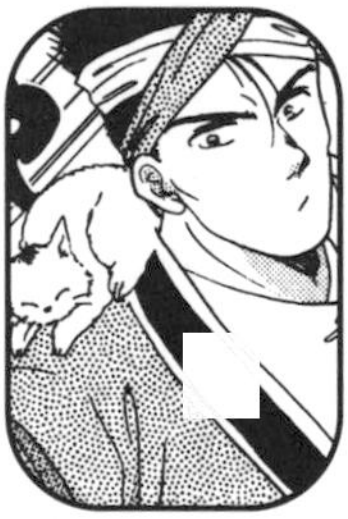

**MITSUKAKE**
A silent healer.

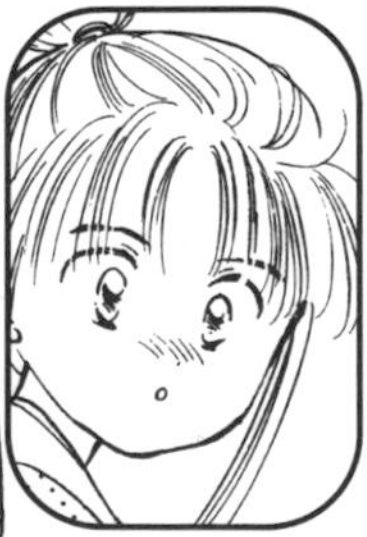

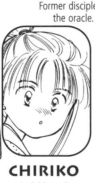

**CHIRIKO**
A child prodigy.

THE FOLLOWERS OF SEIRYU

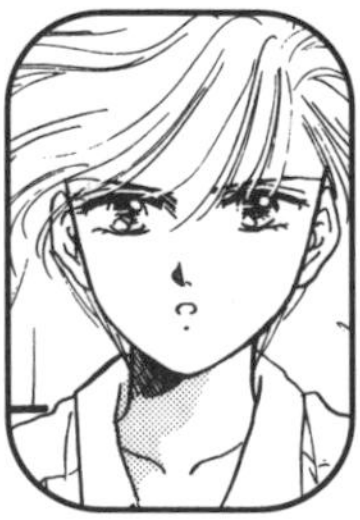

**YUI**
Miaka's former best friend, but now her enemy and the Priestess of Seiryu.

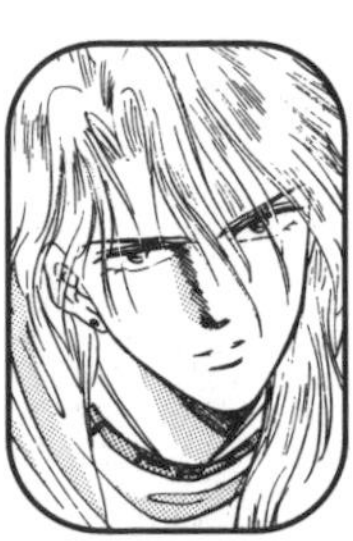

**NAKAGO**
A general of Qu-Dong and a Celestial Warrior of Seiryu.

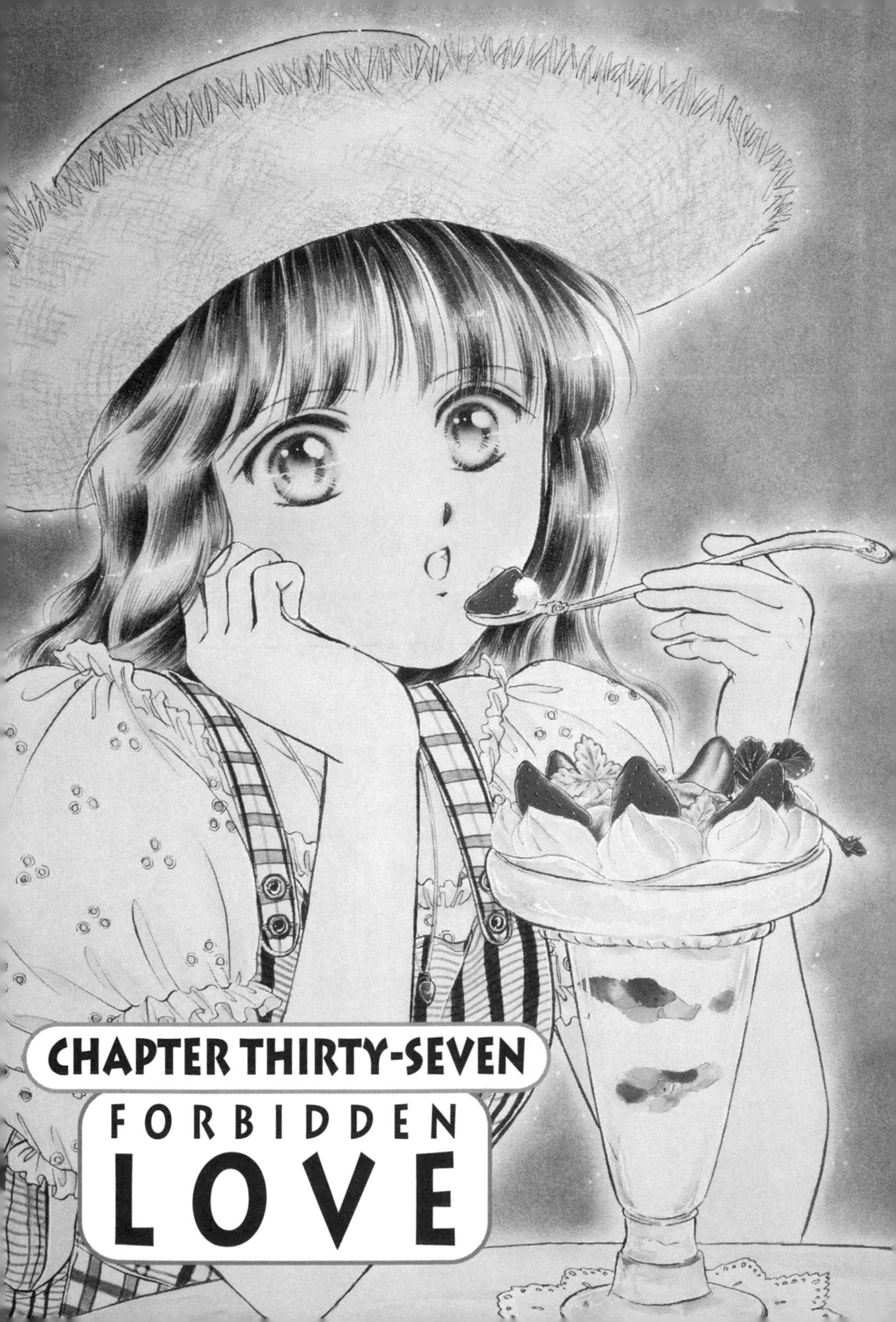
CHAPTER THIRTY-SEVEN
FORBIDDEN
LOVE

MIAO NIOH- AN
妙 寿 安

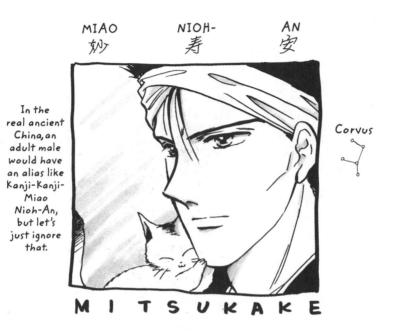

In the real ancient China, an adult male would have an alias like Kanji-Kanji-Miao Nioh-An, but let's just ignore that.

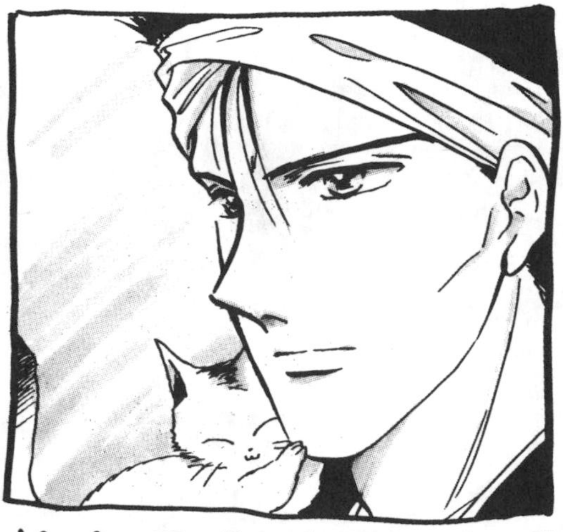

Corvus

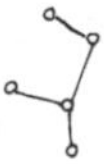

# MITSUKAKE

- Doctor in Shenshan near Changhung in Northern Hong-Nan.
- Age: Currently 22-years old... *looks older though.*
- Personality: Solitary

Was in love with Shao-Huan, the daughter of a landowner in Shengshan, but they were never married.

- Special Power: Healing
- Hobby: Taking care of animals
- Height: 6' 6"
- Blood Type: O

- He's silent, and because he's expressionless most of the time, he's thought to be aloof. But he's actually just shy and doesn't know how to be more outgoing.

He's very kind to the weak, animals, and the elderly. *And kids, and of course the sick.* He's utterly dedicated to healing. A calm, kind man. Deep inside he still cherishes the memory of the late Shao-Huan.

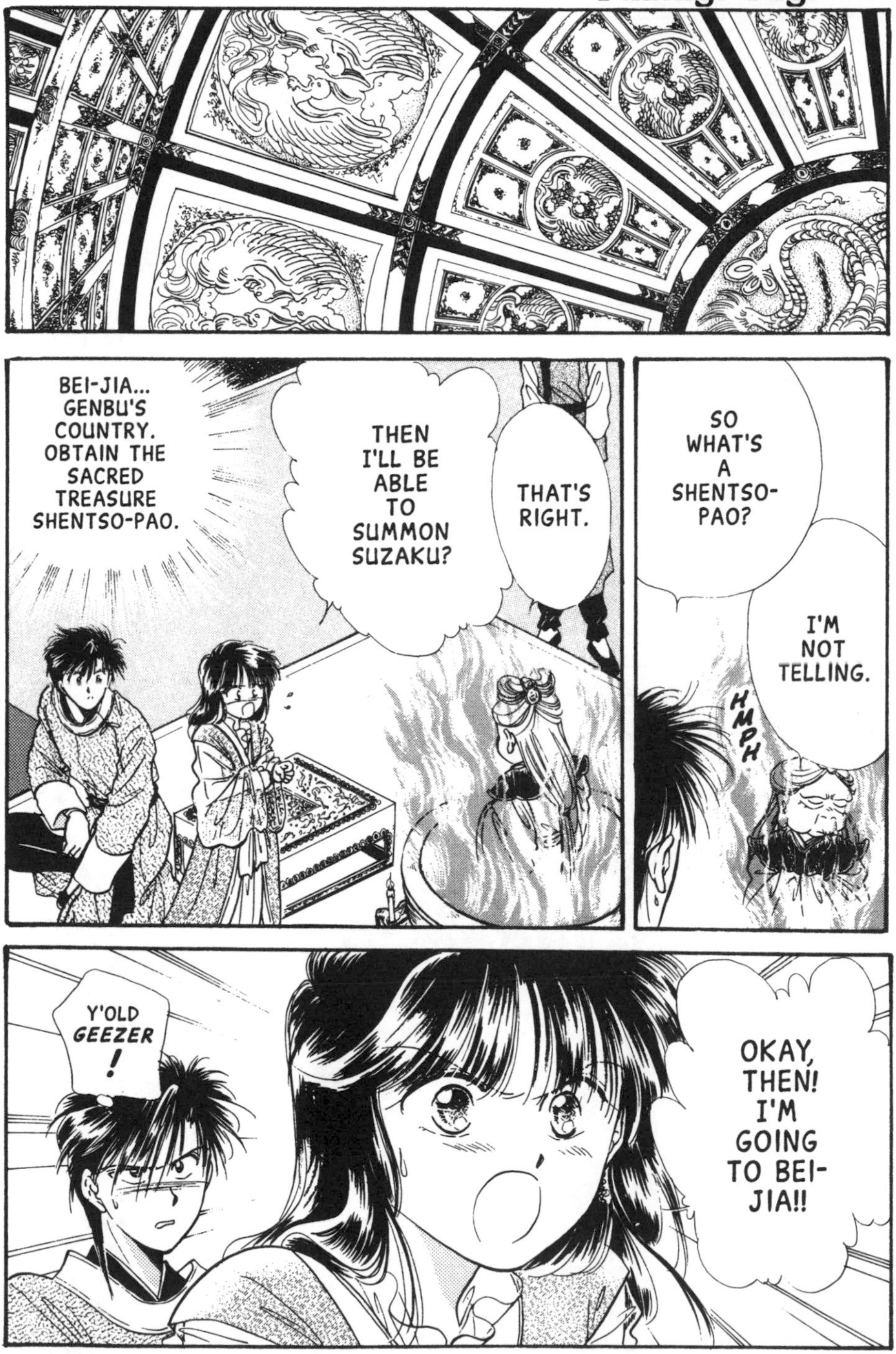
BEI-JIA... GENBU'S COUNTRY. OBTAIN THE SACRED TREASURE SHENTSO-PAO.
THEN I'LL BE ABLE TO SUMMON SUZAKU?
THAT'S RIGHT.
SO WHAT'S A SHENTSO-PAO?
I'M NOT TELLING.
HMPH
Y'OLD *GEEZER*!
OKAY, THEN! I'M GOING TO BEI-JIA!!

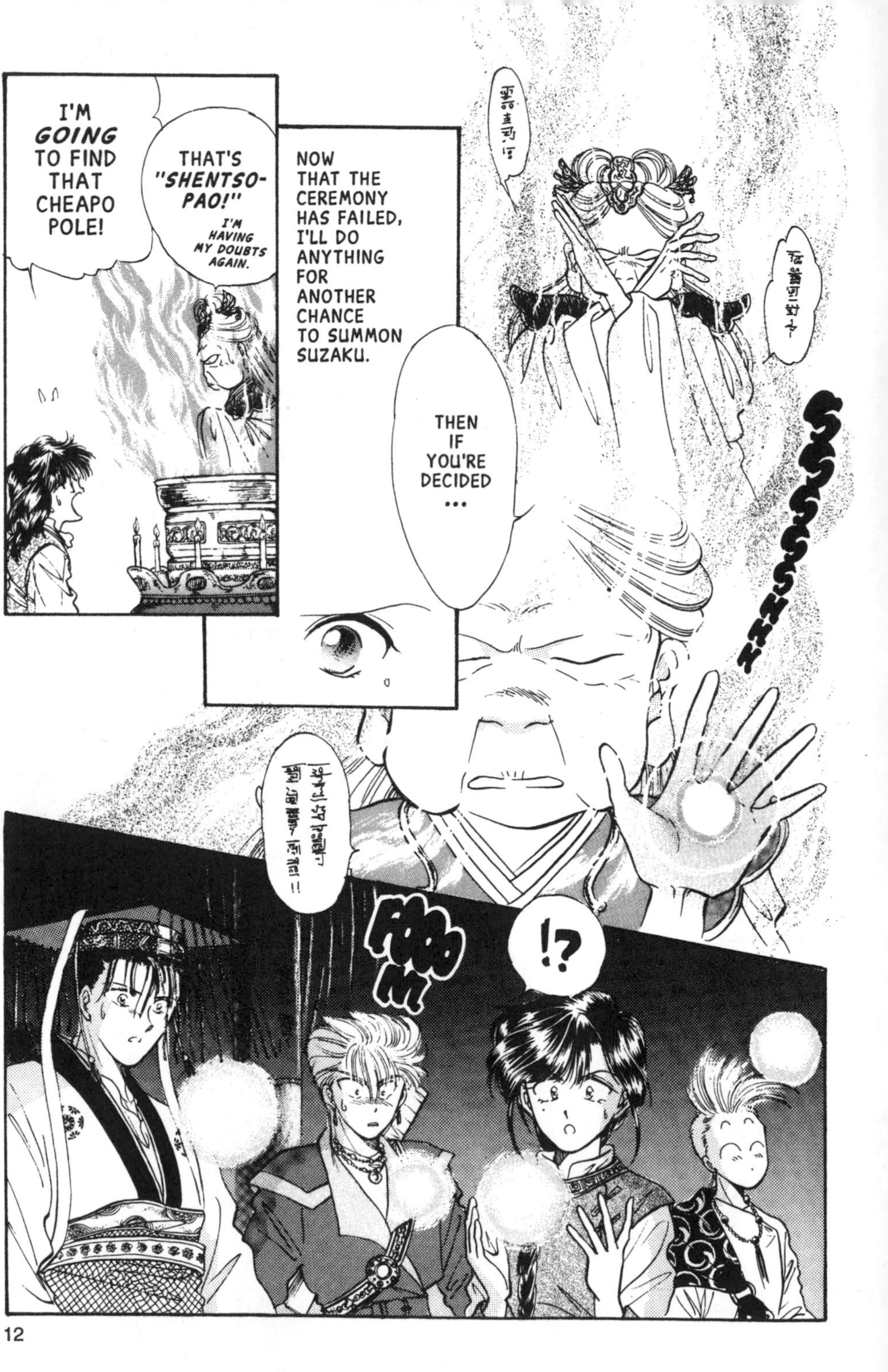
I'M GOING TO FIND THAT CHEAPO POLE!
THAT'S "SHENTSO-PAO!"
I'M HAVING MY DOUBTS AGAIN.
NOW THAT THE CEREMONY HAS FAILED, I'LL DO ANYTHING FOR ANOTHER CHANCE TO SUMMON SUZAKU.
THEN IF YOU'RE DECIDED ...
SSSSSSHHHH
FOOOM
!?

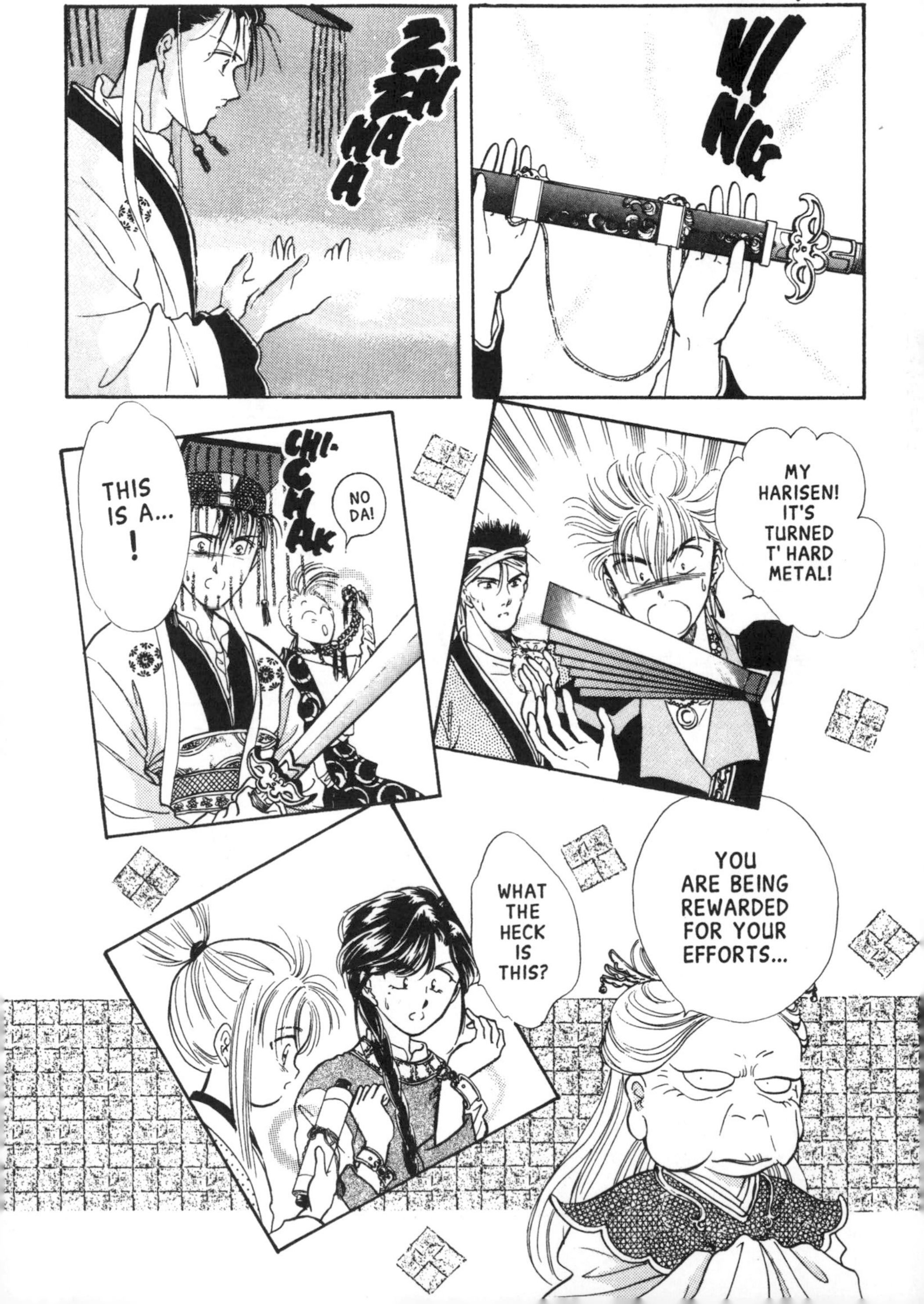
ZZHHAAA
VING
THIS IS A... !
CHI-CHAK
NO DA!
MY HARISEN! IT'S TURNED T' HARD METAL!
WHAT THE HECK IS THIS?
YOU ARE BEING REWARDED FOR YOUR EFFORTS...

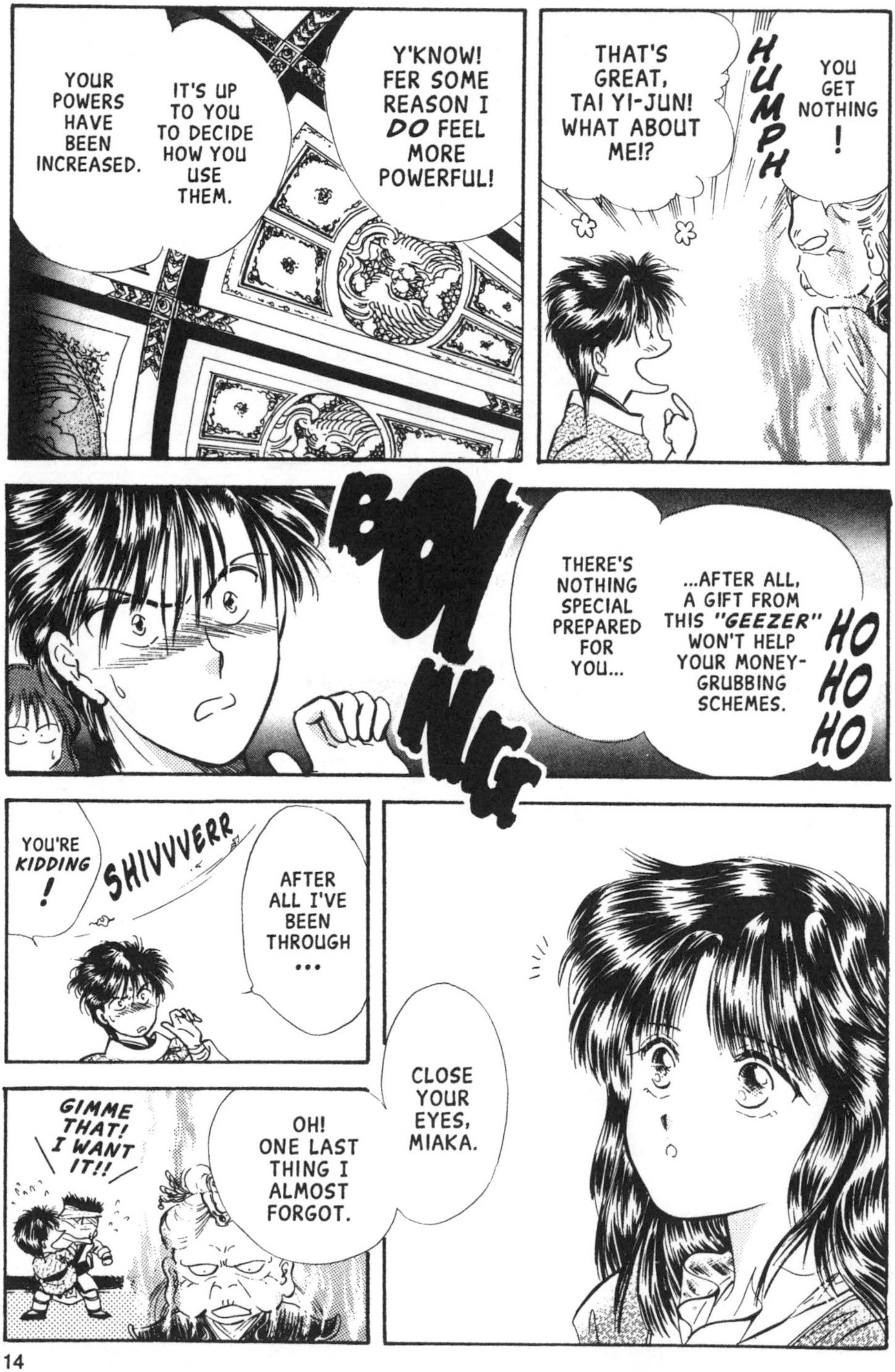
YOUR POWERS HAVE BEEN INCREASED.
IT'S UP TO YOU TO DECIDE HOW YOU USE THEM.
Y'KNOW! FER SOME REASON I DO FEEL MORE POWERFUL!
THAT'S GREAT, TAI YI-JUN! WHAT ABOUT ME!?
HUMPH
YOU GET NOTHING!
BOING
THERE'S NOTHING SPECIAL PREPARED FOR YOU...
...AFTER ALL, A GIFT FROM THIS "GEEZER" WON'T HELP YOUR MONEY-GRUBBING SCHEMES.
HO HO HO
YOU'RE KIDDING!
SHIVVVERR
AFTER ALL I'VE BEEN THROUGH...
GIMME THAT! I WANT IT!!
OH! ONE LAST THING I ALMOST FORGOT.
CLOSE YOUR EYES, MIAKA.

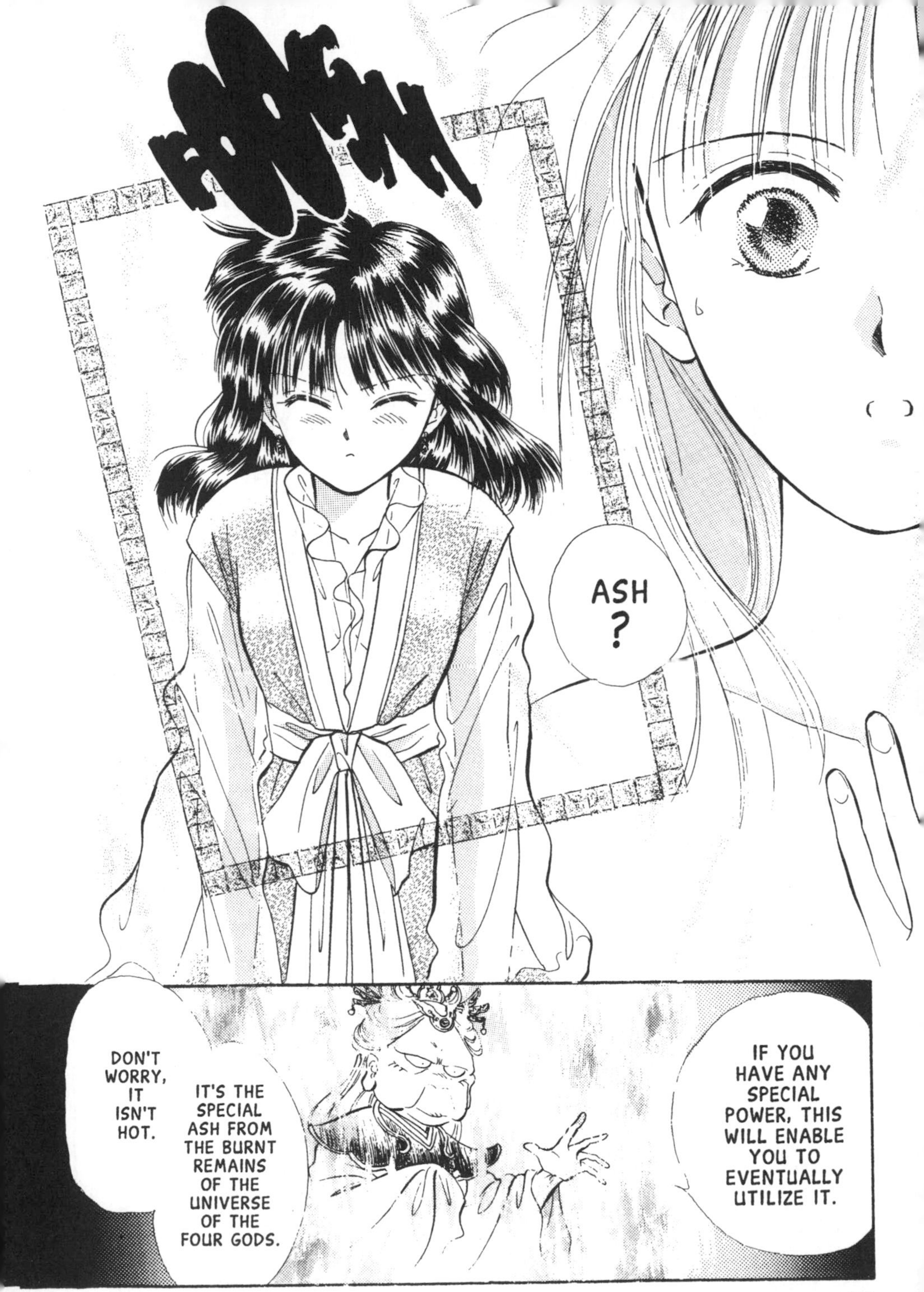
ASH ?
DON'T WORRY, IT ISN'T HOT.
IT'S THE SPECIAL ASH FROM THE BURNT REMAINS OF THE UNIVERSE OF THE FOUR GODS.
IF YOU HAVE ANY SPECIAL POWER, THIS WILL ENABLE YOU TO EVENTUALLY UTILIZE IT.

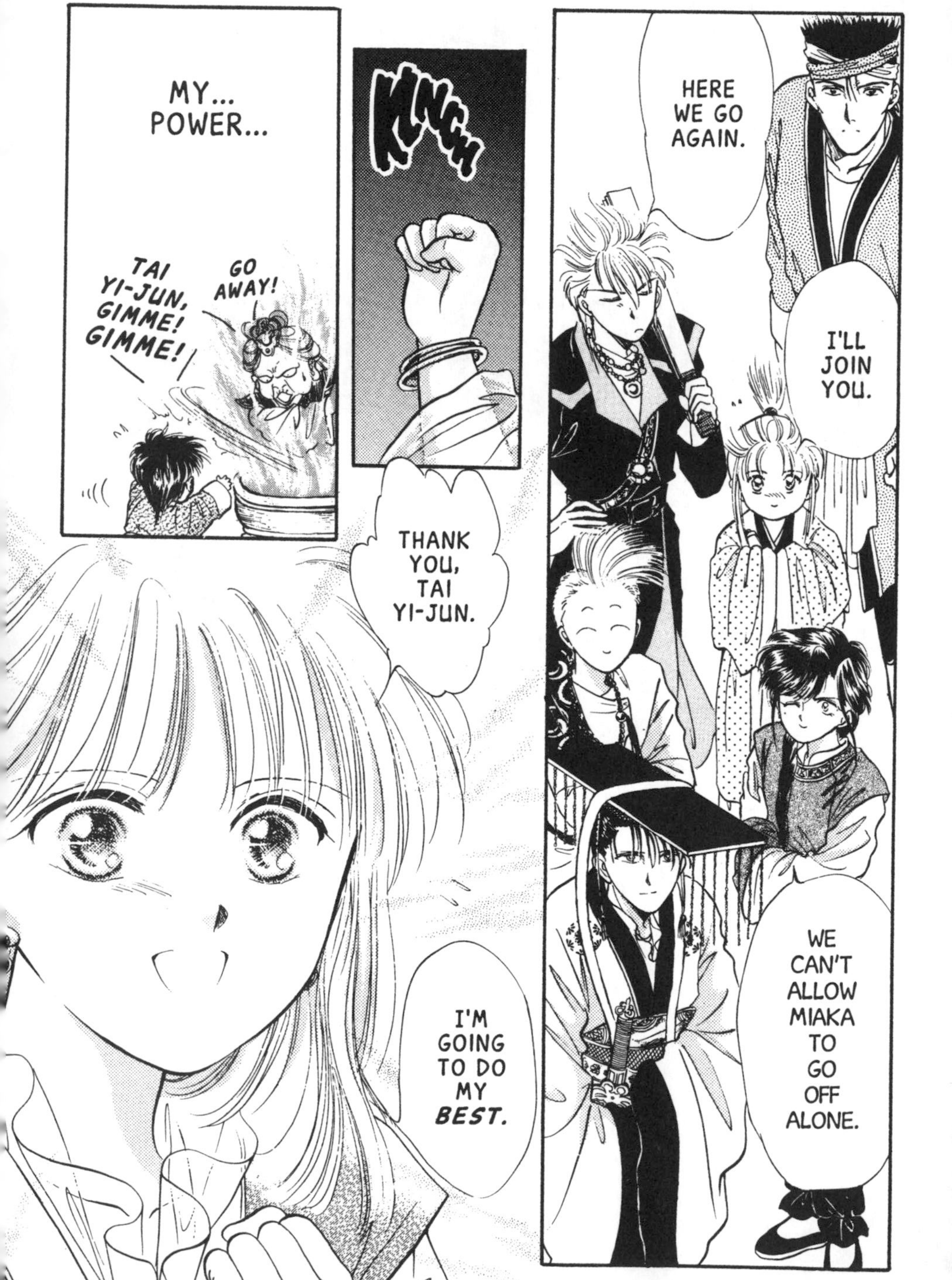
MY... POWER...
TAI YI-JUN, GIMME! GIMME!
GO AWAY!
KLINCH
THANK YOU, TAI YI-JUN.
I'M GOING TO DO MY *BEST.*
HERE WE GO AGAIN.
I'LL JOIN YOU.
WE CAN'T ALLOW MIAKA TO GO OFF ALONE.

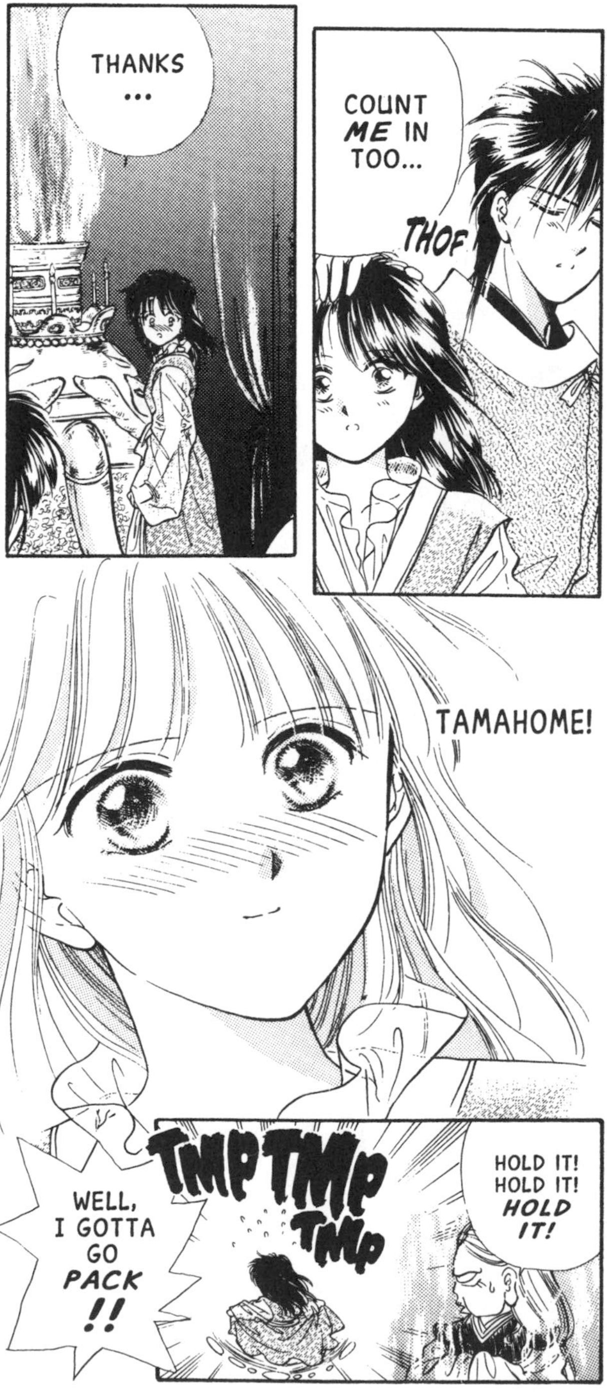
THANKS ...
COUNT *ME* IN TOO...
THOF
TAMAHOME!
WELL, I GOTTA GO *PACK* !!
TMP TMP TMP
HOLD IT! HOLD IT! *HOLD IT!*

Now, we've finally reached Volume 7. Looking over the covers of these graphic novels I can't help but be moved. After finishing chapter 42 (the last chapter in this volume), I went to China to do some research. Only three days after returning, I had to attend a shōjo manga event, so I had a pretty rough summer. I'd like to thank you all for coming to the event. Those of you who live in the provinces, if you're upset the event was held in Tokyo, I'm sure you'll have an opportunity. (Actually I've appeared in events in Sendai, Nagoya, and twice on my home turf in Osaka, so I might show up somewhere in your region.) Some of my fans traveled from far, far away to attend the event, but I have to say I was surprised by the fan who came from Taiwan! She tried so hard to talk to me in Japanese... That's right! Because Fushigi is published in Taiwan I have been receiving the occasional fan mail from over there. Of course I can't read any of it. So I had my editor get a Taiwanese copy of "Prepubescence" (the Japanese title is Shishunki Miman Okotowari, but over there it's "Si Chun Qi Wei Man"). It was incredible because Asuka and the others are all speaking Taiwanese! Even these 1/3rd-page free-talk sections were translated. "Fushigi Yūgi" is called "Meng Huan Yiou Xi" or "Dream Play" (this actually sounds cooler), and the free-talk sections should be translated, too! I would like to thank all my readers in Taiwan!

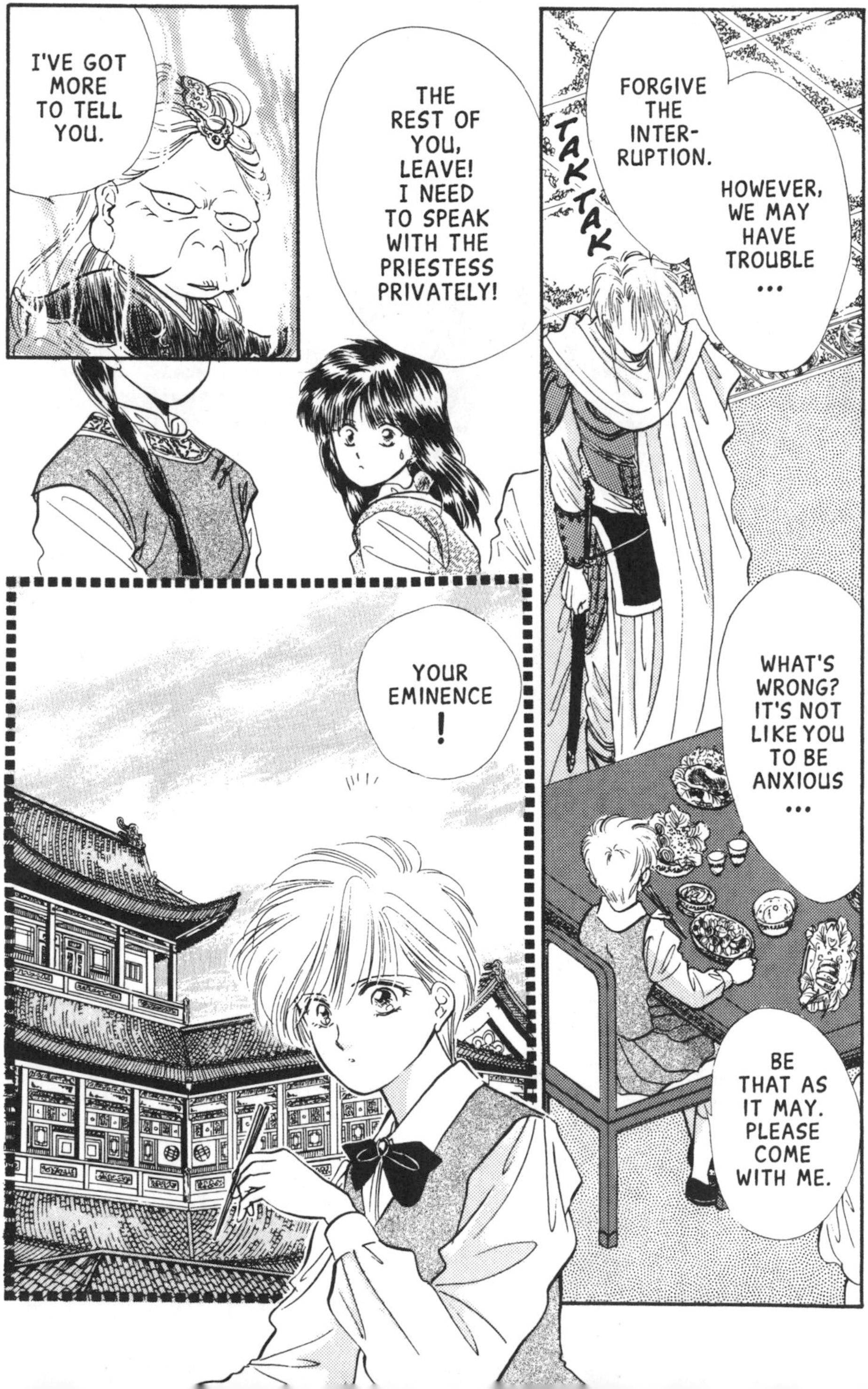
I'VE GOT MORE TO TELL YOU.
THE REST OF YOU, LEAVE! I NEED TO SPEAK WITH THE PRIESTESS PRIVATELY!
YOUR EMINENCE !
TAK TAK
FORGIVE THE INTER-RUPTION.
HOWEVER, WE MAY HAVE TROUBLE ...
WHAT'S WRONG? IT'S NOT LIKE YOU TO BE ANXIOUS ...
BE THAT AS IT MAY. PLEASE COME WITH ME.

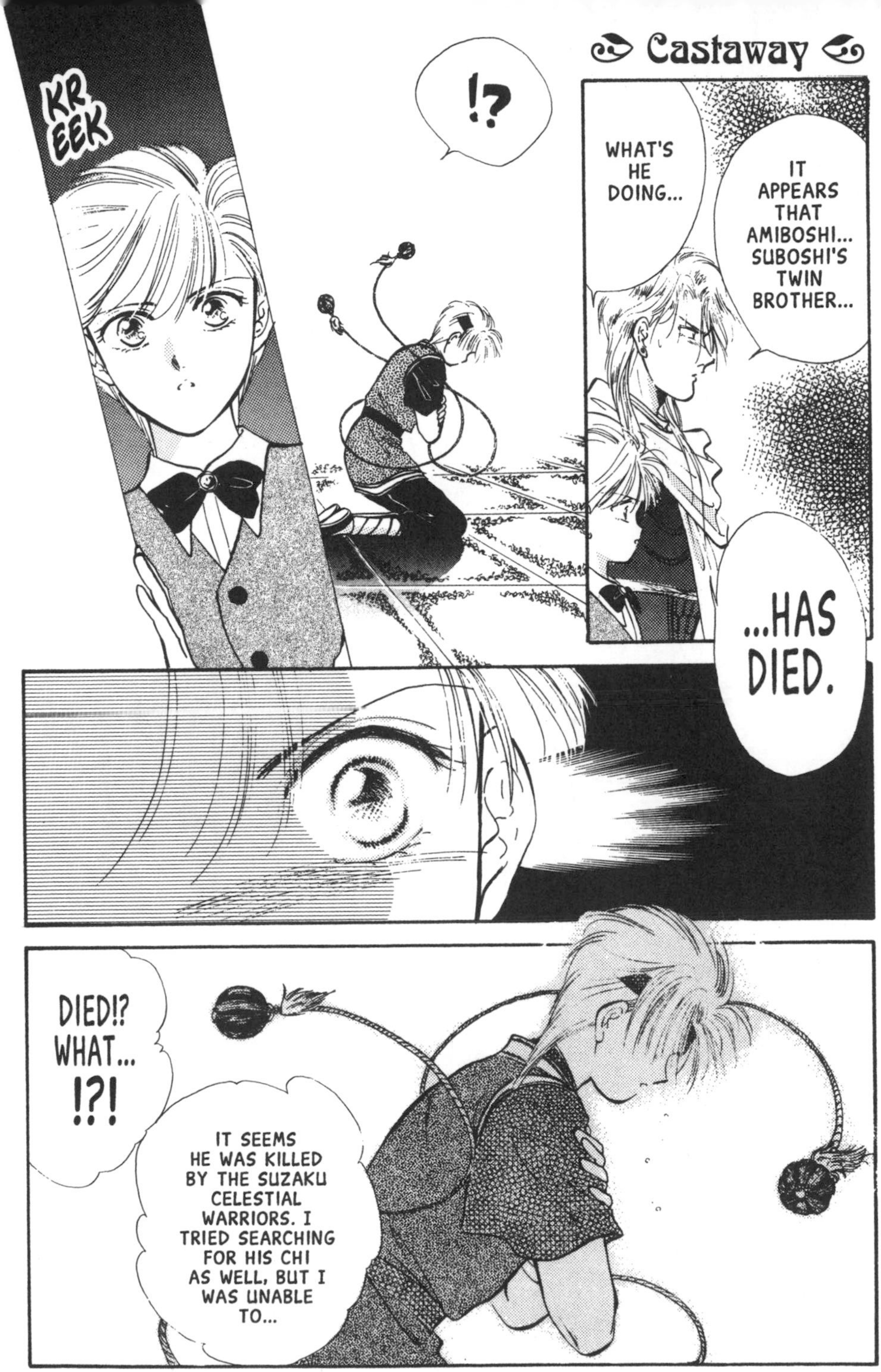
KR EEK
!?
WHAT'S HE DOING...
IT APPEARS THAT AMIBOSHI... SUBOSHI'S TWIN BROTHER...
...HAS DIED.
DIED!? WHAT... !?!
IT SEEMS HE WAS KILLED BY THE SUZAKU CELESTIAL WARRIORS. I TRIED SEARCHING FOR HIS CHI AS WELL, BUT I WAS UNABLE TO...

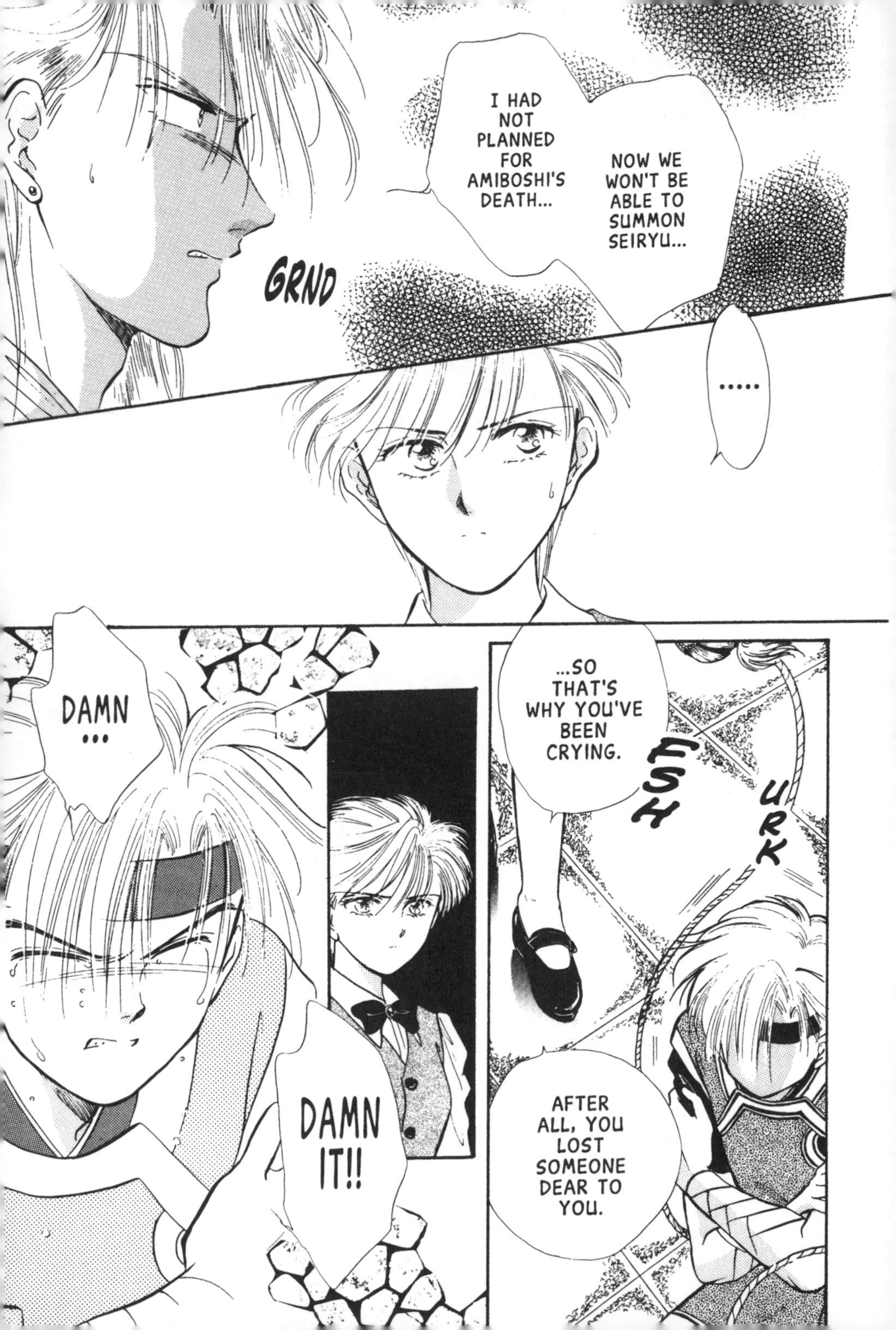
GRND
I HAD NOT PLANNED FOR AMIBOSHI'S DEATH...
NOW WE WON'T BE ABLE TO SUMMON SEIRYU...
.....
DAMN...
DAMN IT!!
...SO THAT'S WHY YOU'VE BEEN CRYING.
FSH
URK
AFTER ALL, YOU LOST SOMEONE DEAR TO YOU.

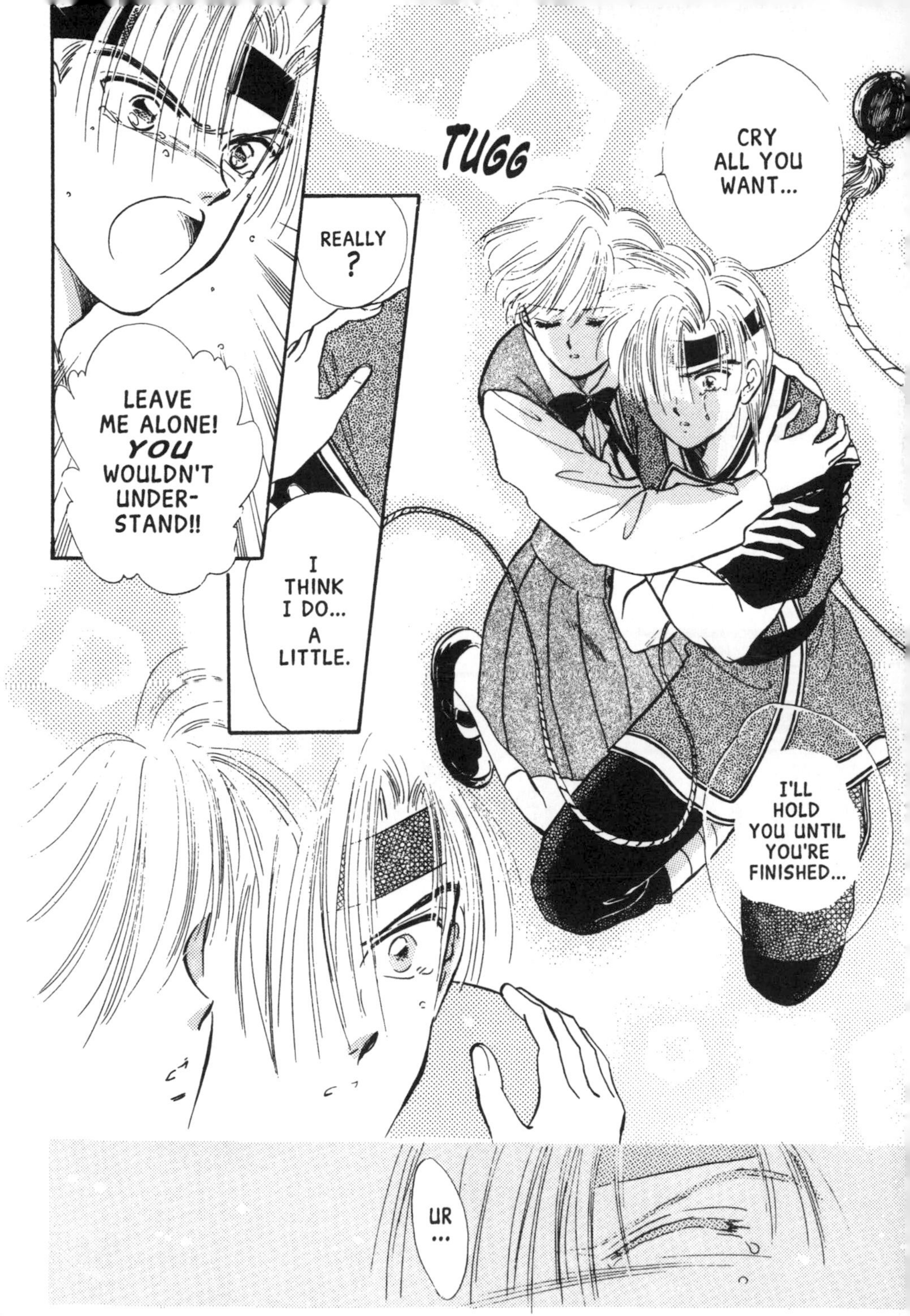
LEAVE ME ALONE! YOU WOULDN'T UNDER-STAND!!
REALLY ?
I THINK I DO... A LITTLE.
TUGG
CRY ALL YOU WANT...
I'LL HOLD YOU UNTIL YOU'RE FINISHED...
UR ...

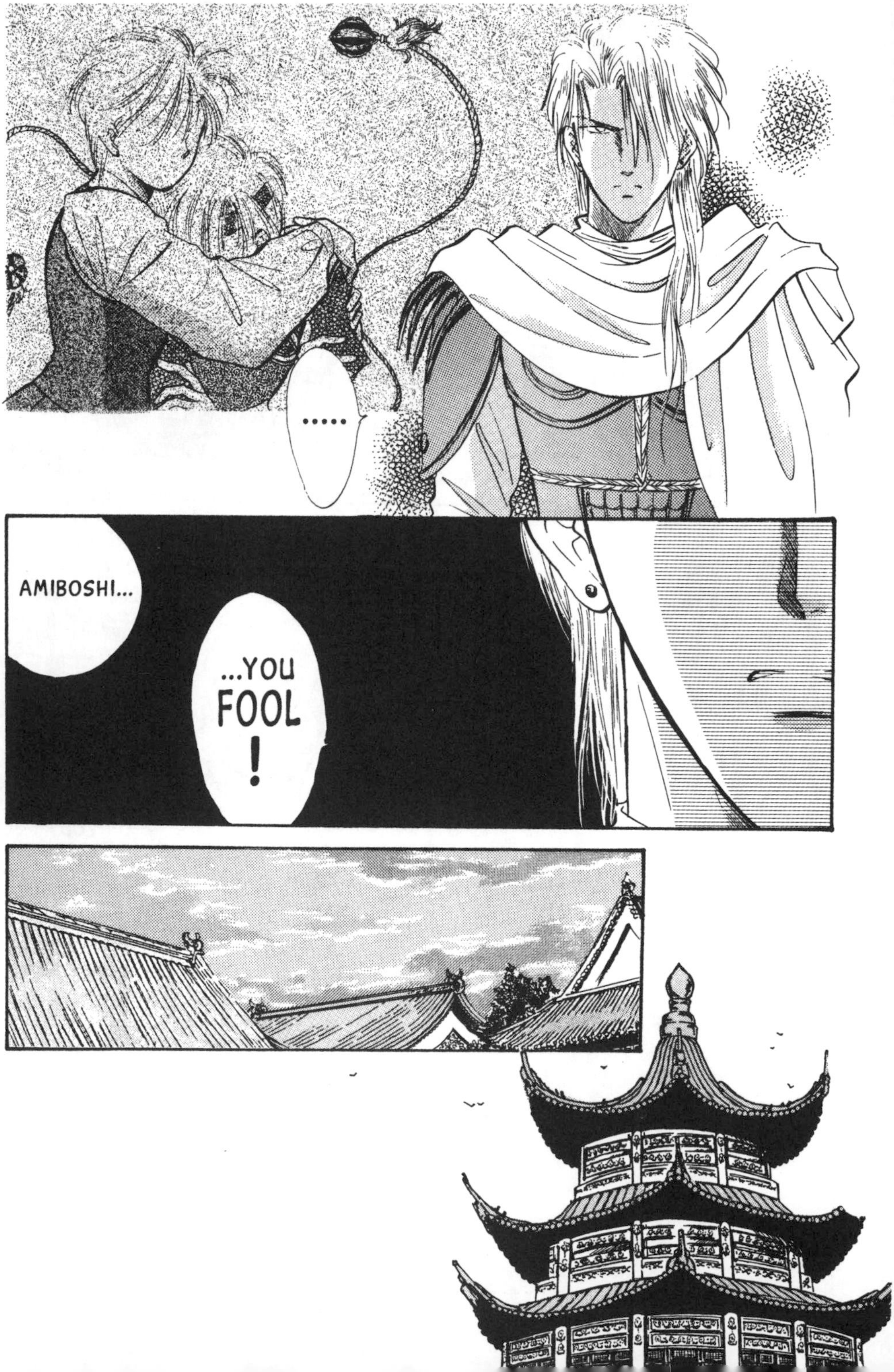
.....
AMIBOSHI...
...YOU FOOL !

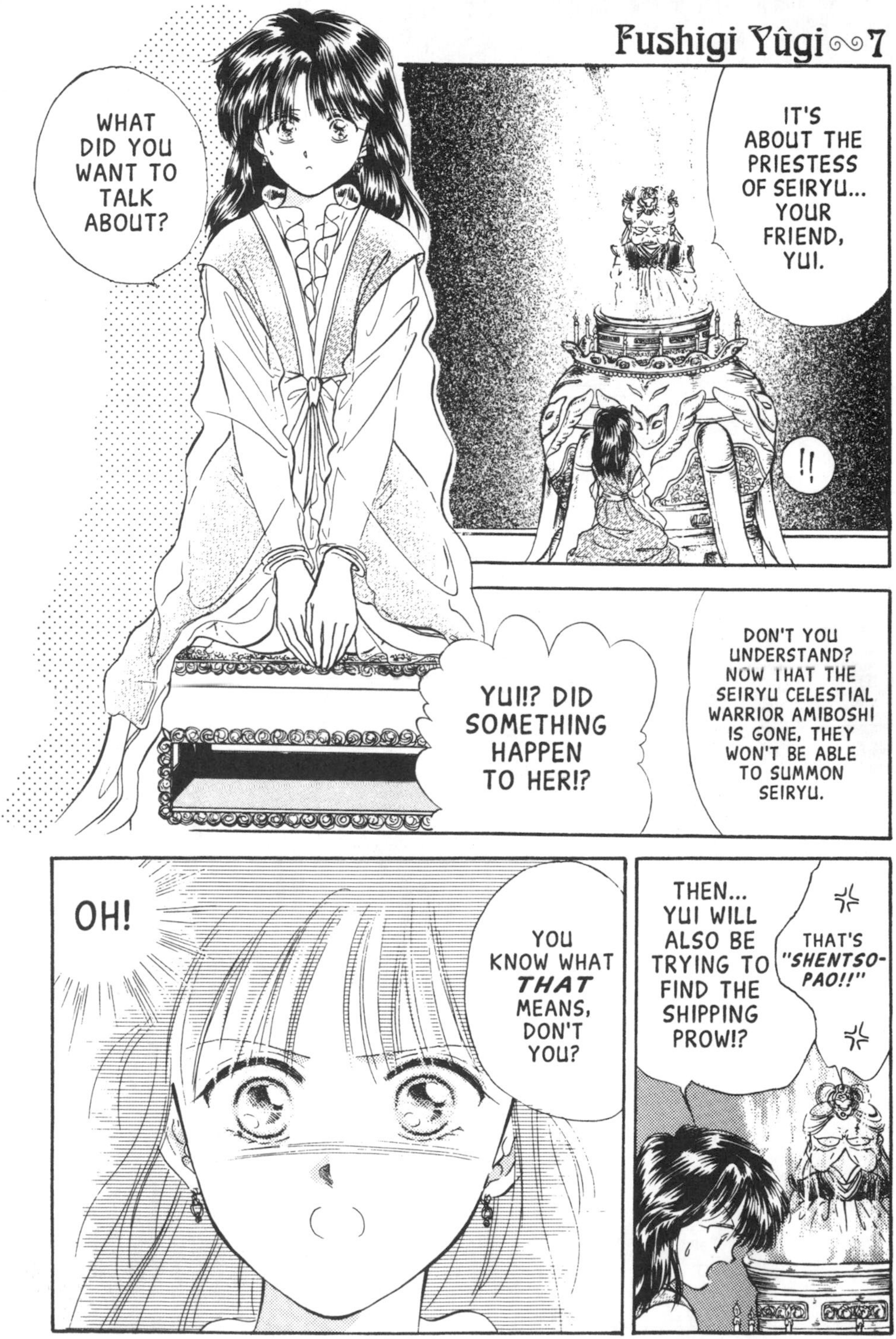
WHAT DID YOU WANT TO TALK ABOUT?
IT'S ABOUT THE PRIESTESS OF SEIRYU... YOUR FRIEND, YUI.
!!
YUI!!? DID SOMETHING HAPPEN TO HER!?
DON'T YOU UNDERSTAND? NOW THAT THE SEIRYU CELESTIAL WARRIOR AMIBOSHI IS GONE, THEY WON'T BE ABLE TO SUMMON SEIRYU.
OH!
YOU KNOW WHAT ***THAT*** MEANS, DON'T YOU?
THEN... YUI WILL ALSO BE TRYING TO FIND THE SHIPPING PROW!?
THAT'S *"SHENTSO-PAO!!"*

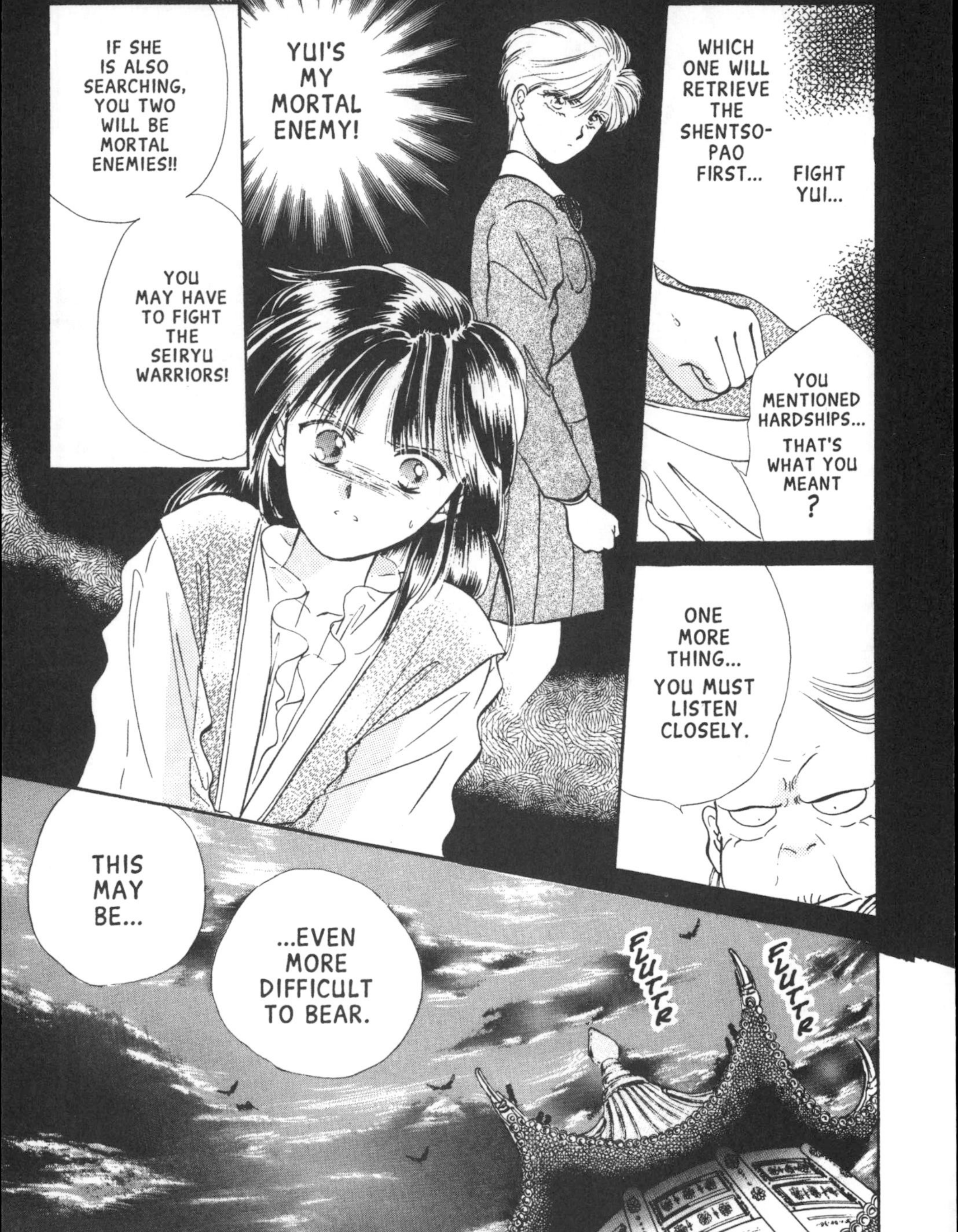
IF SHE IS ALSO SEARCHING, YOU TWO WILL BE MORTAL ENEMIES!!
YUI'S MY MORTAL ENEMY!
YOU MAY HAVE TO FIGHT THE SEIRYU WARRIORS!
WHICH ONE WILL RETRIEVE THE SHENTSO-PAO FIRST...
FIGHT YUI...
YOU MENTIONED HARDSHIPS... THAT'S WHAT YOU MEANT?
ONE MORE THING... YOU MUST LISTEN CLOSELY.
THIS MAY BE...
...EVEN MORE DIFFICULT TO BEAR.
FVUTTR
FVUTTR

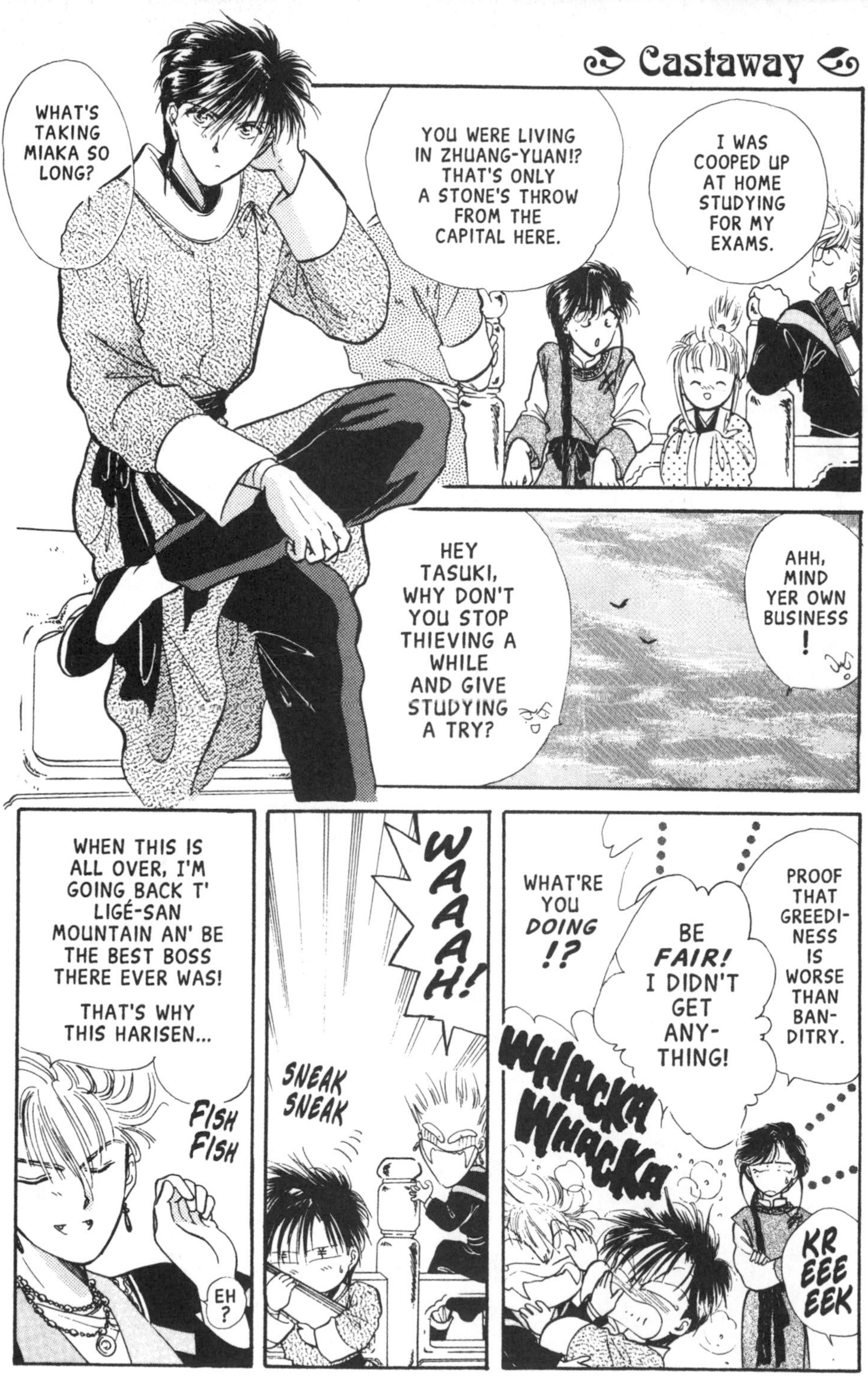
WHAT'S TAKING MIAKA SO LONG?
YOU WERE LIVING IN ZHUANG-YUAN!? THAT'S ONLY A STONE'S THROW FROM THE CAPITAL HERE.
I WAS COOPED UP AT HOME STUDYING FOR MY EXAMS.
HEY TASUKI, WHY DON'T YOU STOP THIEVING A WHILE AND GIVE STUDYING A TRY?
AHH, MIND YER OWN BUSINESS!
WHEN THIS IS ALL OVER, I'M GOING BACK T' LIGÉ-SAN MOUNTAIN AN' BE THE BEST BOSS THERE EVER WAS!
THAT'S WHY THIS HARISEN...
FISH FISH
EH?
WAAAAH!
SNEAK SNEAK
WHAT'RE YOU DOING!?
BE FAIR! I DIDN'T GET ANY-THING!
PROOF THAT GREEDI-NESS IS WORSE THAN BAN-DITRY.
WHACKA WHACKA
KREEEEEK

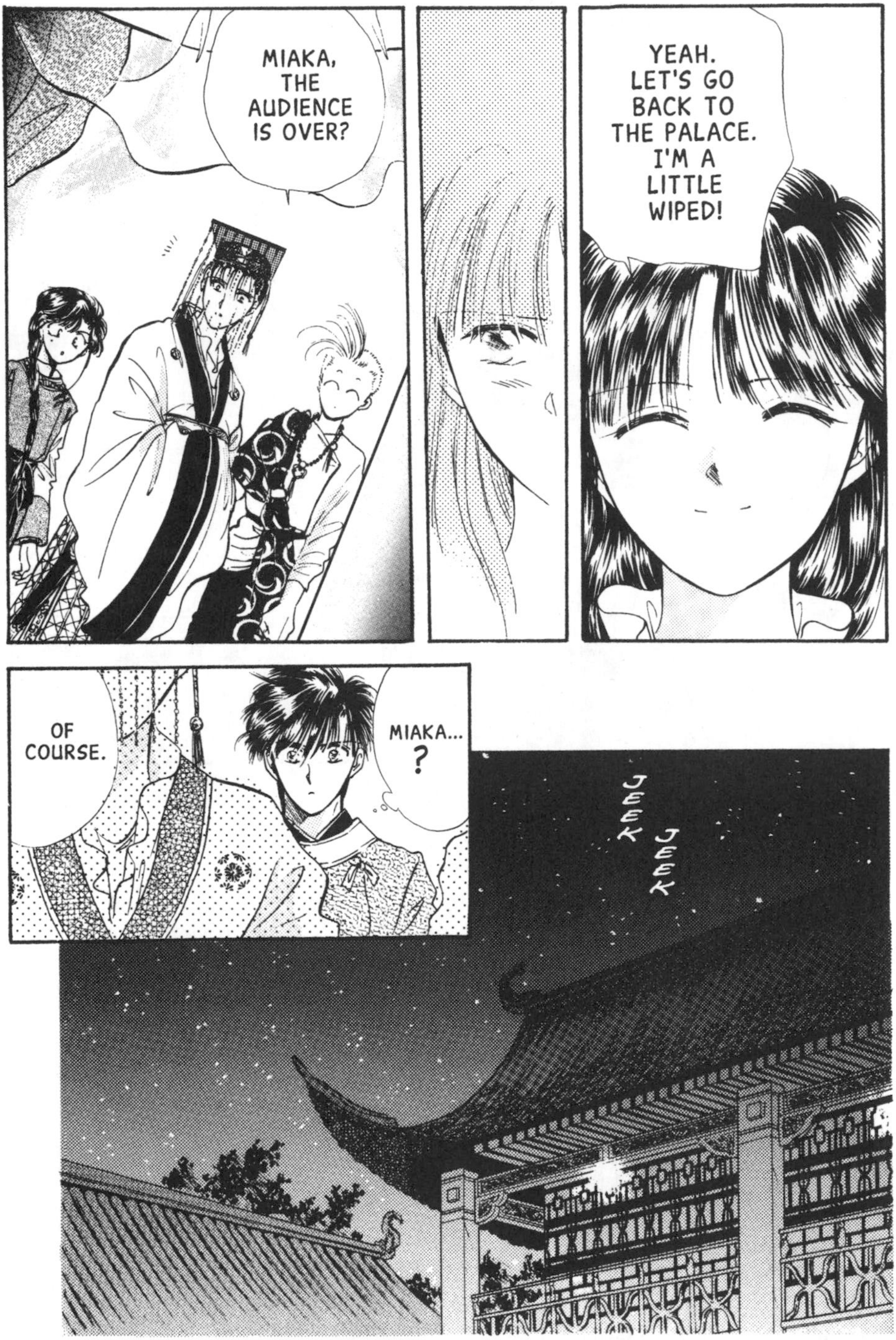
MIAKA, THE AUDIENCE IS OVER?
YEAH. LET'S GO BACK TO THE PALACE. I'M A LITTLE WIPED!
OF COURSE.
MIAKA... ?
JEEK JEEK

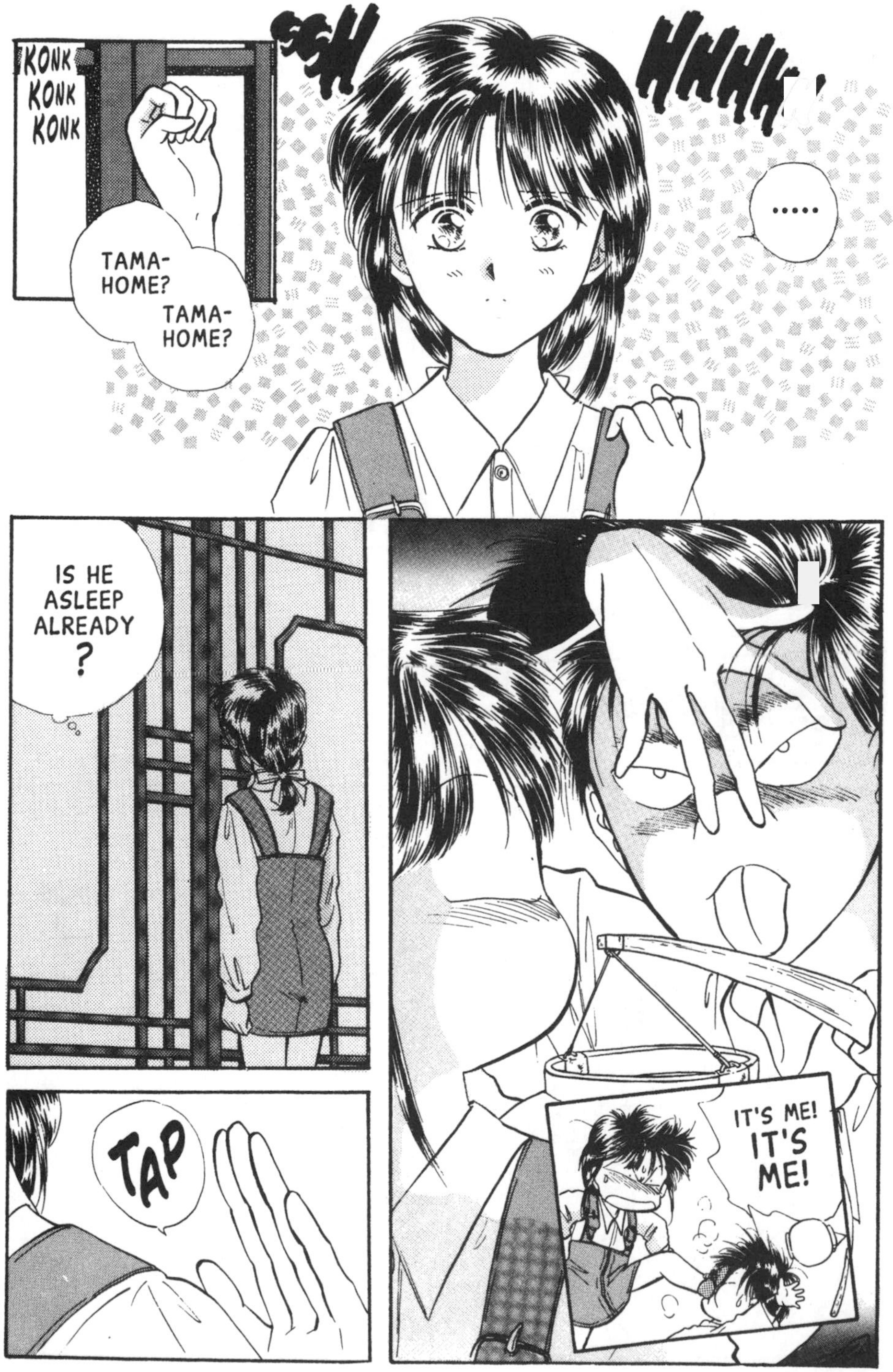
KONK KONK KONK
TAMA-HOME?
TAMA-HOME?
SSH HHHHH
.....
IS HE ASLEEP ALREADY?
TAP
IT'S ME! IT'S ME!

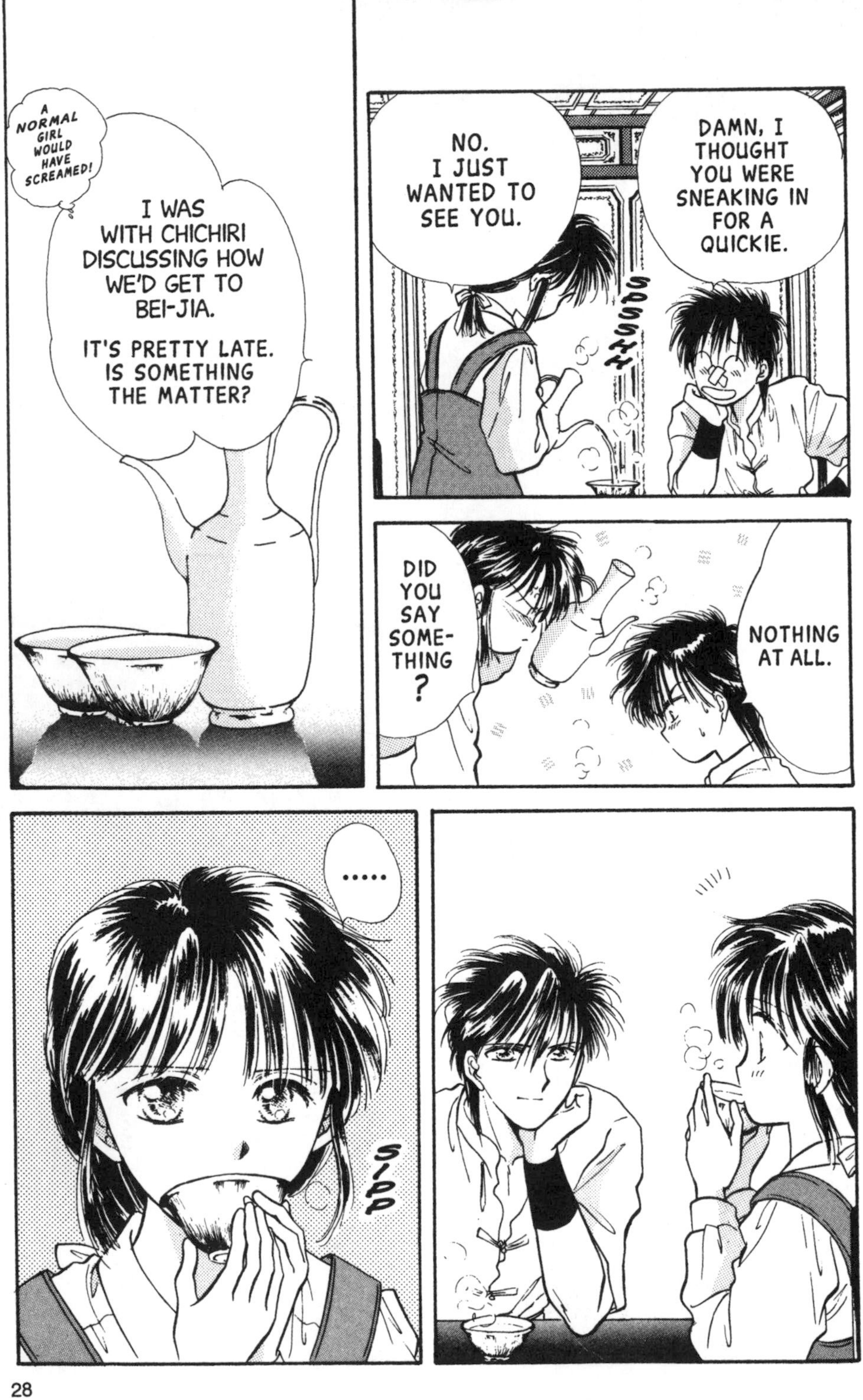
A NORMAL GIRL WOULD HAVE SCREAMED!
I WAS WITH CHICHIRI DISCUSSING HOW WE'D GET TO BEI-JIA.
IT'S PRETTY LATE. IS SOMETHING THE MATTER?
NO. I JUST WANTED TO SEE YOU.
DAMN, I THOUGHT YOU WERE SNEAKING IN FOR A QUICKIE.
SPSSHH
DID YOU SAY SOMETHING?
NOTHING AT ALL.
......
SIPP

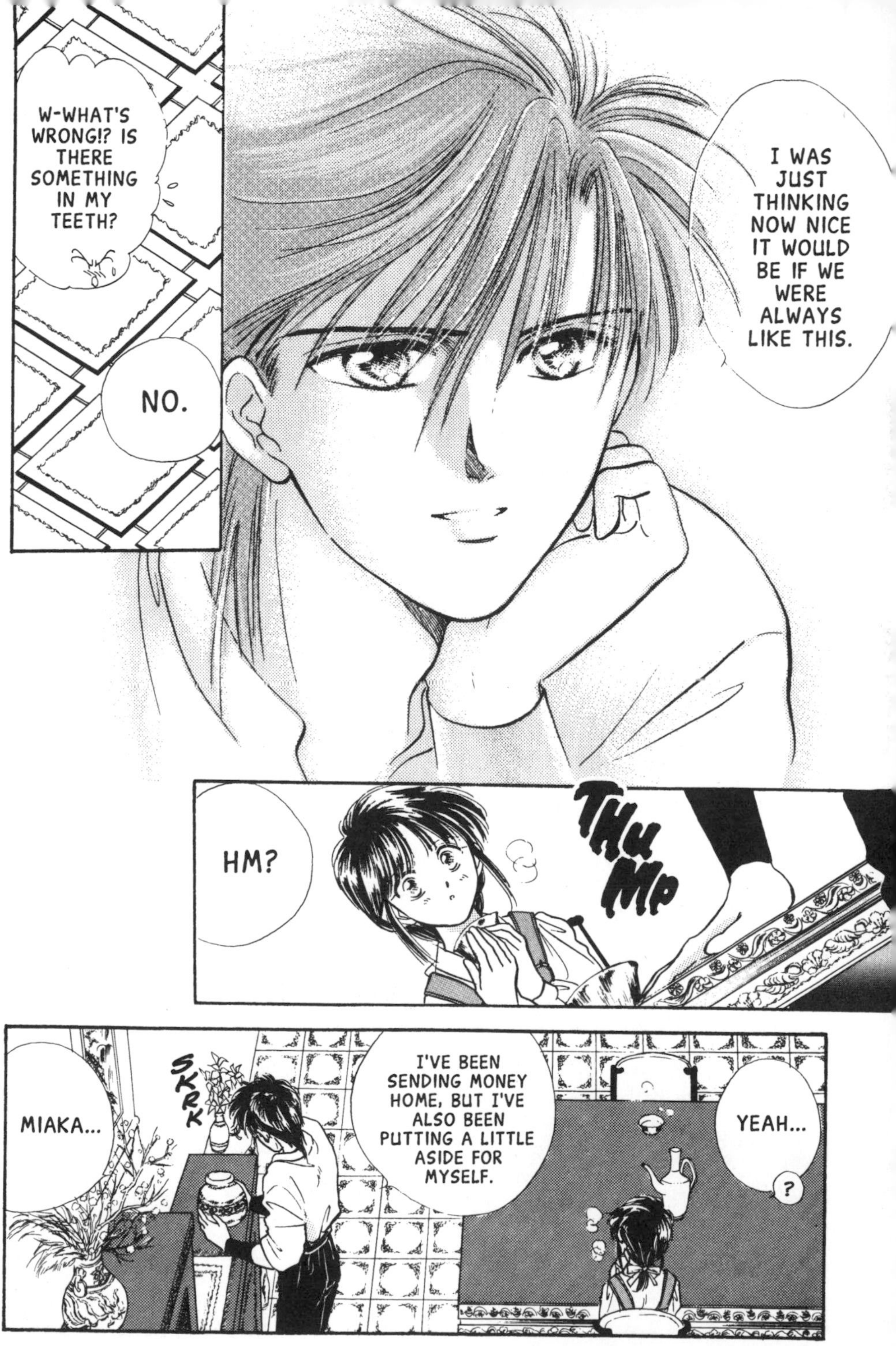
W-WHAT'S WRONG!? IS THERE SOMETHING IN MY TEETH?
NO.
I WAS JUST THINKING NOW NICE IT WOULD BE IF WE WERE ALWAYS LIKE THIS.
HM?
THUMP
MIAKA...
SKRK
I'VE BEEN SENDING MONEY HOME, BUT I'VE ALSO BEEN PUTTING A LITTLE ASIDE FOR MYSELF.
YEAH...
?

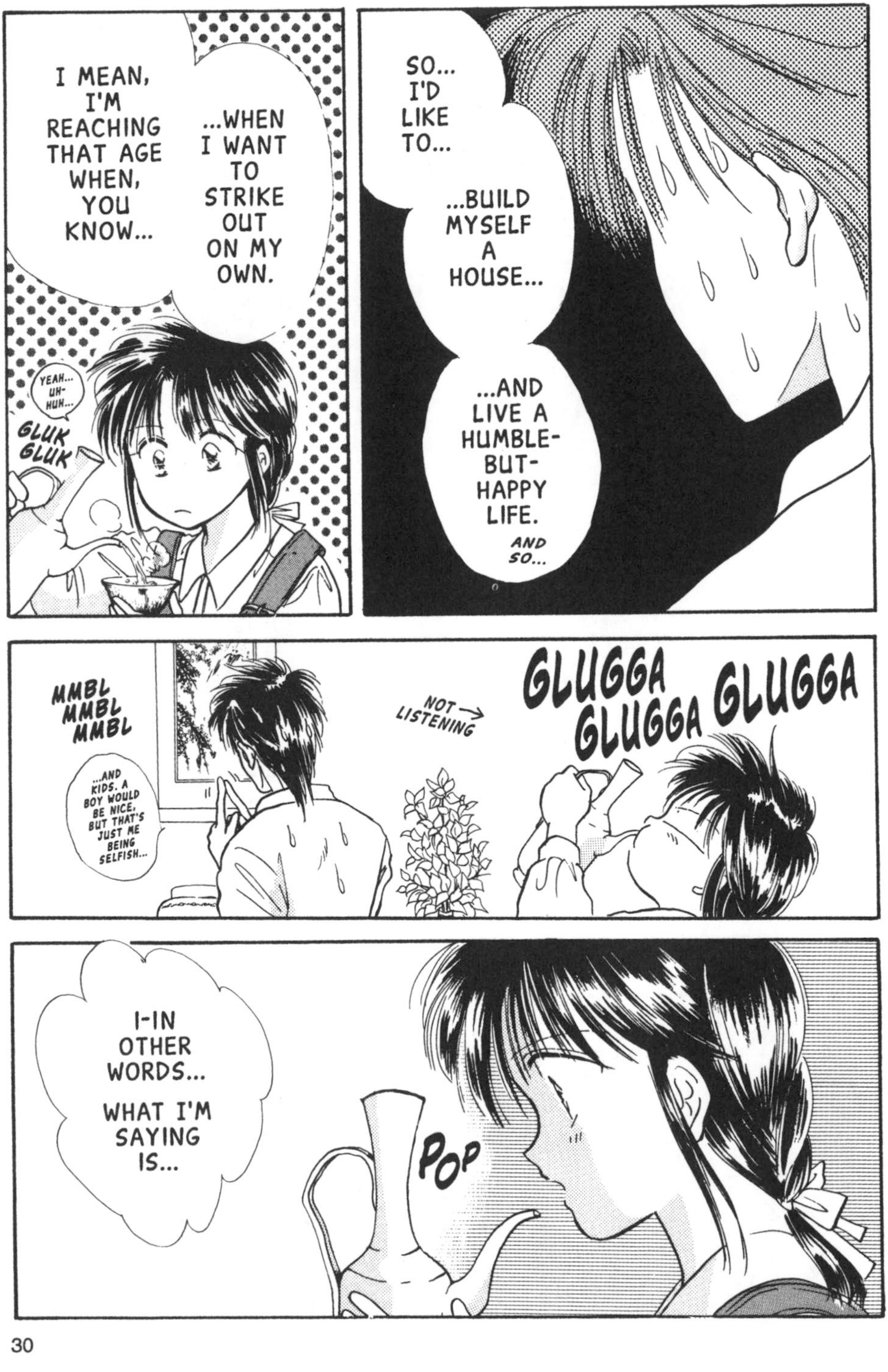
I MEAN, I'M REACHING THAT AGE WHEN, YOU KNOW...
...WHEN I WANT TO STRIKE OUT ON MY OWN.
YEAH... UH-HUH...
GLUK GLUK
SO... I'D LIKE TO...
...BUILD MYSELF A HOUSE...
...AND LIVE A HUMBLE-BUT-HAPPY LIFE.
AND SO...
MMBL MMBL MMBL
...AND KIDS. A BOY WOULD BE NICE, BUT THAT'S JUST ME BEING SELFISH...
NOT LISTENING
GLUGGA GLUGGA GLUGGA GLUGGA
I-IN OTHER WORDS... WHAT I'M SAYING IS...
POP

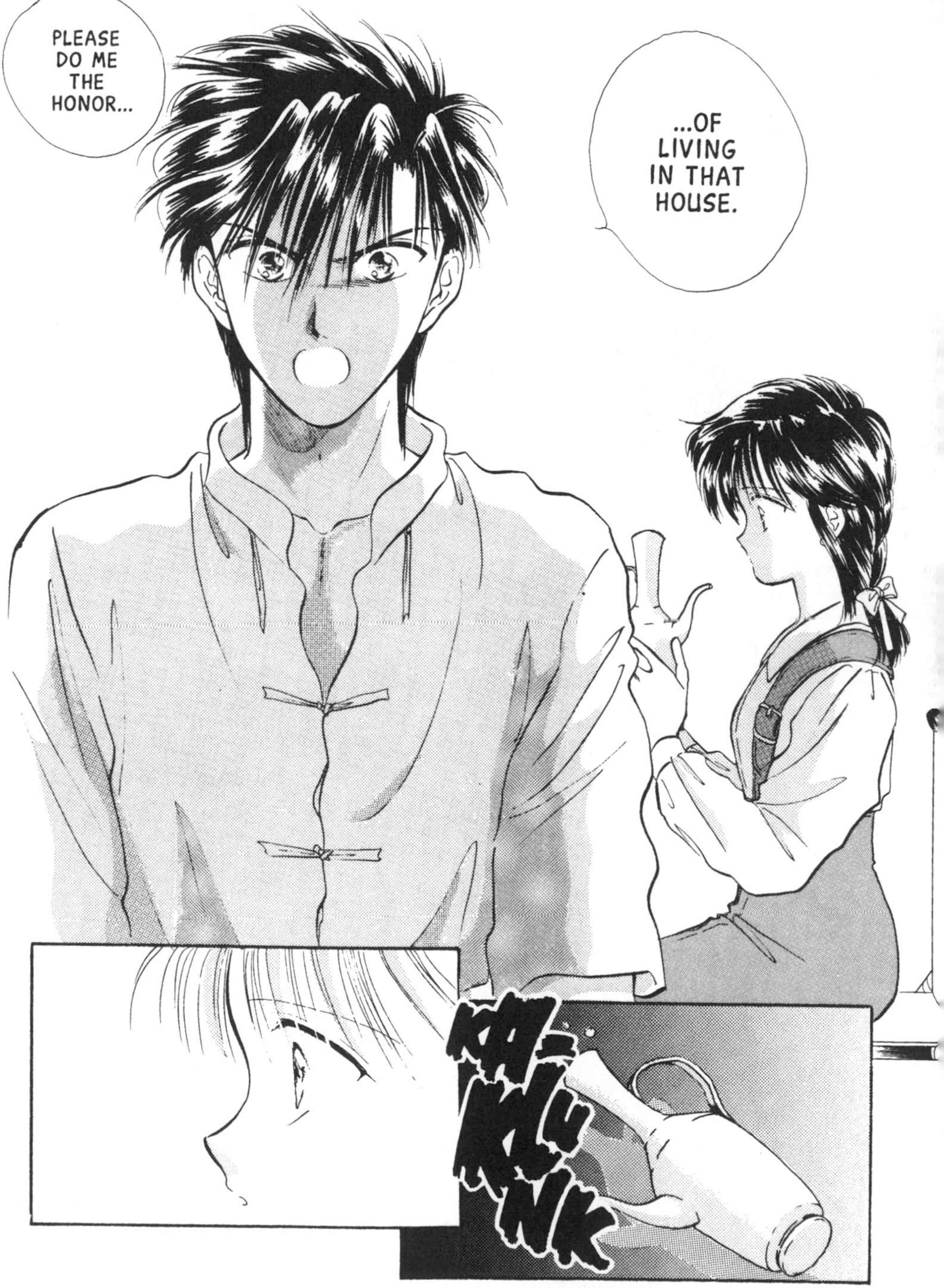
PLEASE DO ME THE HONOR...
...OF LIVING IN THAT HOUSE.
KA-KLUNK

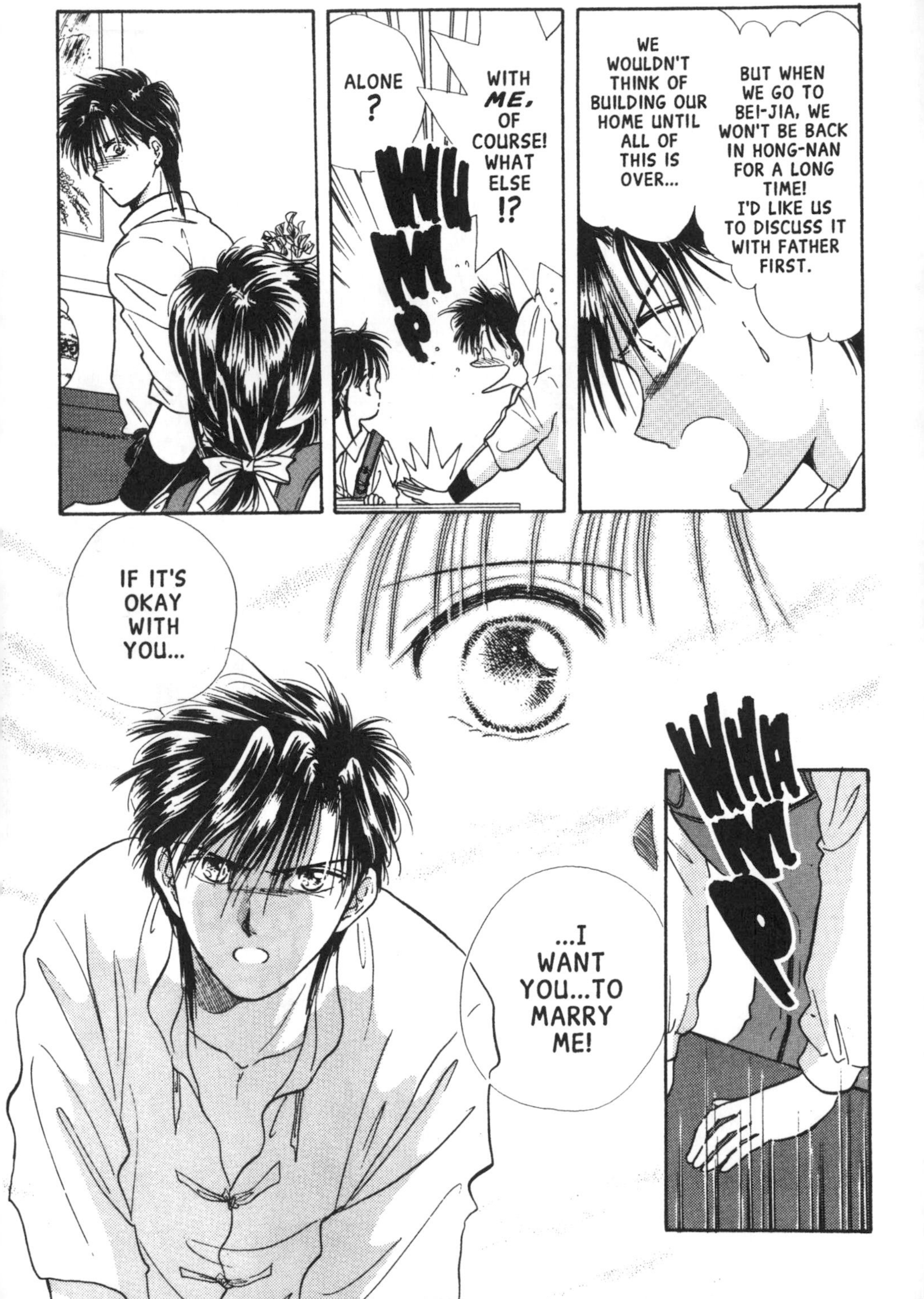
ALONE ?
WITH ME, OF COURSE! WHAT ELSE !?
WHUMP
WE WOULDN'T THINK OF BUILDING OUR HOME UNTIL ALL OF THIS IS OVER...
BUT WHEN WE GO TO BEI-JIA, WE WON'T BE BACK IN HONG-NAN FOR A LONG TIME! I'D LIKE US TO DISCUSS IT WITH FATHER FIRST.
IF IT'S OKAY WITH YOU...
...I WANT YOU...TO MARRY ME!
WHAMP

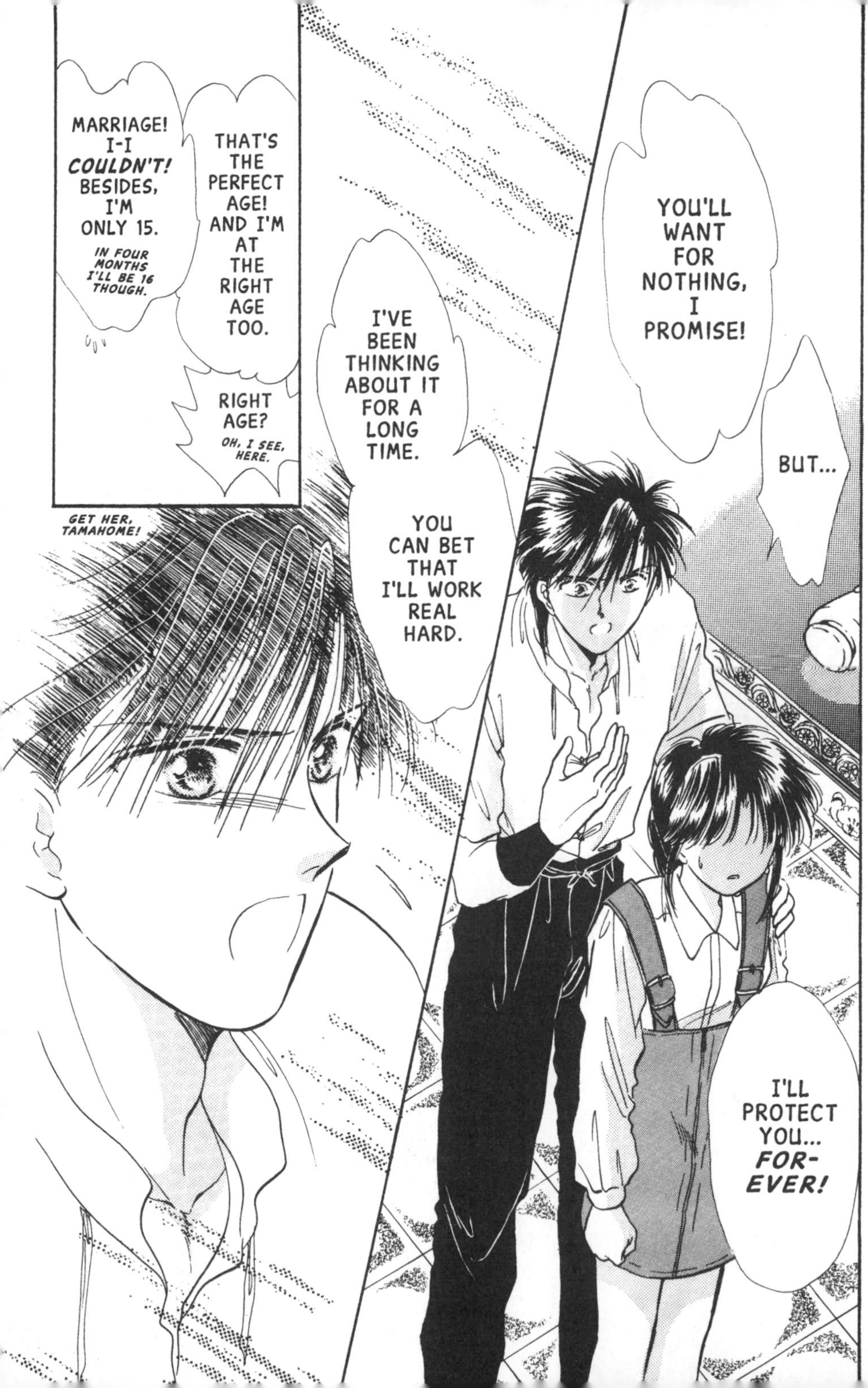
MARRIAGE! I-I COULDN'T! BESIDES, I'M ONLY 15.
IN FOUR MONTHS I'LL BE 16 THOUGH.
THAT'S THE PERFECT AGE! AND I'M AT THE RIGHT AGE TOO.
RIGHT AGE?
OH, I SEE, HERE.
GET HER, TAMAHOME!
I'VE BEEN THINKING ABOUT IT FOR A LONG TIME.
YOU CAN BET THAT I'LL WORK REAL HARD.
YOU'LL WANT FOR NOTHING, I PROMISE!
BUT...
I'LL PROTECT YOU... FOR-EVER!

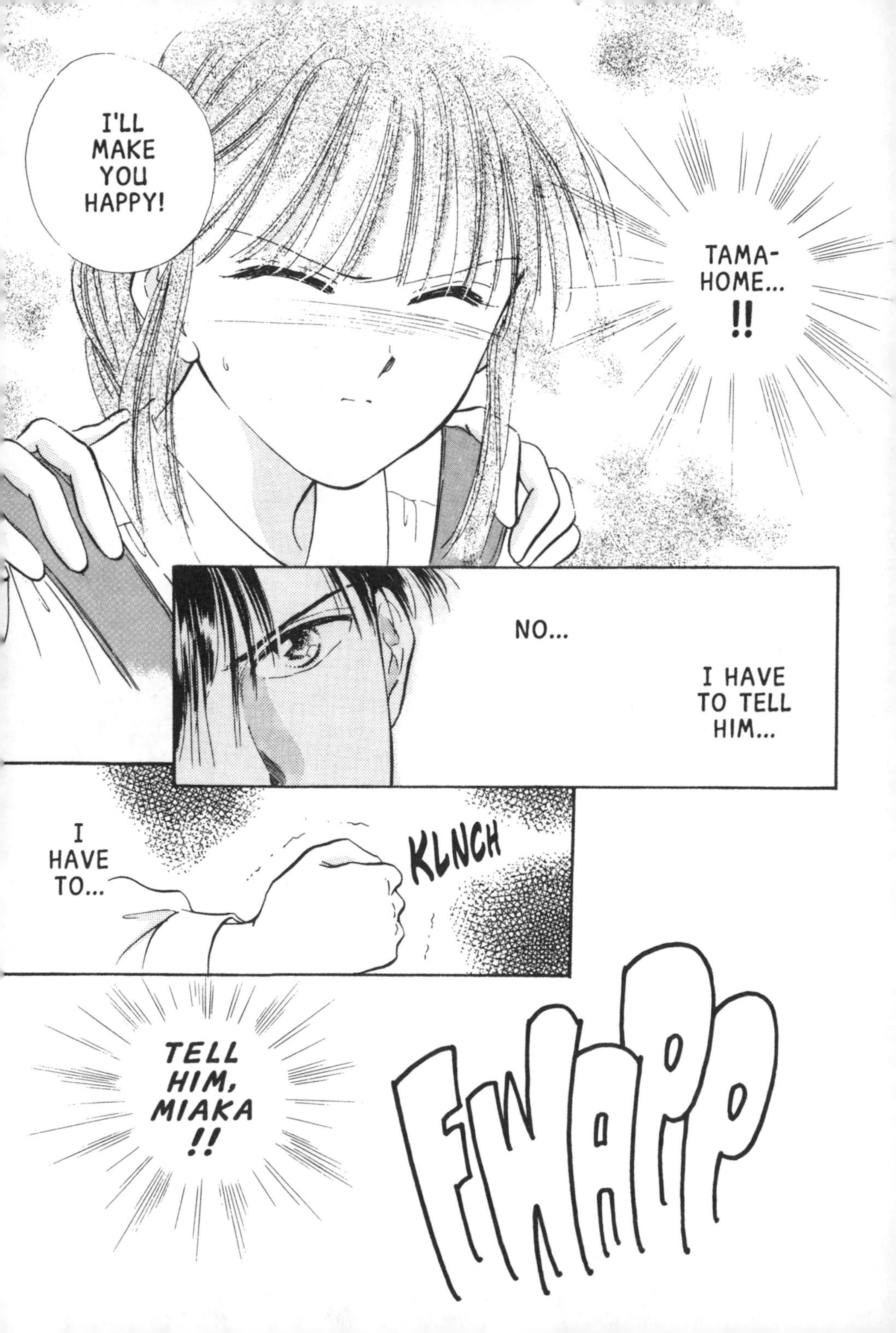
I'LL MAKE YOU HAPPY!
TAMA-HOME... !!
NO...
I HAVE TO TELL HIM...
I HAVE TO...
KLNCH
TELL HIM, MIAKA !!
FWAPPP

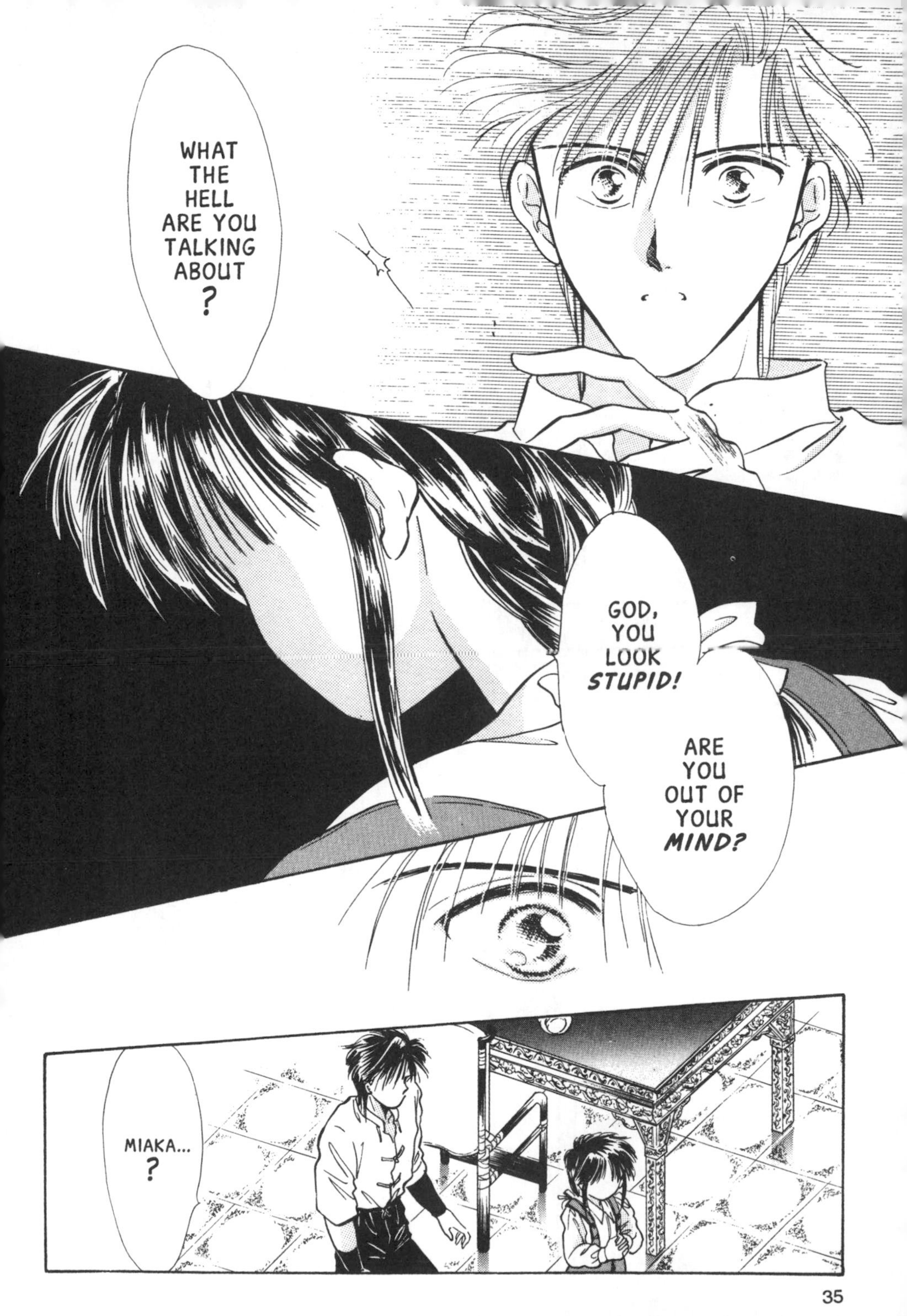
WHAT THE HELL ARE YOU TALKING ABOUT ?
GOD, YOU LOOK *STUPID!*
ARE YOU OUT OF YOUR *MIND?*
MIAKA... ?

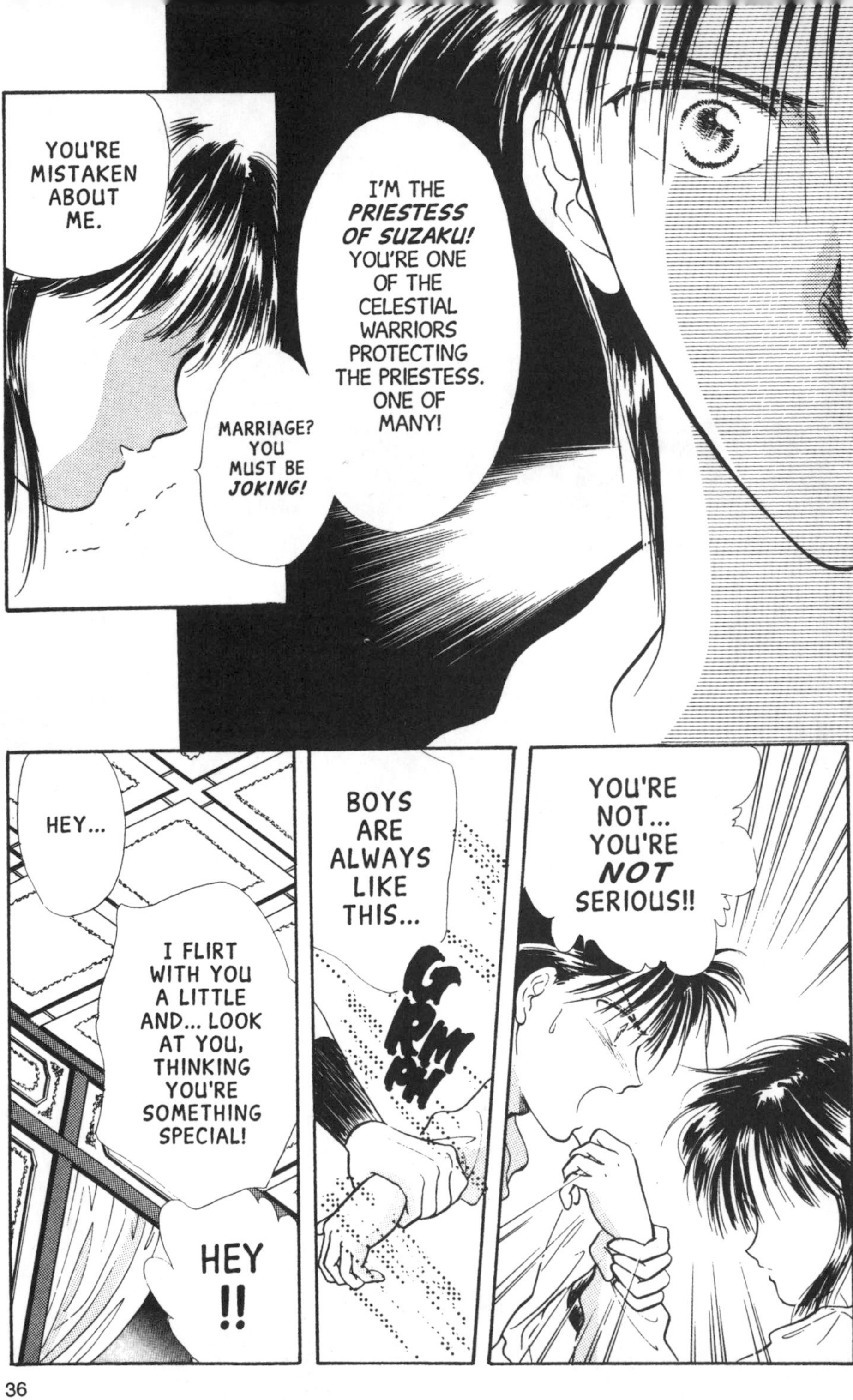

YOU'RE MISTAKEN ABOUT ME.
I'M THE PRIESTESS OF SUZAKU! YOU'RE ONE OF THE CELESTIAL WARRIORS PROTECTING THE PRIESTESS. ONE OF MANY!
MARRIAGE? YOU MUST BE JOKING!
HEY...
I FLIRT WITH YOU A LITTLE AND... LOOK AT YOU, THINKING YOU'RE SOMETHING SPECIAL!
HEY !!
BOYS ARE ALWAYS LIKE THIS...
GRMPH
YOU'RE NOT... YOU'RE NOT SERIOUS!!

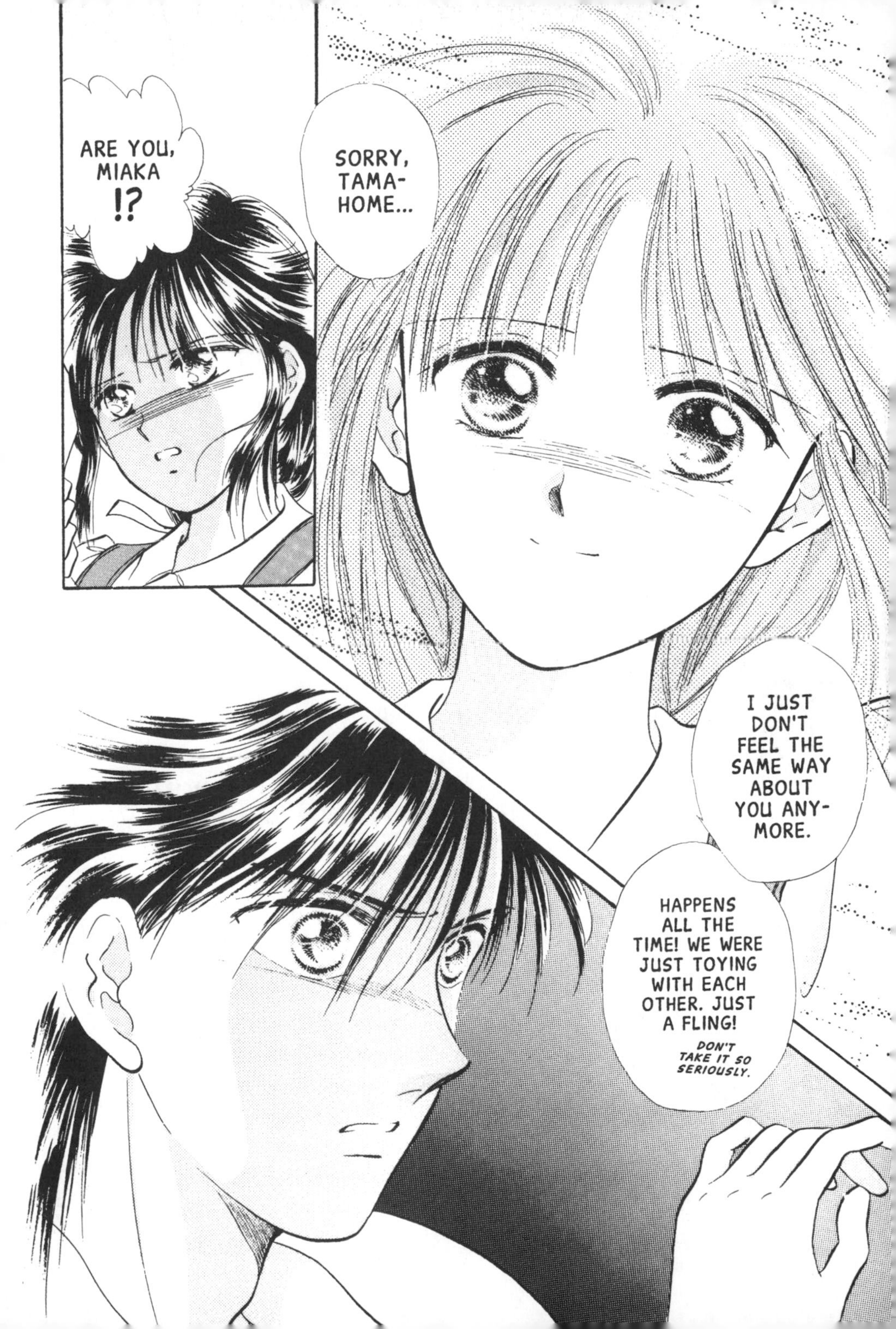
ARE YOU, MIAKA !?
SORRY, TAMA-HOME...
I JUST DON'T FEEL THE SAME WAY ABOUT YOU ANY-MORE.
HAPPENS ALL THE TIME! WE WERE JUST TOYING WITH EACH OTHER. JUST A FLING!
DON'T TAKE IT SO SERIOUSLY.

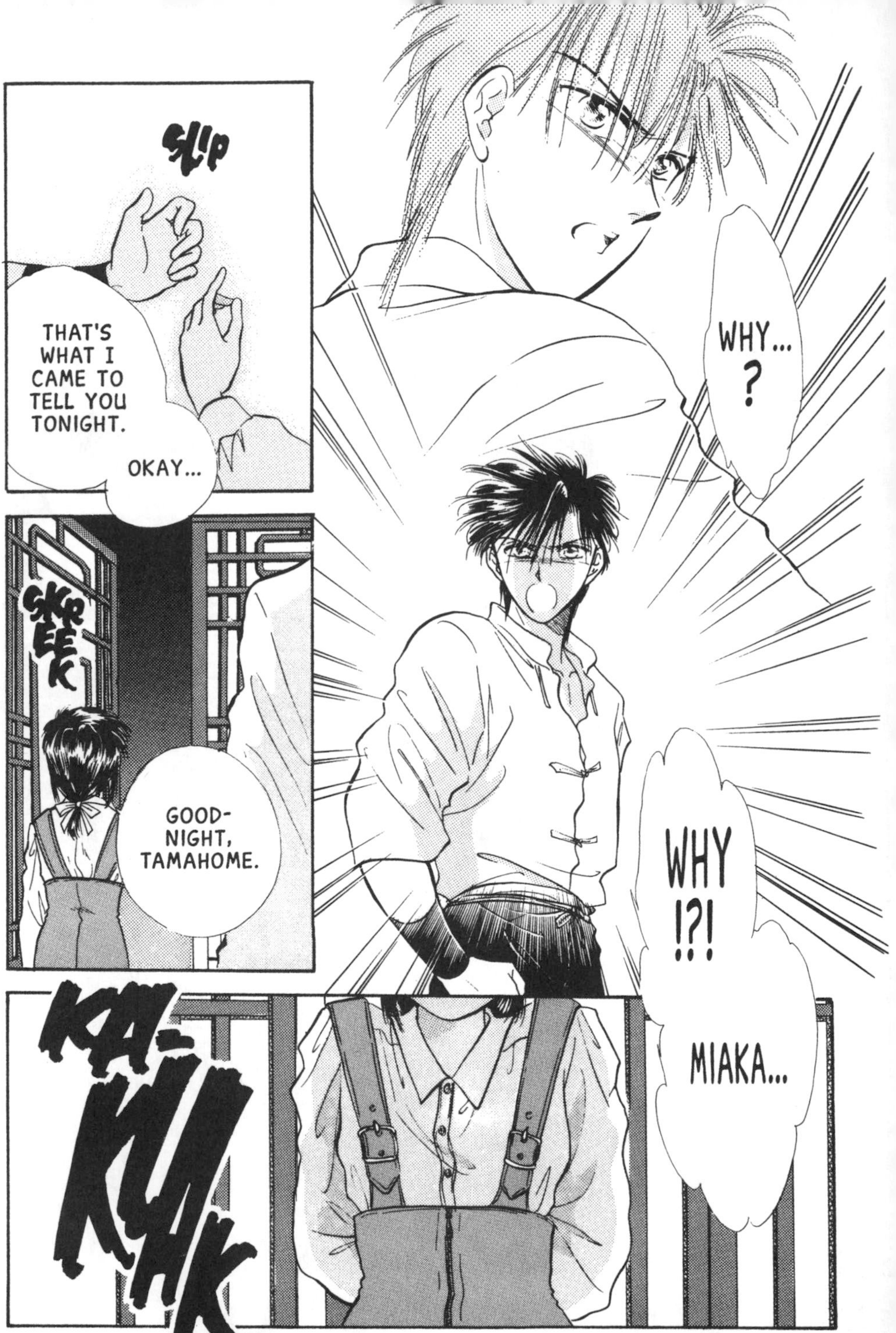
SLIP
THAT'S WHAT I CAME TO TELL YOU TONIGHT.
OKAY...
SKREEEK
GOOD-NIGHT, TAMAHOME.
WHY...?
WHY!?!
MIAKA...
KA-KUNK

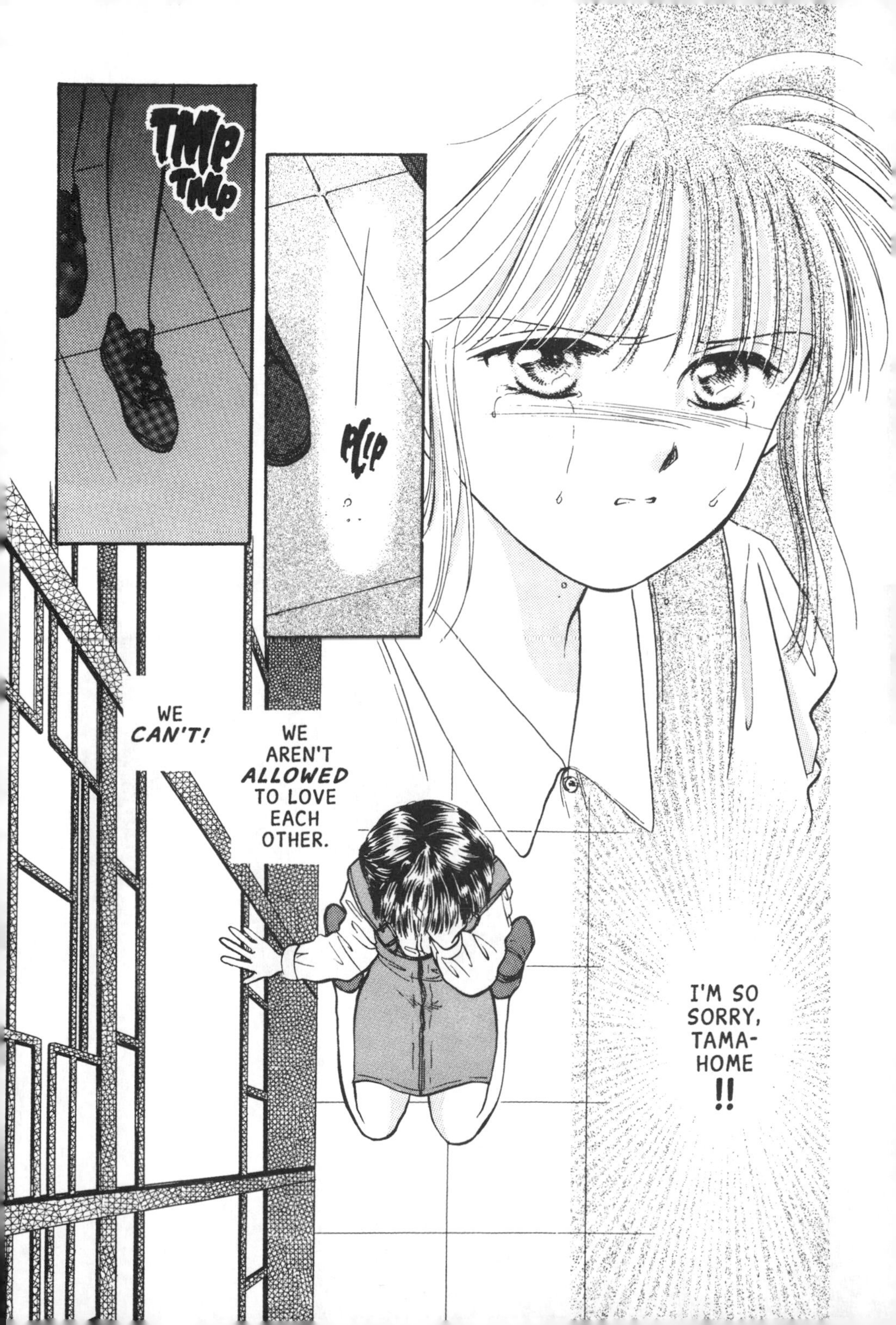
TMP TMP
PLIP
WE CAN'T!
WE AREN'T ALLOWED TO LOVE EACH OTHER.
I'M SO SORRY, TAMAHOME!!

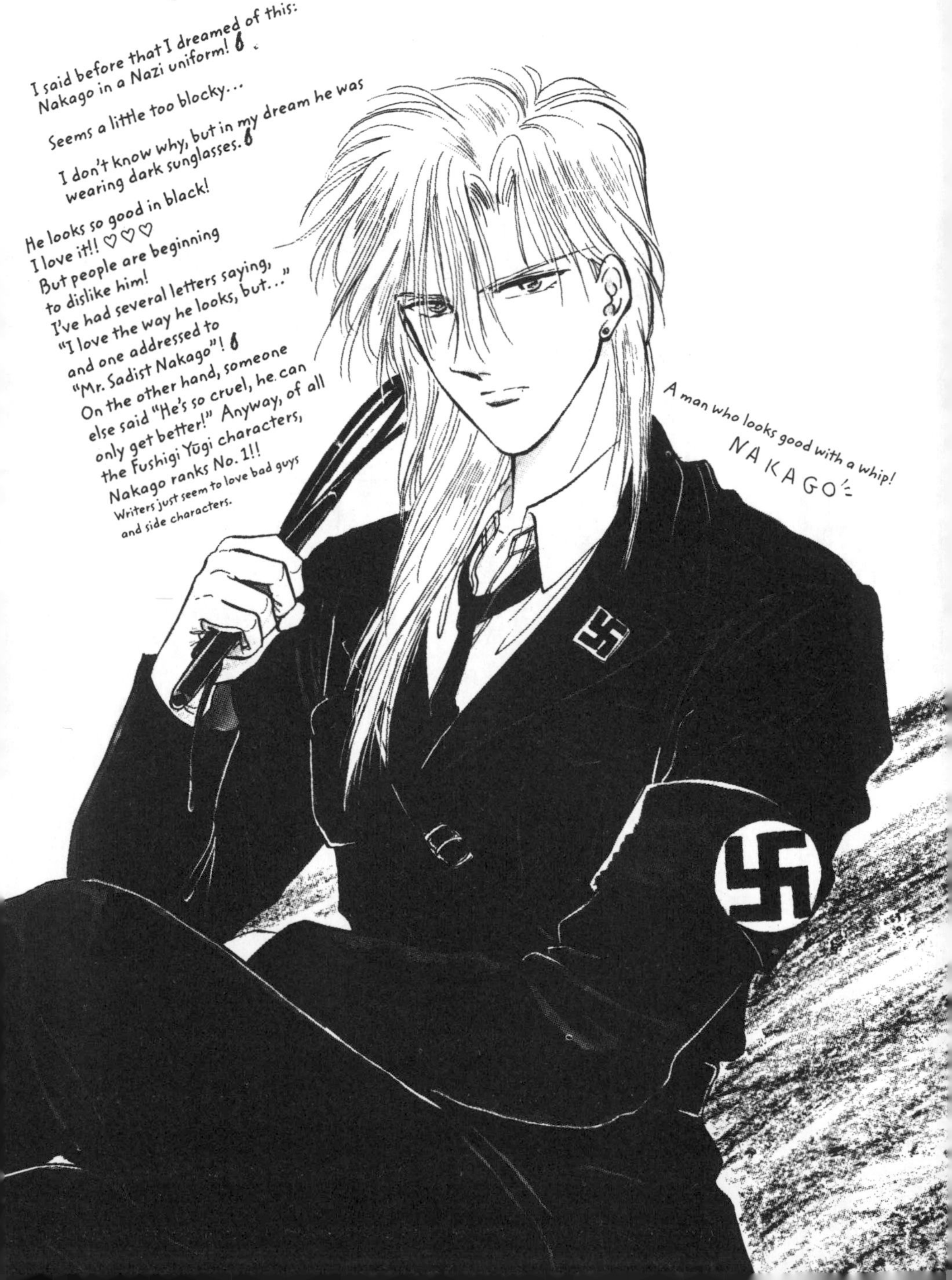
I said before that I dreamed of this:
Nakago in a Nazi uniform!
Seems a little too blocky...
I don't know why, but in my dream he was
wearing dark sunglasses.
He looks so good in black!
I love it!! ♡♡♡
But people are beginning
to dislike him!
I've had several letters saying,
"I love the way he looks, but..."
and one addressed to
"Mr. Sadist Nakago"!
On the other hand, someone
else said "He's so cruel, he can
only get better!" Anyway, of all
the Fushigi Yūgi characters,
Nakago ranks No. 1!!
Writers just seem to love bad guys
and side characters.
A man who looks good with a whip!
NAKAGO

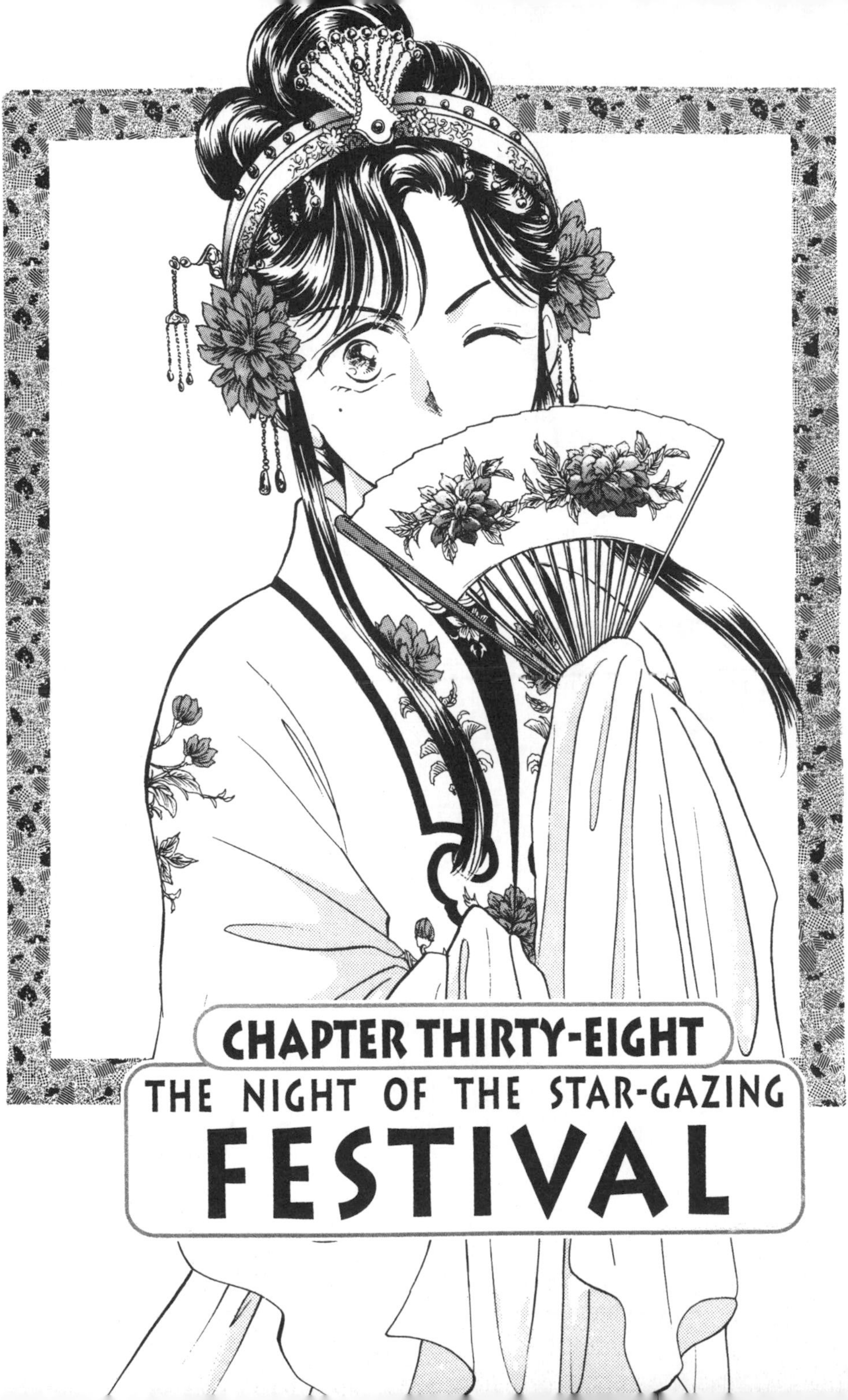

# CHAPTER THIRTY-EIGHT
# THE NIGHT OF THE STAR-GAZING FESTIVAL

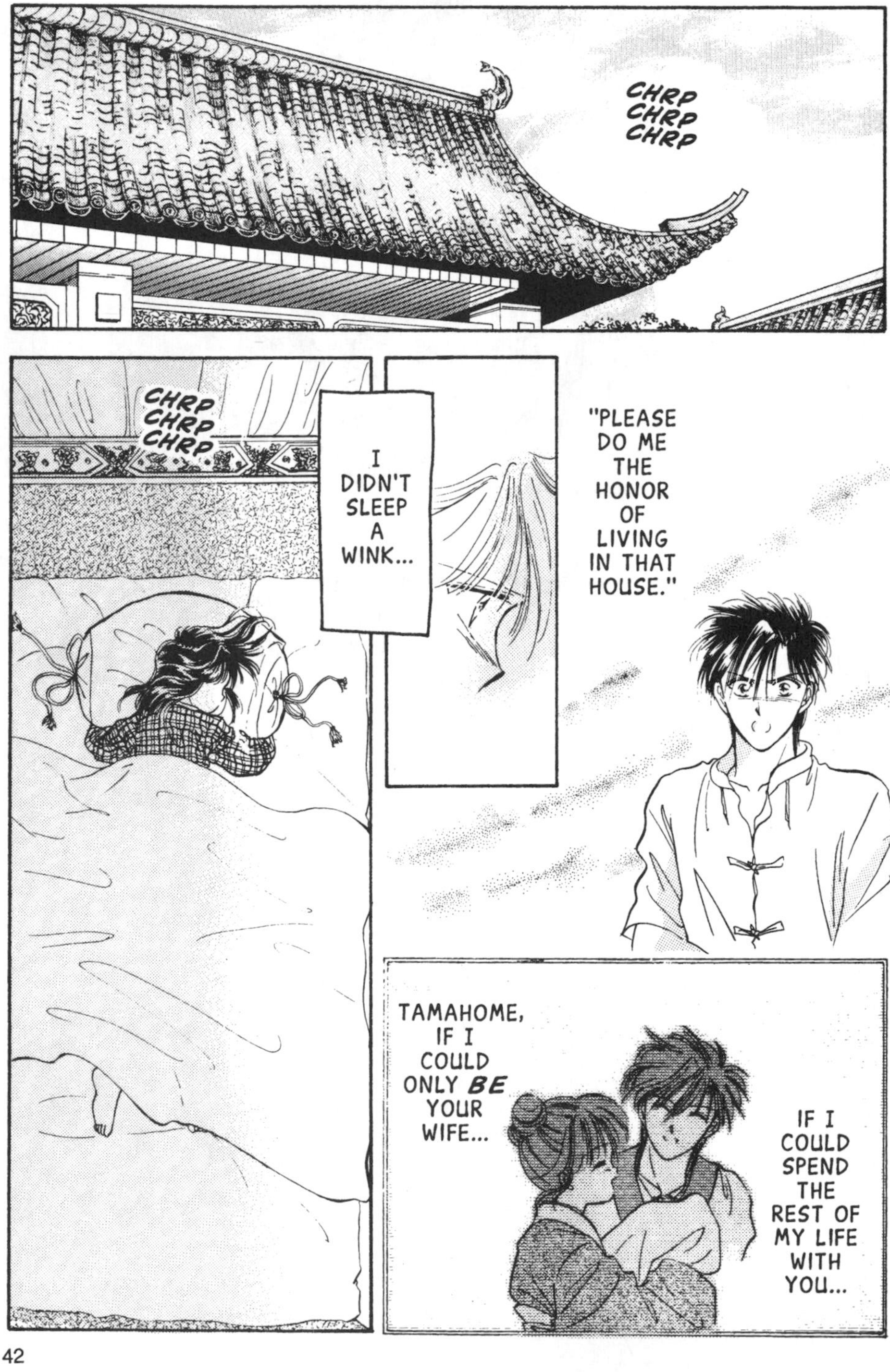
CHRP CHRP CHRP
CHRP CHRP CHRP
I DIDN'T SLEEP A WINK...
"PLEASE DO ME THE HONOR OF LIVING IN THAT HOUSE."
TAMAHOME, IF I COULD ONLY *BE* YOUR WIFE...
IF I COULD SPEND THE REST OF MY LIFE WITH YOU...

BUT I CAN'T...

...I JUST CAN'T.

FWAHH

YO...

GOOD MORNING, MIAKA.

OH. 'MORNING.

HEY, MIAKA. I WAS TALKING TO TASUKI. LET'S GO TO THE TOWN SQUARE! THERE'S A STAR-GAZING FESTIVAL TONIGHT!

WE ONLY HAVE A DAY OR TWO LEFT IN HONG-NAN, SO *COME ON!!*

Now, I'm going to tell you how I ended up owning a dog. It first started as an impulse-- I just wanted a dog. Then I started getting specific thinking a small one would be nice. We once took care of my uncle's Yorkshire Terrier for a couple days, so I automatically thought, "That breed was the one to get!" They're supposed to be pretty smart as far as dogs go... A tiny, fist-sized, trembling, three-month-old puppy arrived. By the way, she's female. As for her name... my parents were required to register her name at the shop, so the best they could come up with was "Yû." They're such space heads using MY name! So we're giving her name a different kanji character. (I just noticed recently how it's the same "Yû" for Fushigi Yûgi.)

I have to say, it's really hard to train dogs. ♪ (I hope potty training goes okay.) When she doesn't behave, we have to spank and scold her. But she's so tiny and cute, it's hard! So now, it's been six months, and she hasn't grown much at all. (Well, compared to the beginning when she was smaller than a slipper, I guess she has...) She's not really crazy about food. Maybe she doesn't have much of an appetite, or maybe she's just fickle. She never cries, even when she's hungry or anything. But she stares at you when you say something to her, so maybe she knows more than she's letting on.

SMILE

GOOD MORNING, TAMA-HOME.

......

THERE'S A FESTIVAL TONIGHT.

TUMP

LET'S ALL GO TOGETHER, OKAY?

IT'S BEST FOR US THIS WAY.

I HAVE TO THINK ABOUT...

...HOW THE PRIESTESS OF SEIRYU AND I "WILL BE MORTAL ENEMIES!!"

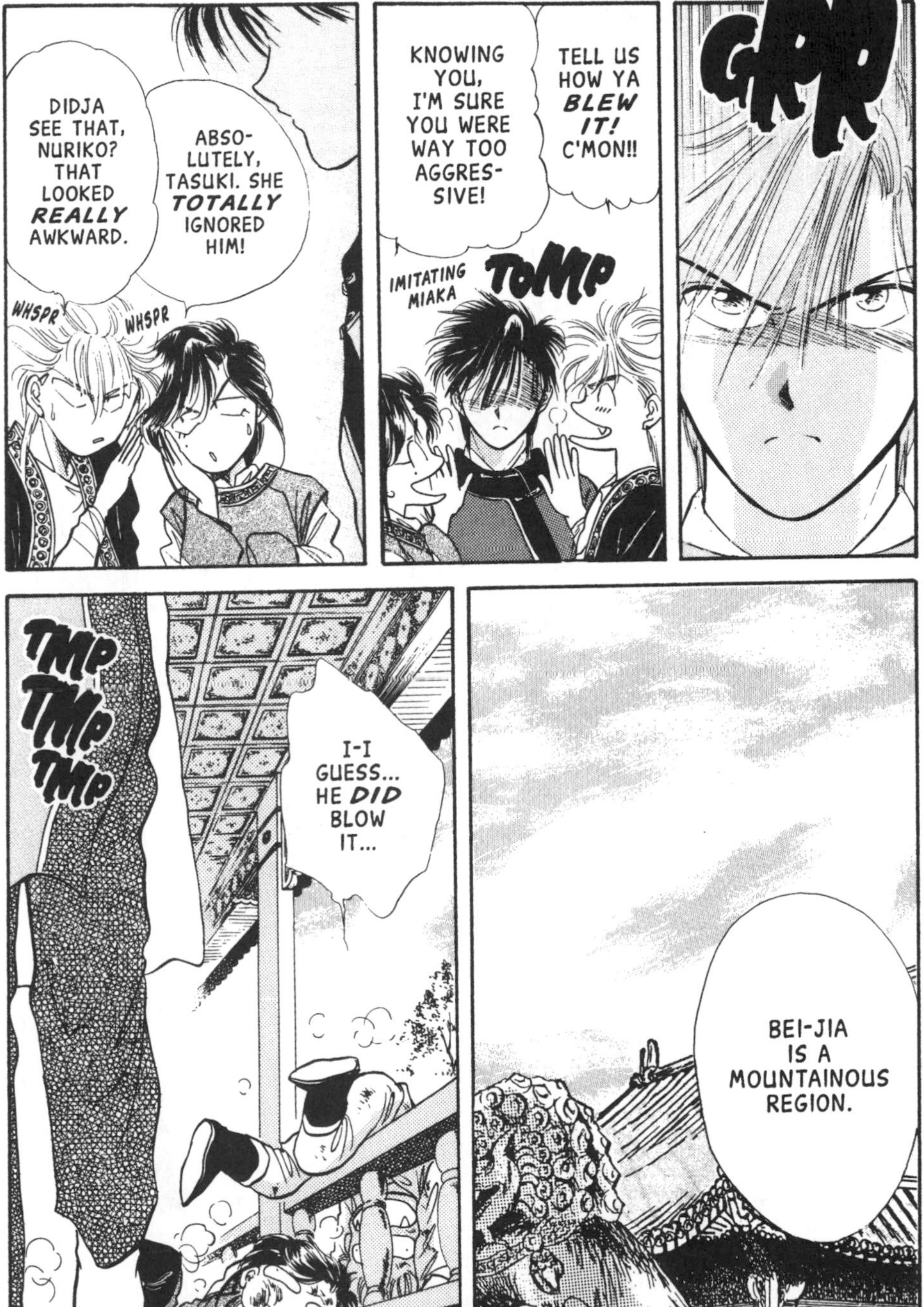
DIDJA SEE THAT, NURIKO? THAT LOOKED REALLY AWKWARD.
ABSO-LUTELY, TASUKI. SHE TOTALLY IGNORED HIM!
WHSPR
WHSPR
KNOWING YOU, I'M SURE YOU WERE WAY TOO AGGRES-SIVE!
TELL US HOW YA BLEW IT! C'MON!!
IMITATING MIAKA
TOMP
GRR
TMP TMP TMP
I-I GUESS... HE DID BLOW IT...
BEI-JIA IS A MOUNTAINOUS REGION.

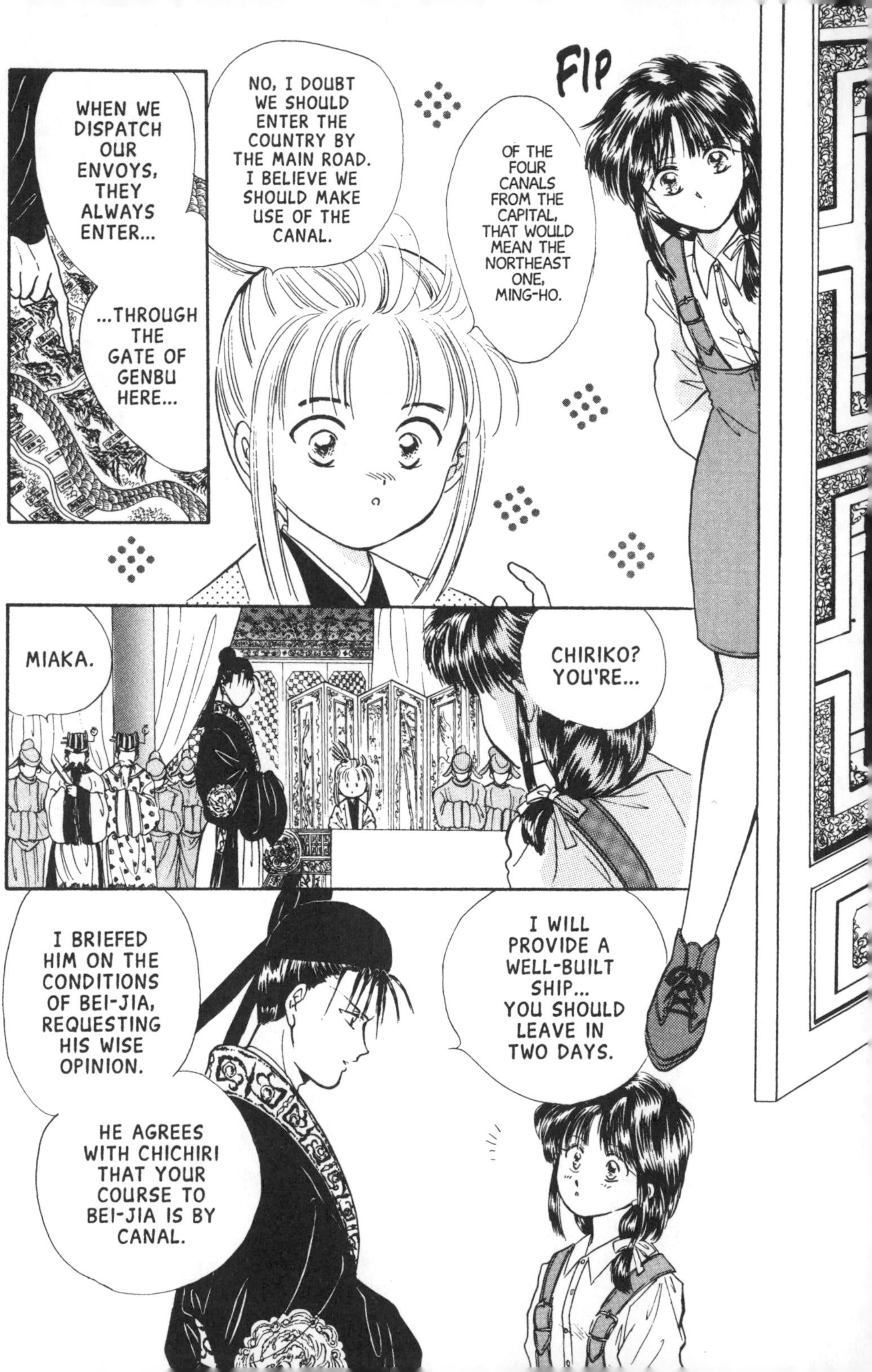
WHEN WE DISPATCH OUR ENVOYS, THEY ALWAYS ENTER...
...THROUGH THE GATE OF GENBU HERE...
NO, I DOUBT WE SHOULD ENTER THE COUNTRY BY THE MAIN ROAD. I BELIEVE WE SHOULD MAKE USE OF THE CANAL.
OF THE FOUR CANALS FROM THE CAPITAL, THAT WOULD MEAN THE NORTHEAST ONE, MING-HO.
FLP
MIAKA.
CHIRIKO? YOU'RE...
I BRIEFED HIM ON THE CONDITIONS OF BEI-JIA, REQUESTING HIS WISE OPINION.
HE AGREES WITH CHICHIRI THAT YOUR COURSE TO BEI-JIA IS BY CANAL.
I WILL PROVIDE A WELL-BUILT SHIP... YOU SHOULD LEAVE IN TWO DAYS.

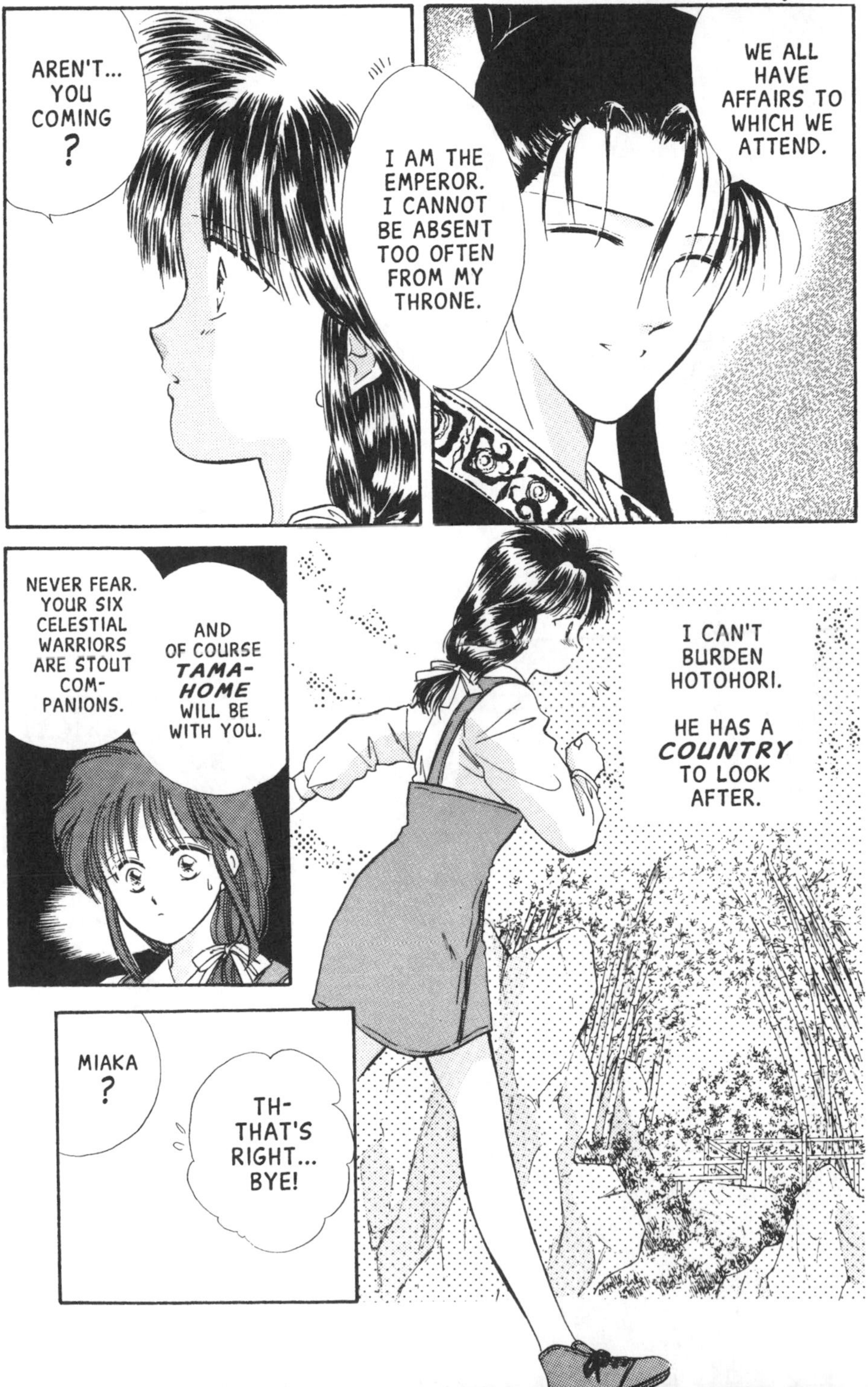
AREN'T... YOU COMING?
I AM THE EMPEROR. I CANNOT BE ABSENT TOO OFTEN FROM MY THRONE.
WE ALL HAVE AFFAIRS TO WHICH WE ATTEND.
NEVER FEAR. YOUR SIX CELESTIAL WARRIORS ARE STOUT COM-PANIONS.
AND OF COURSE *TAMA-HOME* WILL BE WITH YOU.
MIAKA?
TH-THAT'S RIGHT... BYE!
I CAN'T BURDEN HOTOHORI.
HE HAS A *COUNTRY* TO LOOK AFTER.

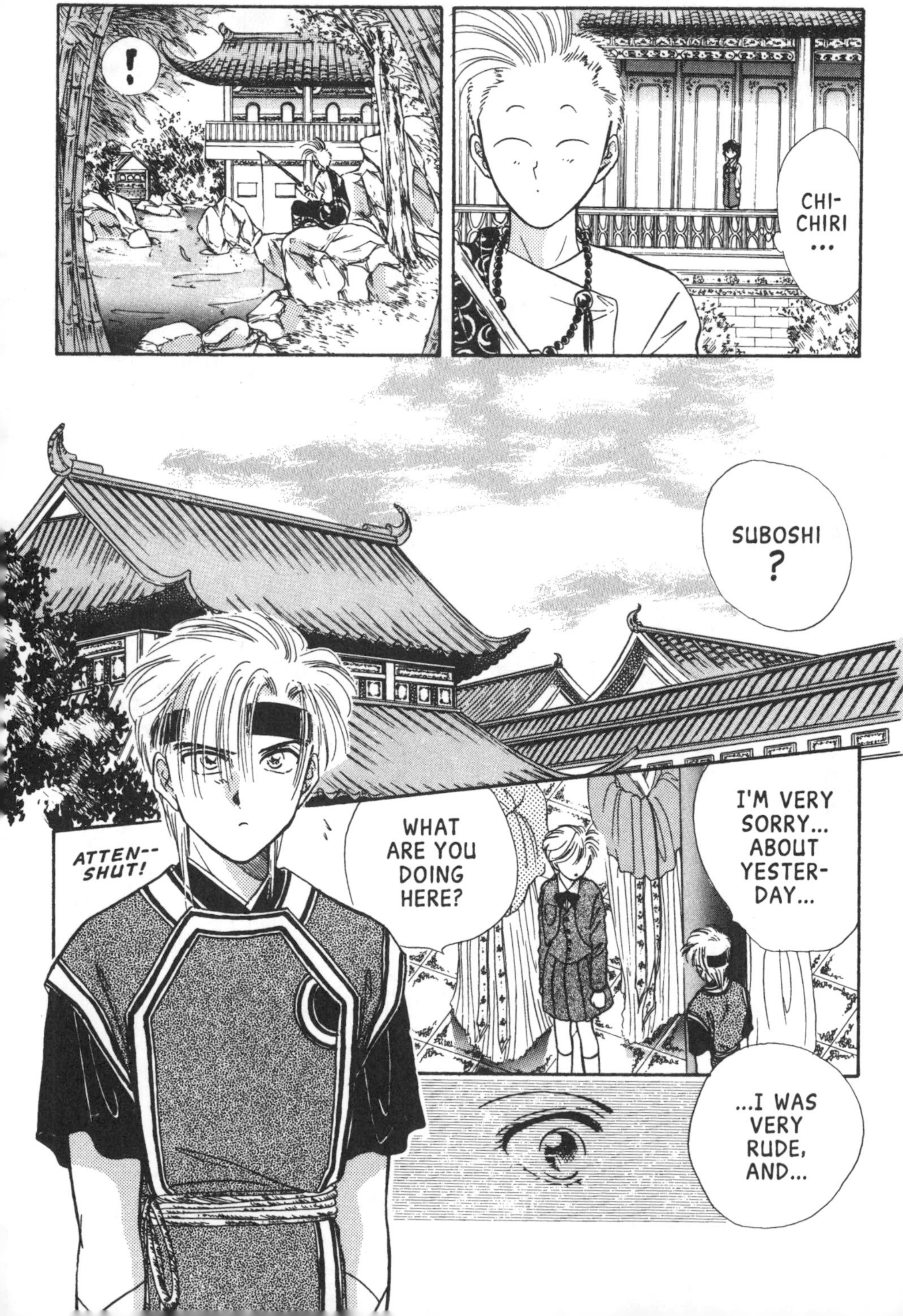
!
CHI-CHIRI...
SUBOSHI?
ATTEN--SHUT!
WHAT ARE YOU DOING HERE?
I'M VERY SORRY... ABOUT YESTER-DAY...
...I WAS VERY RUDE, AND...

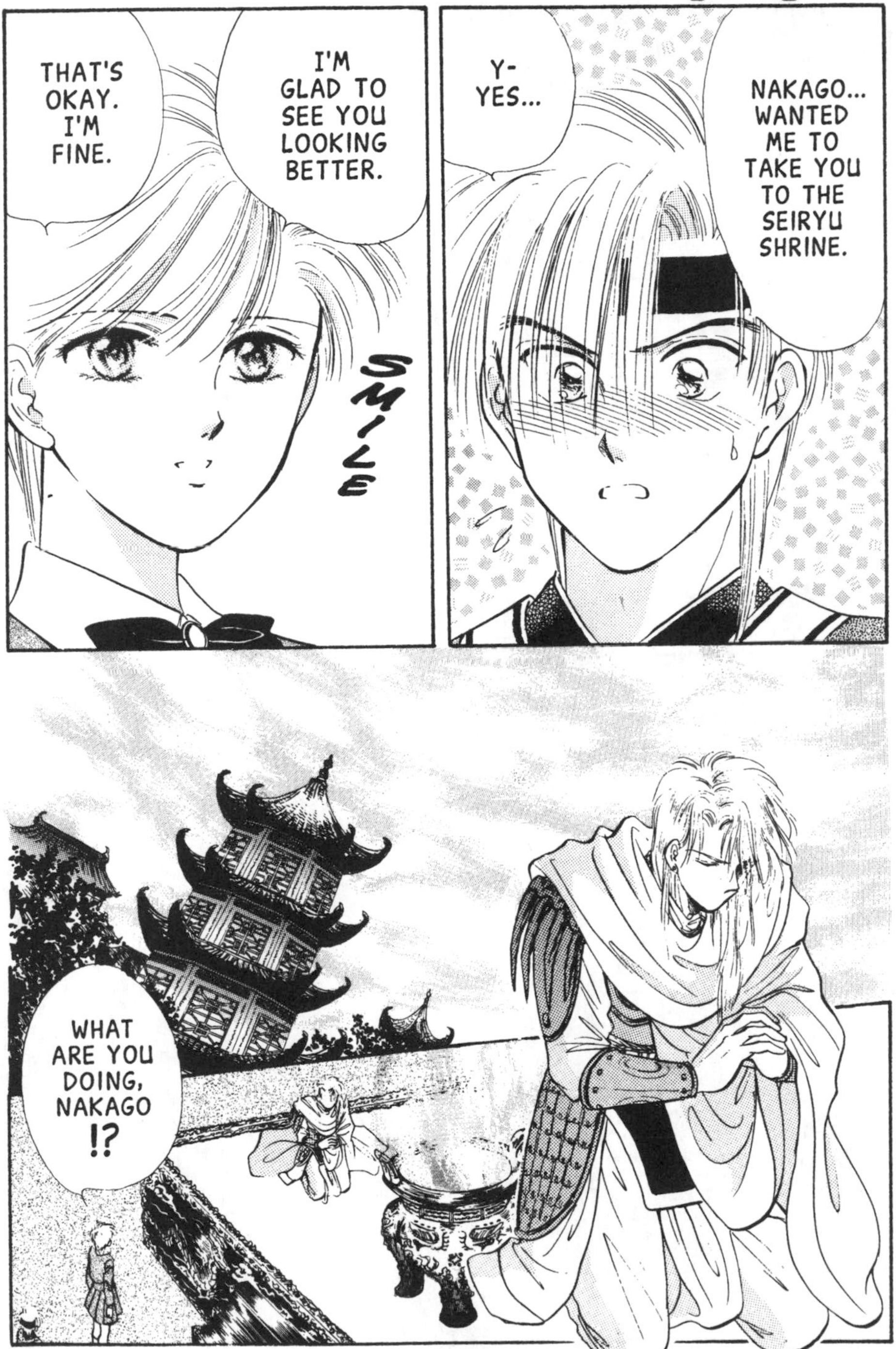
THAT'S OKAY. I'M FINE.
I'M GLAD TO SEE YOU LOOKING BETTER.
SMILE
Y-YES...
NAKAGO... WANTED ME TO TAKE YOU TO THE SEIRYU SHRINE.
WHAT ARE YOU DOING, NAKAGO !?

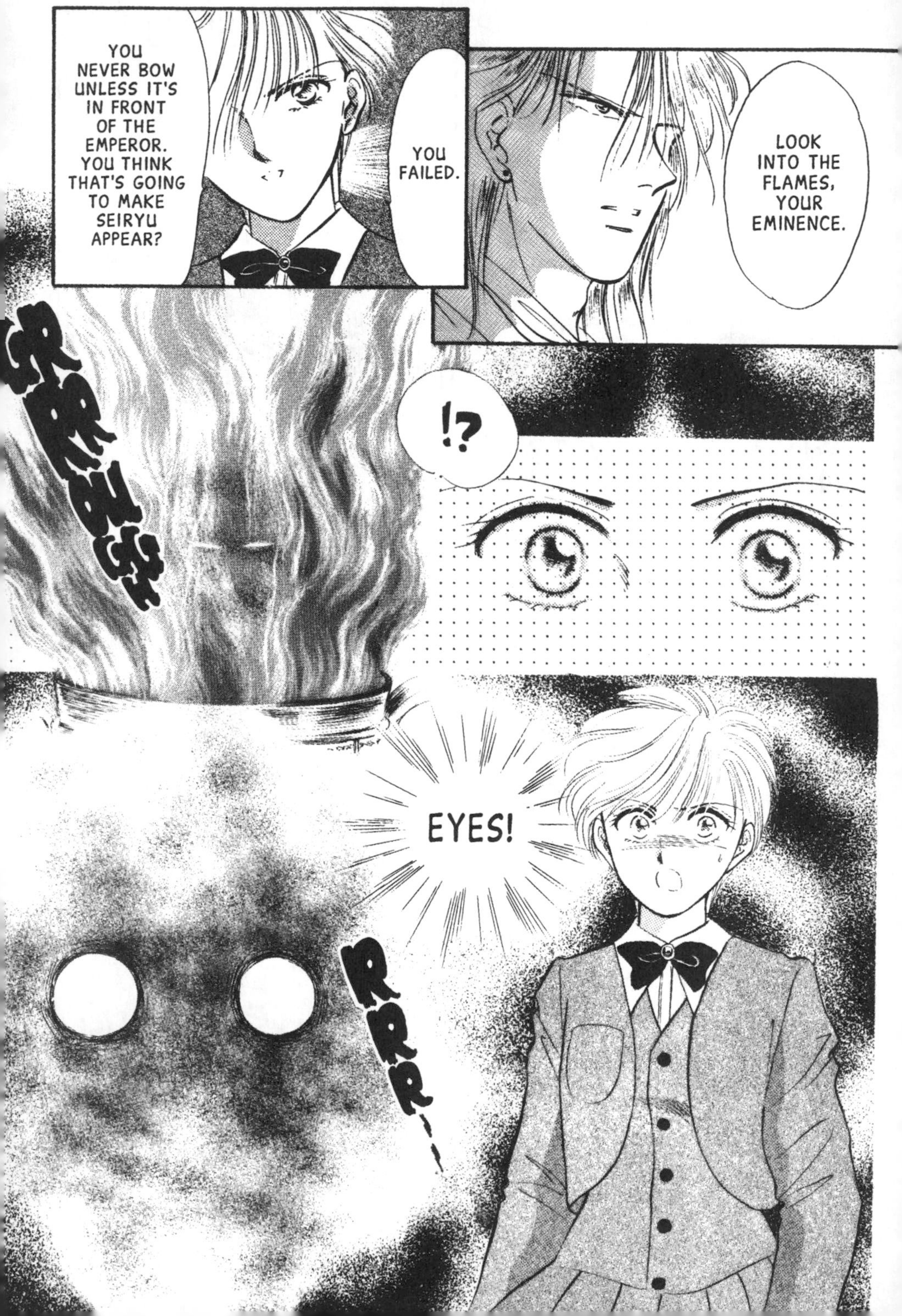
YOU NEVER BOW UNLESS IT'S IN FRONT OF THE EMPEROR. YOU THINK THAT'S GOING TO MAKE SEIRYU APPEAR?
YOU FAILED.
LOOK INTO THE FLAMES, YOUR EMINENCE.
!?
EYES!
RRR--

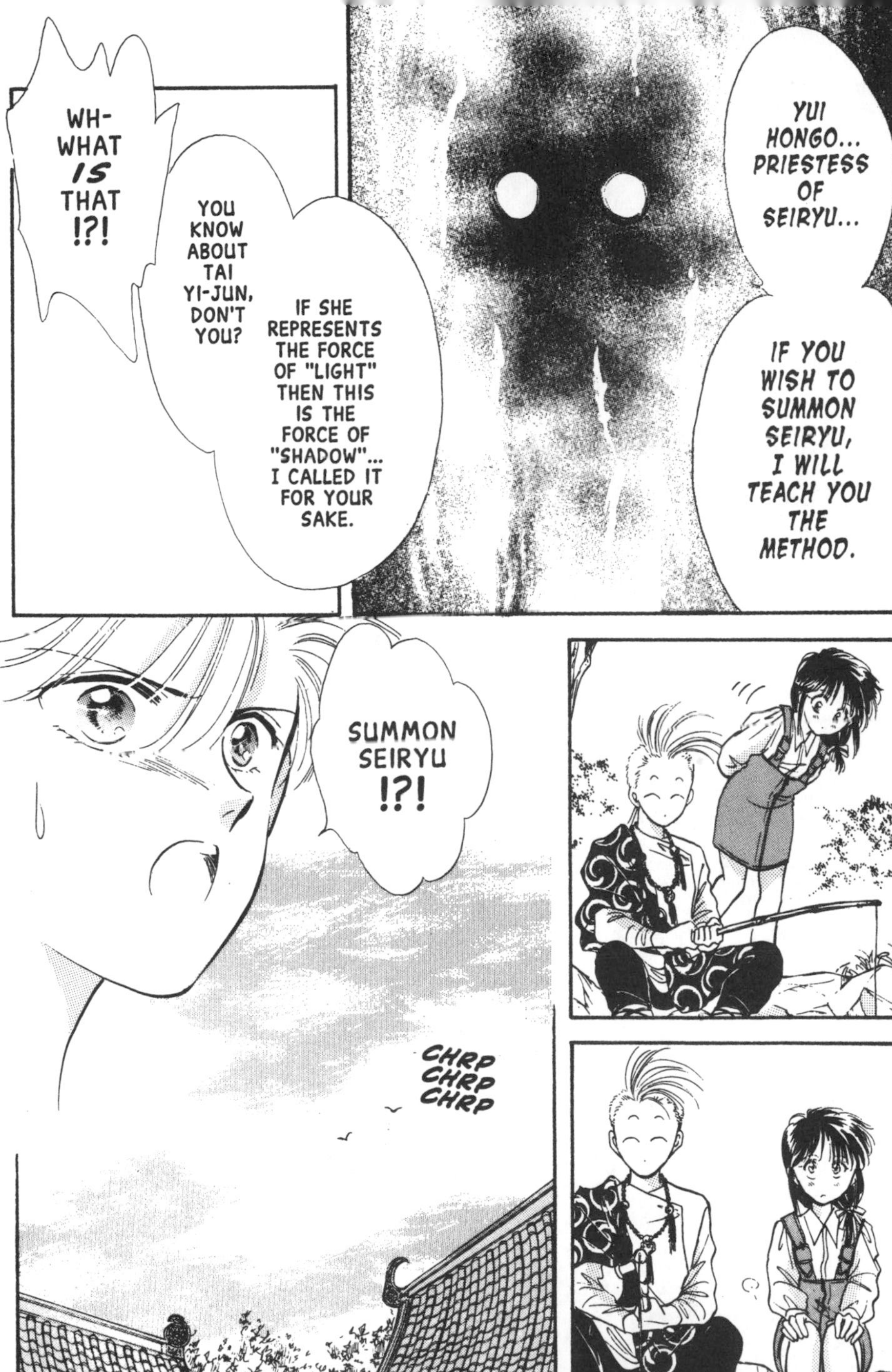
WH-WHAT IS THAT !?!
YOU KNOW ABOUT TAI YI-JUN, DON'T YOU?
IF SHE REPRESENTS THE FORCE OF "LIGHT" THEN THIS IS THE FORCE OF "SHADOW"... I CALLED IT FOR YOUR SAKE.
YUI HONGO... PRIESTESS OF SEIRYU...
IF YOU WISH TO SUMMON SEIRYU, I WILL TEACH YOU THE METHOD.
SUMMON SEIRYU !?!
CHRP CHRP CHRP

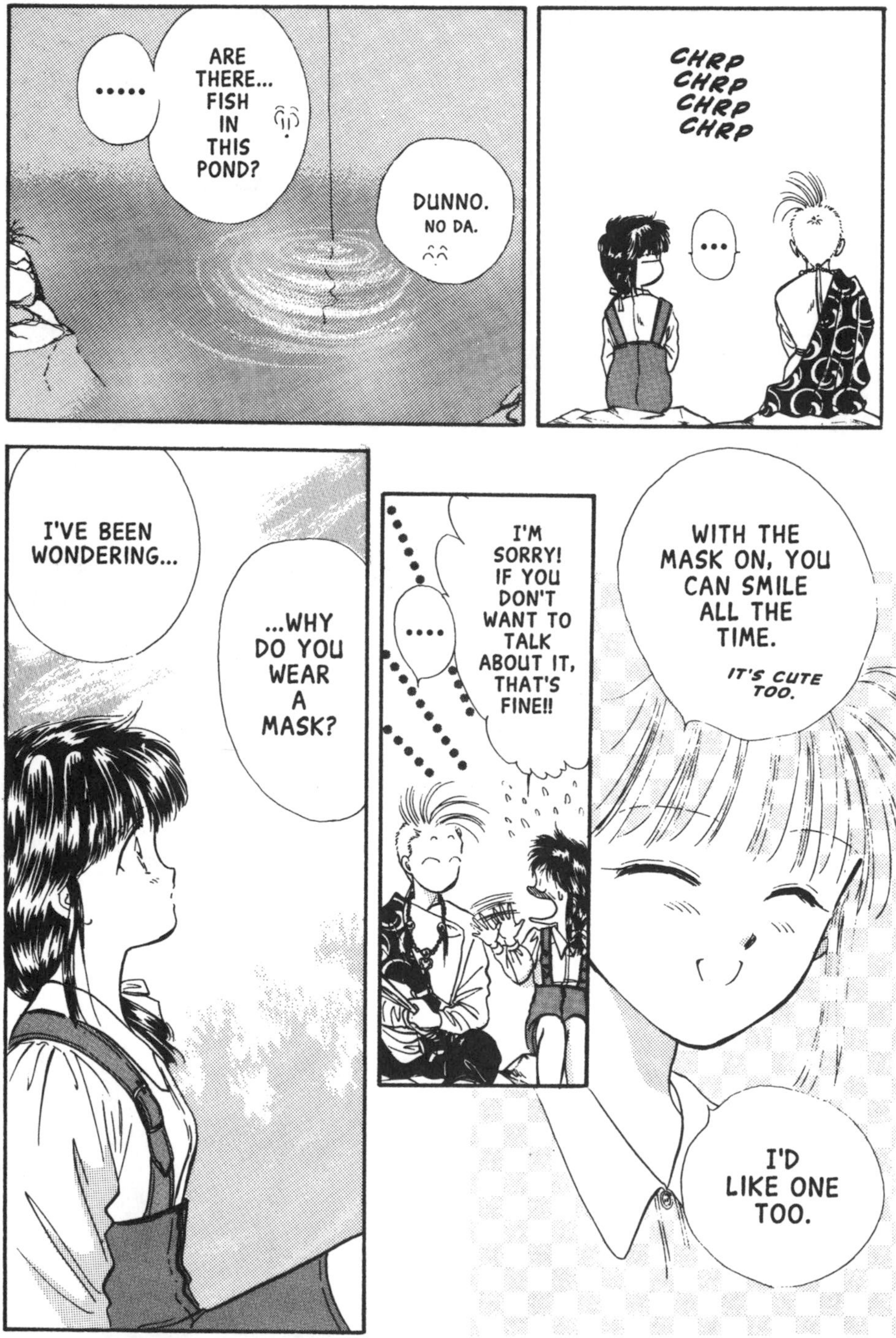
.....
ARE THERE... FISH IN THIS POND?
DUNNO. NO DA.
CHRP CHRP CHRP CHRP
...
I'VE BEEN WONDERING...
...WHY DO YOU WEAR A MASK?
....
I'M SORRY! IF YOU DON'T WANT TO TALK ABOUT IT, THAT'S FINE!!
WITH THE MASK ON, YOU CAN SMILE ALL THE TIME.
IT'S CUTE TOO.
I'D LIKE ONE TOO.

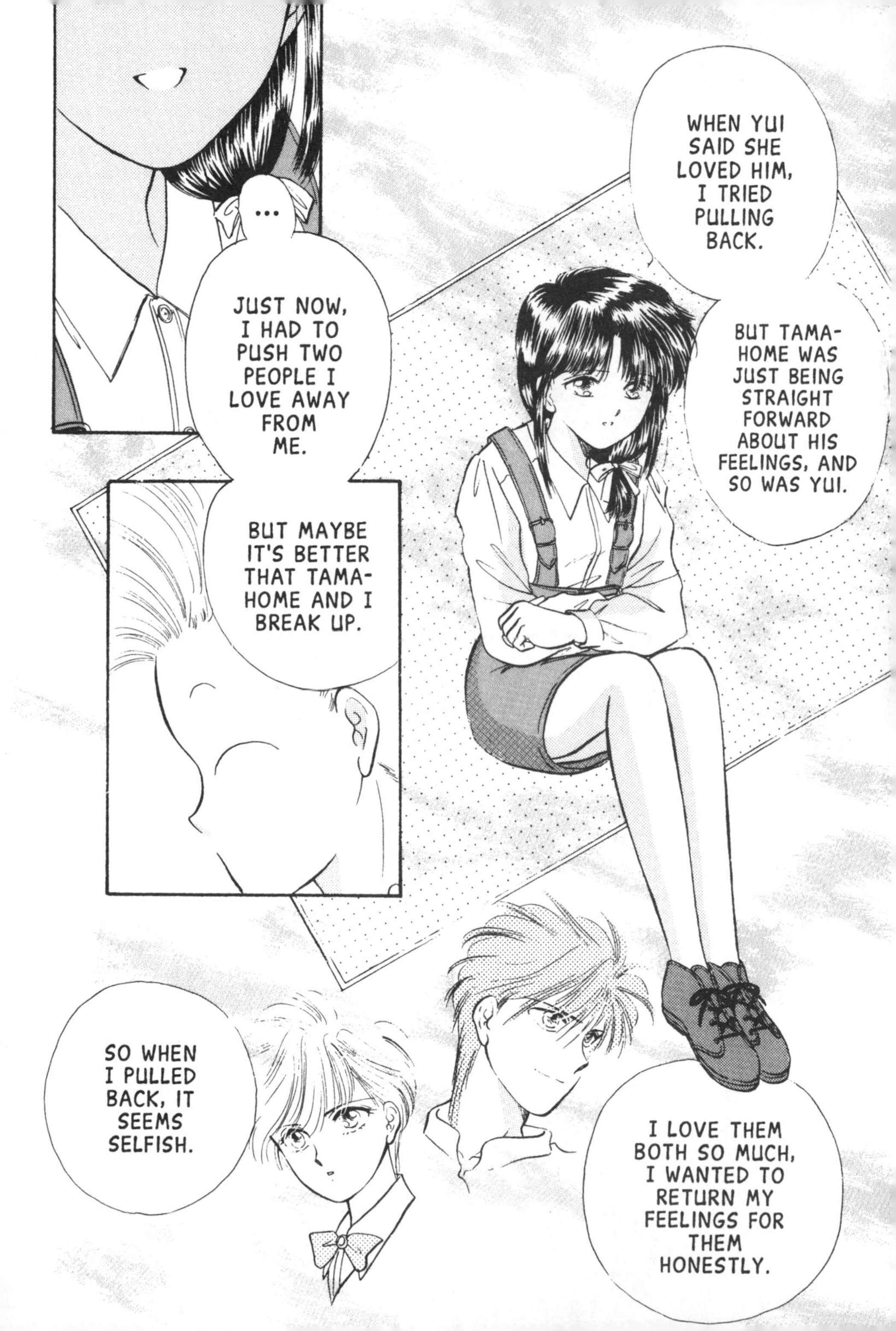
...
JUST NOW, I HAD TO PUSH TWO PEOPLE I LOVE AWAY FROM ME.
WHEN YUI SAID SHE LOVED HIM, I TRIED PULLING BACK.
BUT TAMA-HOME WAS JUST BEING STRAIGHT FORWARD ABOUT HIS FEELINGS, AND SO WAS YUI.
BUT MAYBE IT'S BETTER THAT TAMA-HOME AND I BREAK UP.
SO WHEN I PULLED BACK, IT SEEMS SELFISH.
I LOVE THEM BOTH SO MUCH, I WANTED TO RETURN MY FEELINGS FOR THEM HONESTLY.

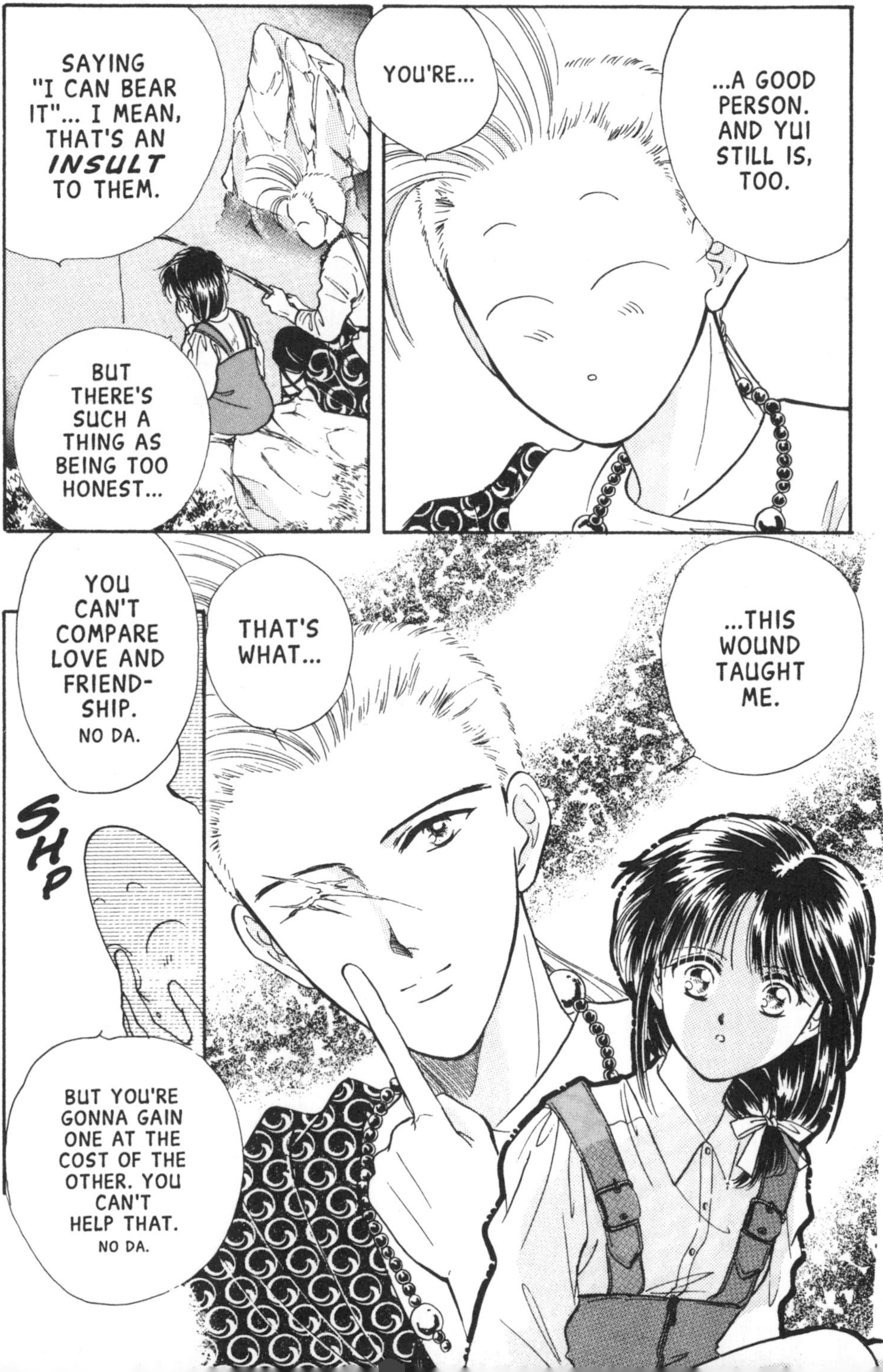
SAYING "I CAN BEAR IT"... I MEAN, THAT'S AN INSULT TO THEM.
BUT THERE'S SUCH A THING AS BEING TOO HONEST...
YOU'RE...
...A GOOD PERSON. AND YUI STILL IS, TOO.
YOU CAN'T COMPARE LOVE AND FRIEND-SHIP. NO DA.
SHP
BUT YOU'RE GONNA GAIN ONE AT THE COST OF THE OTHER. YOU CAN'T HELP THAT. NO DA.
THAT'S WHAT...
...THIS WOUND TAUGHT ME.

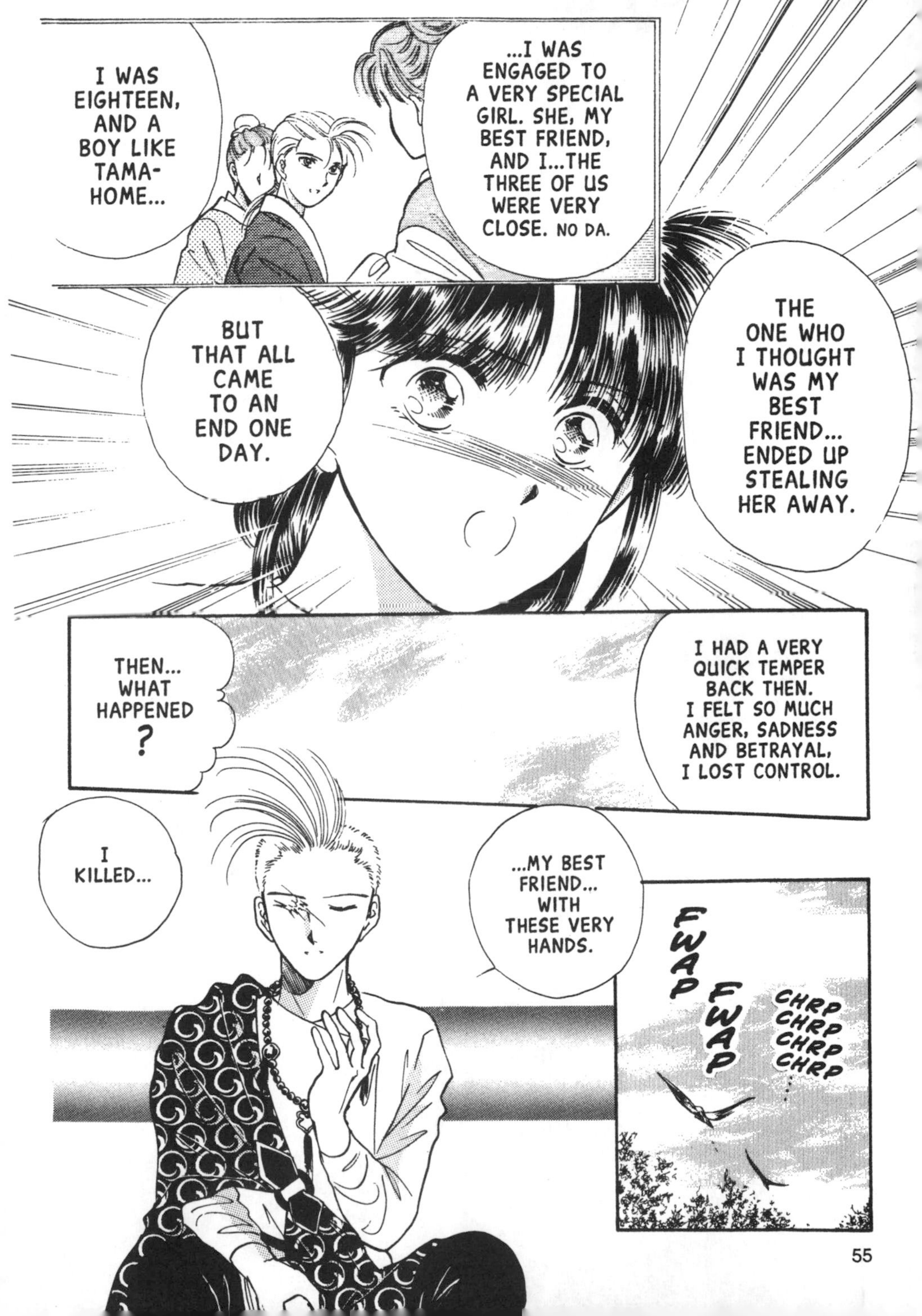
I WAS EIGHTEEN, AND A BOY LIKE TAMA-HOME...
...I WAS ENGAGED TO A VERY SPECIAL GIRL. SHE, MY BEST FRIEND, AND I...THE THREE OF US WERE VERY CLOSE. NO DA.
BUT THAT ALL CAME TO AN END ONE DAY.
THE ONE WHO I THOUGHT WAS MY BEST FRIEND... ENDED UP STEALING HER AWAY.
THEN... WHAT HAPPENED?
I HAD A VERY QUICK TEMPER BACK THEN. I FELT SO MUCH ANGER, SADNESS AND BETRAYAL, I LOST CONTROL.
I KILLED...
...MY BEST FRIEND... WITH THESE VERY HANDS.
FWAP
FWAP
CHRP CHRP CHRP CHRP

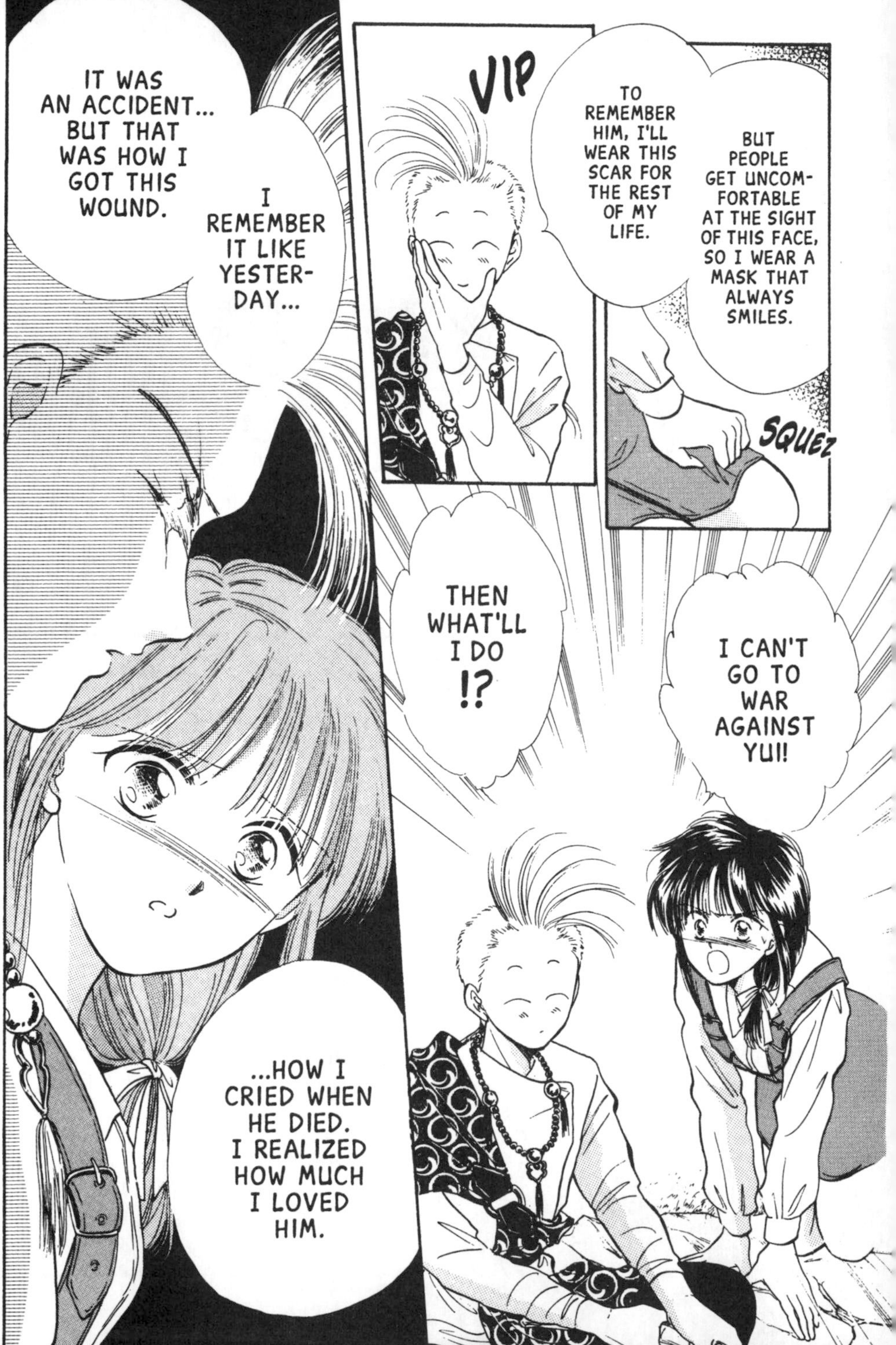
IT WAS AN ACCIDENT... BUT THAT WAS HOW I GOT THIS WOUND.
I REMEMBER IT LIKE YESTER-DAY...
...HOW I CRIED WHEN HE DIED. I REALIZED HOW MUCH I LOVED HIM.
VIP
TO REMEMBER HIM, I'LL WEAR THIS SCAR FOR THE REST OF MY LIFE.
BUT PEOPLE GET UNCOM-FORTABLE AT THE SIGHT OF THIS FACE, SO I WEAR A MASK THAT ALWAYS SMILES.
SQUEZ
THEN WHAT'LL I DO !?
I CAN'T GO TO WAR AGAINST YUI!

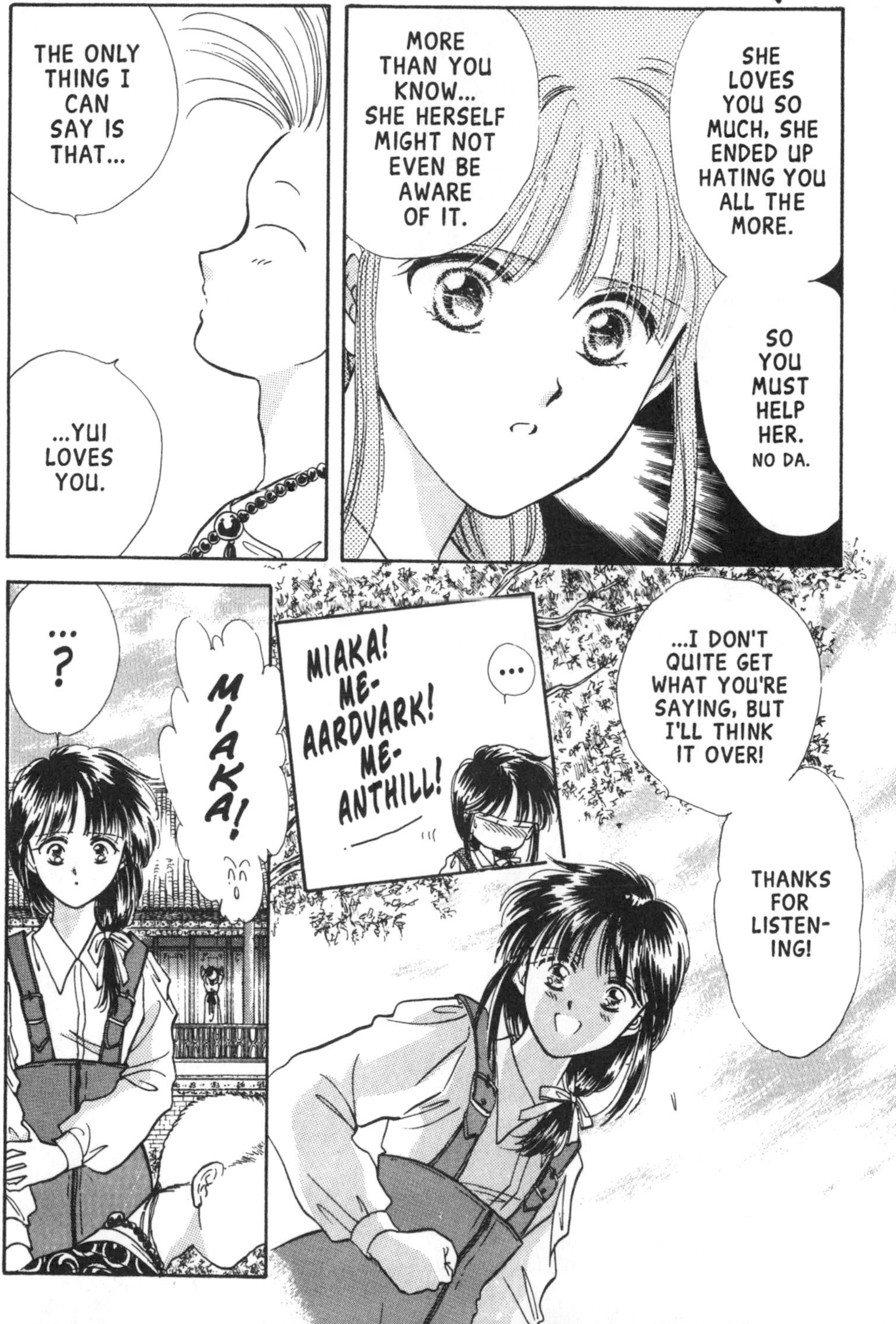
THE ONLY THING I CAN SAY IS THAT...
...YUI LOVES YOU.
MORE THAN YOU KNOW... SHE HERSELF MIGHT NOT EVEN BE AWARE OF IT.
SHE LOVES YOU SO MUCH, SHE ENDED UP HATING YOU ALL THE MORE.
SO YOU MUST HELP HER. NO DA.
...?
MIAKA!
MIAKA! ME-AARDVARK! ME-ANTHILL!
...
...I DON'T QUITE GET WHAT YOU'RE SAYING, BUT I'LL THINK IT OVER!
THANKS FOR LISTEN-ING!

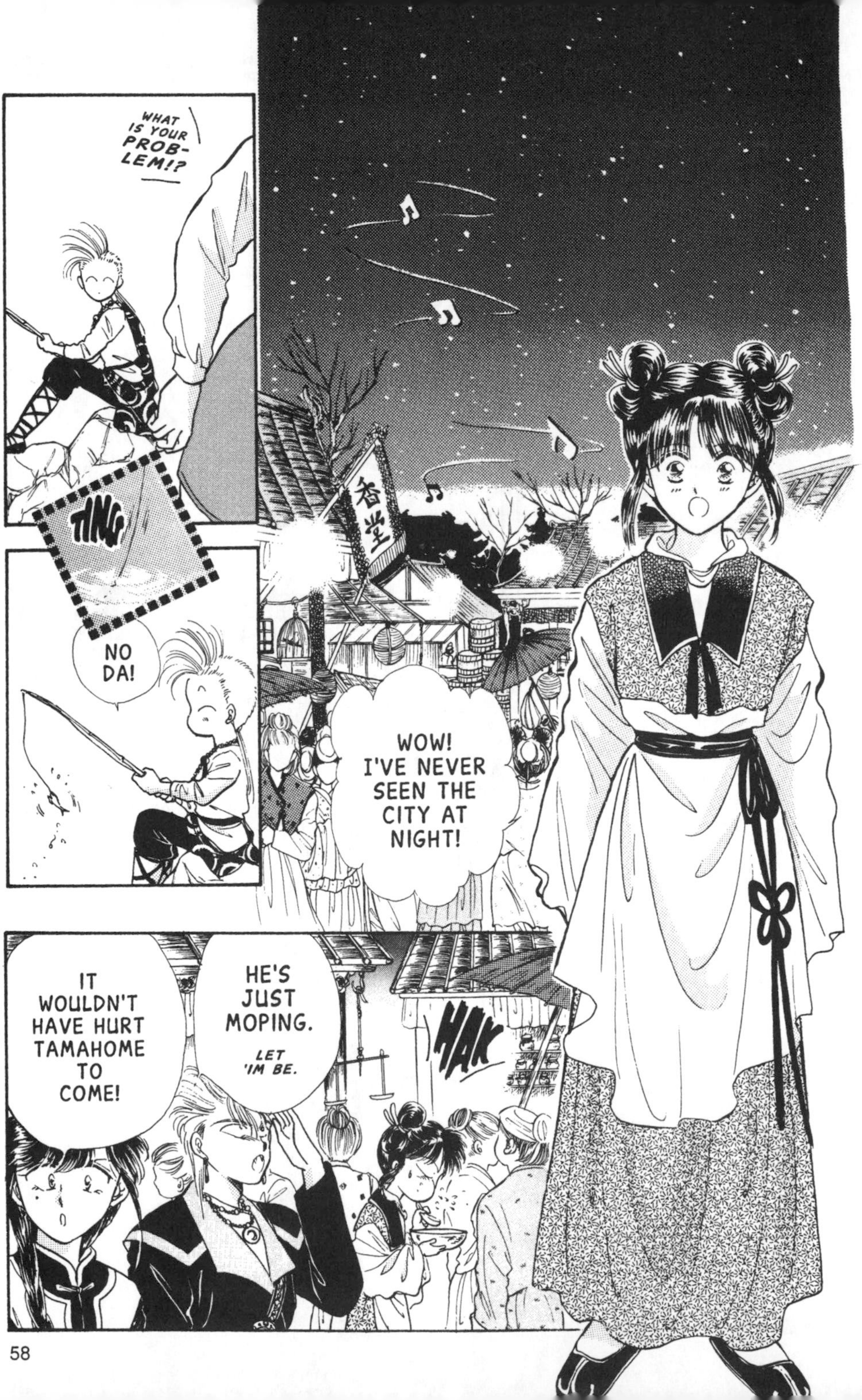
WHAT IS YOUR PROB-LEM!?
TING
NO DA!
香堂
WOW! I'VE NEVER SEEN THE CITY AT NIGHT!
IT WOULDN'T HAVE HURT TAMAHOME TO COME!
HE'S JUST MOPING.
LET 'IM BE.
HAK

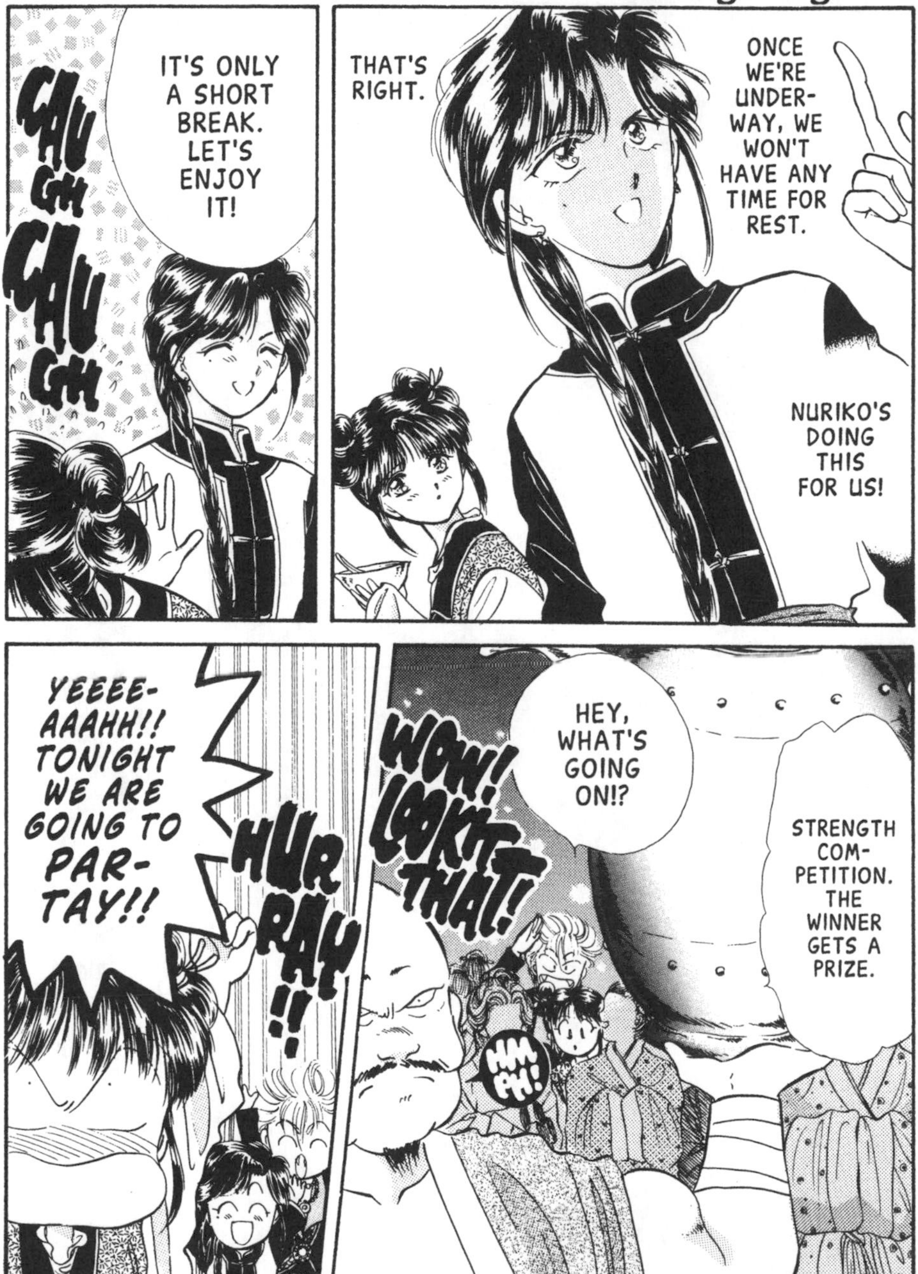
GAUGH GAUGH
IT'S ONLY A SHORT BREAK. LET'S ENJOY IT!
THAT'S RIGHT.
ONCE WE'RE UNDER-WAY, WE WON'T HAVE ANY TIME FOR REST.
NURIKO'S DOING THIS FOR US!
YEEEE-AAAHH!! TONIGHT WE ARE GOING TO PAR-TAY!!
HURRAY!!
WOW! LOOKIT THAT!
HEY, WHAT'S GOING ON!?
HMPH!
STRENGTH COM-PETITION. THE WINNER GETS A PRIZE.

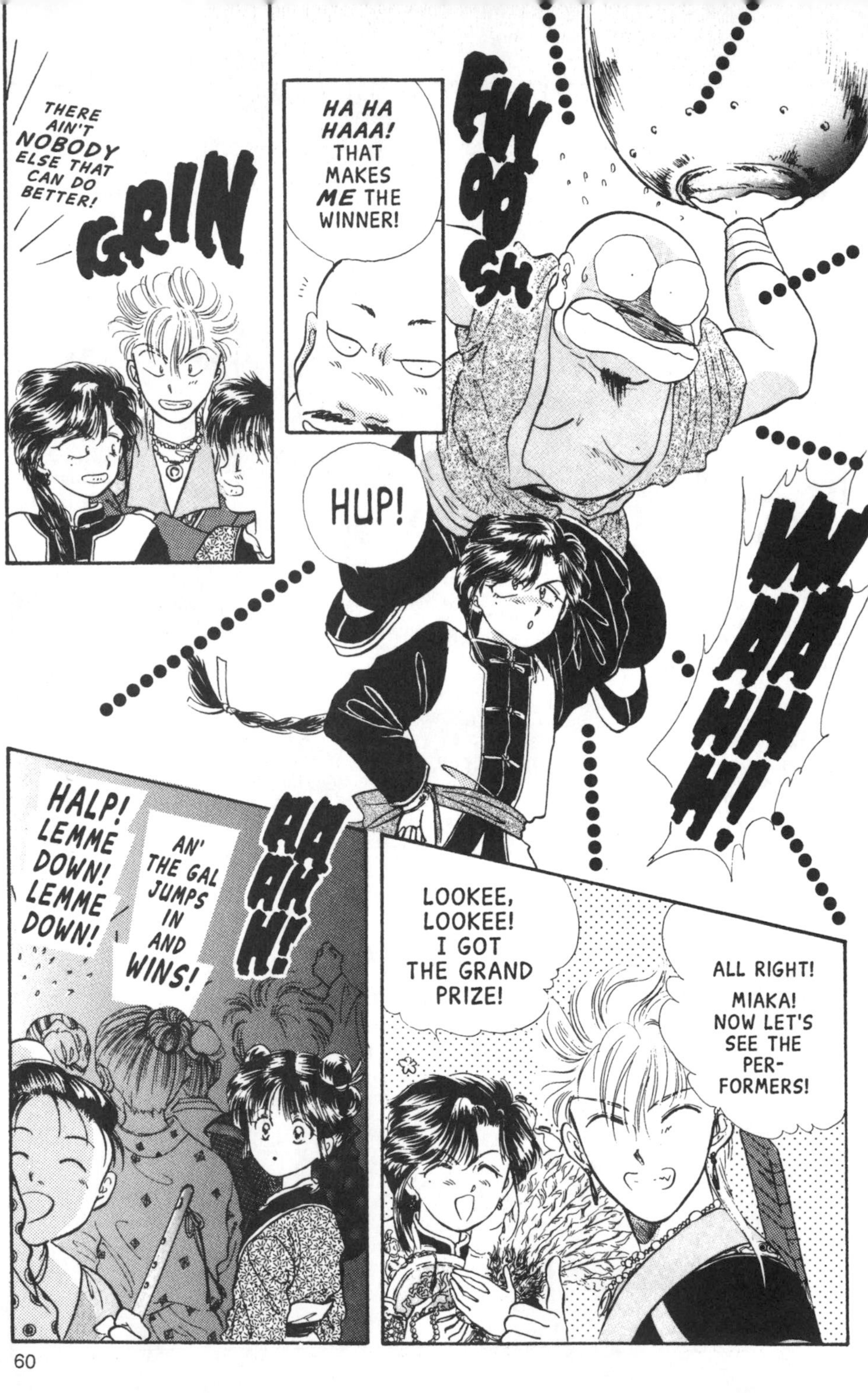

THERE AIN'T NOBODY ELSE THAT CAN DO BETTER!
GRIN
HA HA HAAA! THAT MAKES ME THE WINNER!
FWOOSH
HUP!
WAAAHHH!
HALP! LEMME DOWN! LEMME DOWN!
AN' THE GAL JUMPS IN AND WINS!
AAAHHH!
LOOKEE, LOOKEE! I GOT THE GRAND PRIZE!
ALL RIGHT! MIAKA! NOW LET'S SEE THE PER-FORMERS!

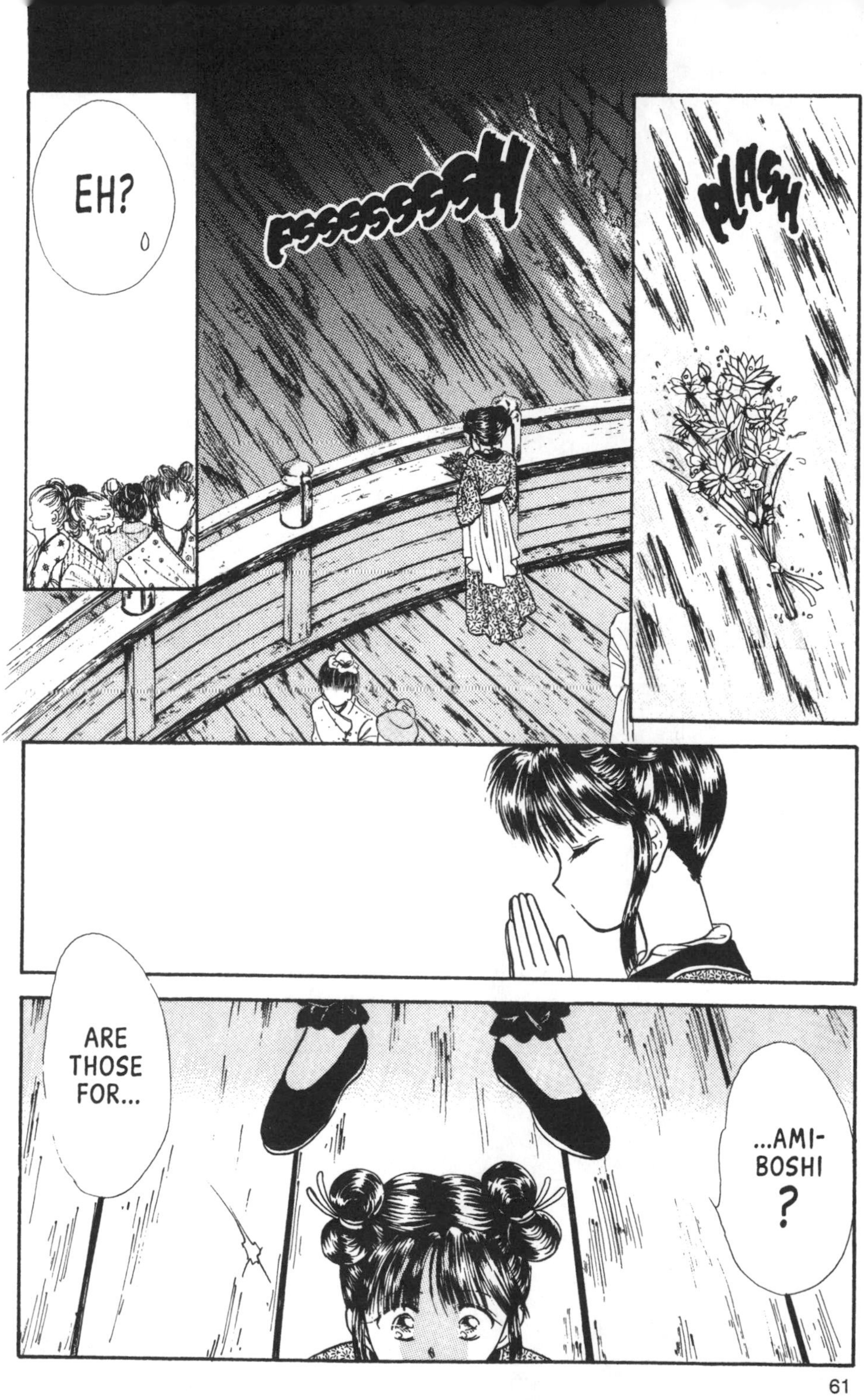

EH?
FSSSSSSSSH
PLASH
ARE THOSE FOR...
...AMI-BOSHI ?

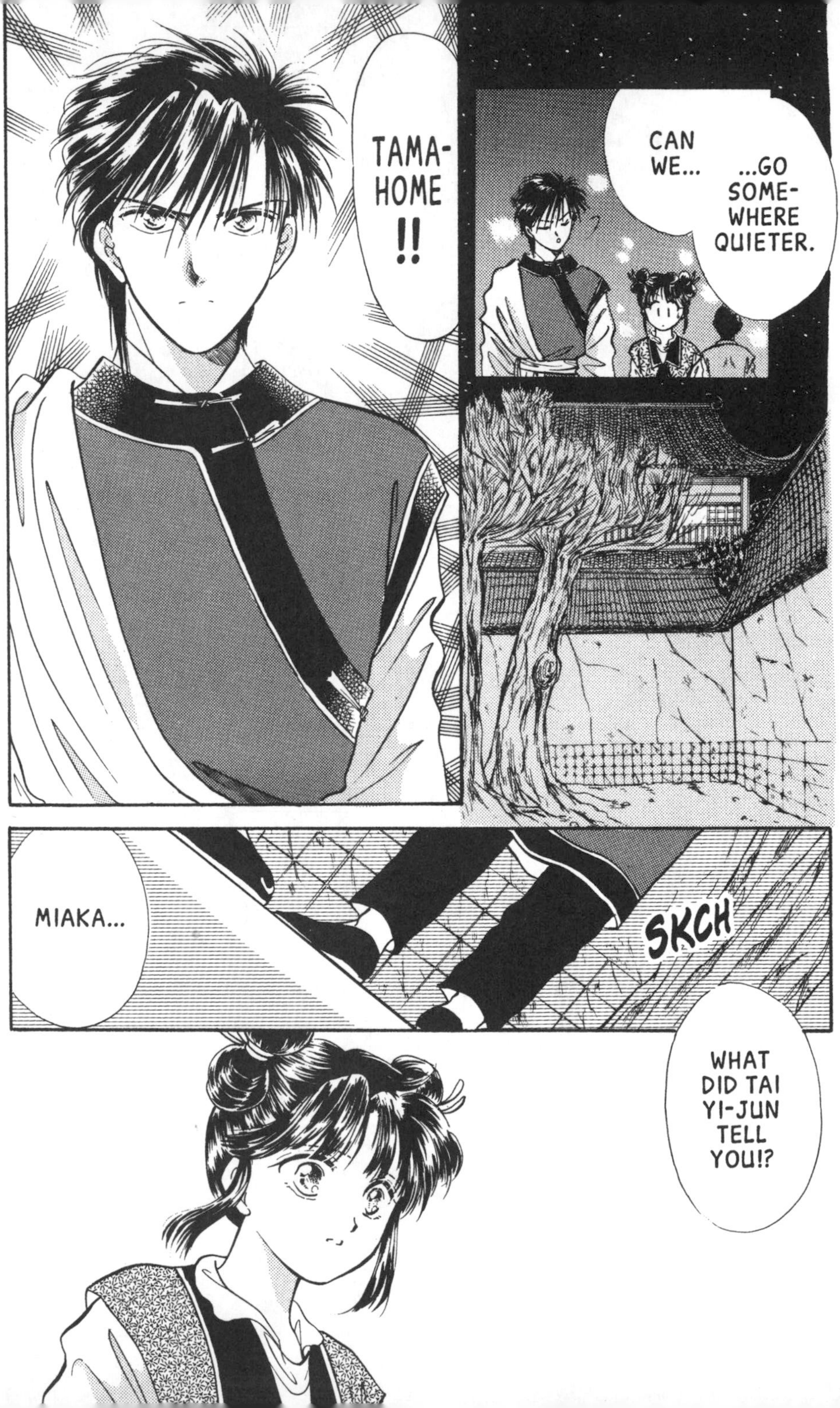
TAMA-HOME!!
CAN WE...
...GO SOMEWHERE QUIETER.
MIAKA...
SKCH
WHAT DID TAI YI-JUN TELL YOU!?

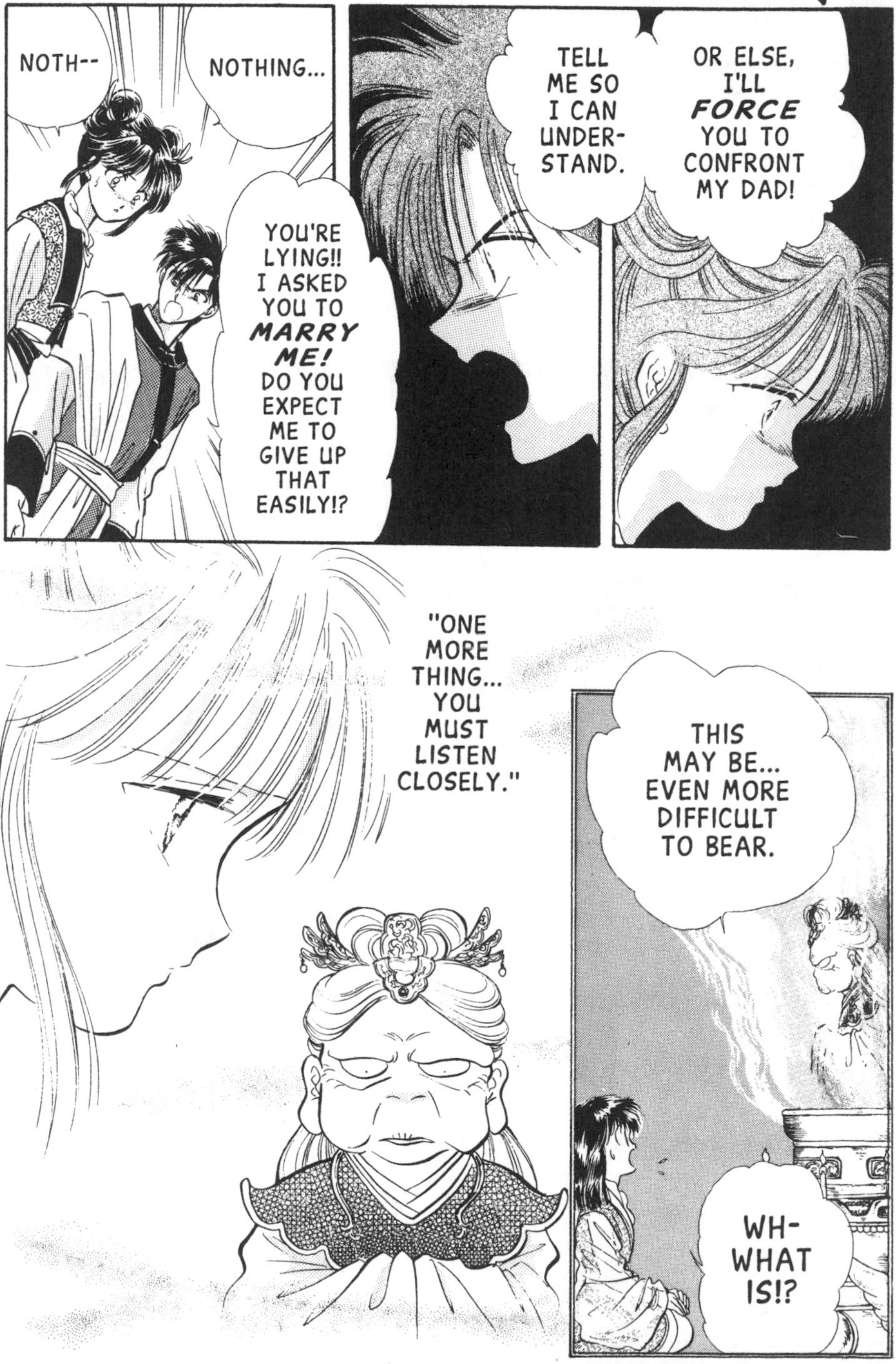
NOTH--
NOTHING...
YOU'RE LYING!! I ASKED YOU TO MARRY ME! DO YOU EXPECT ME TO GIVE UP THAT EASILY!?
TELL ME SO I CAN UNDER-STAND.
OR ELSE, I'LL FORCE YOU TO CONFRONT MY DAD!
"ONE MORE THING... YOU MUST LISTEN CLOSELY."
THIS MAY BE... EVEN MORE DIFFICULT TO BEAR.
WH-WHAT IS!?

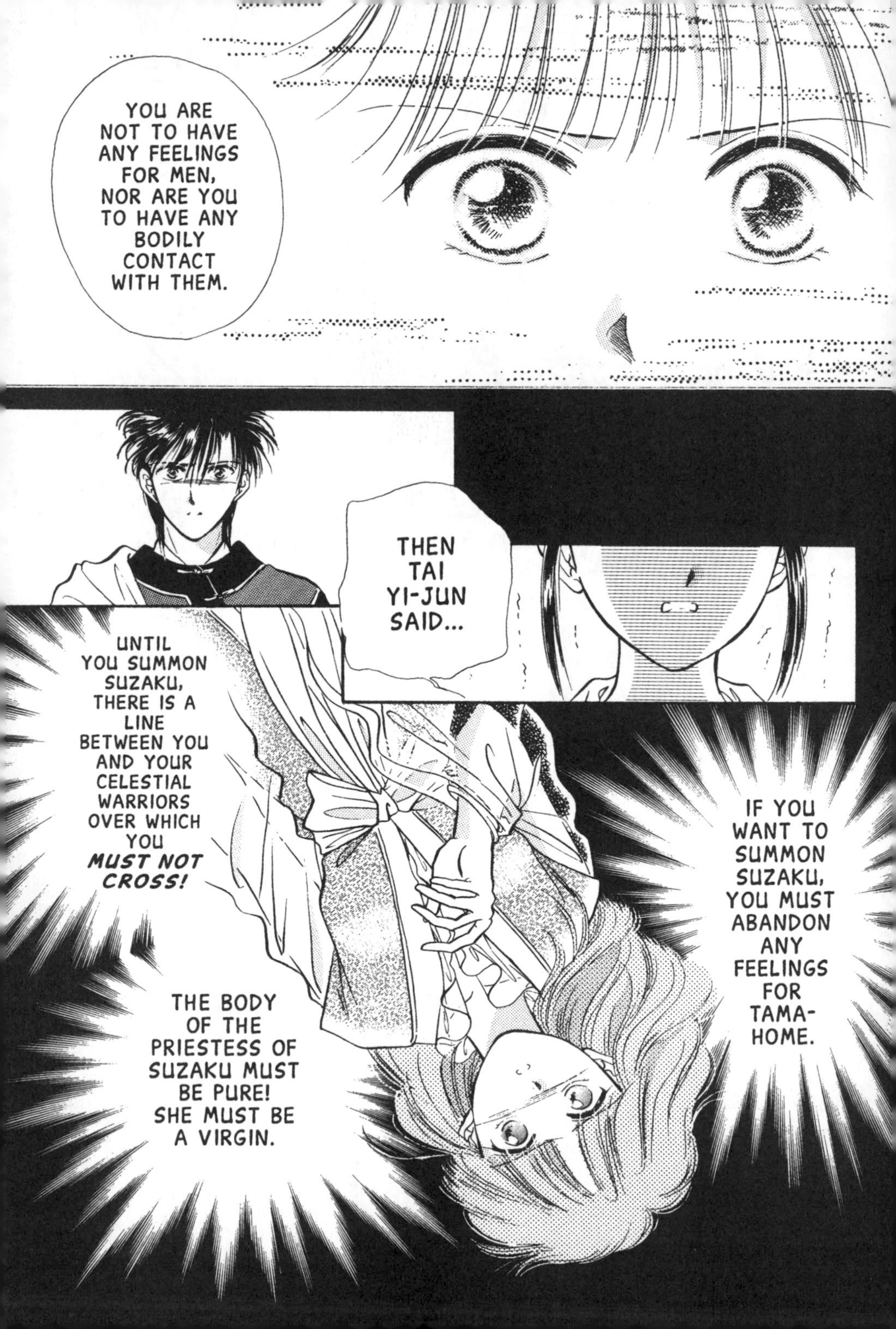
YOU ARE NOT TO HAVE ANY FEELINGS FOR MEN, NOR ARE YOU TO HAVE ANY BODILY CONTACT WITH THEM.
THEN TAI YI-JUN SAID...
UNTIL YOU SUMMON SUZAKU, THERE IS A LINE BETWEEN YOU AND YOUR CELESTIAL WARRIORS OVER WHICH YOU ***MUST NOT CROSS!***
IF YOU WANT TO SUMMON SUZAKU, YOU MUST ABANDON ANY FEELINGS FOR TAMA-HOME.
THE BODY OF THE PRIESTESS OF SUZAKU MUST BE PURE! SHE MUST BE A VIRGIN.

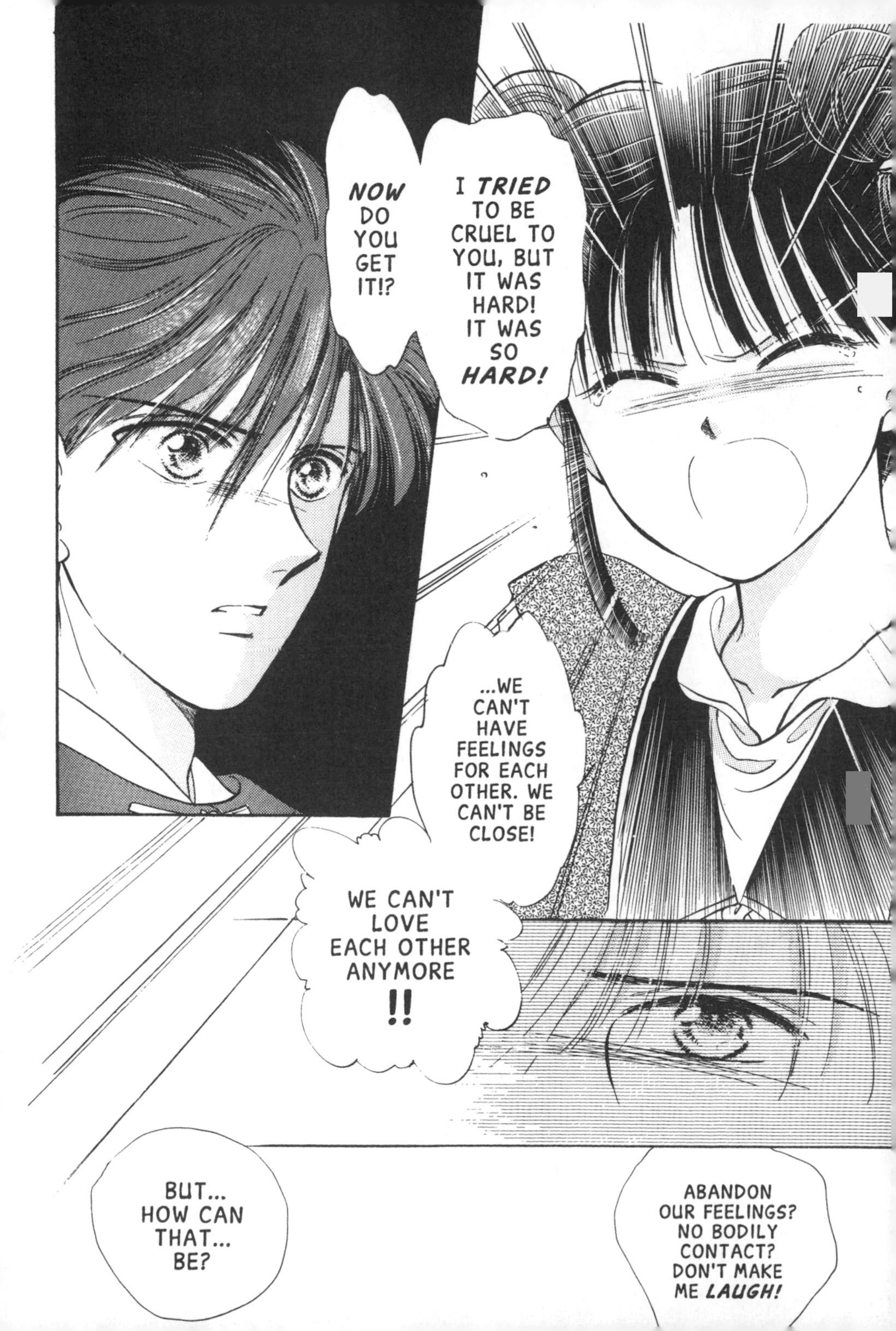
NOW DO YOU GET IT!?
I TRIED TO BE CRUEL TO YOU, BUT IT WAS HARD! IT WAS SO HARD!
...WE CAN'T HAVE FEELINGS FOR EACH OTHER. WE CAN'T BE CLOSE!
WE CAN'T LOVE EACH OTHER ANYMORE !!
BUT... HOW CAN THAT... BE?
ABANDON OUR FEELINGS? NO BODILY CONTACT? DON'T MAKE ME LAUGH!

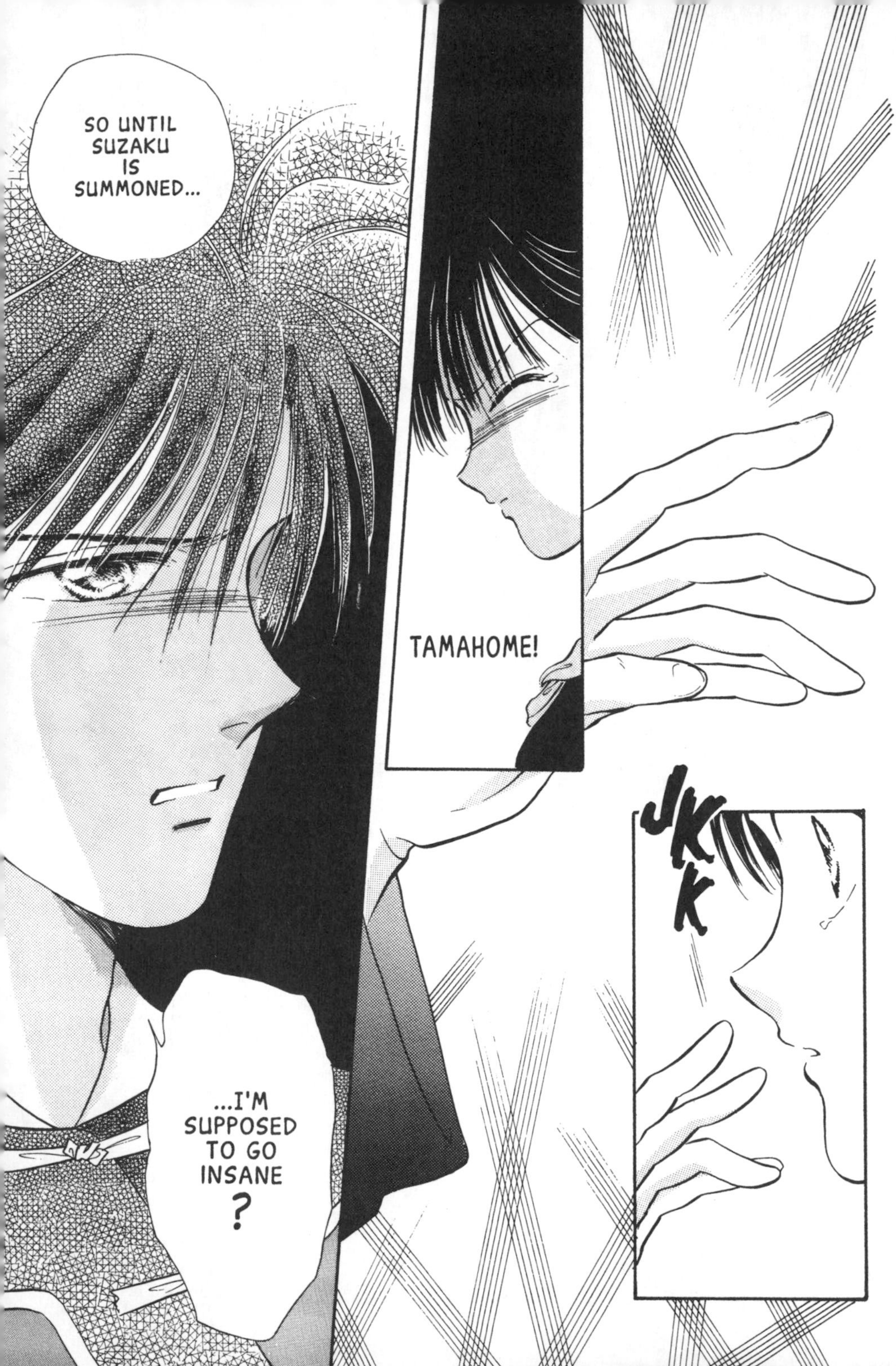
SO UNTIL SUZAKU IS SUMMONED...
...I'M SUPPOSED TO GO INSANE?
TAMAHOME!
JKK

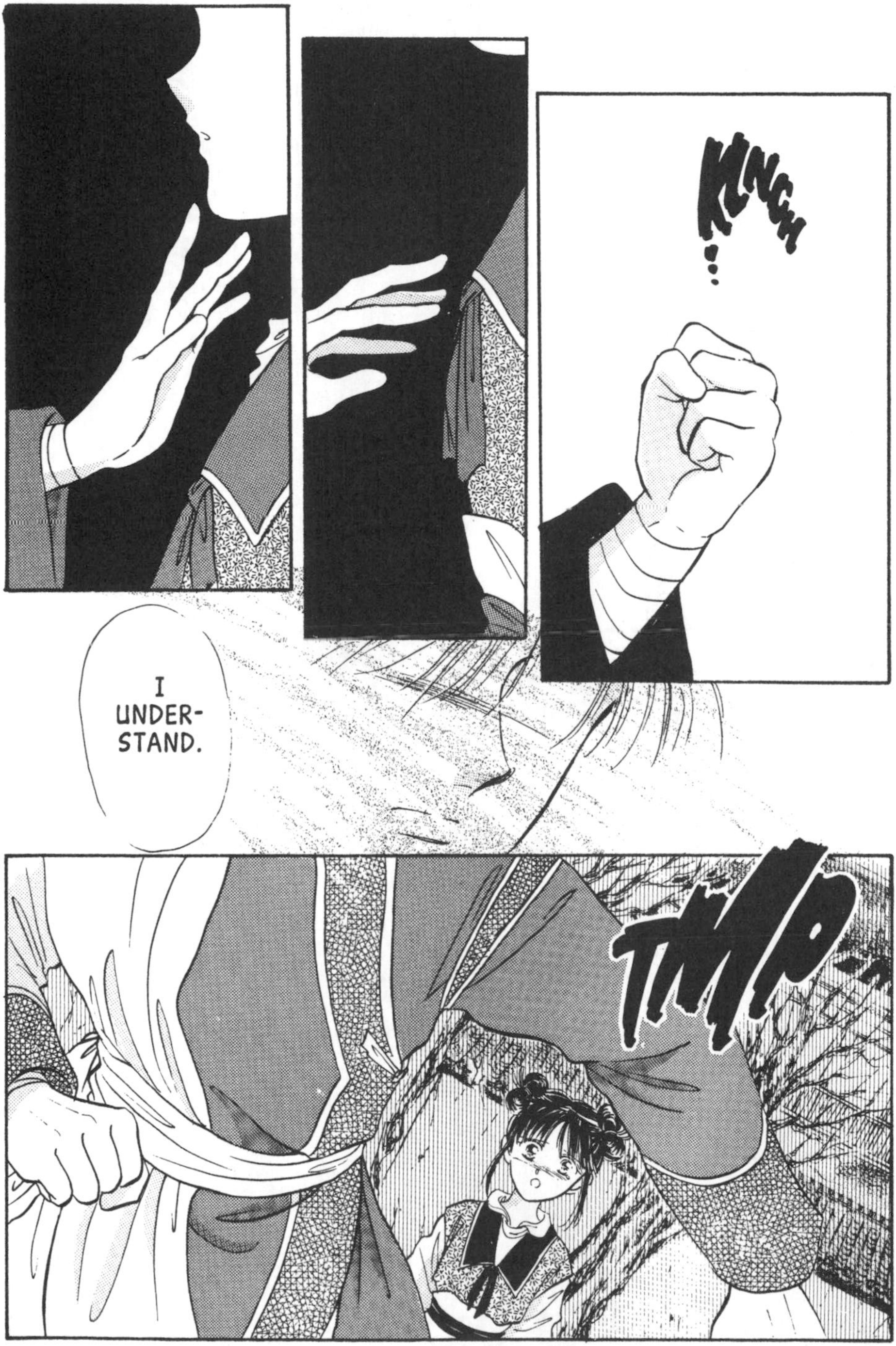
KLNCH
I UNDER-STAND.
THMP

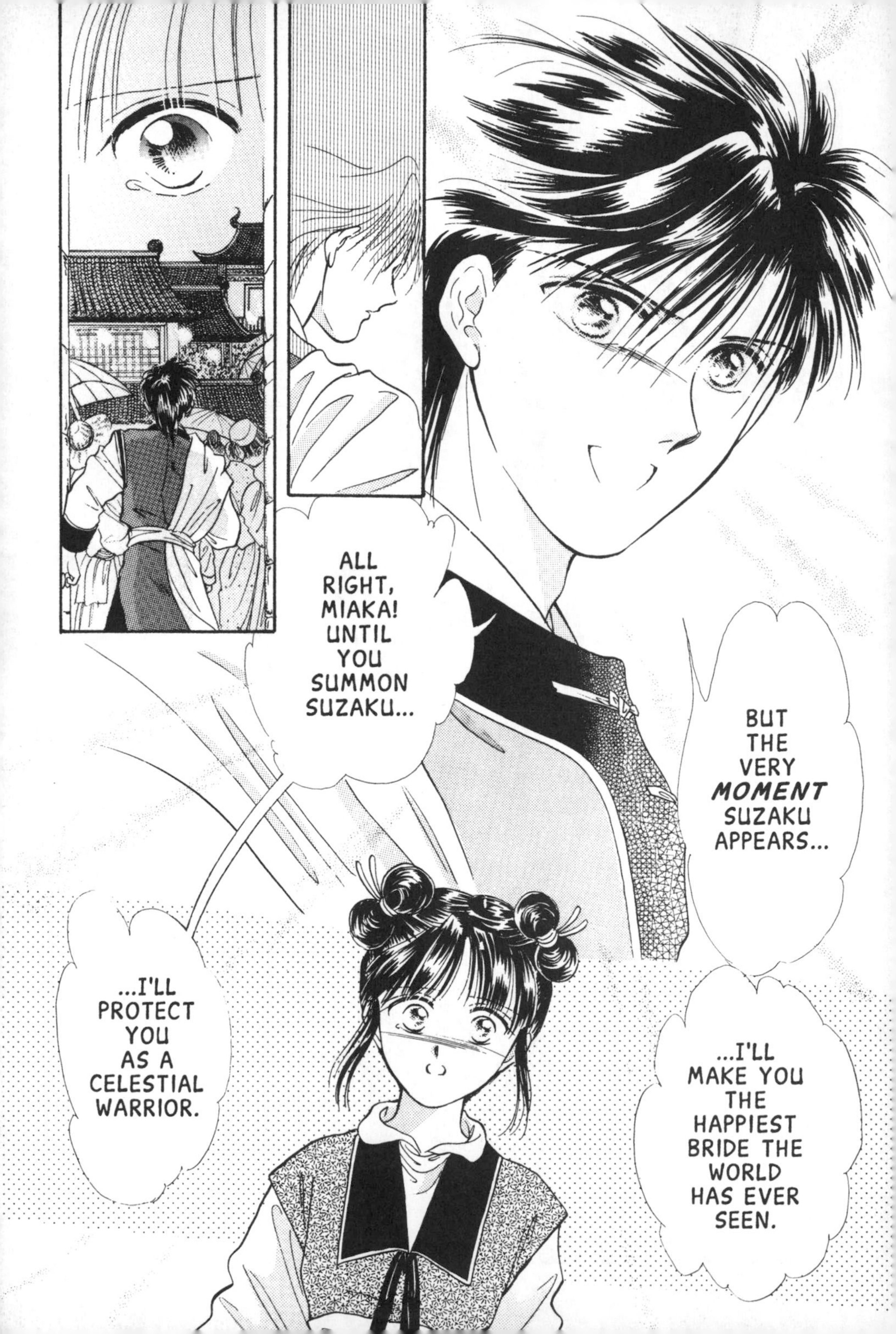
ALL RIGHT, MIAKA! UNTIL YOU SUMMON SUZAKU...
...I'LL PROTECT YOU AS A CELESTIAL WARRIOR.
BUT THE VERY ***MOMENT*** SUZAKU APPEARS...
...I'LL MAKE YOU THE HAPPIEST BRIDE THE WORLD HAS EVER SEEN.

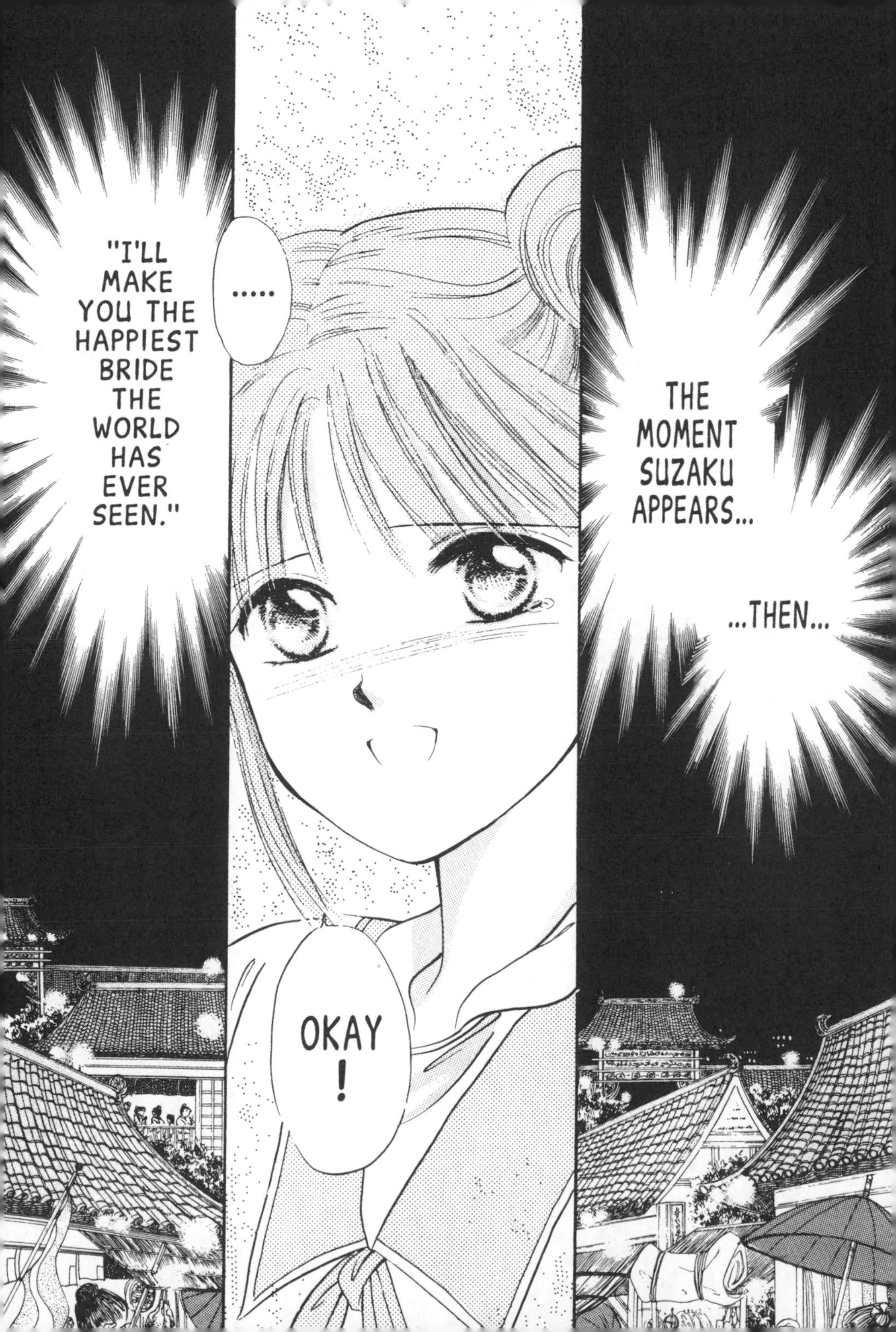
"I'LL MAKE YOU THE HAPPIEST BRIDE THE WORLD HAS EVER SEEN."
.....
OKAY!
THE MOMENT SUZAKU APPEARS...
...THEN...

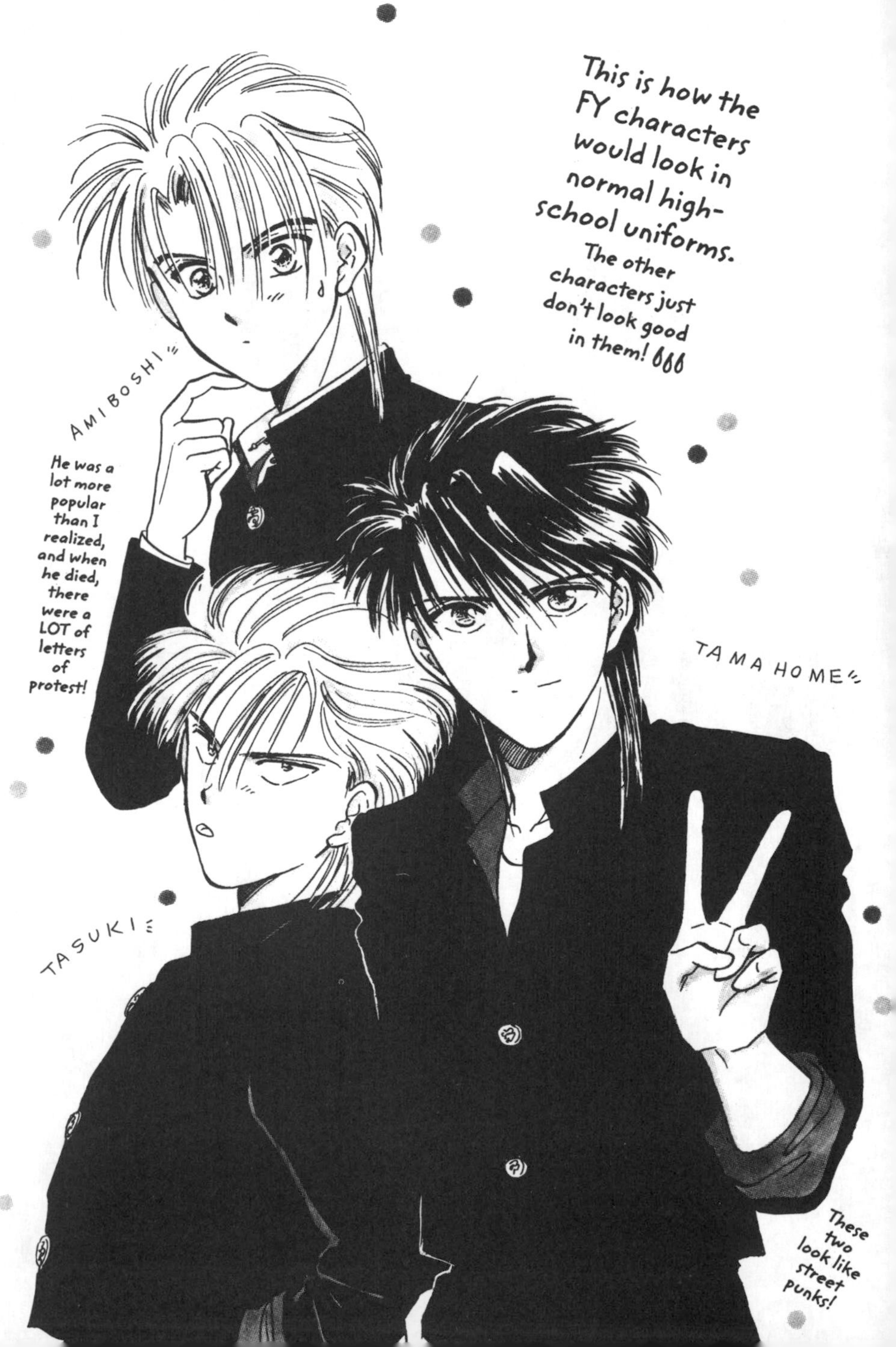
This is how the FY characters would look in normal high-school uniforms.
The other characters just don't look good in them! ôôô
AMIBOSHI
He was a lot more popular than I realized, and when he died, there were a LOT of letters of protest!
TAMAHOME
TASUKI
These two look like street punks!

# CHAPTER THIRTY-NINE

# FRAIL SMILE

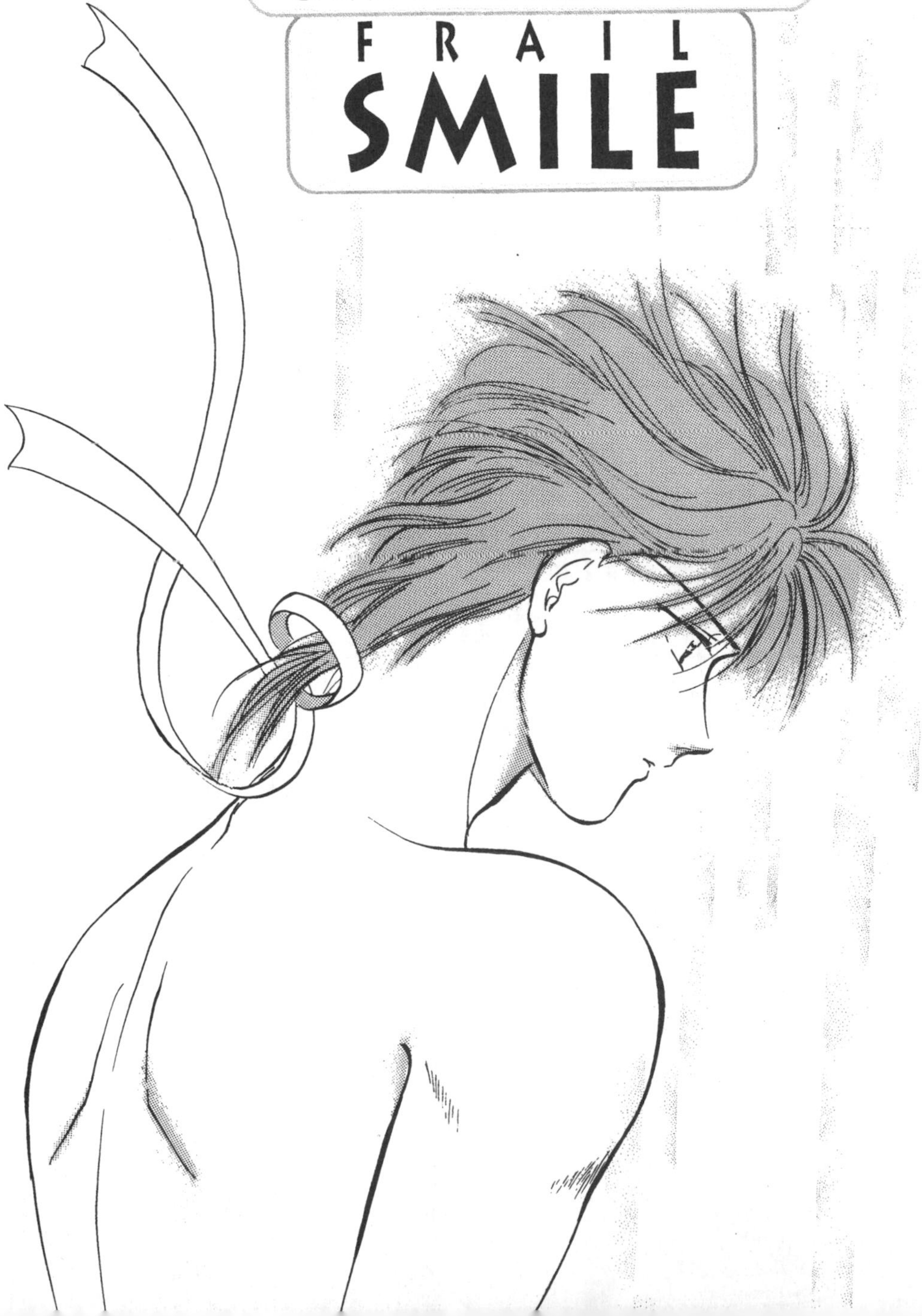

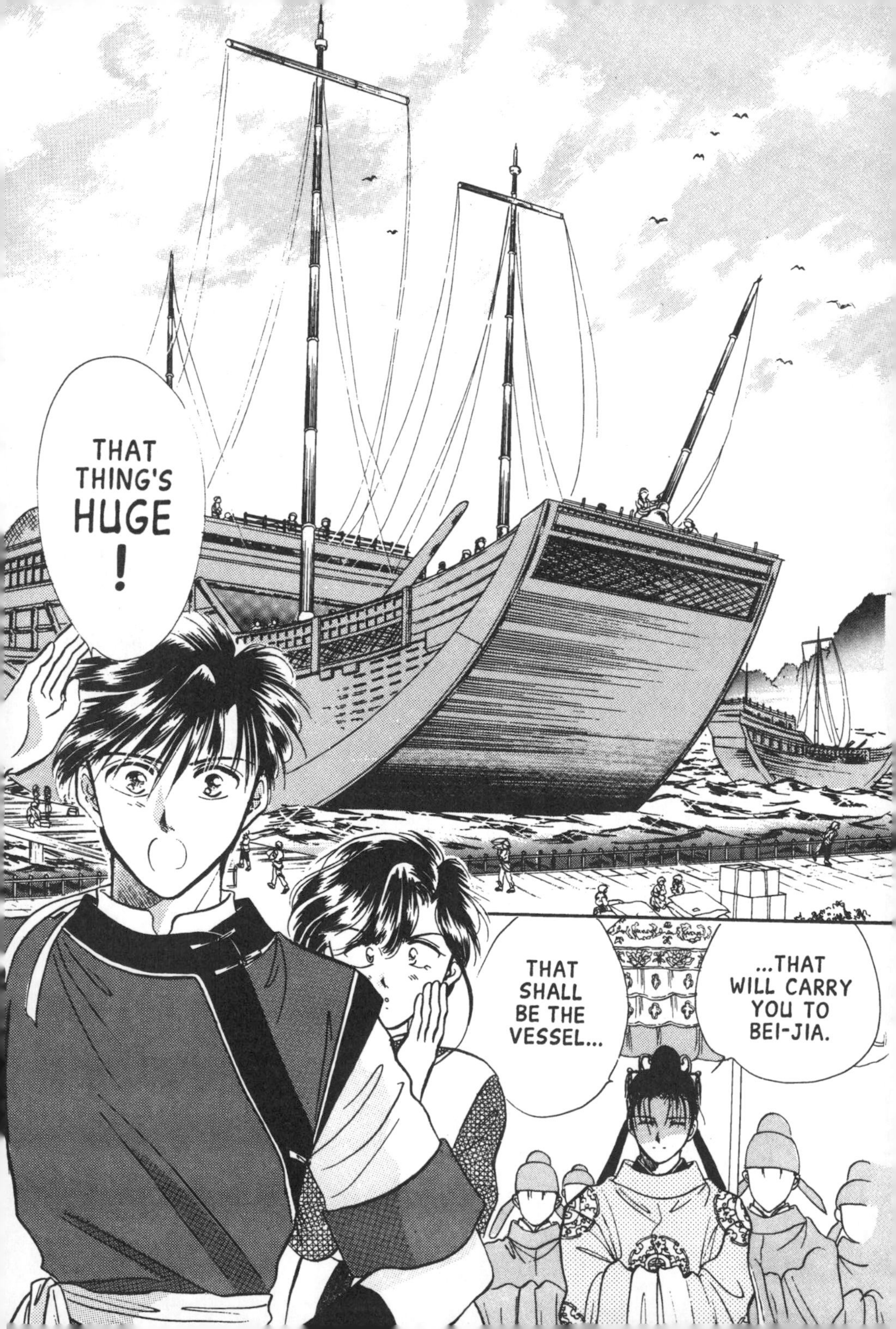
THAT THING'S HUGE !
THAT SHALL BE THE VESSEL...
...THAT WILL CARRY YOU TO BEI-JIA.

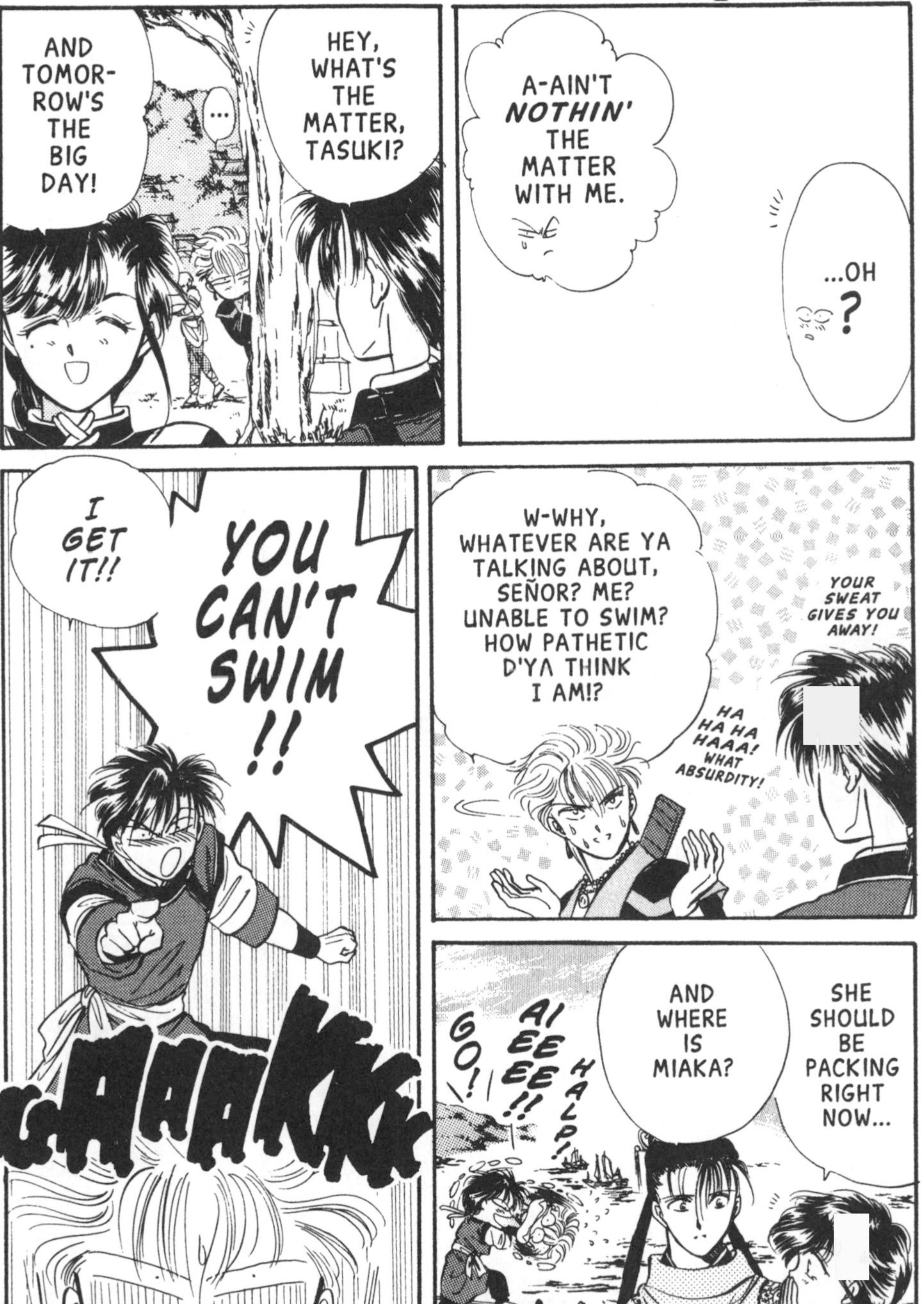
AND TOMOR-ROW'S THE BIG DAY!
...
HEY, WHAT'S THE MATTER, TASUKI?
A-AIN'T *NOTHIN'* THE MATTER WITH ME.
...OH
?
I GET IT!!
YOU CAN'T SWIM!!
GAAAKKK
W-WHY, WHATEVER ARE YA TALKING ABOUT, SEÑOR? ME? UNABLE TO SWIM? HOW PATHETIC D'YA THINK I AM!?
YOUR SWEAT GIVES YOU AWAY!
HA HA HA HAAA! WHAT ABSURDITY!
GO!
AIEEEEE!!
HALP!
AND WHERE IS MIAKA?
SHE SHOULD BE PACKING RIGHT NOW...

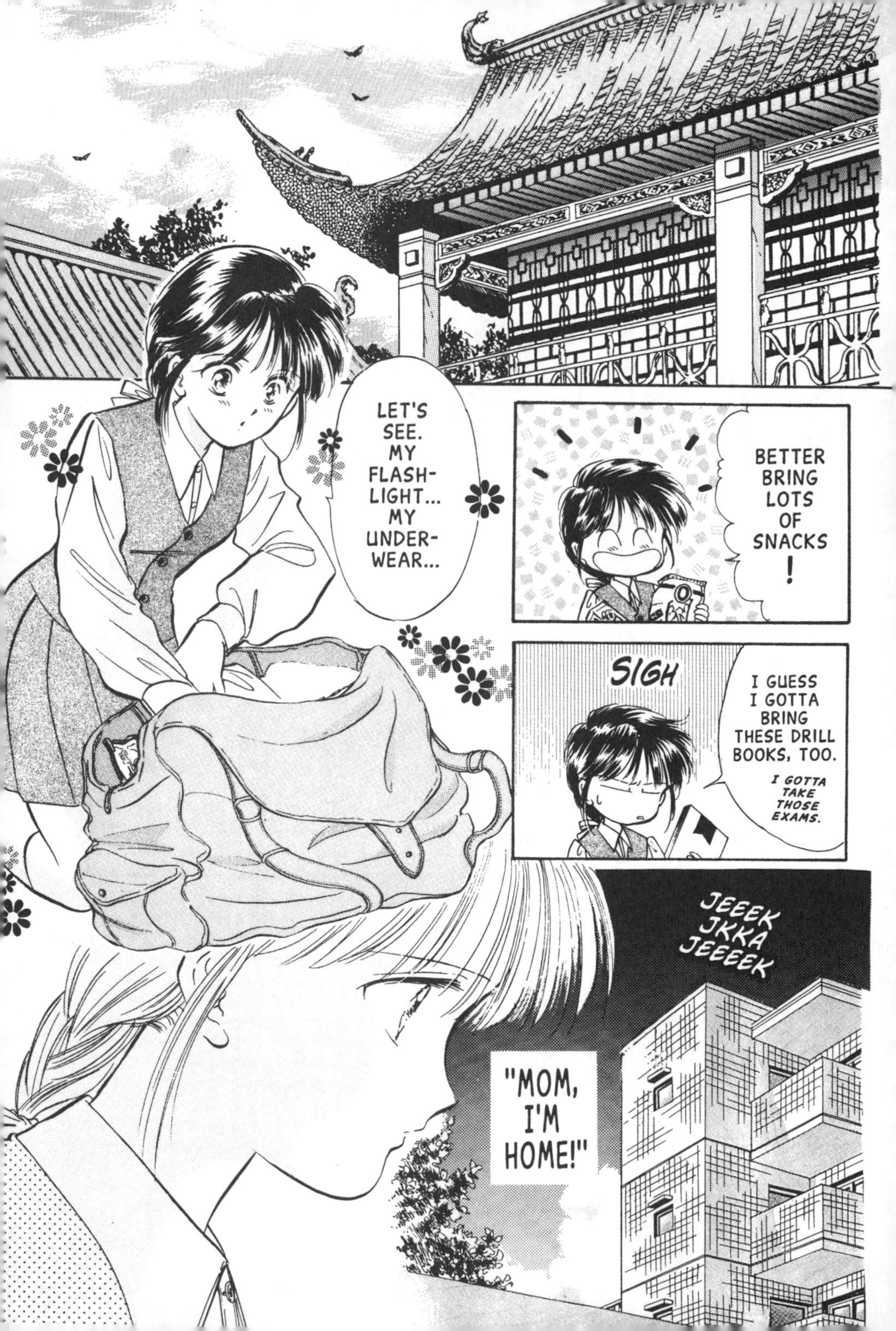
LET'S SEE. MY FLASH-LIGHT... MY UNDER-WEAR...
BETTER BRING LOTS OF SNACKS!
SIGH
I GUESS I GOTTA BRING THESE DRILL BOOKS, TOO.
I GOTTA TAKE THOSE EXAMS.
JEEEK JKKA JEEEEK
"MOM, I'M HOME!"

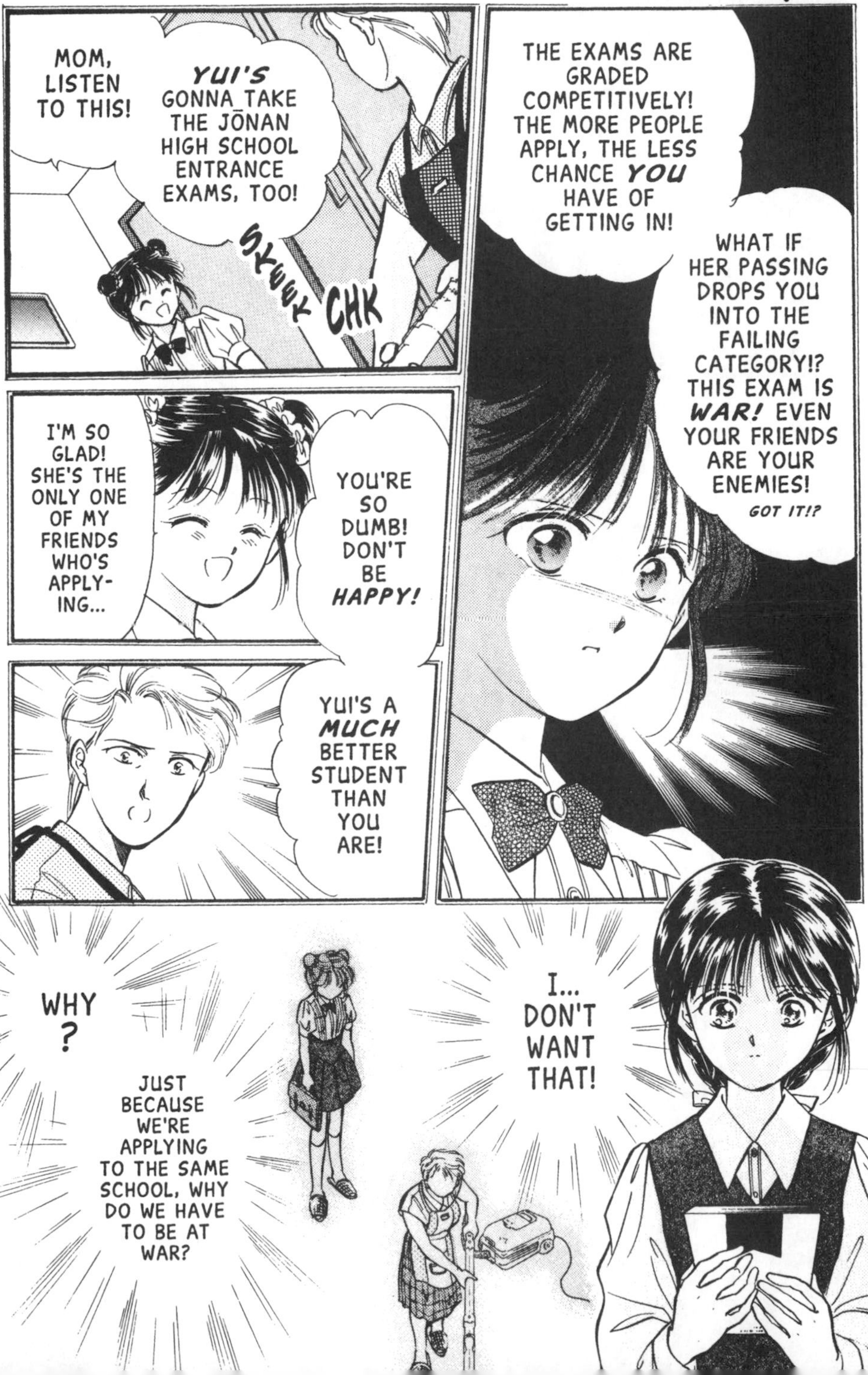
MOM, LISTEN TO THIS!
YUI'S GONNA TAKE THE JŌNAN HIGH SCHOOL ENTRANCE EXAMS, TOO!
SKEEK
CHK
I'M SO GLAD! SHE'S THE ONLY ONE OF MY FRIENDS WHO'S APPLYING...
YOU'RE SO DUMB! DON'T BE HAPPY!
YUI'S A MUCH BETTER STUDENT THAN YOU ARE!
THE EXAMS ARE GRADED COMPETITIVELY! THE MORE PEOPLE APPLY, THE LESS CHANCE YOU HAVE OF GETTING IN!
WHAT IF HER PASSING DROPS YOU INTO THE FAILING CATEGORY!? THIS EXAM IS WAR! EVEN YOUR FRIENDS ARE YOUR ENEMIES!
GOT IT!?
WHY ?
JUST BECAUSE WE'RE APPLYING TO THE SAME SCHOOL, WHY DO WE HAVE TO BE AT WAR?
I... DON'T WANT THAT!

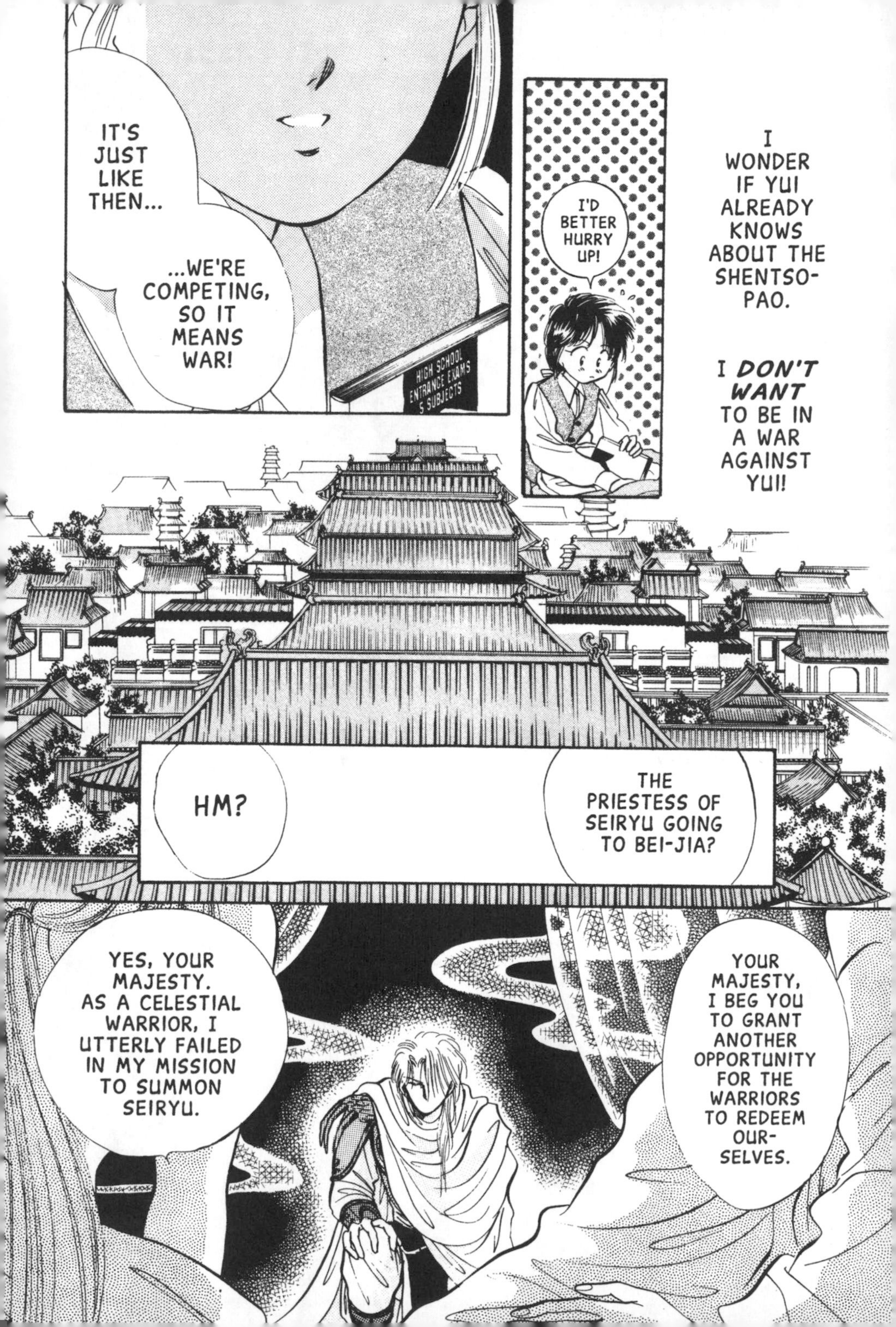
IT'S JUST LIKE THEN...
...WE'RE COMPETING, SO IT MEANS WAR!
HIGH SCHOOL ENTRANCE EXAMS 5 SUBJECTS
I'D BETTER HURRY UP!
I WONDER IF YUI ALREADY KNOWS ABOUT THE SHENTSO-PAO.
I *DON'T WANT* TO BE IN A WAR AGAINST YUI!
HM?
THE PRIESTESS OF SEIRYU GOING TO BEI-JIA?
YES, YOUR MAJESTY. AS A CELESTIAL WARRIOR, I UTTERLY FAILED IN MY MISSION TO SUMMON SEIRYU.
YOUR MAJESTY, I BEG YOU TO GRANT ANOTHER OPPORTUNITY FOR THE WARRIORS TO REDEEM OUR-SELVES.

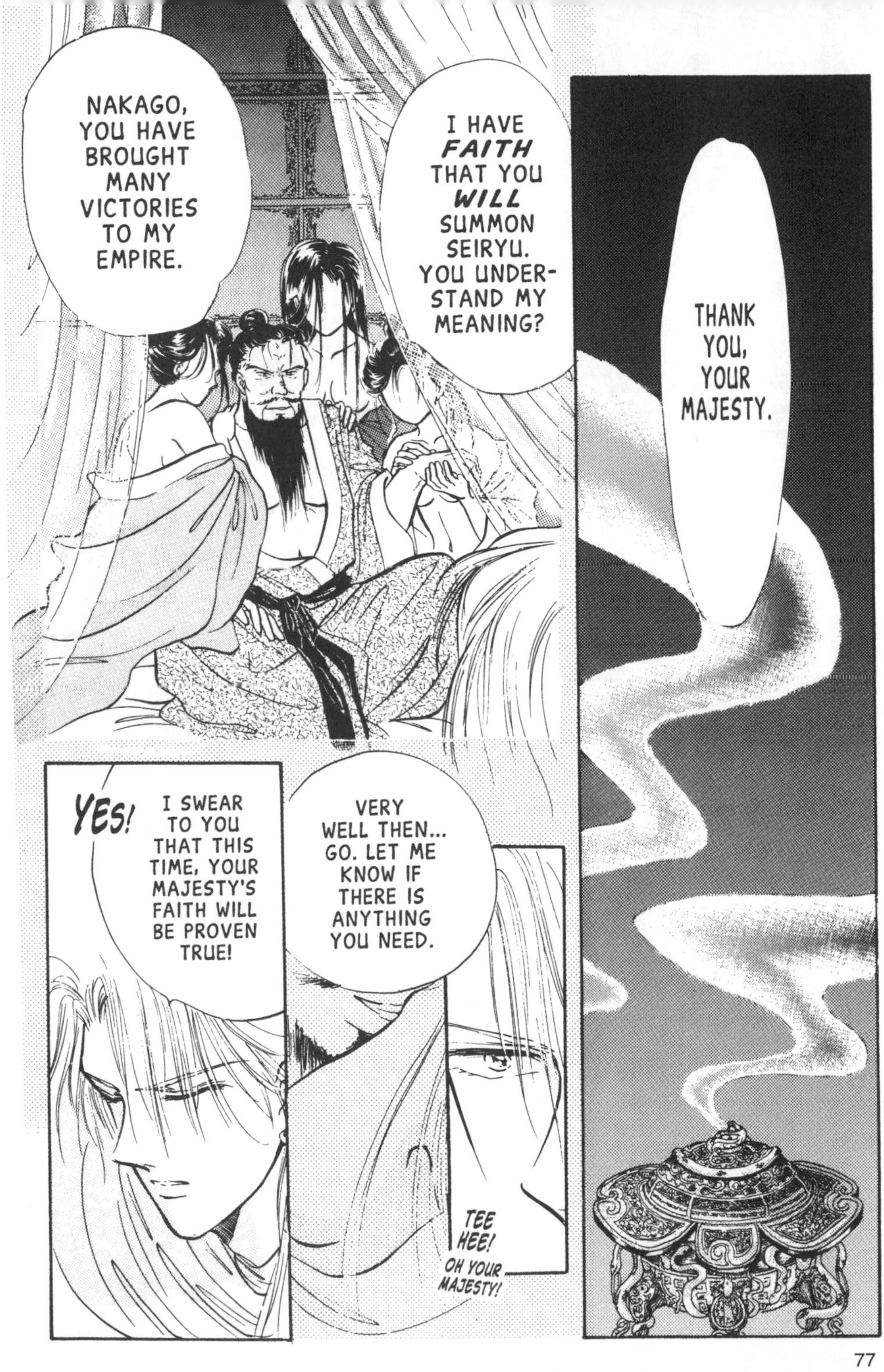
NAKAGO, YOU HAVE BROUGHT MANY VICTORIES TO MY EMPIRE.
I HAVE FAITH THAT YOU WILL SUMMON SEIRYU. YOU UNDERSTAND MY MEANING?
YES!
I SWEAR TO YOU THAT THIS TIME, YOUR MAJESTY'S FAITH WILL BE PROVEN TRUE!
VERY WELL THEN... GO. LET ME KNOW IF THERE IS ANYTHING YOU NEED.
TEE HEE!
OH YOUR MAJESTY!
THANK YOU, YOUR MAJESTY.

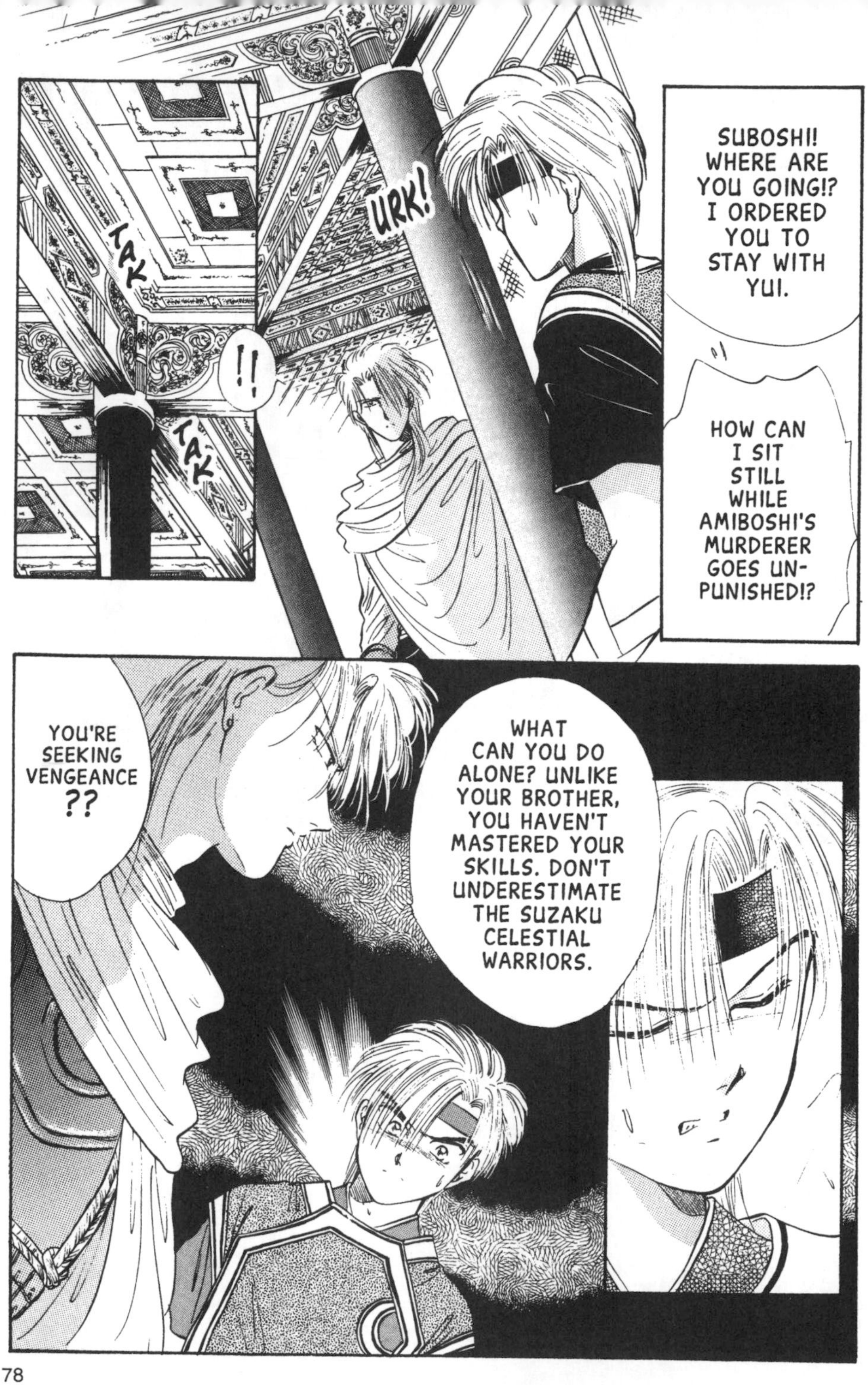
TAK
TAK
!!
URK!
SUBOSHI! WHERE ARE YOU GOING!? I ORDERED YOU TO STAY WITH YUI.
HOW CAN I SIT STILL WHILE AMIBOSHI'S MURDERER GOES UN-PUNISHED!?
YOU'RE SEEKING VENGEANCE ??
WHAT CAN YOU DO ALONE? UNLIKE YOUR BROTHER, YOU HAVEN'T MASTERED YOUR SKILLS. DON'T UNDERESTIMATE THE SUZAKU CELESTIAL WARRIORS.

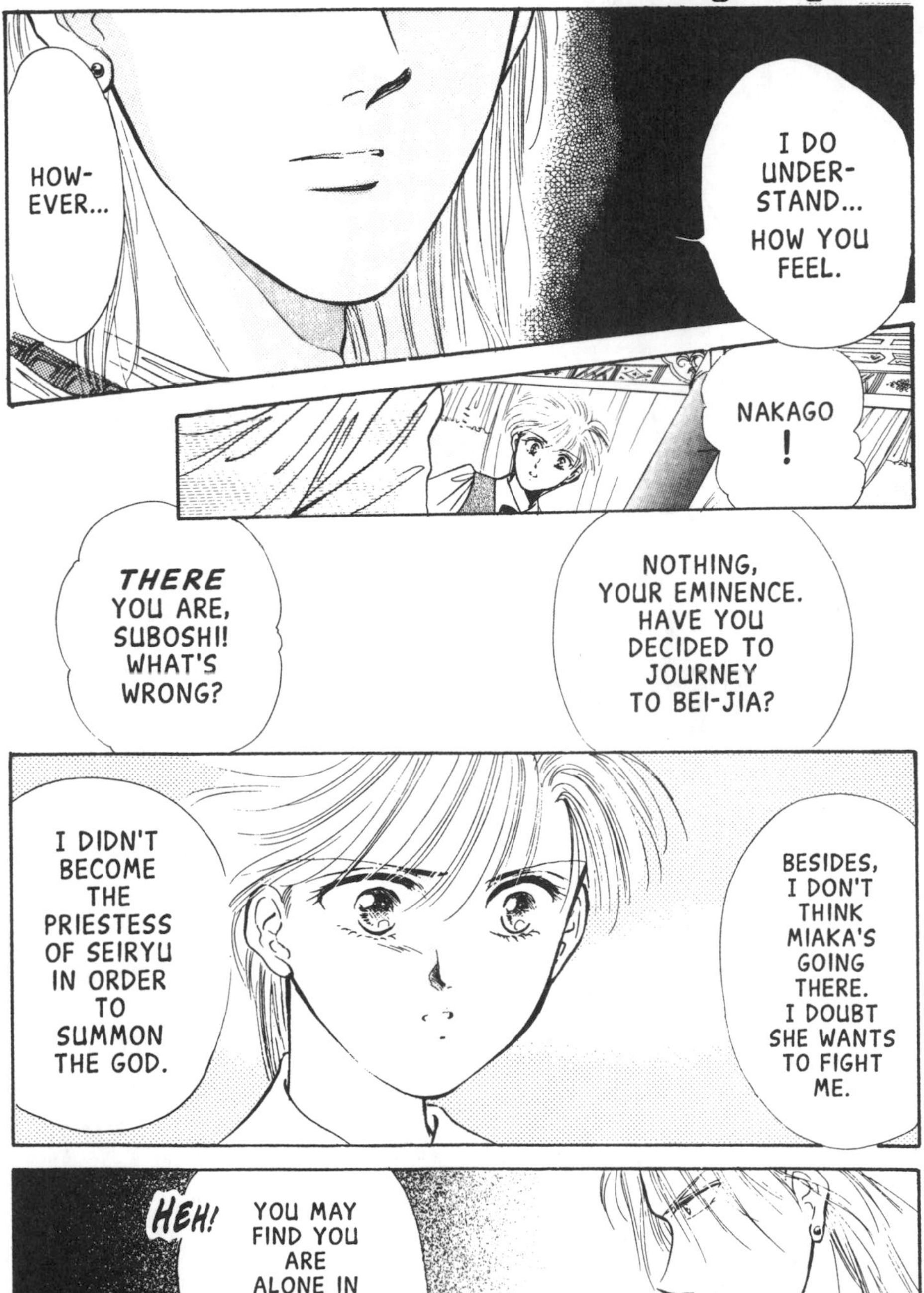
I DO UNDER-STAND... HOW YOU FEEL.
HOW-EVER...
NAKAGO!
THERE YOU ARE, SUBOSHI! WHAT'S WRONG?
NOTHING, YOUR EMINENCE. HAVE YOU DECIDED TO JOURNEY TO BEI-JIA?
I DIDN'T BECOME THE PRIESTESS OF SEIRYU IN ORDER TO SUMMON THE GOD.
BESIDES, I DON'T THINK MIAKA'S GOING THERE. I DOUBT SHE WANTS TO FIGHT ME.
HEH!
YOU MAY FIND YOU ARE ALONE IN THAT ASSUMPTION.

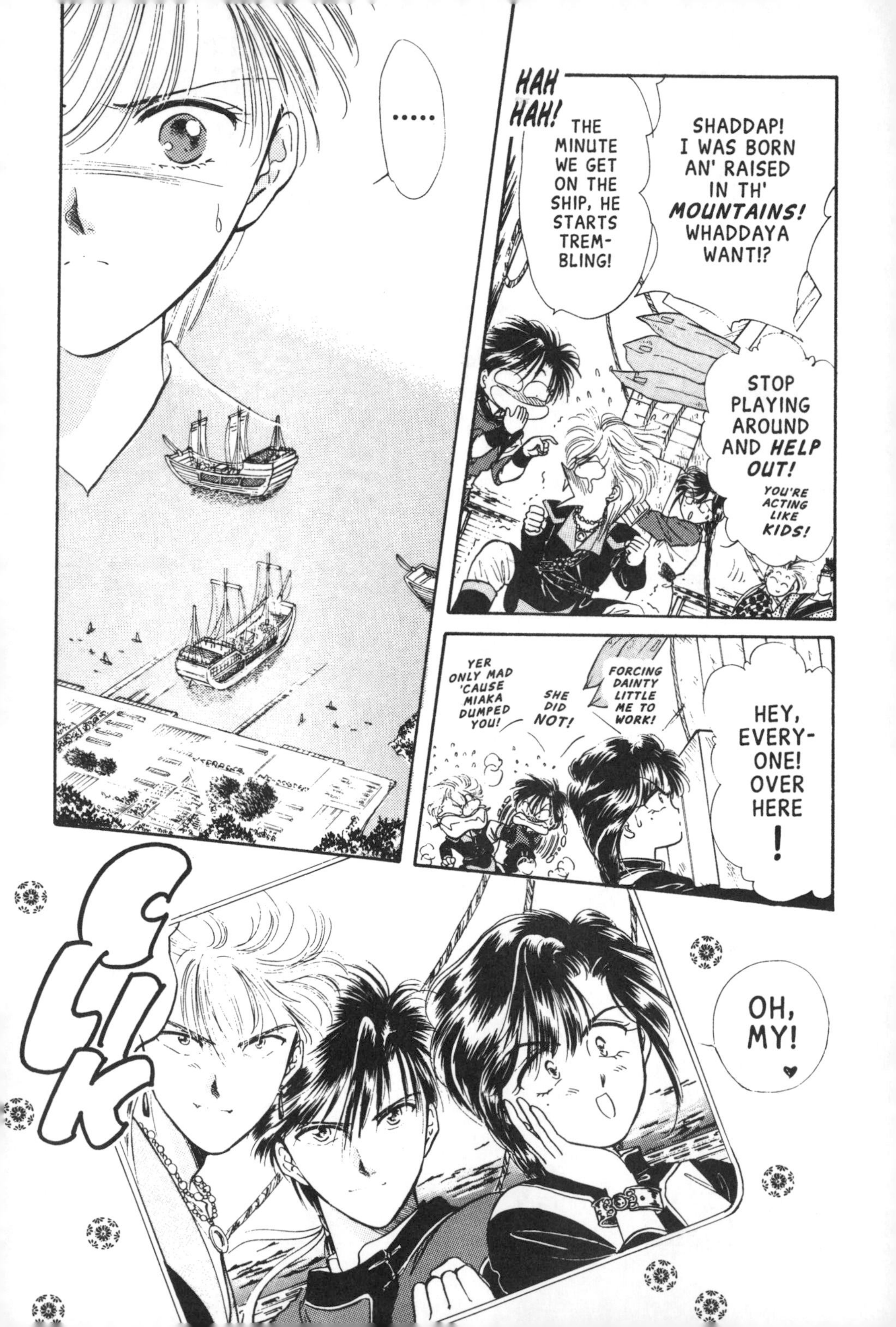
......
HAH HAH!
THE MINUTE WE GET ON THE SHIP, HE STARTS TREM-BLING!
SHADDAP! I WAS BORN AN' RAISED IN TH' MOUNTAINS! WHADDAYA WANT!?
STOP PLAYING AROUND AND HELP OUT!
YOU'RE ACTING LIKE KIDS!
YER ONLY MAD 'CAUSE MIAKA DUMPED YOU!
SHE DID NOT!
FORCING DAINTY LITTLE ME TO WORK!
HEY, EVERY-ONE! OVER HERE!
CLINK
OH, MY!

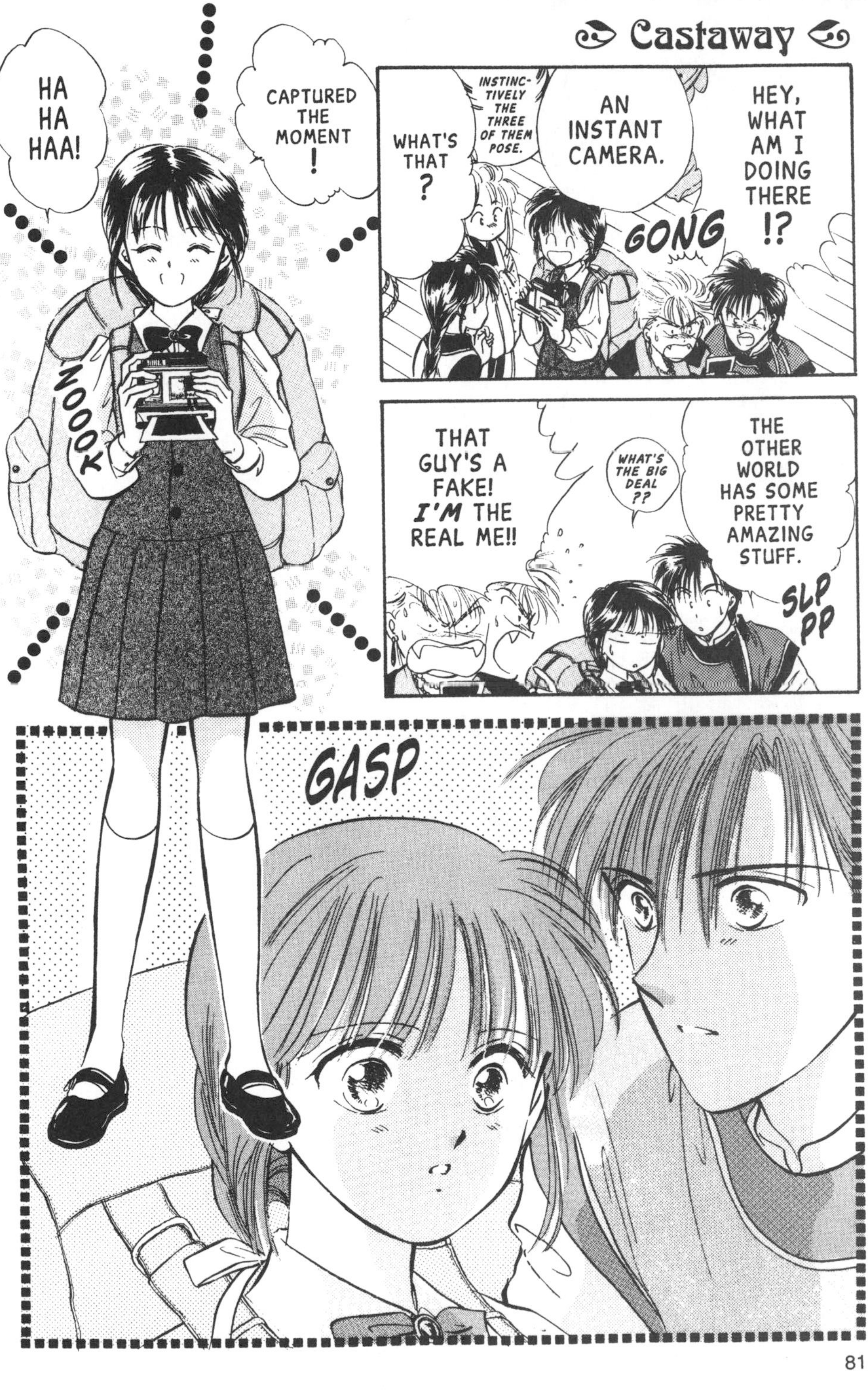
HA HA HAA!
CAPTURED THE MOMENT!
NOOOK
WHAT'S THAT?
INSTINCTIVELY THE THREE OF THEM POSE.
AN INSTANT CAMERA.
HEY, WHAT AM I DOING THERE!?
GONG
THAT GUY'S A FAKE! I'M THE REAL ME!!
WHAT'S THE BIG DEAL??
THE OTHER WORLD HAS SOME PRETTY AMAZING STUFF.
SLPPP
GASP

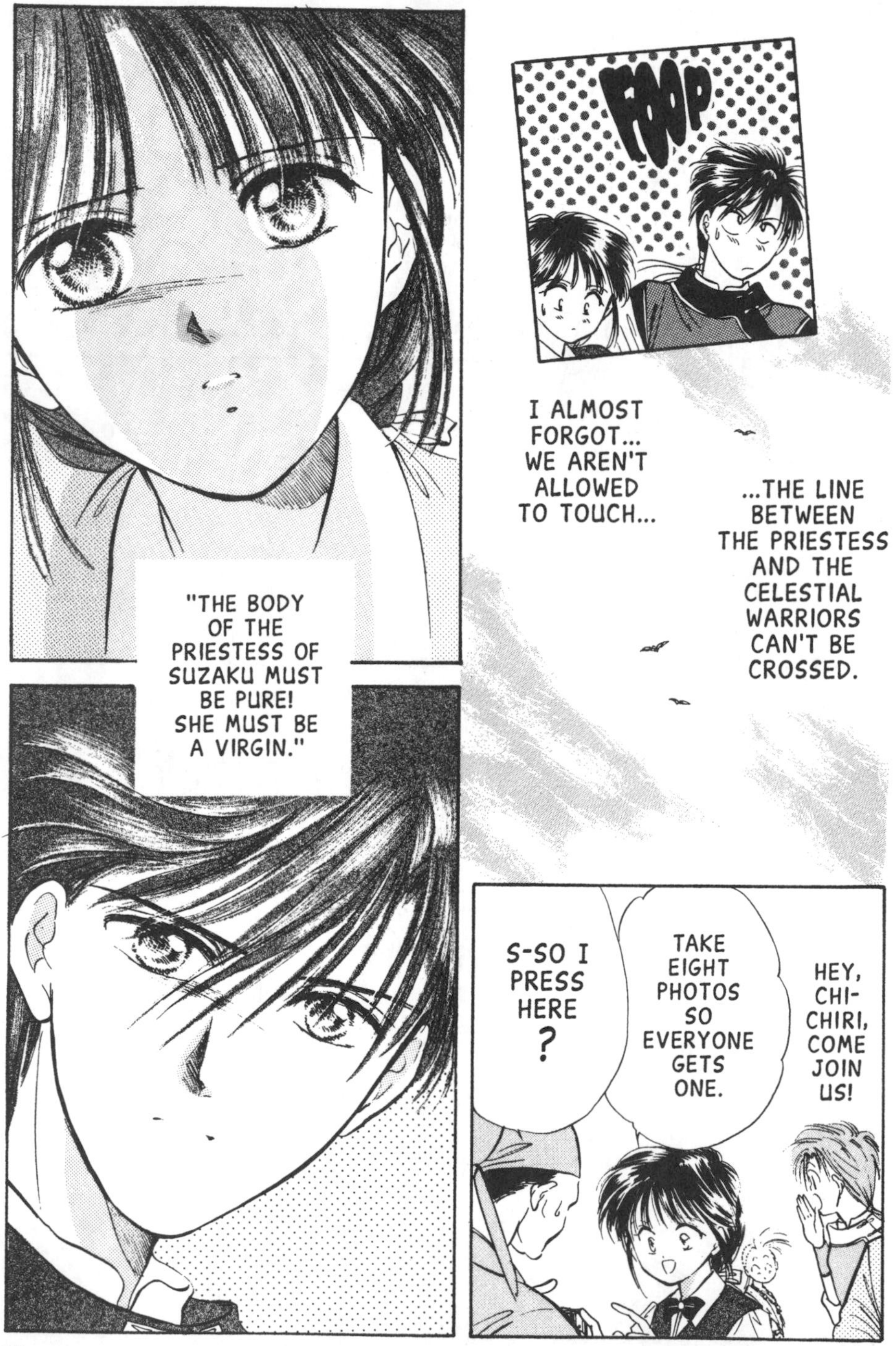
FOOP
I ALMOST FORGOT... WE AREN'T ALLOWED TO TOUCH...
...THE LINE BETWEEN THE PRIESTESS AND THE CELESTIAL WARRIORS CAN'T BE CROSSED.
"THE BODY OF THE PRIESTESS OF SUZAKU MUST BE PURE! SHE MUST BE A VIRGIN."
S-SO I PRESS HERE?
TAKE EIGHT PHOTOS SO EVERYONE GETS ONE.
HEY, CHI-CHIRI, COME JOIN US!

CLIK!

↑ PUTTING ON A SMILE

LOOK HOW CLOSE WE ARE, BUT...

I KNOW I GOTTA SUMMON SUZAKU, BUT I DON'T WANT TO FIGHT YUI!!

WHAT'M I SUPPOSED TO DO!?

BAM BAM BAM

WHAT'S WRONG WITH HER??

SHE'S PROBABLY HUNGRY AGAIN.

TAMA-HOME...

A THOUGHT CAME TO US LAST NIGHT...

...CON-CERNING YOUR FAMILY.

WHAT?

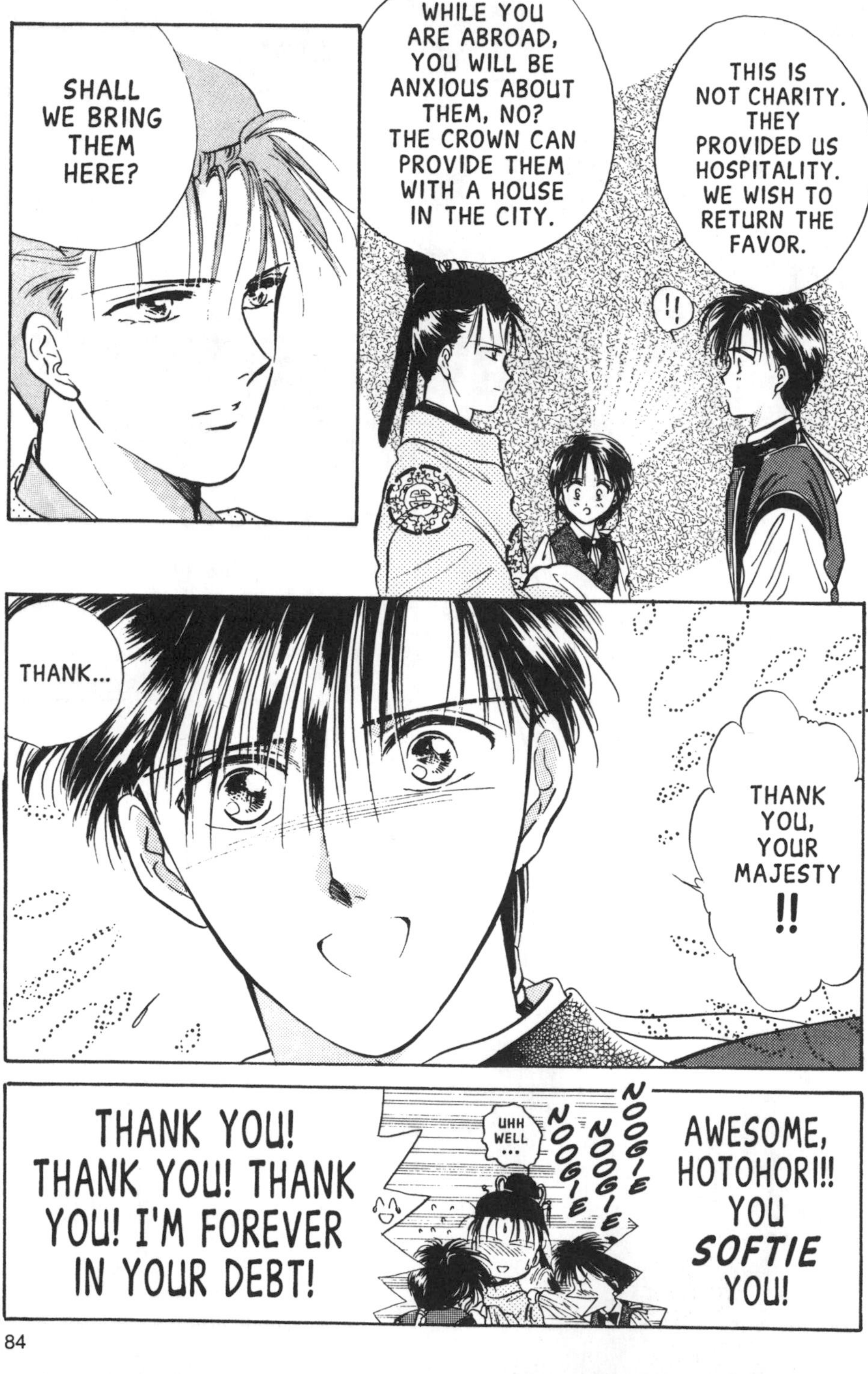

SHALL WE BRING THEM HERE?
WHILE YOU ARE ABROAD, YOU WILL BE ANXIOUS ABOUT THEM, NO? THE CROWN CAN PROVIDE THEM WITH A HOUSE IN THE CITY.
THIS IS NOT CHARITY. THEY PROVIDED US HOSPITALITY. WE WISH TO RETURN THE FAVOR.
!!
THANK...
THANK YOU, YOUR MAJESTY !!
THANK YOU! THANK YOU! THANK YOU! I'M FOREVER IN YOUR DEBT!
UHH WELL ...
NOOGIE
NOOGIE
NOOGIE
AWESOME, HOTOHORI!!! YOU SOFTIE YOU!

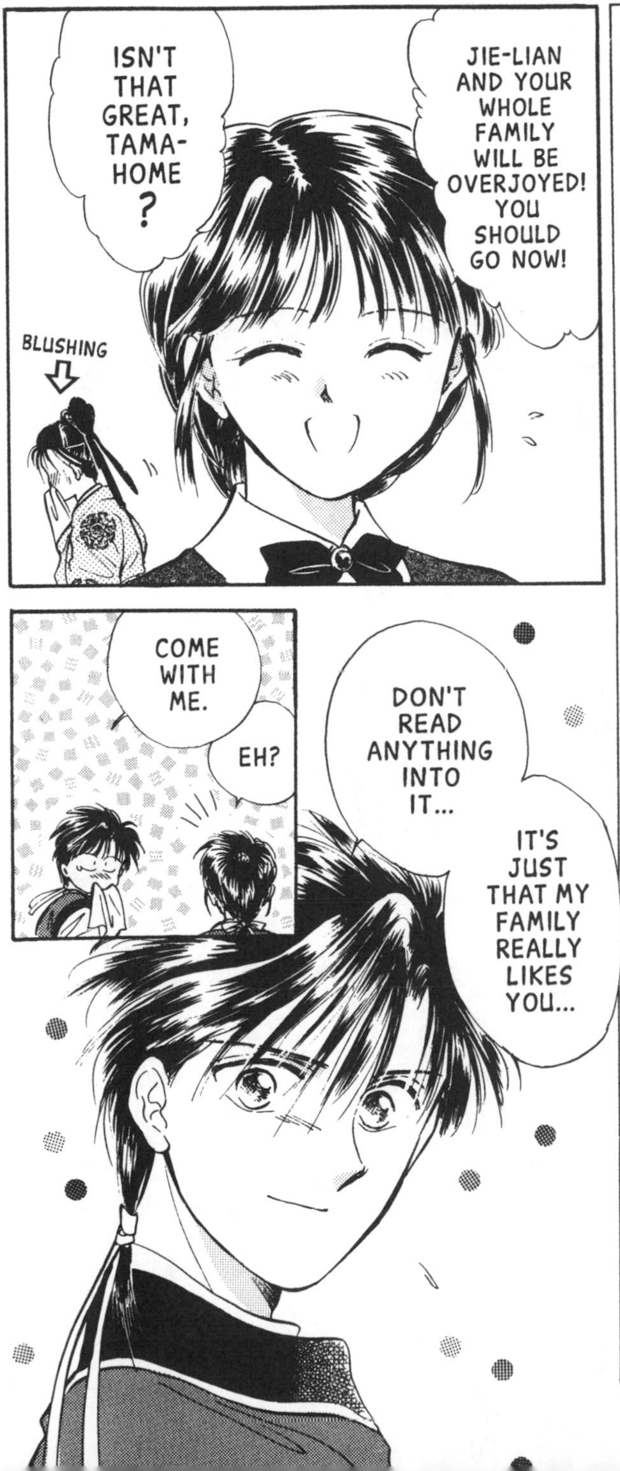
ISN'T THAT GREAT, TAMA-HOME ?
JIE-LIAN AND YOUR WHOLE FAMILY WILL BE OVERJOYED! YOU SHOULD GO NOW!
BLUSHING
COME WITH ME.
EH?
DON'T READ ANYTHING INTO IT...
IT'S JUST THAT MY FAMILY REALLY LIKES YOU...

Most dogs like to be hugged, right? Ours doesn't. I wonder why. She loves sleeping on the futon. She'll lie on a towel like a pillow or use it to cover up like a blanket. Sometimes I can't help but think, "Are you human or what!?"
I didn't realize how cute dogs can be. But now I know why pet owners the world over are so crazy about their cats and dogs--on international TV and the like. The pets become part of the family.
A friend of mine was telling me how dogs emit alpha waves (?), so they have a stress-reducing effect when you pet them. I don't know if that's true, but it is true that hugging dogs or petting them does make you feel better, even when you're angry. Also when you stare at their kind eyes, you feel all warm inside. Animals are so wonderful. But when they pass away, it can be painful.
I heard a story about a kid who brought his pet dog, who had just died, to the toy store and asked the owner there to "Please, fix him." Come on! Animals aren't machines! I'm sure teaching children about the importance of life and death is a difficult undertaking, but give me a break! Someone else stuck his dead dog in a microwave to warm it.
*Let's get with it, people!*

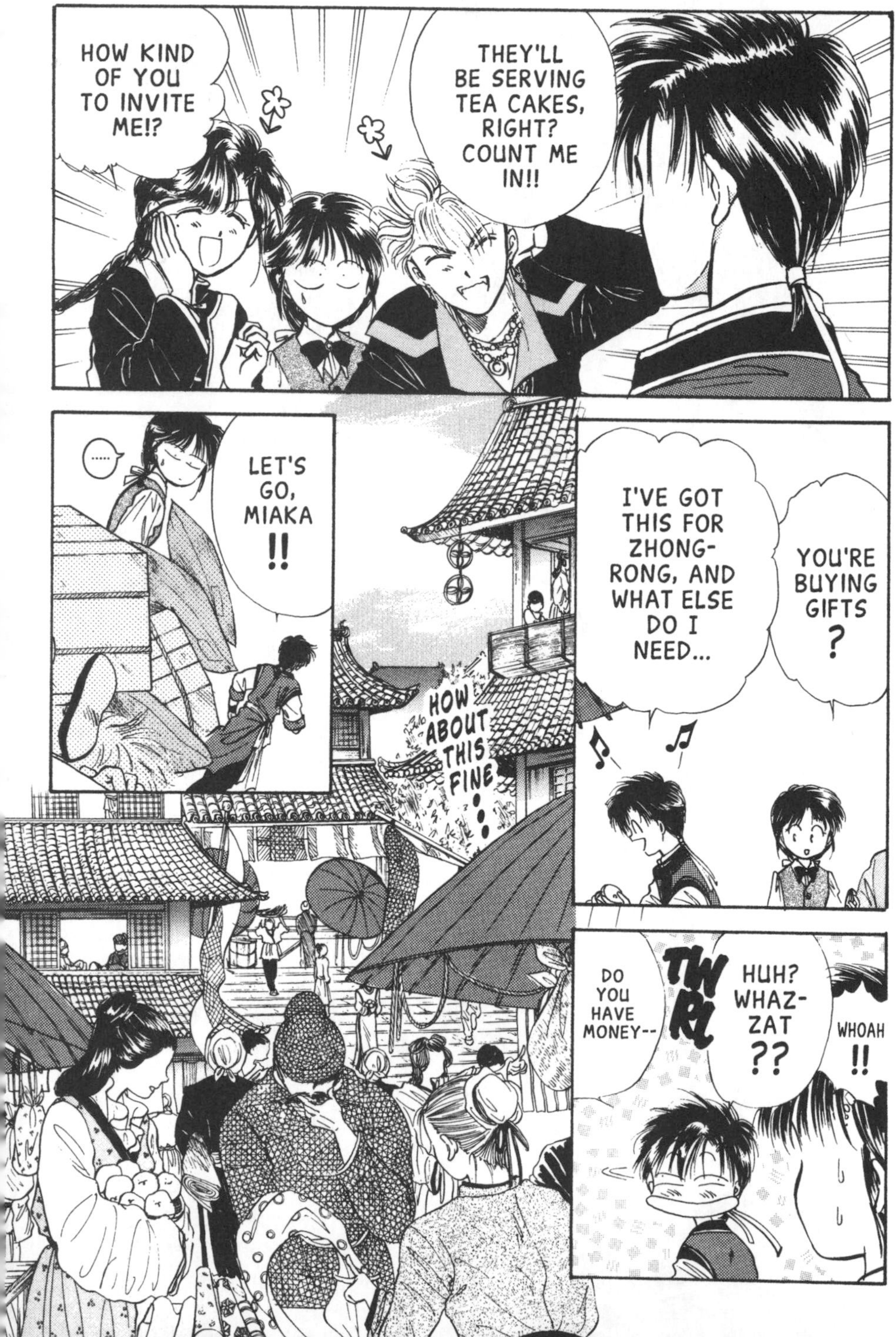
HOW KIND OF YOU TO INVITE ME!?
THEY'LL BE SERVING TEA CAKES, RIGHT? COUNT ME IN!!
......
LET'S GO, MIAKA !!
HOW ABOUT THIS FINE...
I'VE GOT THIS FOR ZHONG-RONG, AND WHAT ELSE DO I NEED...
YOU'RE BUYING GIFTS ?
DO YOU HAVE MONEY--
TWIRL
HUH? WHAZ-ZAT ??
WHOAH !!

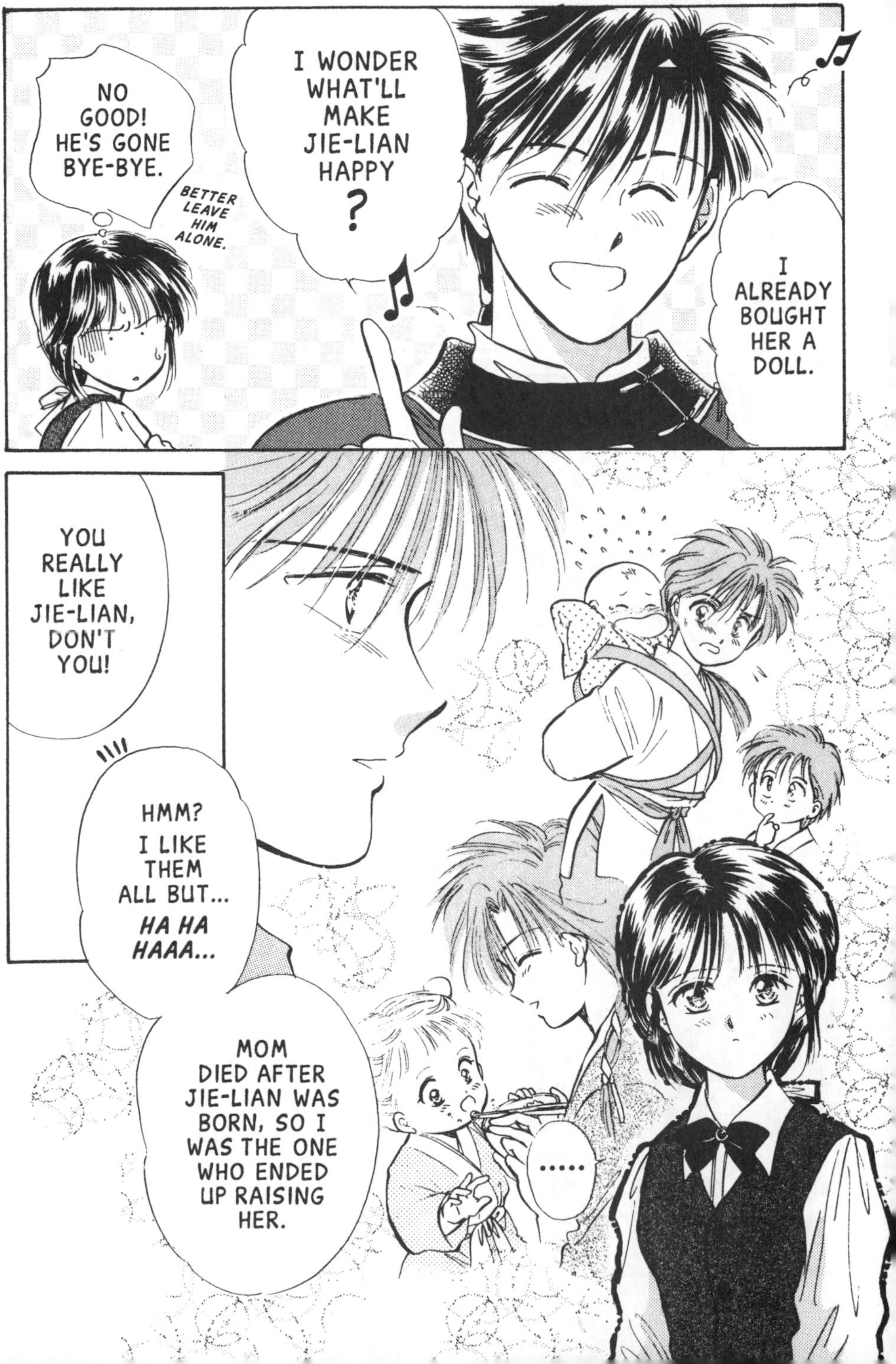
NO GOOD! HE'S GONE BYE-BYE.
BETTER LEAVE HIM ALONE.
I WONDER WHAT'LL MAKE JIE-LIAN HAPPY?
I ALREADY BOUGHT HER A DOLL.
YOU REALLY LIKE JIE-LIAN, DON'T YOU!
HMM? I LIKE THEM ALL BUT... HA HA HAAA...
MOM DIED AFTER JIE-LIAN WAS BORN, SO I WAS THE ONE WHO ENDED UP RAISING HER.
.....

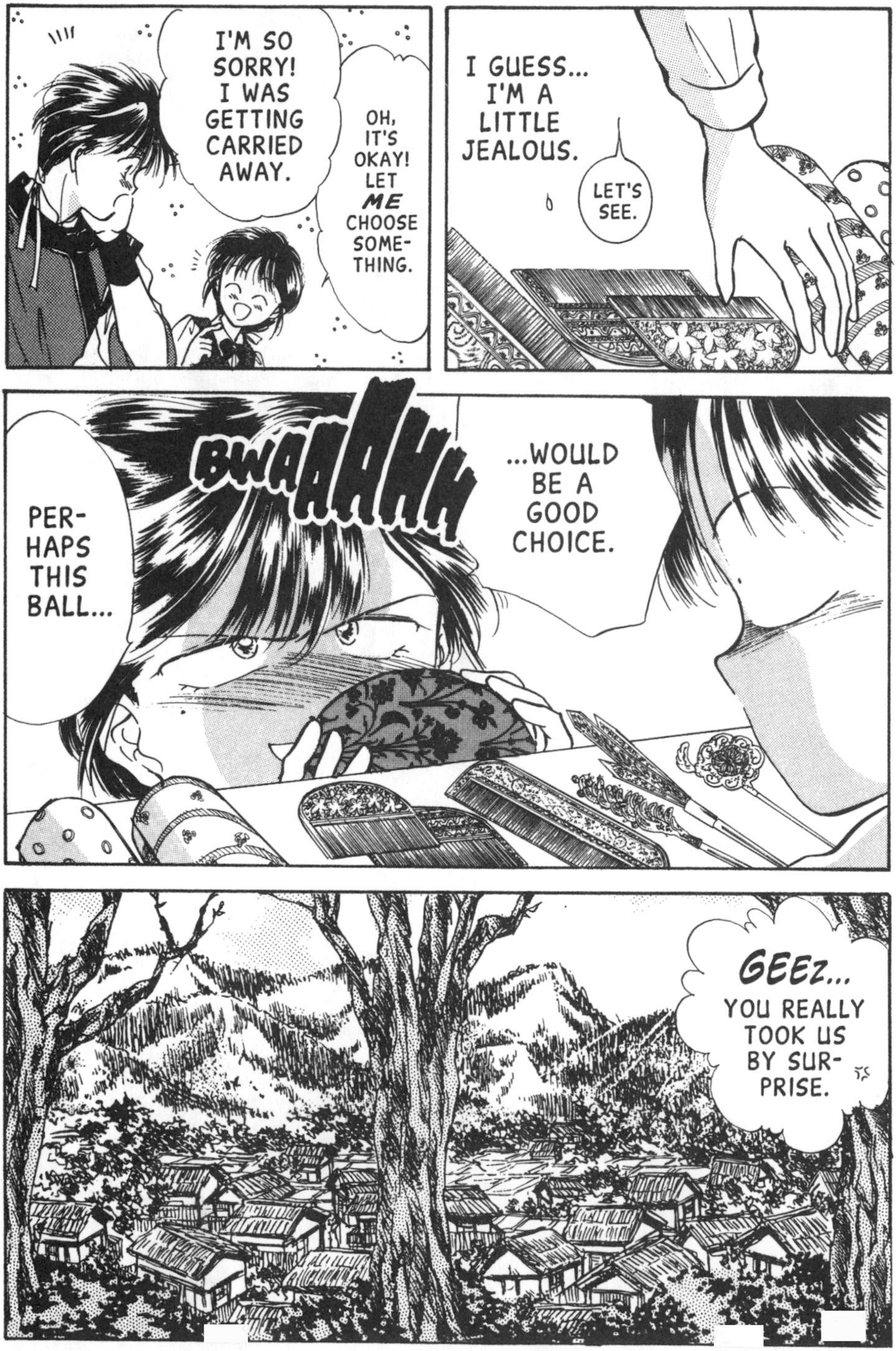
I'M SO SORRY! I WAS GETTING CARRIED AWAY.
OH, IT'S OKAY! LET *ME* CHOOSE SOME-THING.
I GUESS... I'M A LITTLE JEALOUS.
LET'S SEE.
PER-HAPS THIS BALL...
BWAAAHHH
...WOULD BE A GOOD CHOICE.
GEEZ... YOU REALLY TOOK US BY SUR-PRISE.

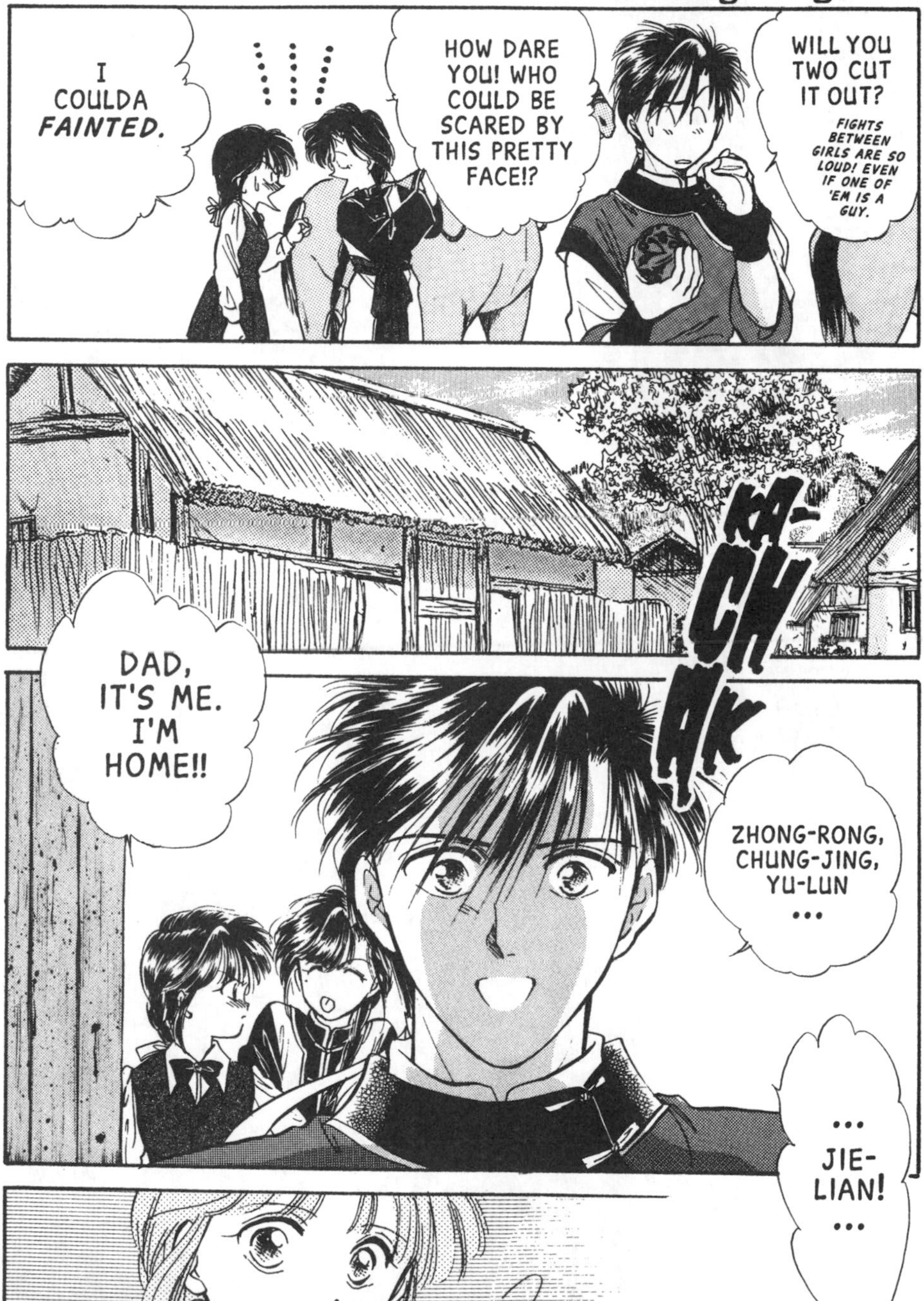
I COULDA FAINTED.
...
HOW DARE YOU! WHO COULD BE SCARED BY THIS PRETTY FACE!?
WILL YOU TWO CUT IT OUT?
FIGHTS BETWEEN GIRLS ARE SO LOUD! EVEN IF ONE OF 'EM IS A GUY.
KA-CHAK
DAD, IT'S ME. I'M HOME!!
ZHONG-RONG, CHUNG-JING, YU-LUN ...
... JIE-LIAN! ...

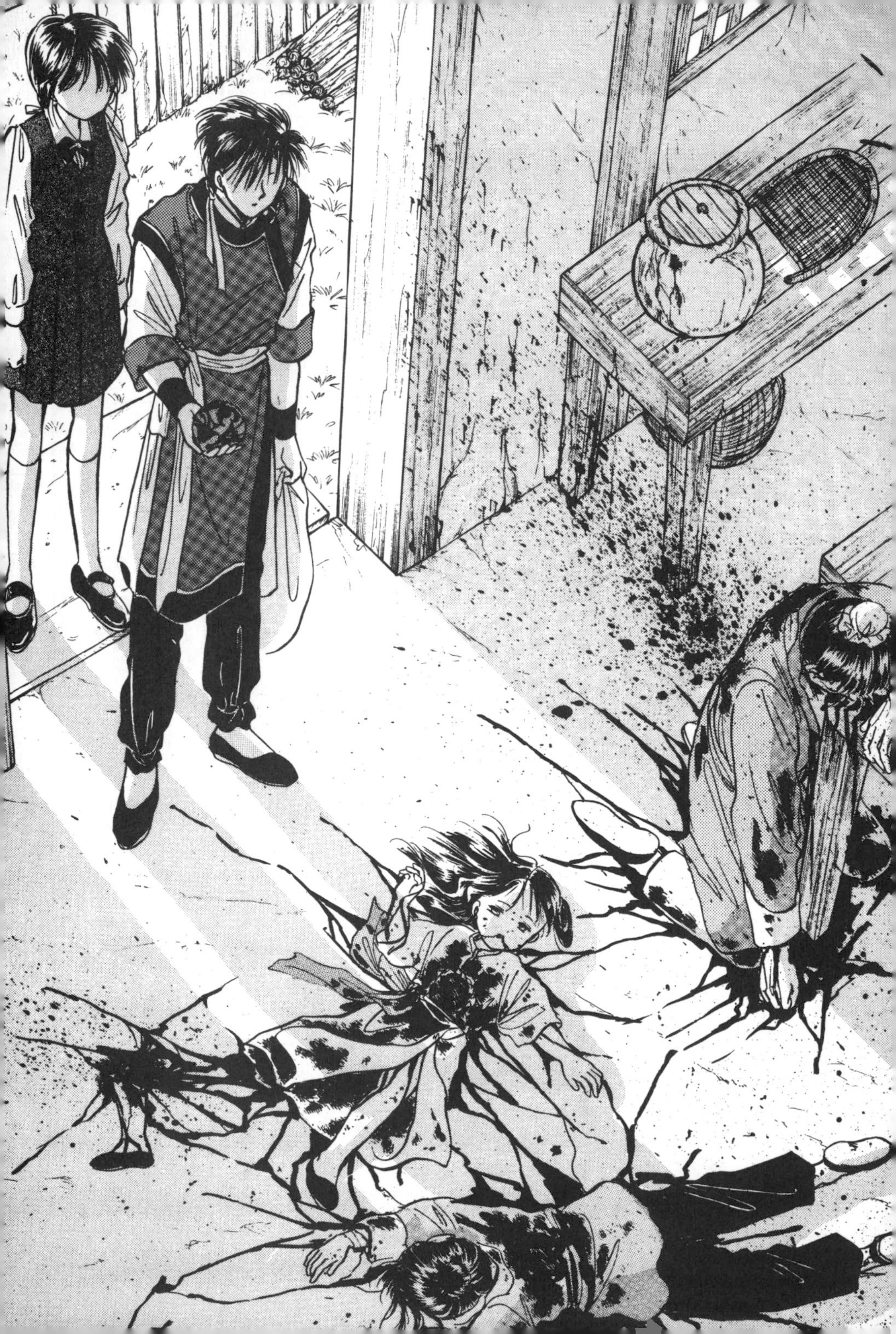

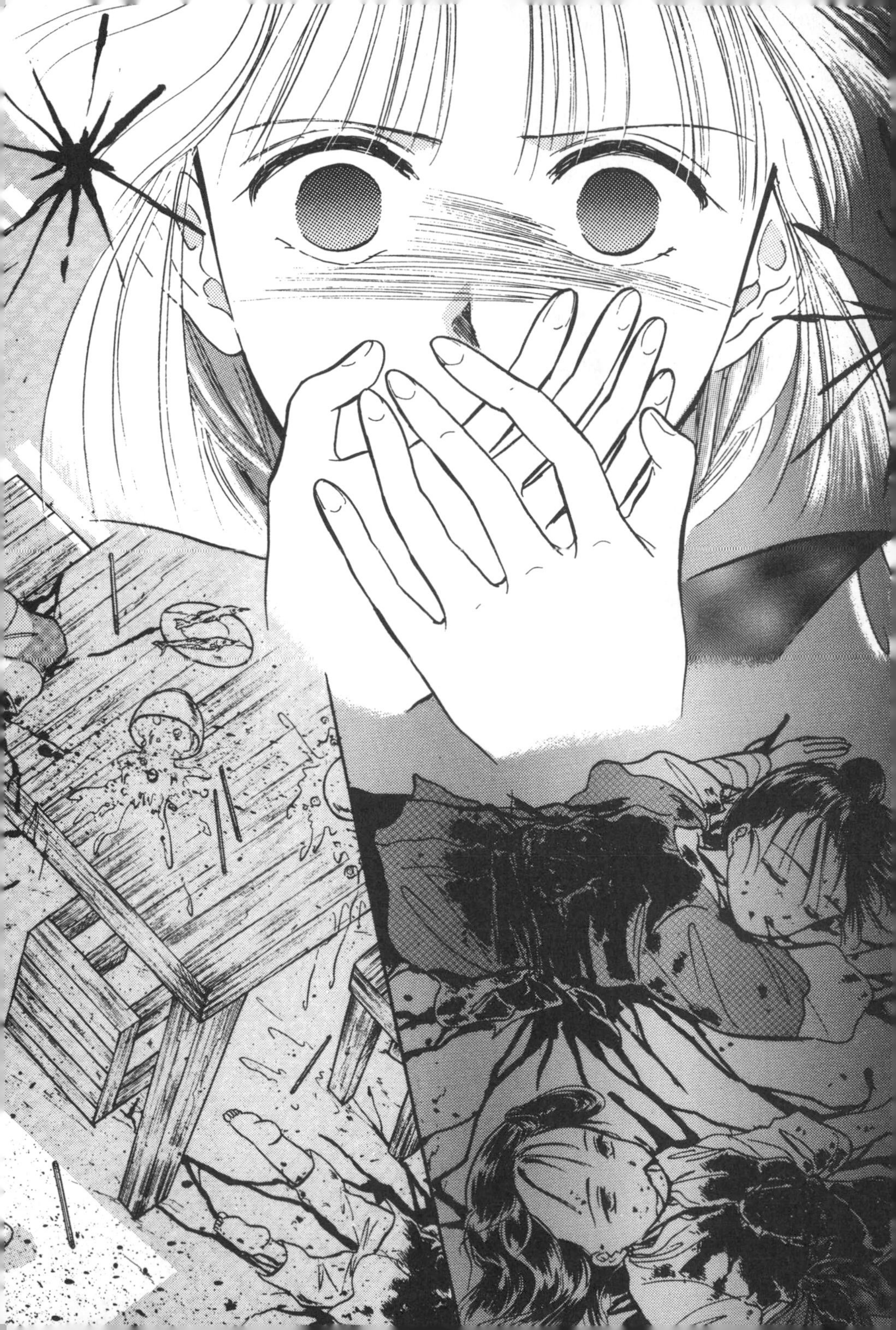

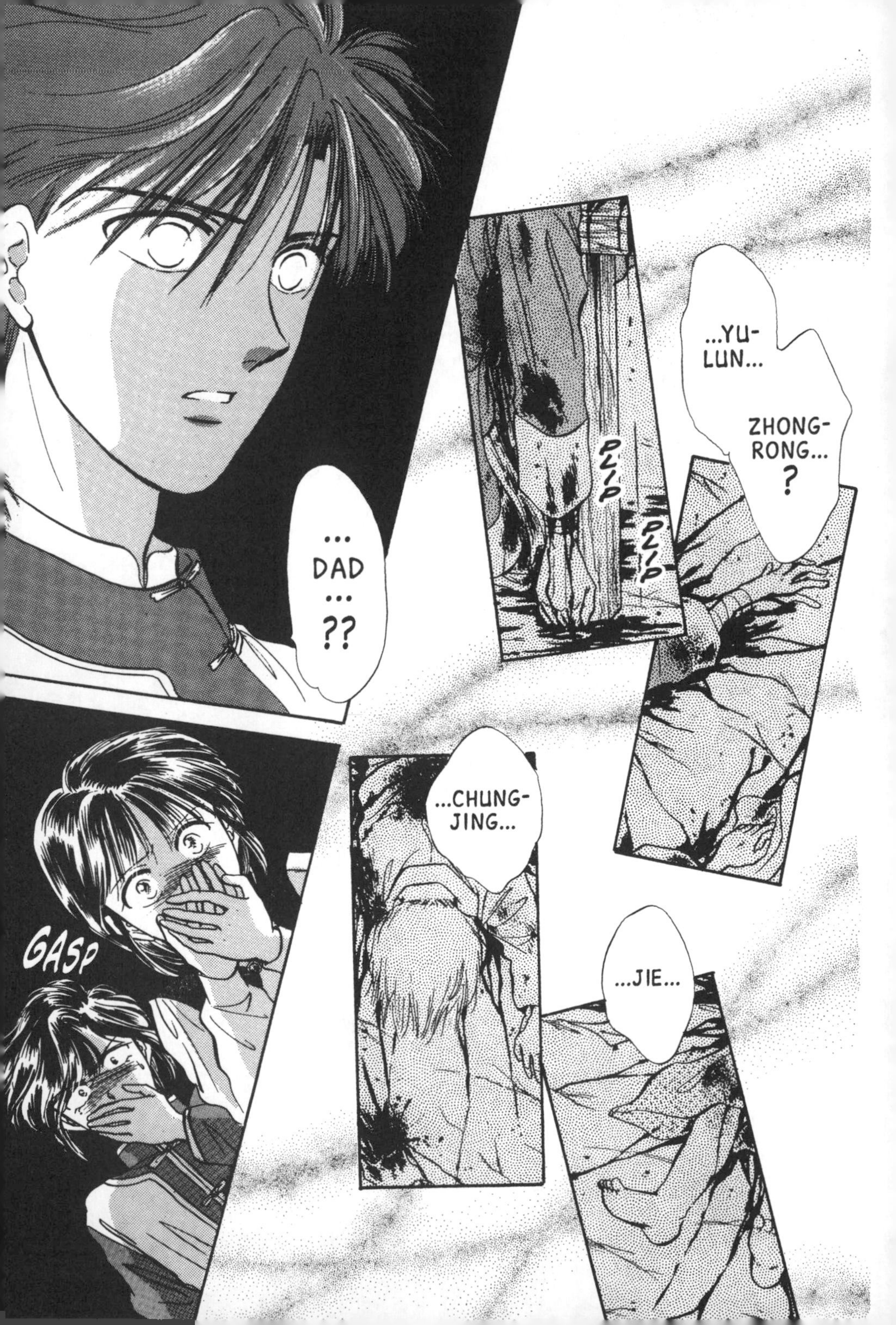

PLIP
PLIP
...YU-LUN...
ZHONG-RONG...?
...DAD...??
...CHUNG-JING...
...JIE...
GASP

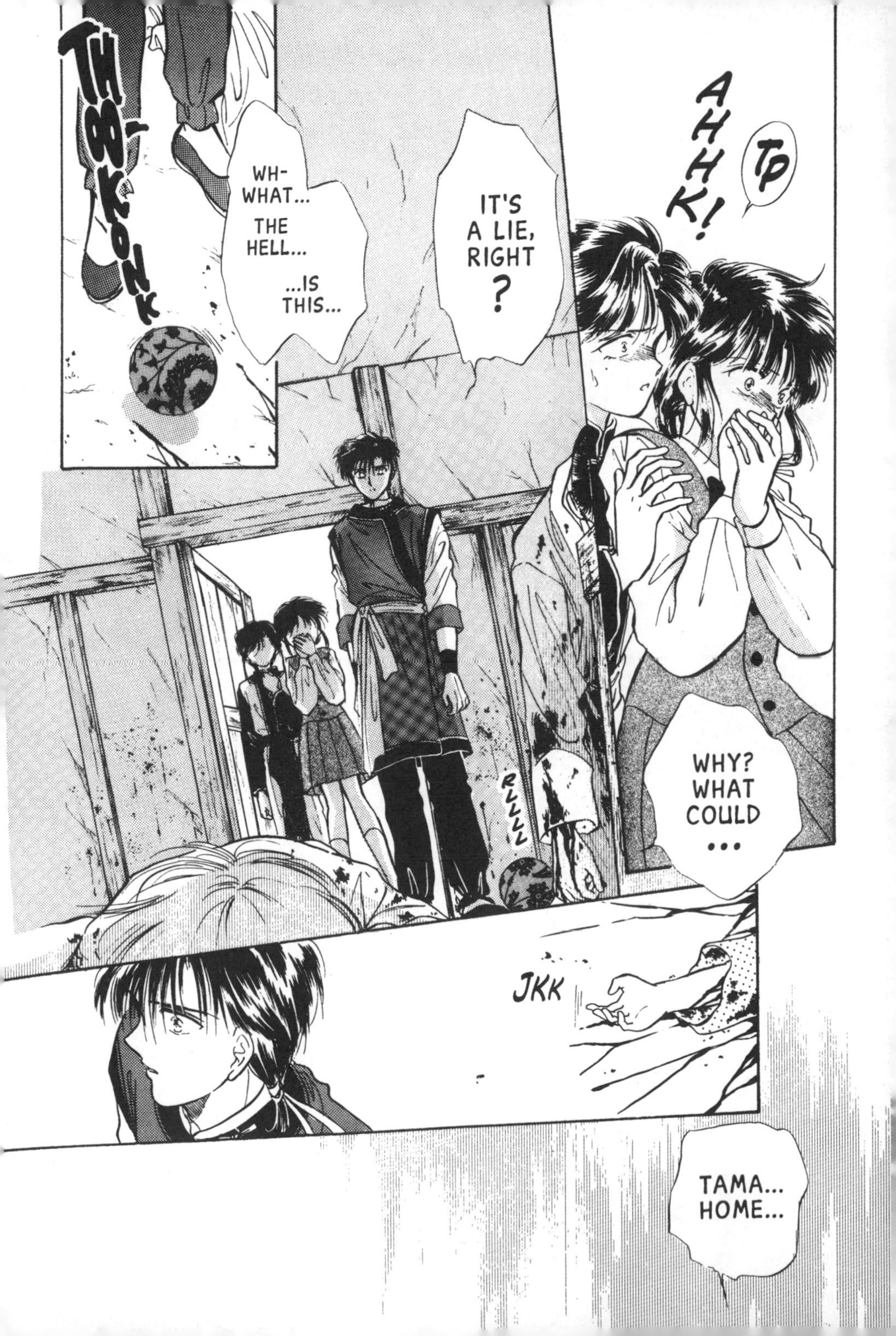
Tp
AHHHK!
IT'S A LIE, RIGHT?
WH-WHAT... THE HELL... ...IS THIS...
THOO-KONK
WHY? WHAT COULD ...
RLLL
JKK
TAMA... HOME...

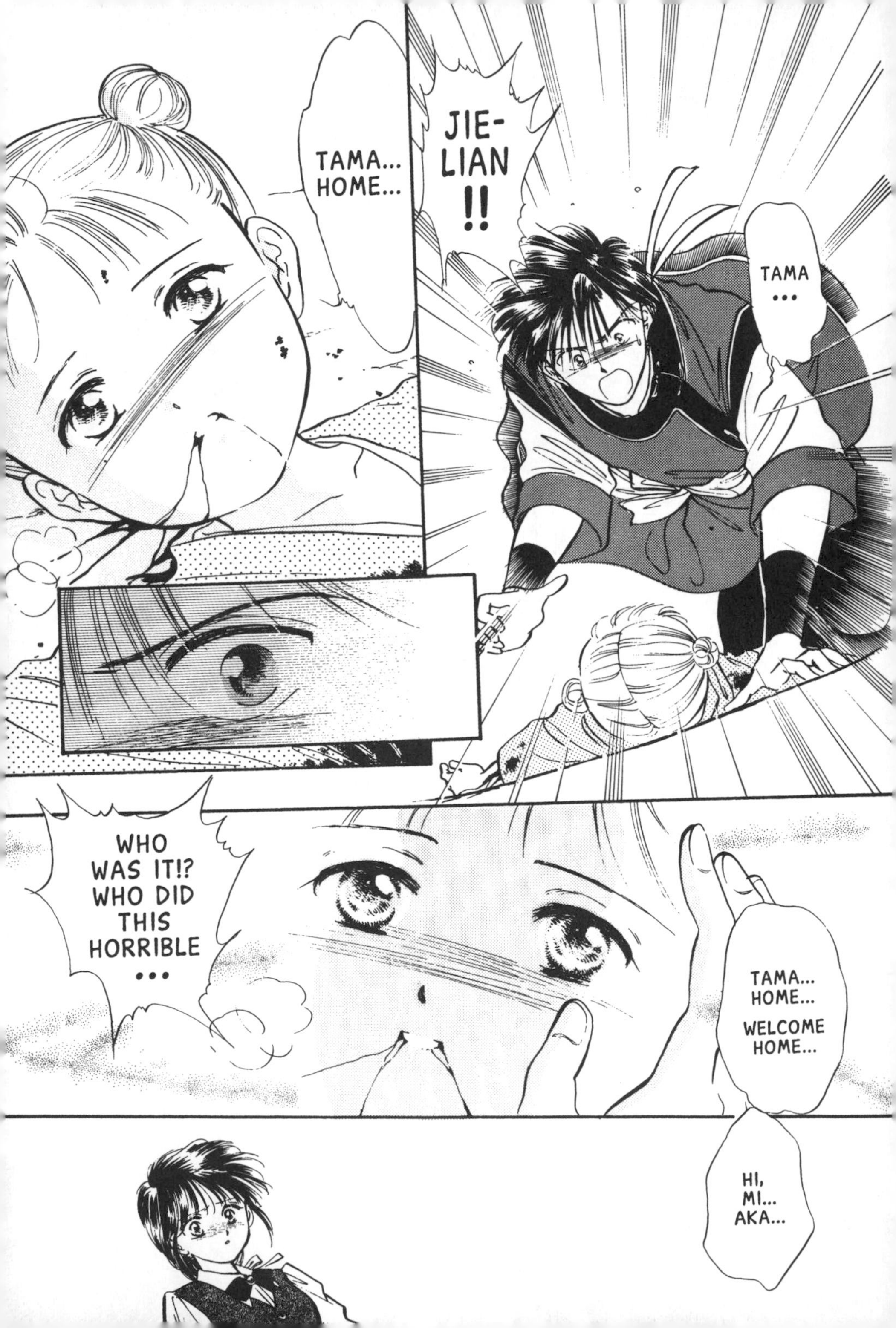
TAMA... HOME...
JIE-LIAN !!
TAMA ...
WHO WAS IT!? WHO DID THIS HORRIBLE ...
TAMA... HOME... WELCOME HOME...
HI, MI... AKA...

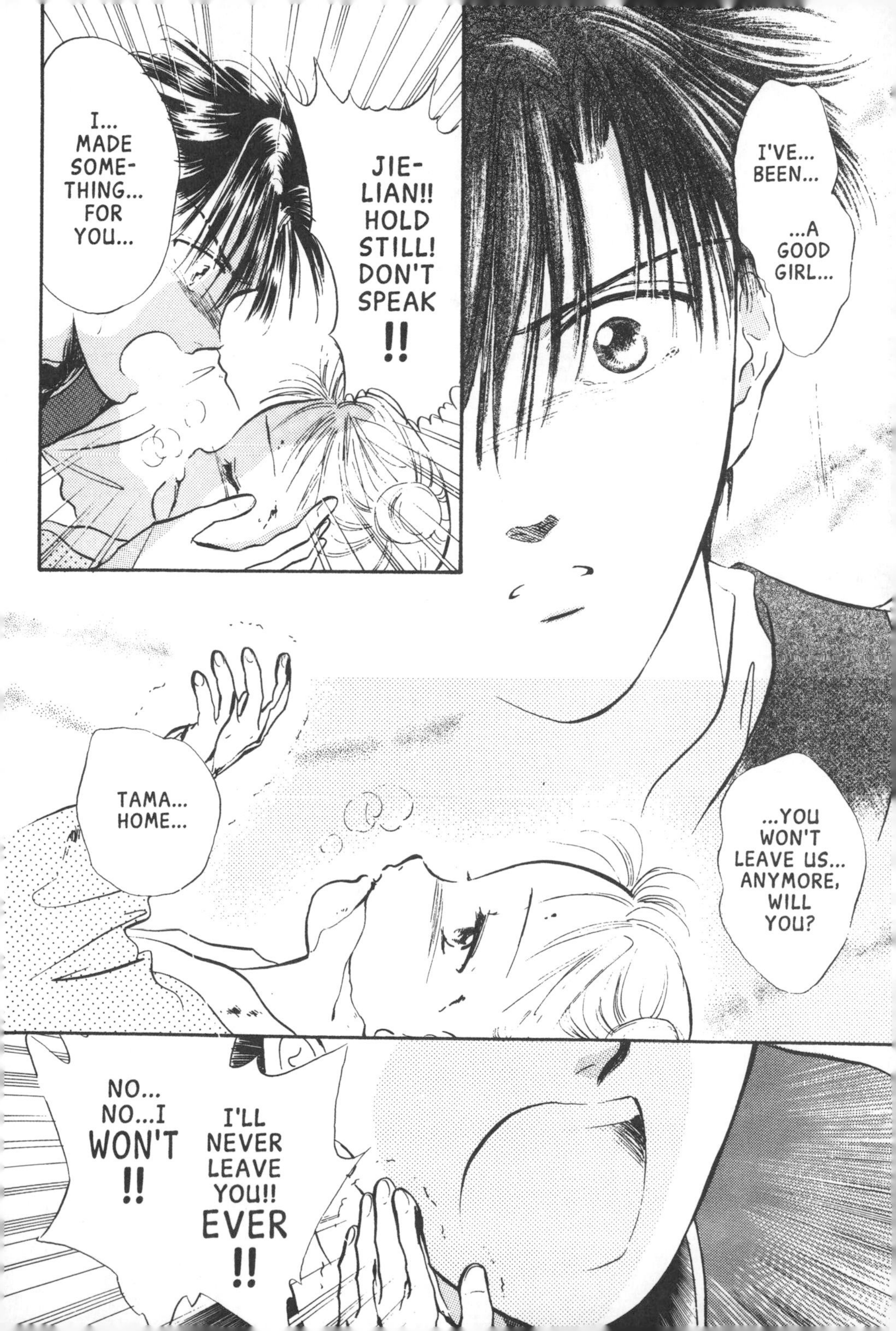
I... MADE SOME-THING... FOR YOU...
JIE-LIAN!! HOLD STILL! DON'T SPEAK!!
I'VE... BEEN...
...A GOOD GIRL...
TAMA... HOME...
...YOU WON'T LEAVE US... ANYMORE, WILL YOU?
NO... NO...I WON'T!!
I'LL NEVER LEAVE YOU!! EVER!!

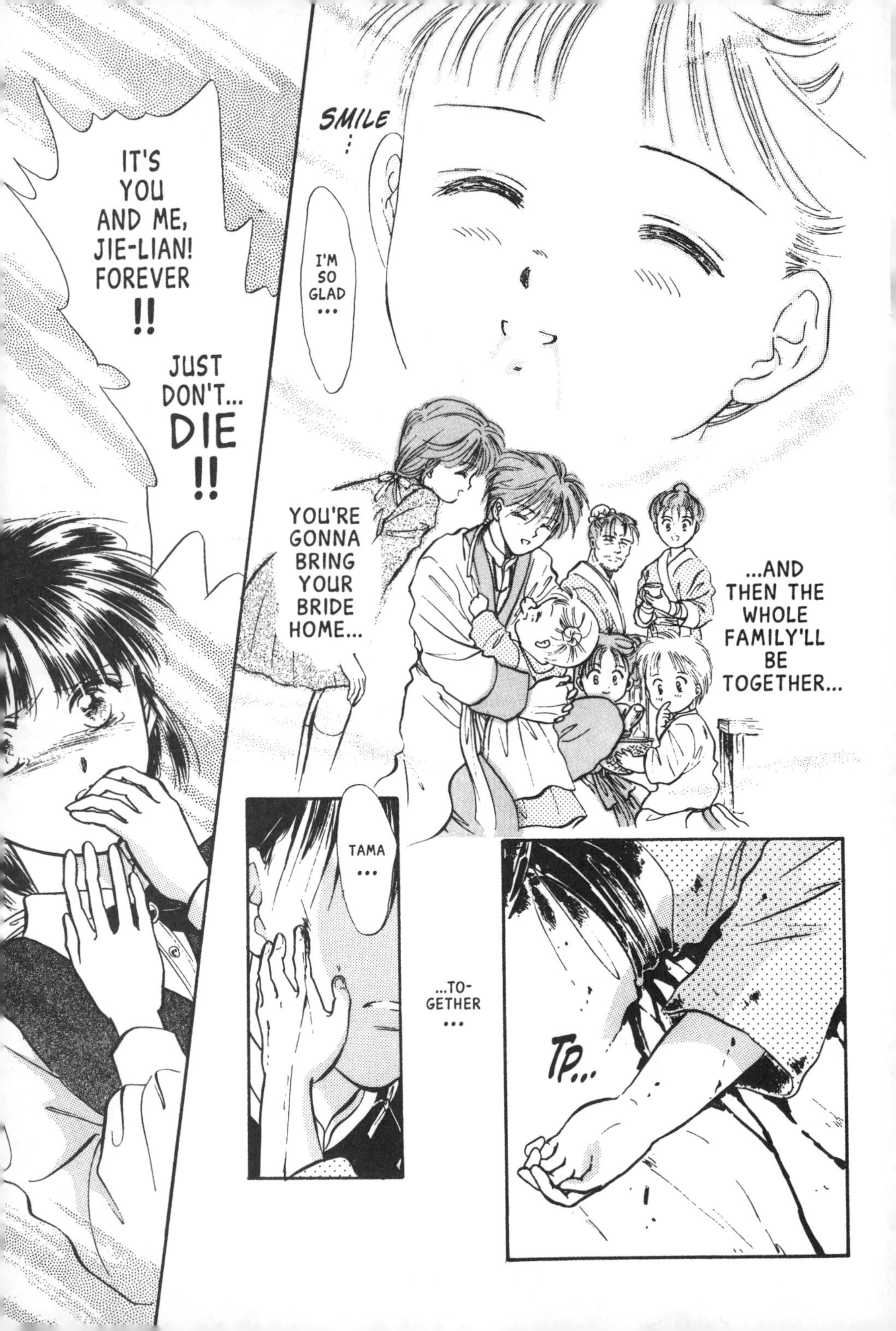
IT'S YOU AND ME, JIE-LIAN! FOREVER!!
JUST DON'T... DIE!!
SMILE
I'M SO GLAD...
YOU'RE GONNA BRING YOUR BRIDE HOME...
...AND THEN THE WHOLE FAMILY'LL BE TOGETHER...
TAMA...
...TO-GETHER...
TP...

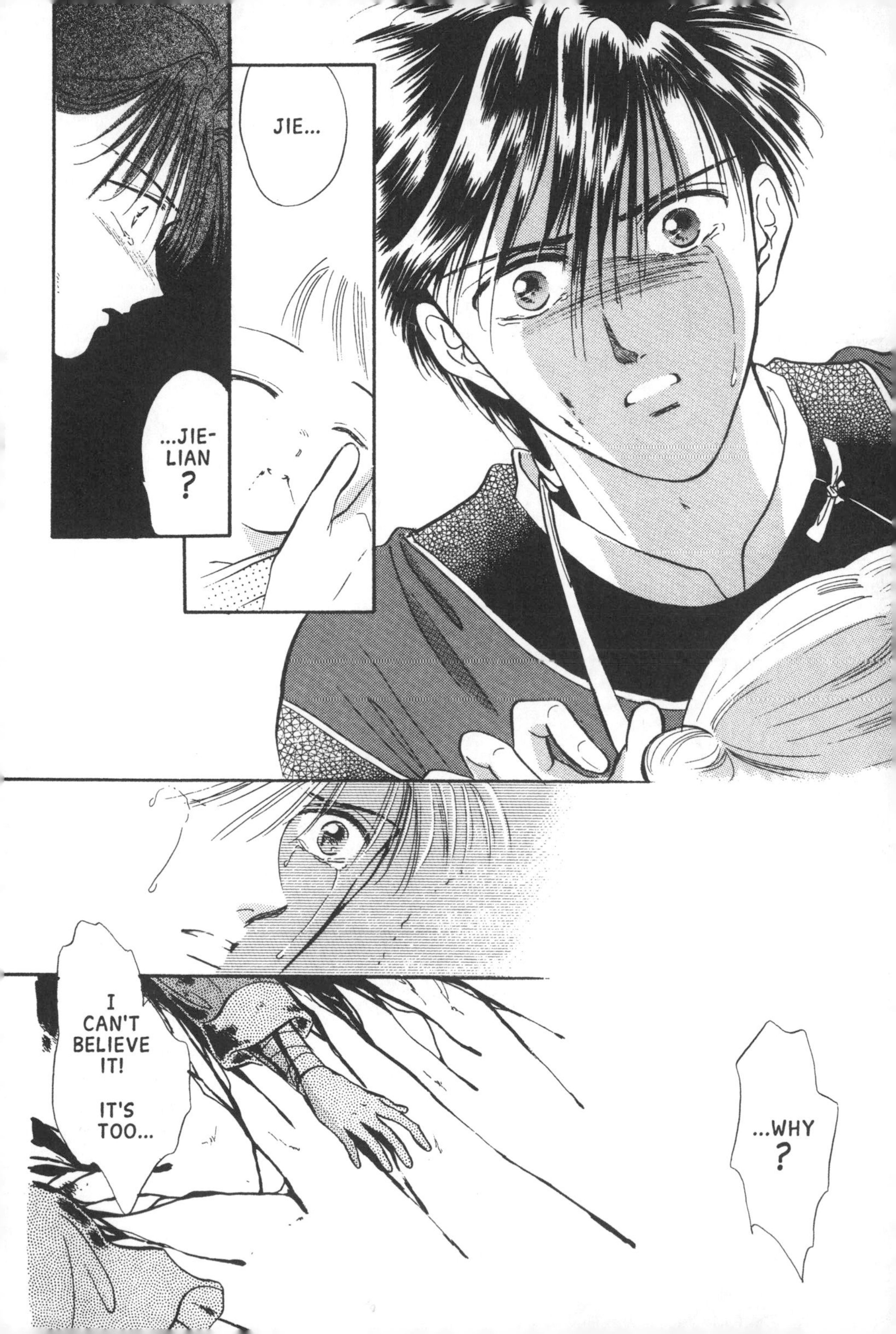

...JIE-LIAN?
JIE...
I CAN'T BELIEVE IT!
IT'S TOO...
...WHY?

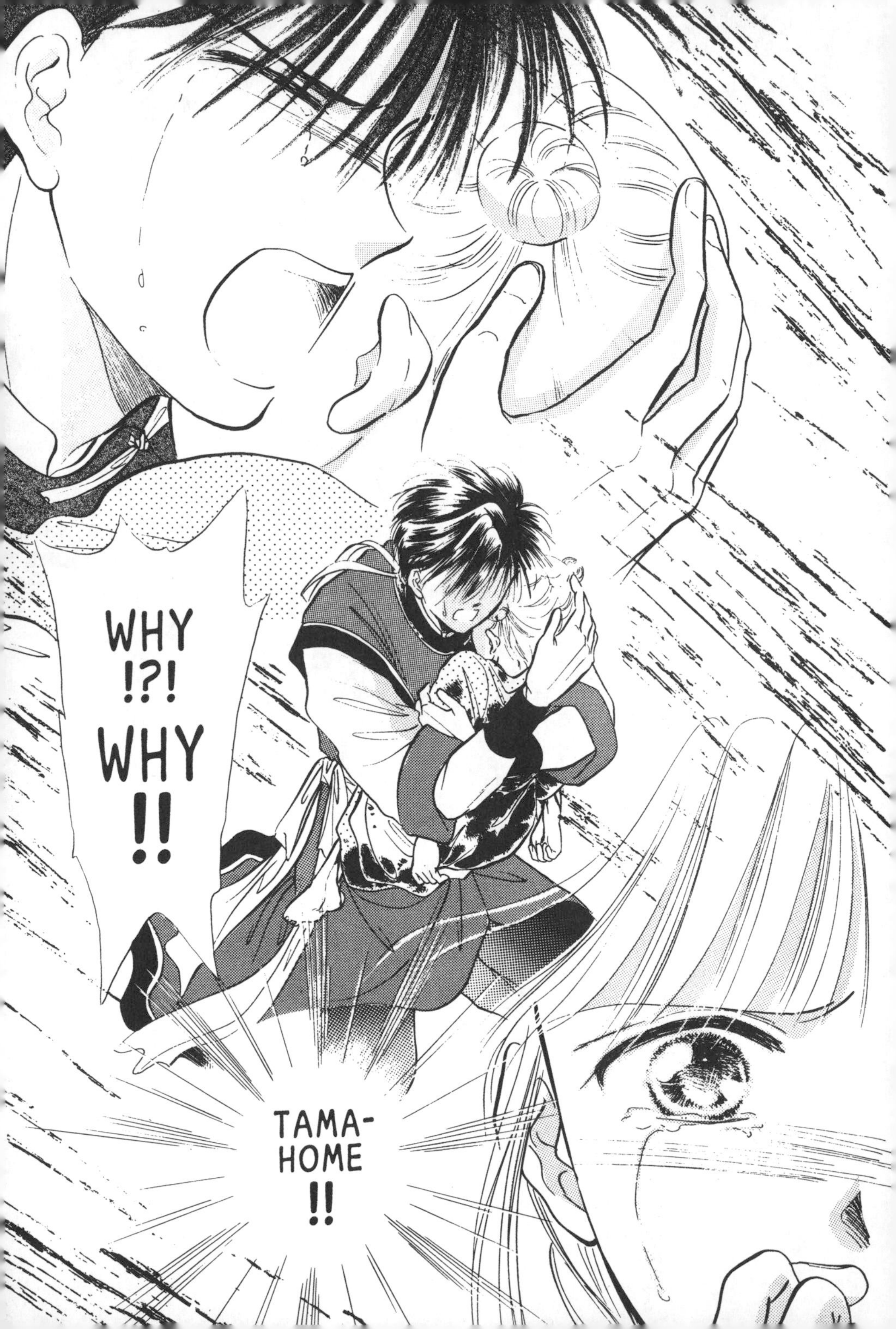
WHY !?! WHY !!
TAMA-HOME !!

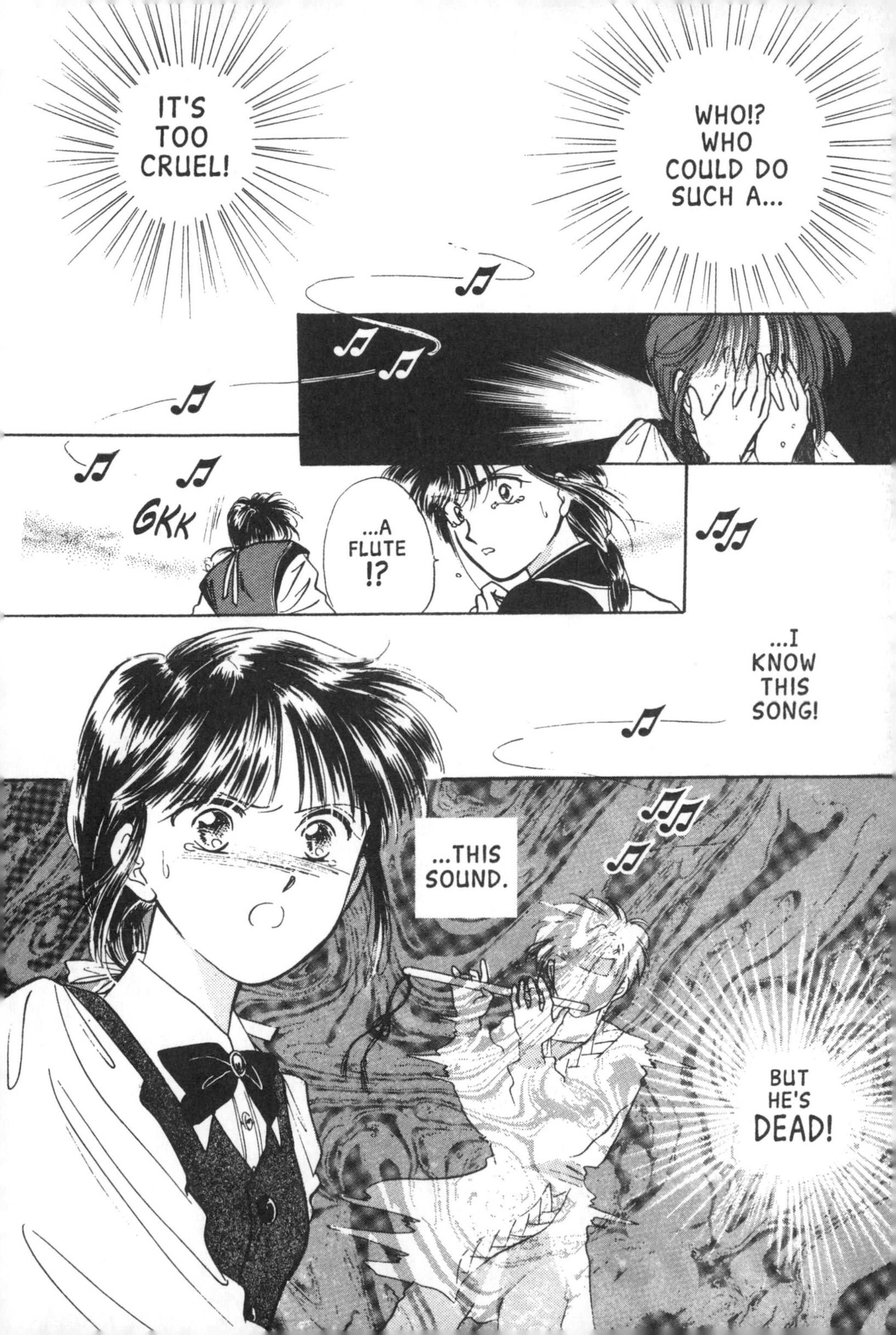
IT'S TOO CRUEL!
WHO!? WHO COULD DO SUCH A...
GKK
...A FLUTE !?
...I KNOW THIS SONG!
...THIS SOUND.
BUT HE'S DEAD!

# CHAPTER FORTY

# VOW ON A GRAVE

SESSIONS
SNOWBOARD
shop

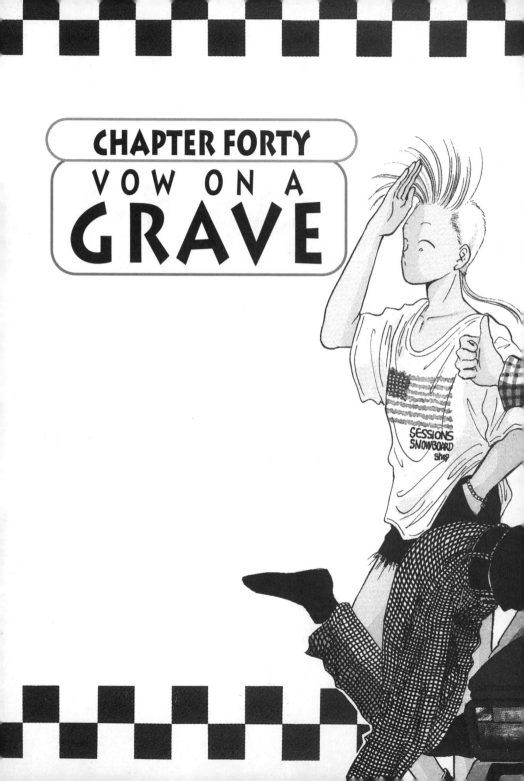

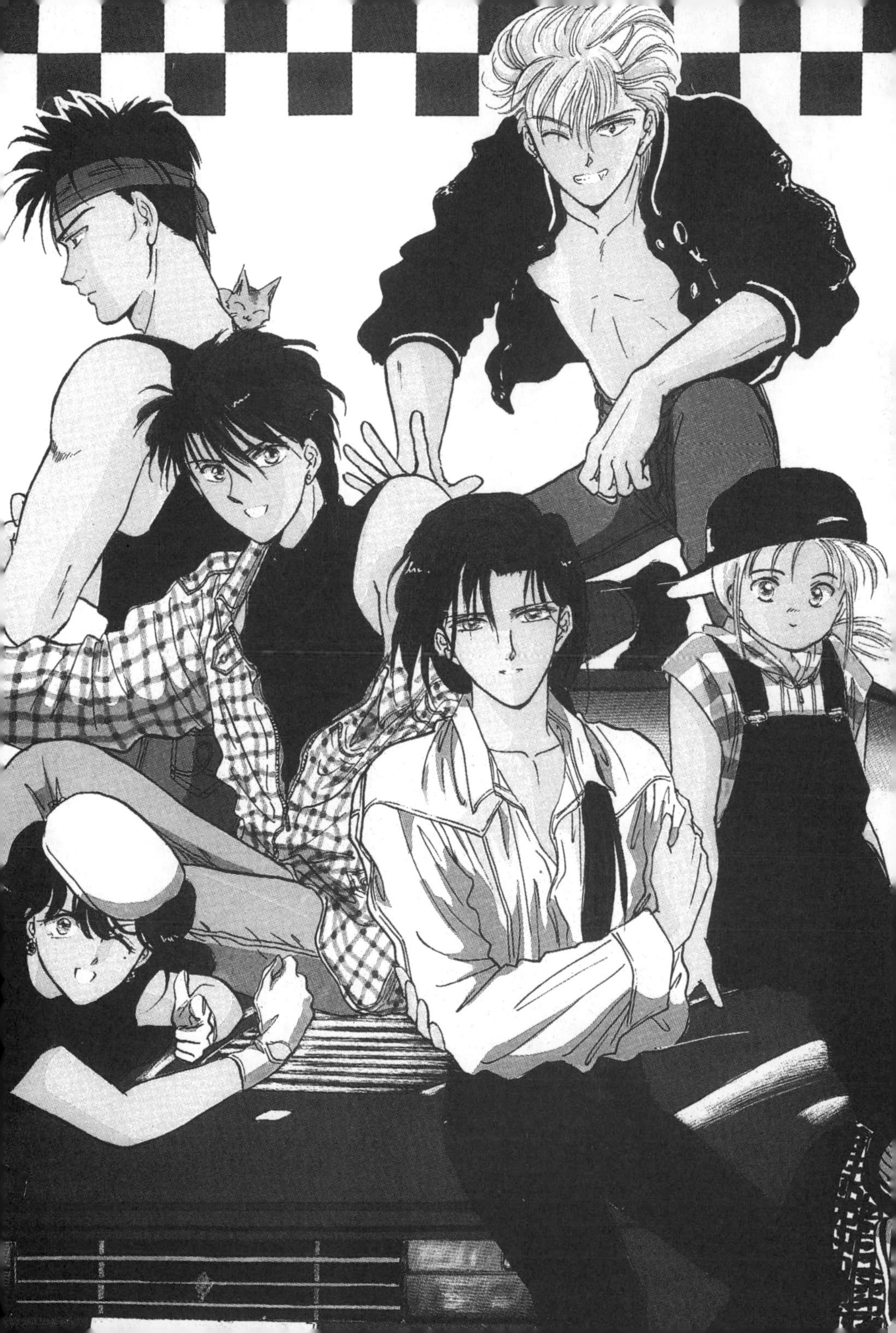

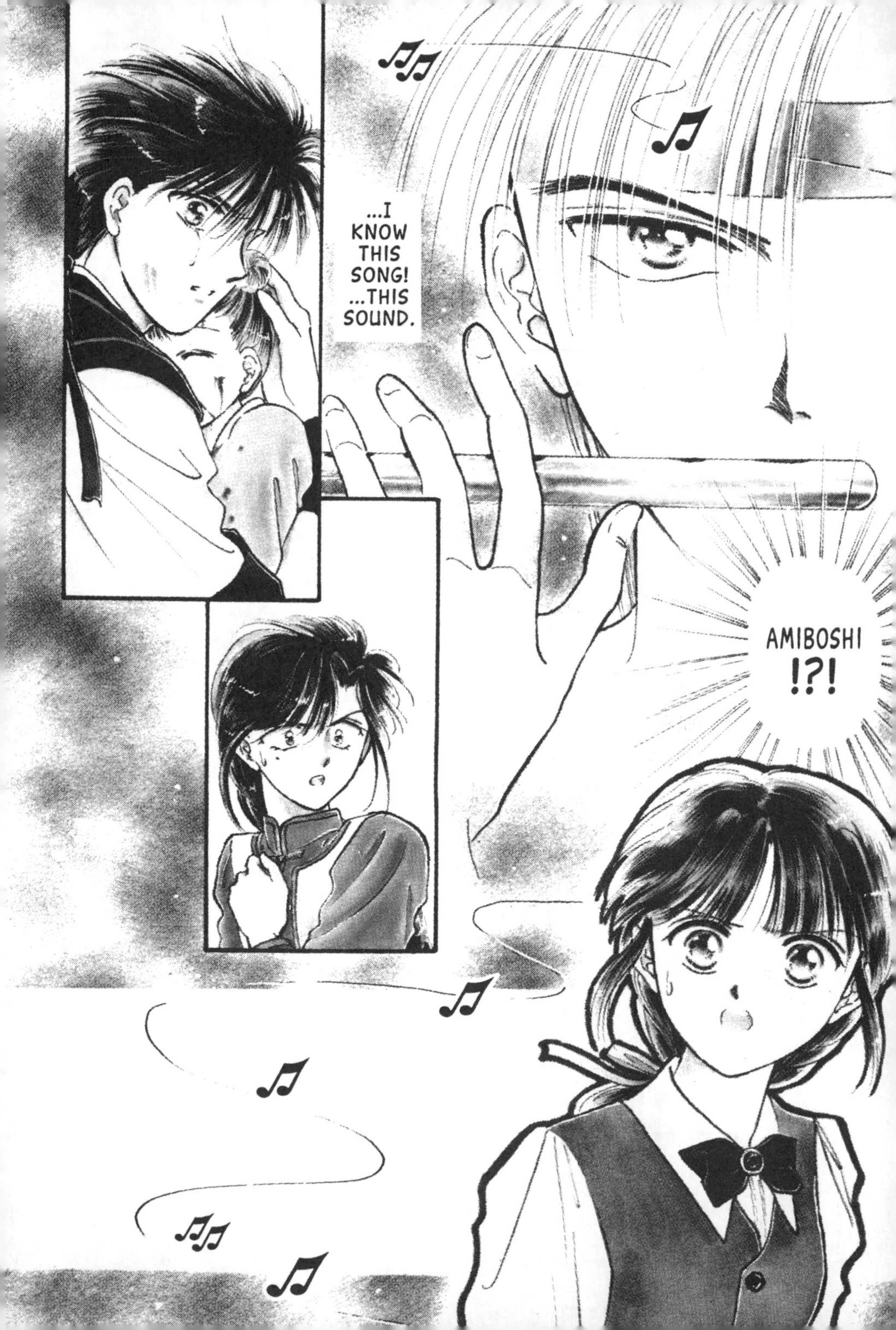
...I KNOW THIS SONG! ...THIS SOUND.
AMIBOSHI !?!

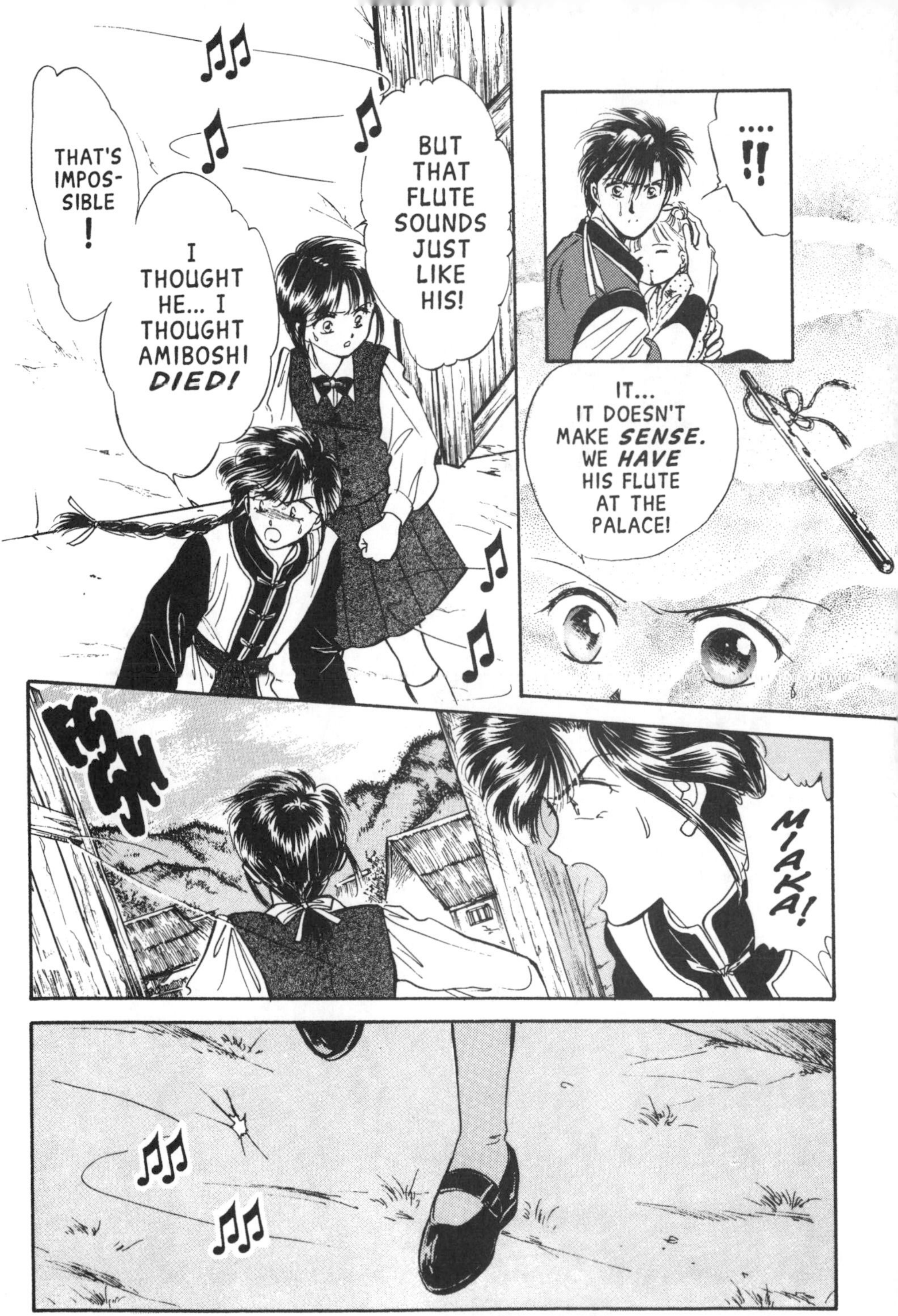
THAT'S IMPOSSIBLE!
I THOUGHT HE... I THOUGHT AMIBOSHI *DIED!*
BUT THAT FLUTE SOUNDS JUST LIKE HIS!
....!!
IT... IT DOESN'T MAKE *SENSE.* WE *HAVE* HIS FLUTE AT THE PALACE!
MIAKA!

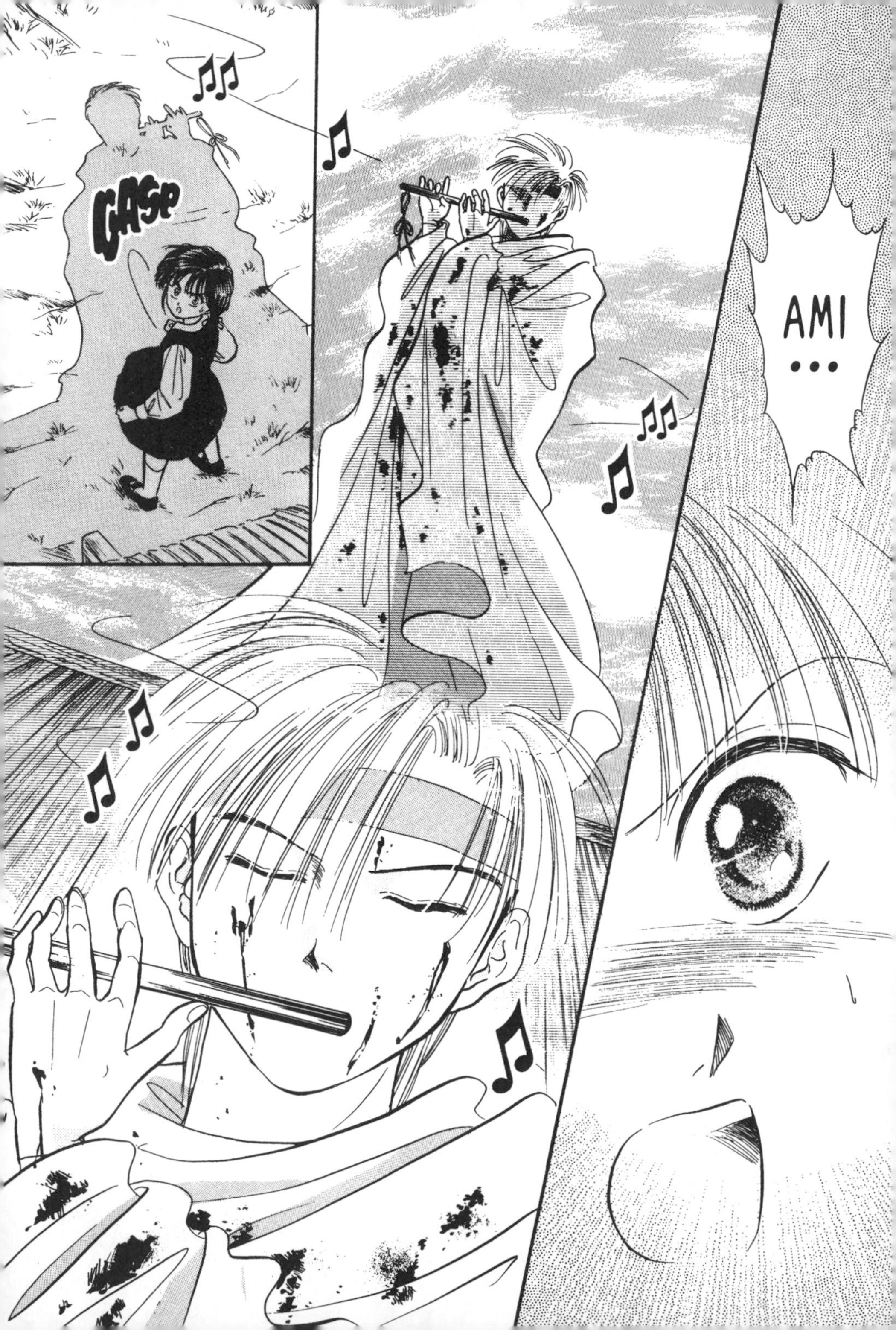
GASP
AMI ...

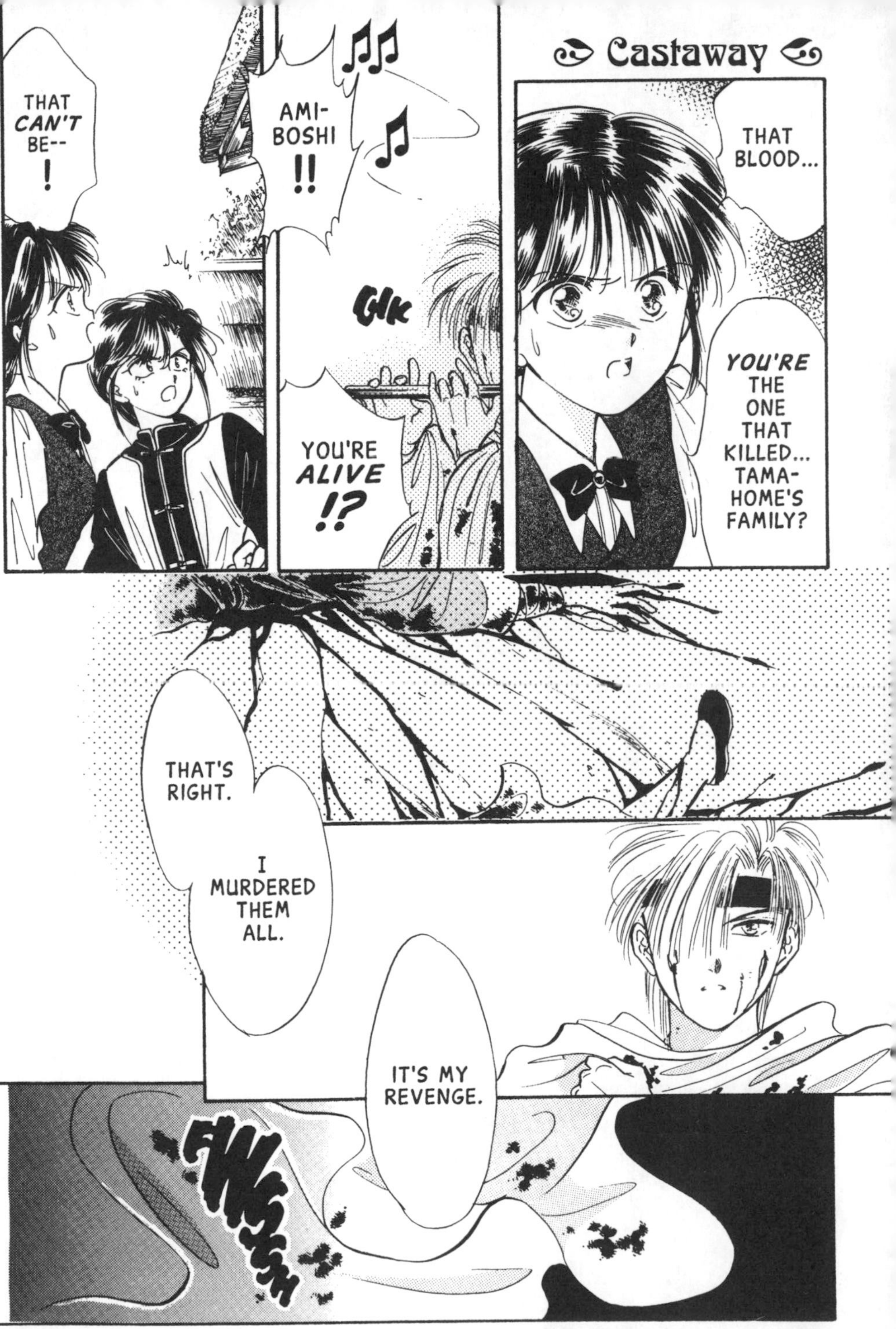
THAT *CAN'T* BE-- !
AMI-BOSHI !!
GHK
YOU'RE *ALIVE* !?
THAT BLOOD...
*YOU'RE* THE ONE THAT KILLED... TAMA-HOME'S FAMILY?
THAT'S RIGHT.
I MURDERED THEM ALL.
IT'S MY REVENGE.

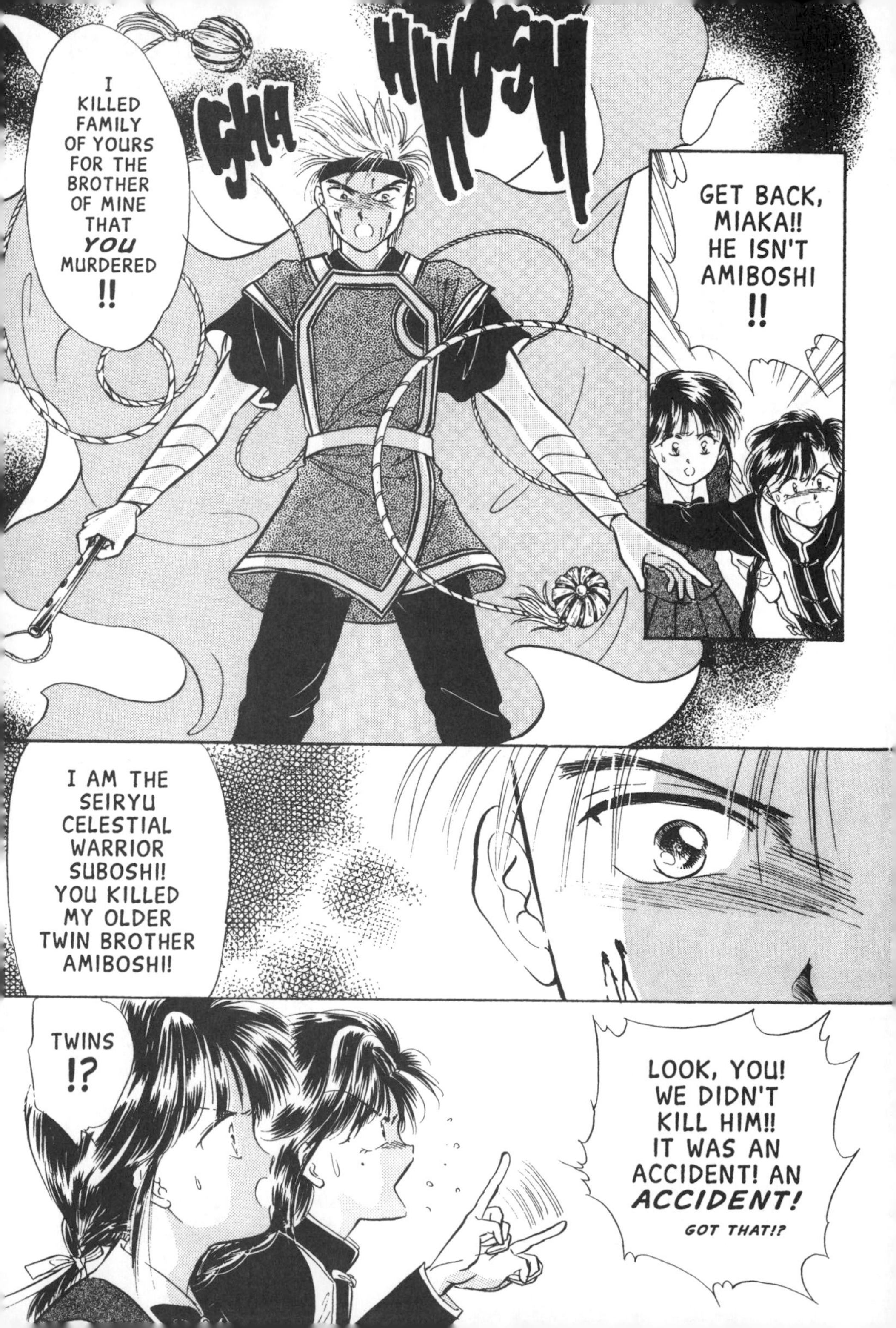

I KILLED FAMILY OF YOURS FOR THE BROTHER OF MINE THAT *YOU* MURDERED !!
GHA
HWOOSH
GET BACK, MIAKA!! HE ISN'T AMIBOSHI !!
I AM THE SEIRYU CELESTIAL WARRIOR SUBOSHI!! YOU KILLED MY OLDER TWIN BROTHER AMIBOSHI!!
TWINS !?
LOOK, YOU! WE DIDN'T KILL HIM!! IT WAS AN ACCIDENT! AN ***ACCIDENT!***
*GOT THAT!?*

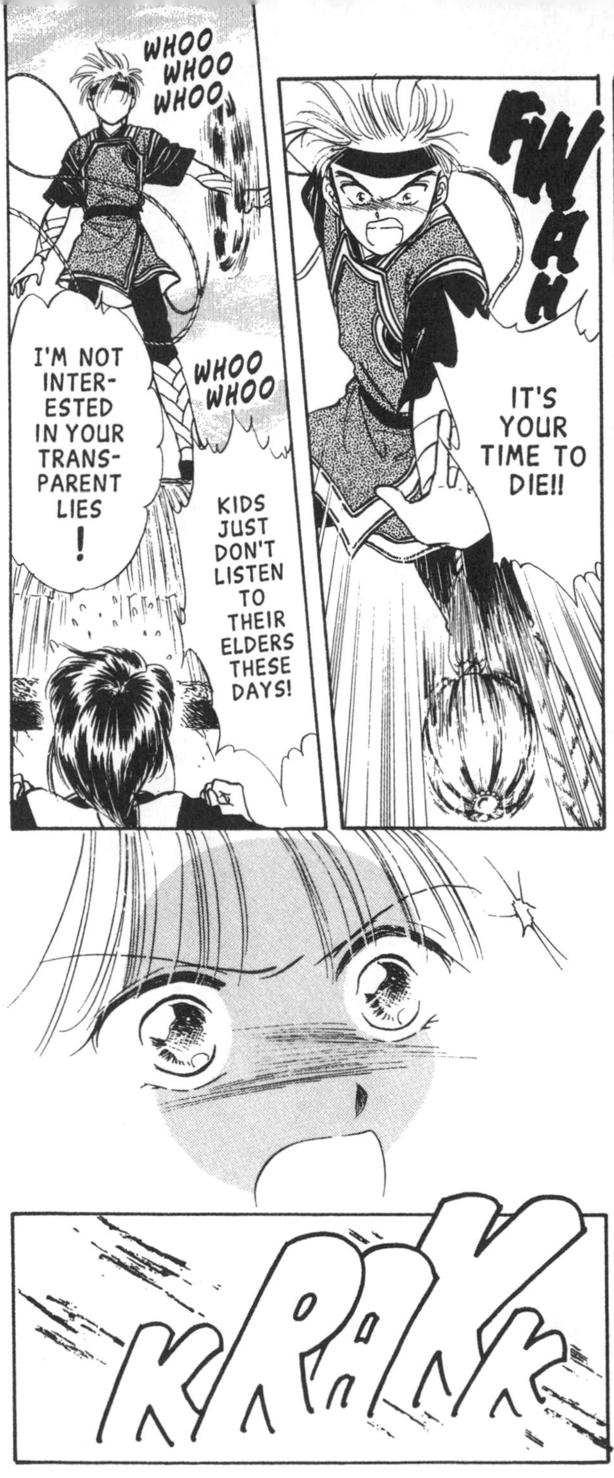
WHOO WHOO WHOO
I'M NOT INTER-ESTED IN YOUR TRANS-PARENT LIES!
WHOO WHOO
KIDS JUST DON'T LISTEN TO THEIR ELDERS THESE DAYS!
FWAH
IT'S YOUR TIME TO DIE!!
KRAPANK

Speaking of life, I remember that there was quite a reaction to "The Jie-Lian Family Massacre" (that sounds weird) in this episode... One letter began "It can't be true," and ended "It's too terrible!" Apparently, her friend was reading it lying down and lost her contact lens from crying. Of course, I couldn't draw it without crying too, you know! You might ask, "Then why did you have to draw it!?" Well, that's how stories work (THAT'S the reason?). Tamahome, who watched Jie-Lian die in his arms with no way to help her, must be the saddest one though...
Getting back to my dog, while I was at my office (near my house), Yū, who just learned how to climb the stairs, fell from the second floor. My mother immediately came to the rescue, and as soon as she saw Yū not moving with her tongue hanging out, she thought it was dead! Yū was only unconscious though. She moved a little, and my mother held her until the vet arrived. In the meantime, Yū was trying to tell her something in a strange voice. *An excuse!?* My mom, the one who yells most in our family, started crying, afraid that Yū might die. She was put on an IV at the vet's and recovered...
*It totally freaked me out.*

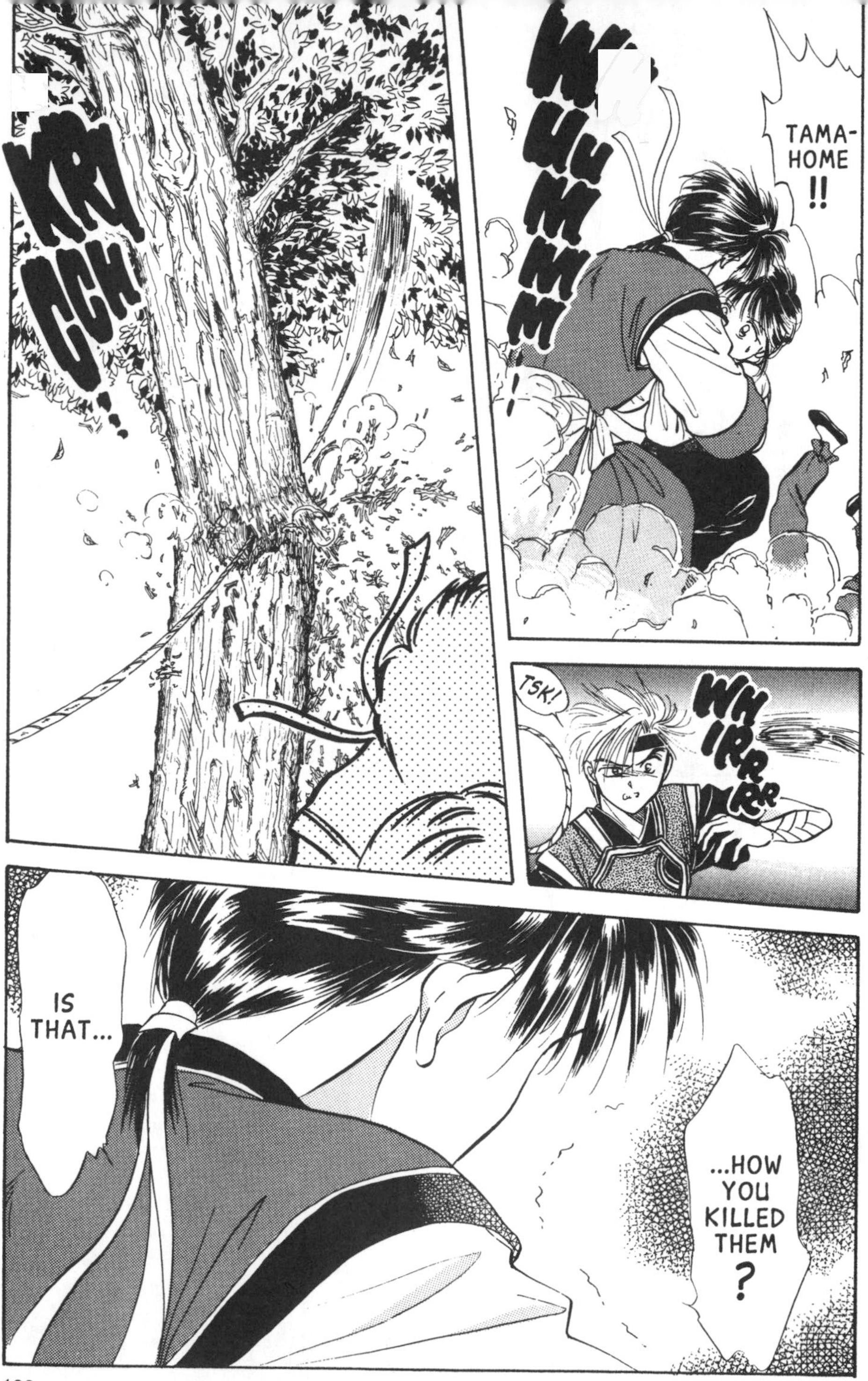
KRYCCH!!
WHUMMMM!!
TAMA-HOME!!
TSK!
WHIRRRR
IS THAT...
...HOW YOU KILLED THEM?

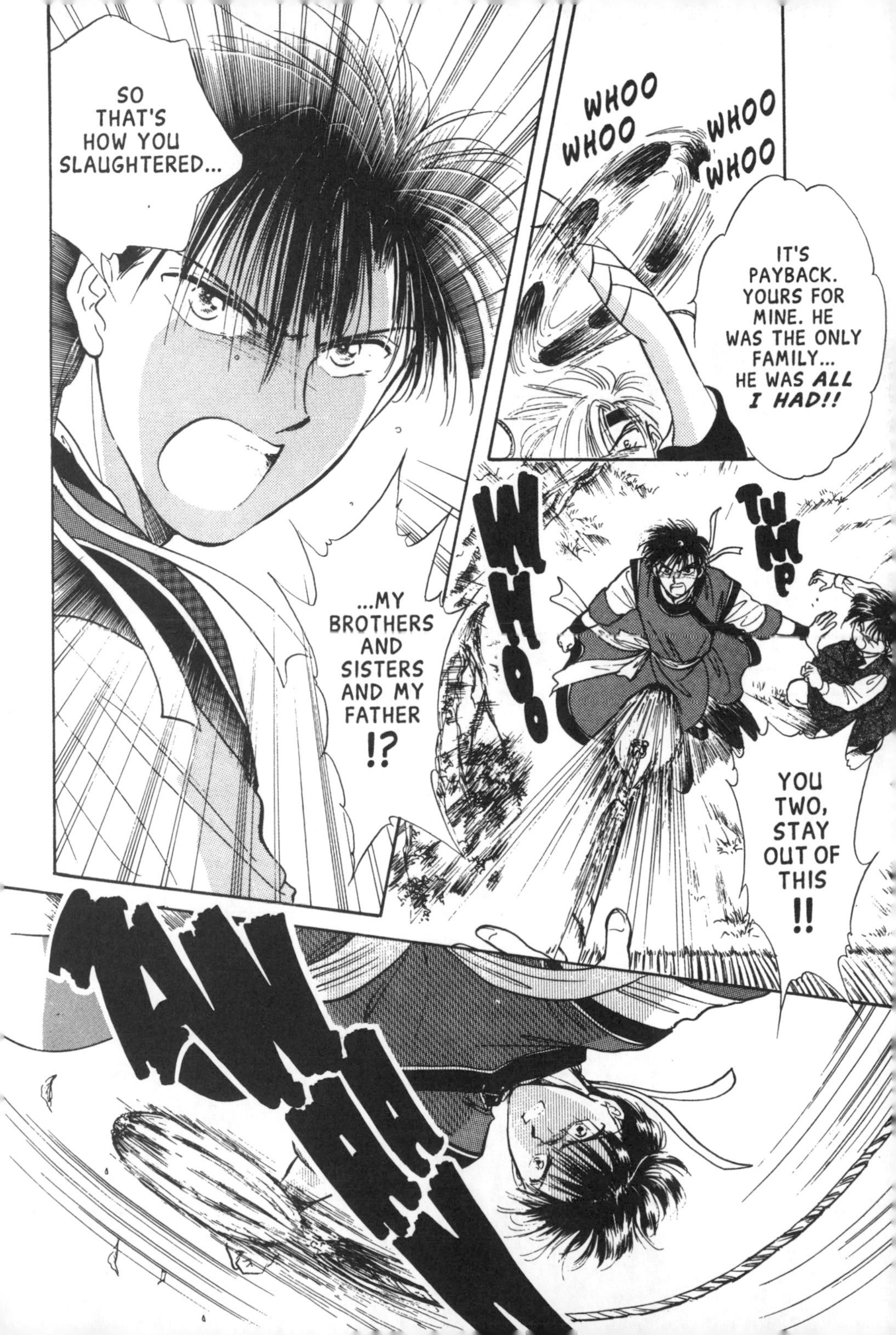
SO THAT'S HOW YOU SLAUGHTERED...
...MY BROTHERS AND SISTERS AND MY FATHER !?
WHOO WHOO
WHOO WHOO
IT'S PAYBACK. YOURS FOR MINE. HE WAS THE ONLY FAMILY... HE WAS ALL I HAD!!
WHOOO
TUMP
YOU TWO, STAY OUT OF THIS !!

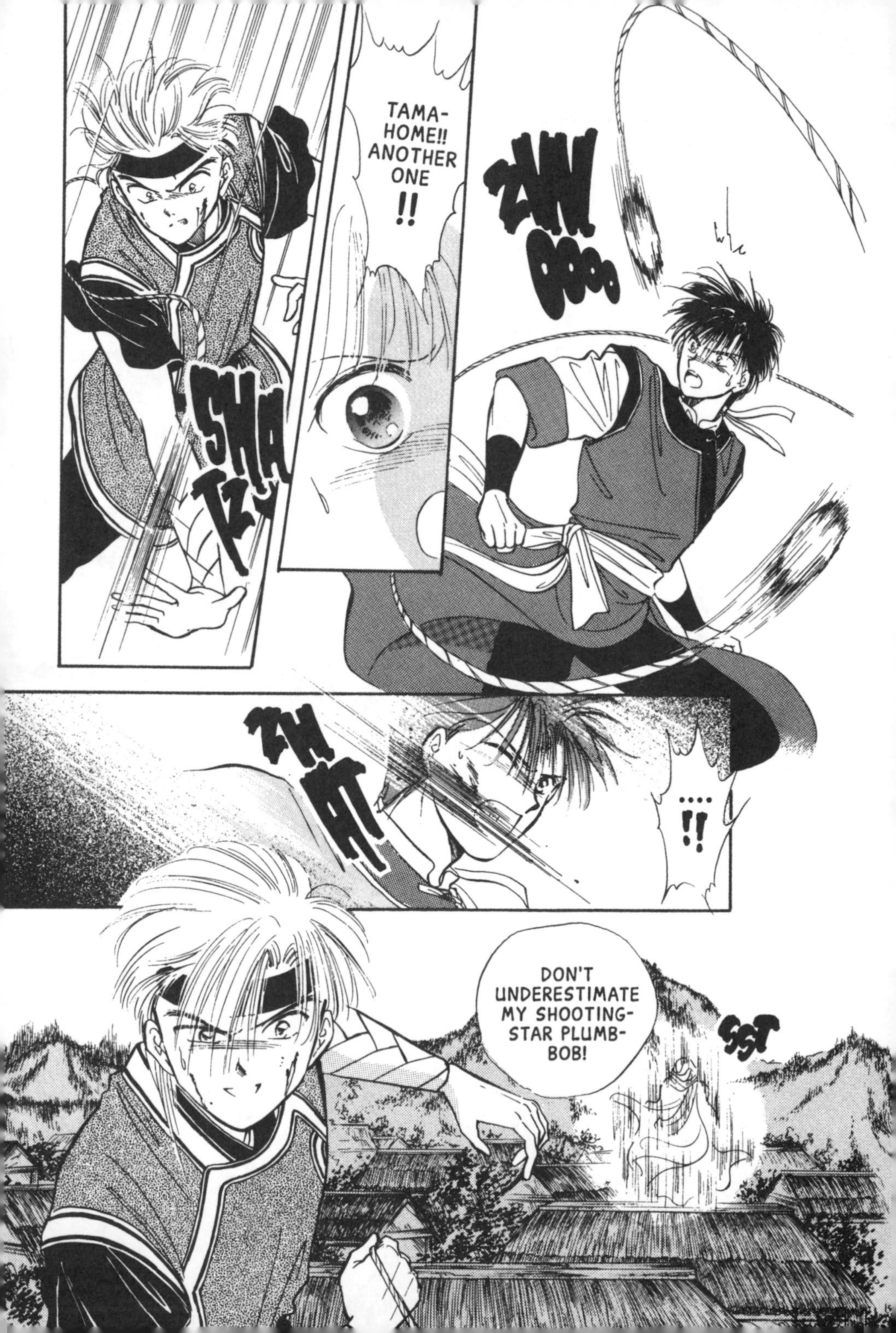
TAMA-HOME!! ANOTHER ONE !!
ZHAT
....!!
DON'T UNDERESTIMATE MY SHOOTING-STAR PLUMB-BOB!
SST

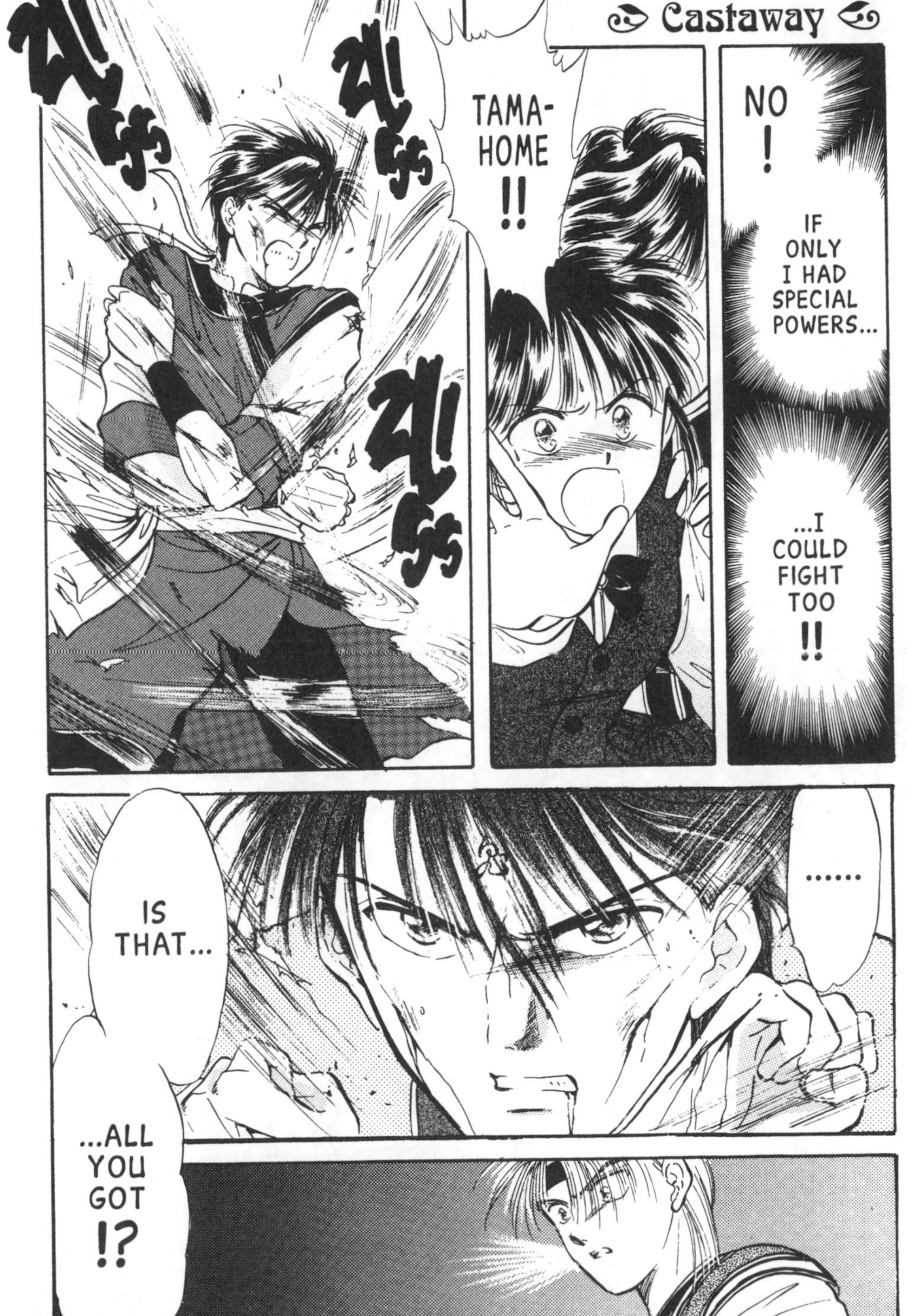
TAMA-
HOME
!!
NO
!
IF ONLY I HAD SPECIAL POWERS...
...I COULD FIGHT TOO
!!
IS THAT...
......
...ALL YOU GOT
!?

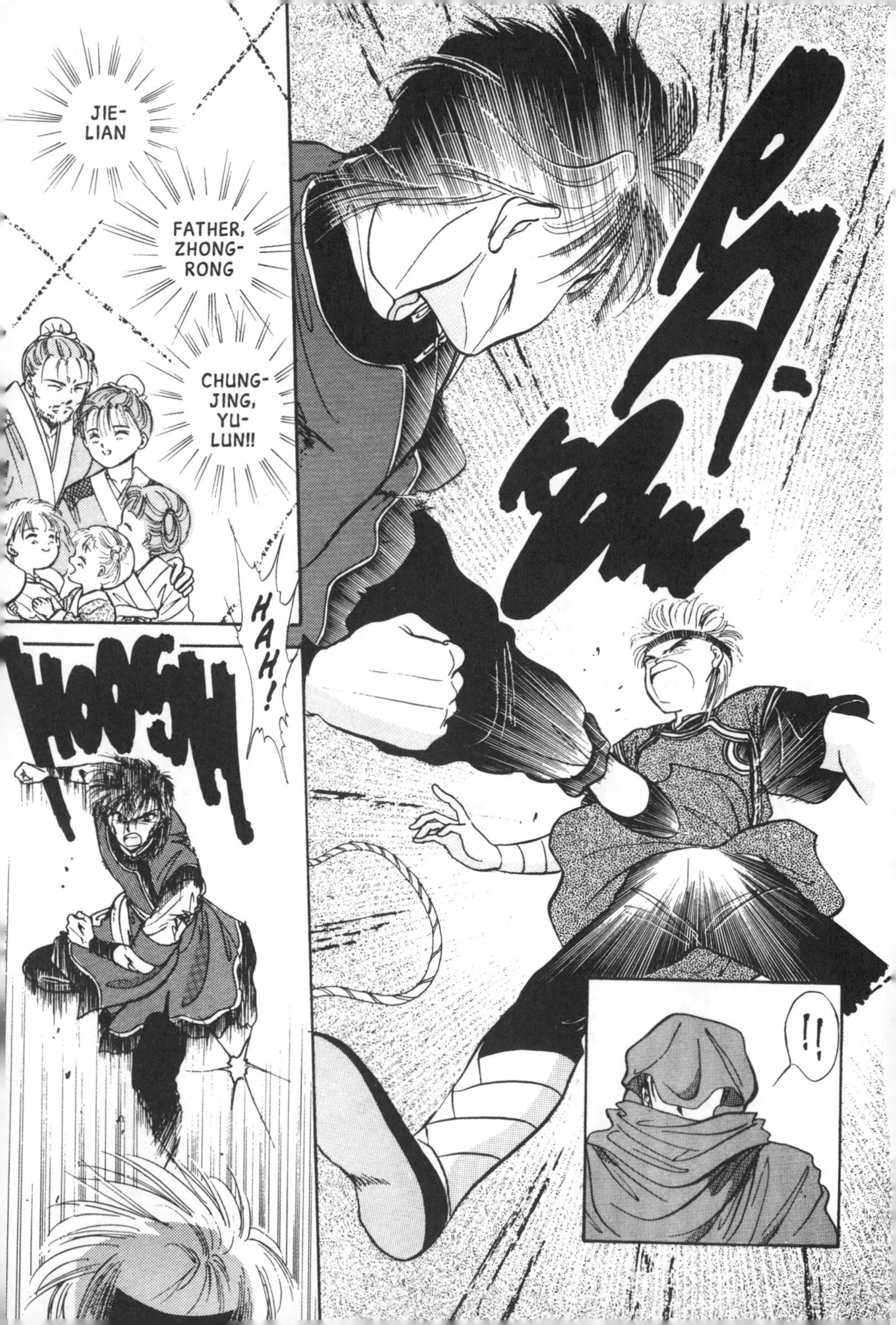
JIE-
LIAN
FATHER,
ZHONG-
RONG
CHUNG-
JING,
YU-
LUN!!
HOOSH
HAH!
PA-BAM
!!

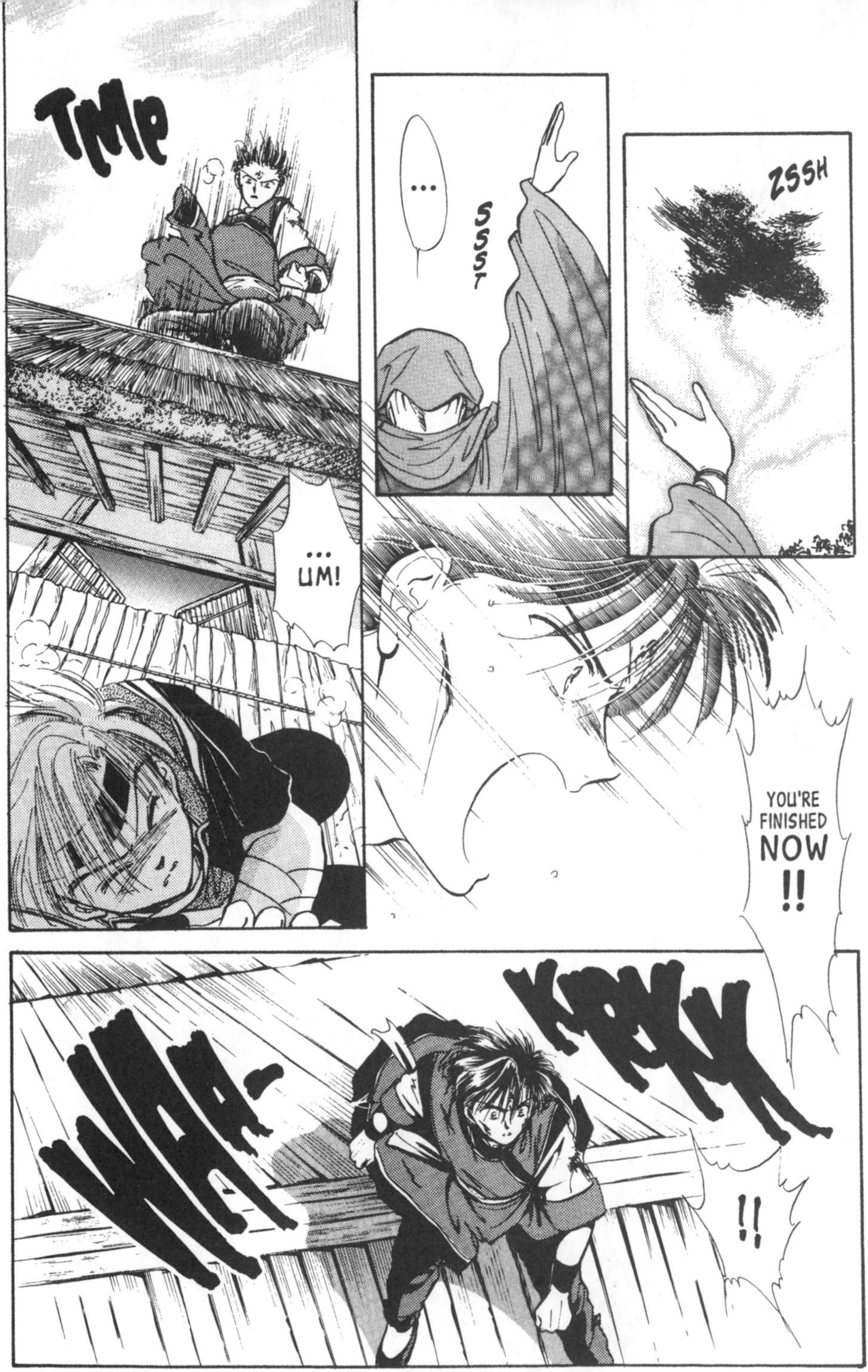
TMP
... UM!
...
SSST
ZSSH
YOU'RE FINISHED NOW !!
WHA-
!!

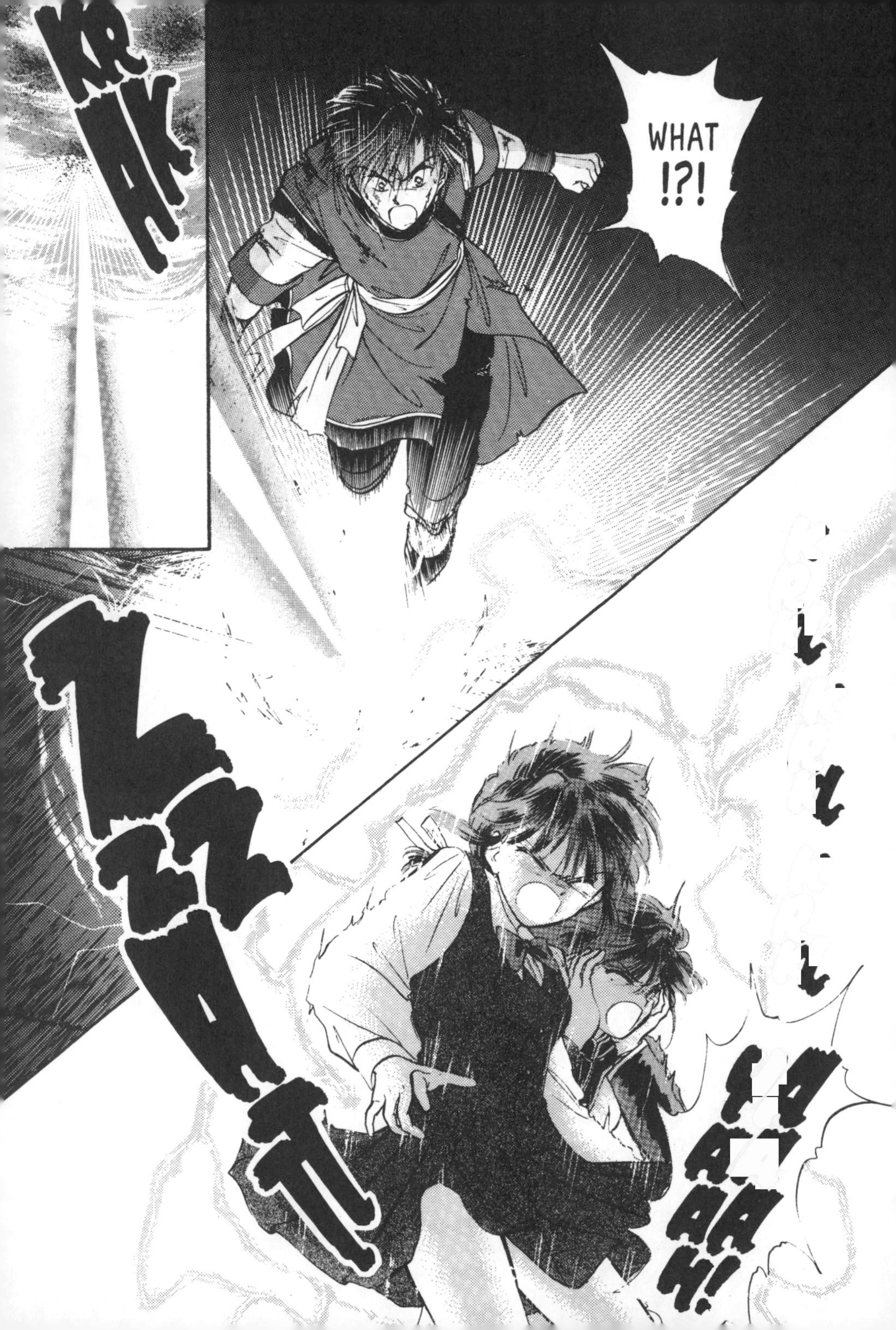
KRAKK
WHAT !?!
ZZZAT!

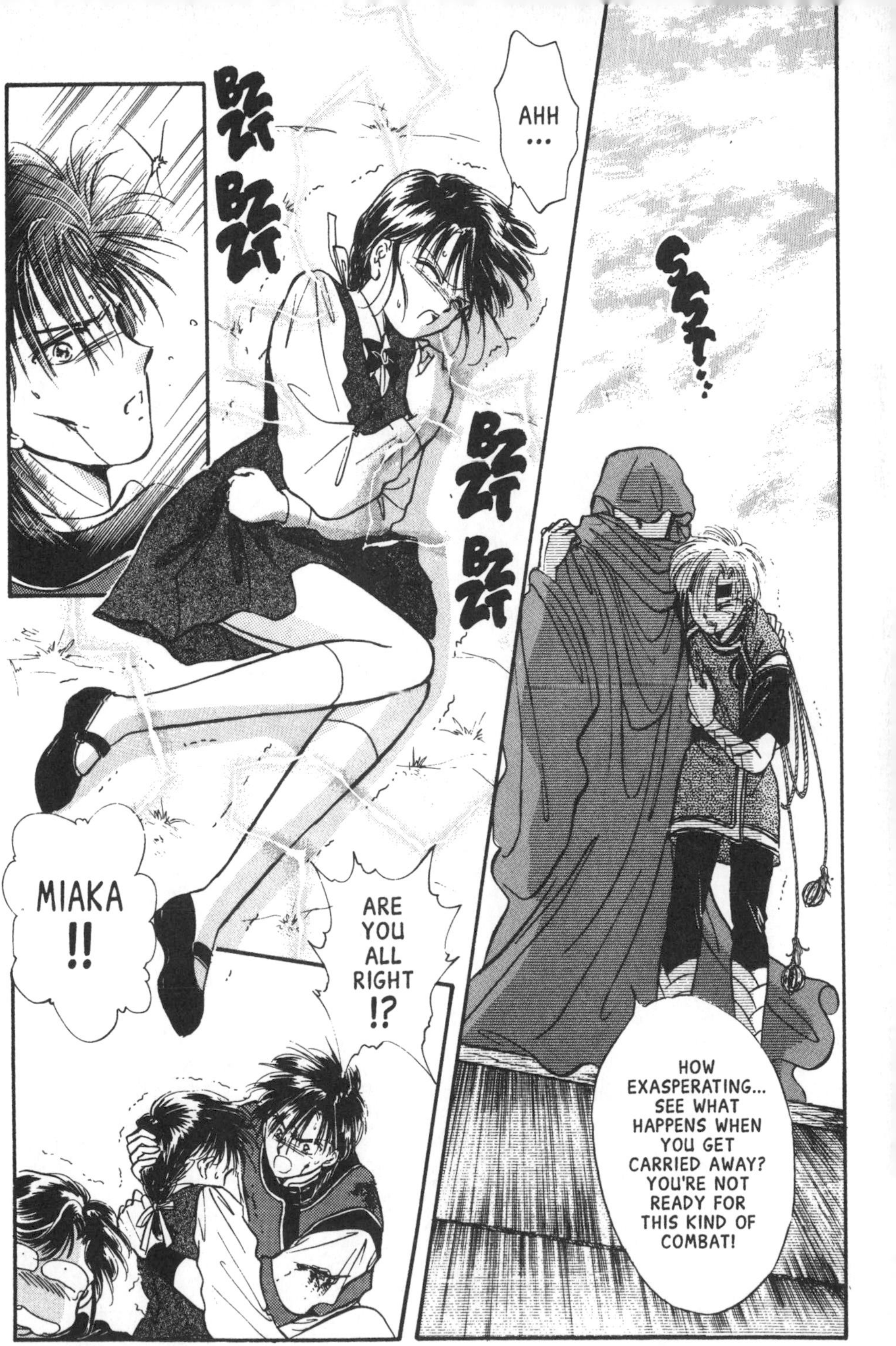
BZZT BZZT
AHH...
BZZT BZZT
MIAKA!!
ARE YOU ALL RIGHT!?
SSSST...
HOW EXASPERATING... SEE WHAT HAPPENS WHEN YOU GET CARRIED AWAY? YOU'RE NOT READY FOR THIS KIND OF COMBAT!

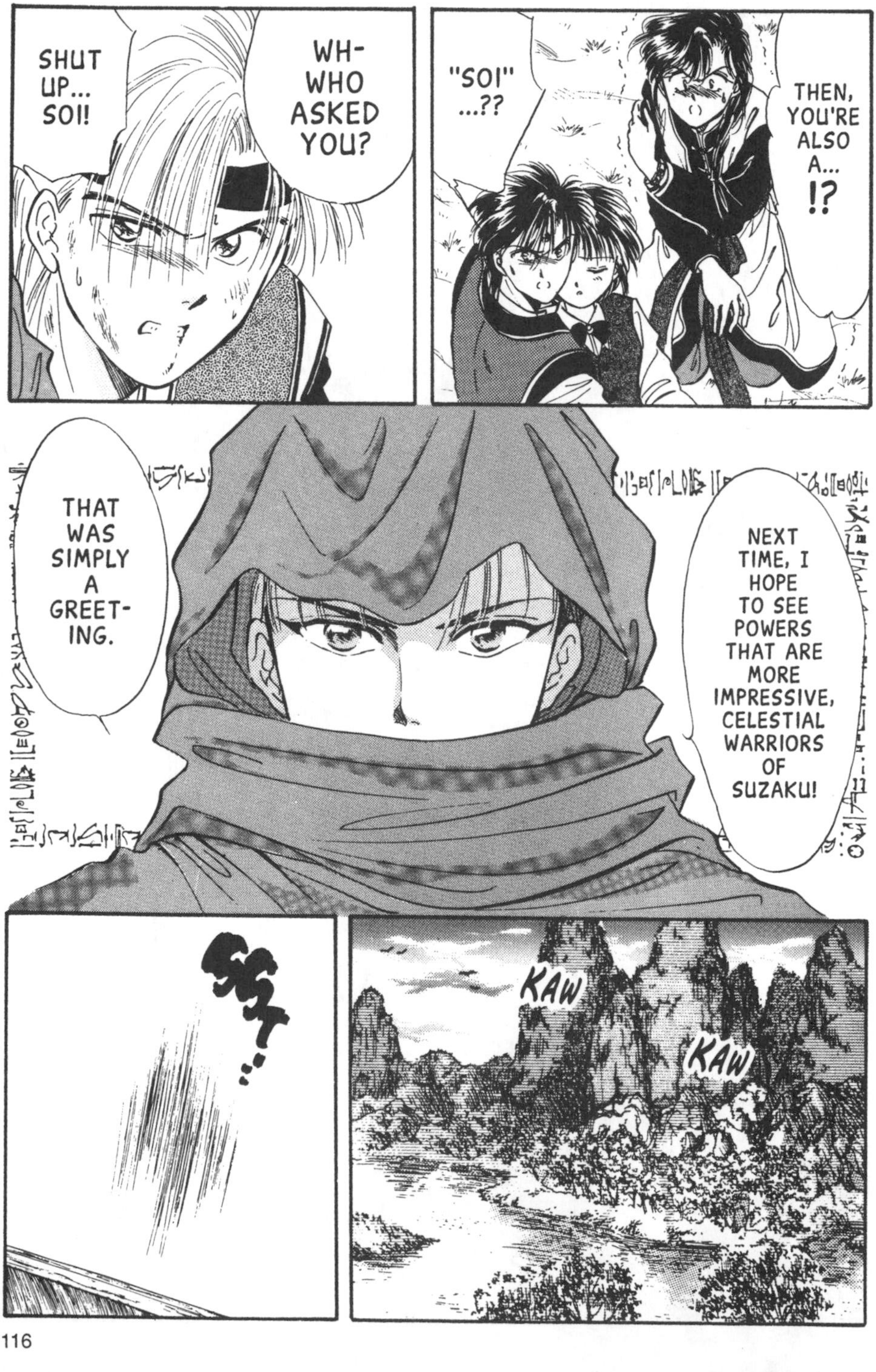
SHUT UP... SOI!
WH- WHO ASKED YOU?
"SOI" ...??
THEN, YOU'RE ALSO A... !?
THAT WAS SIMPLY A GREET- ING.
NEXT TIME, I HOPE TO SEE POWERS THAT ARE MORE IMPRESSIVE, CELESTIAL WARRIORS OF SUZAKU!
SSST...
KAW
KAW

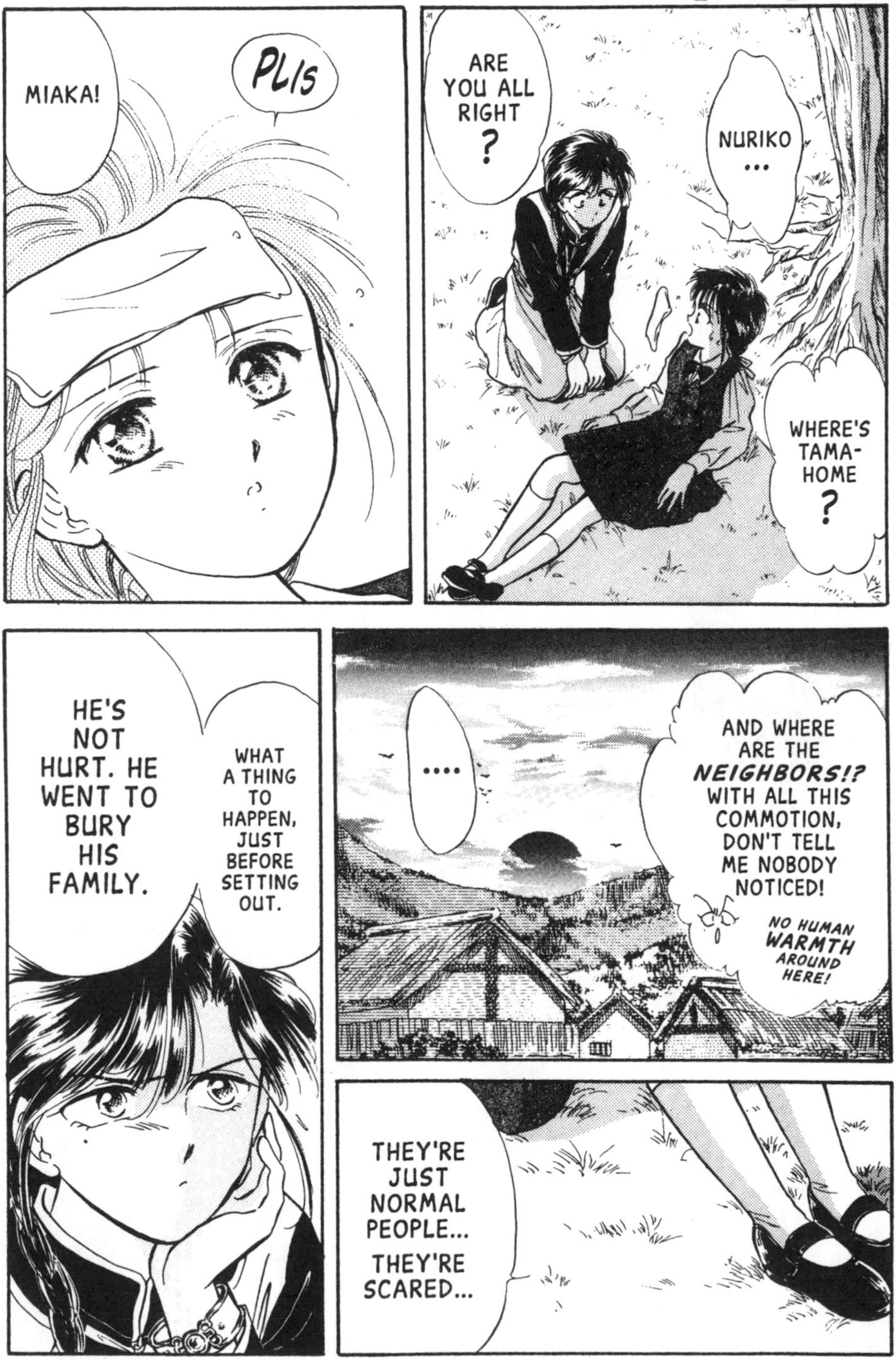
MIAKA!
PLIS
ARE YOU ALL RIGHT?
NURIKO...
WHERE'S TAMA-HOME?
HE'S NOT HURT. HE WENT TO BURY HIS FAMILY.
WHAT A THING TO HAPPEN, JUST BEFORE SETTING OUT.
....
AND WHERE ARE THE ***NEIGHBORS!?*** WITH ALL THIS COMMOTION, DON'T TELL ME NOBODY NOTICED!
NO HUMAN ***WARMTH*** AROUND HERE!
THEY'RE JUST NORMAL PEOPLE... THEY'RE SCARED...

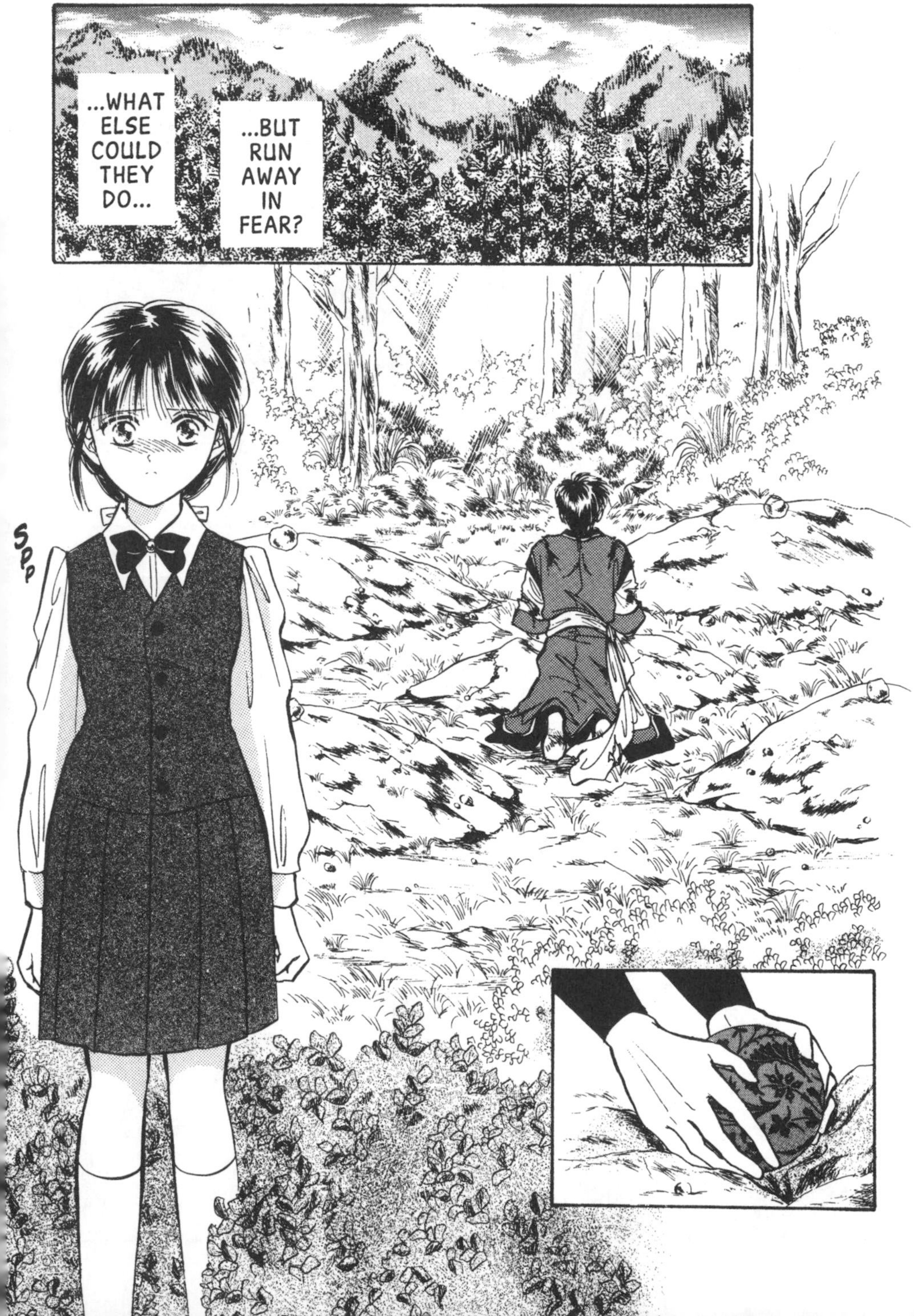
...WHAT ELSE COULD THEY DO...
...BUT RUN AWAY IN FEAR?
SPP

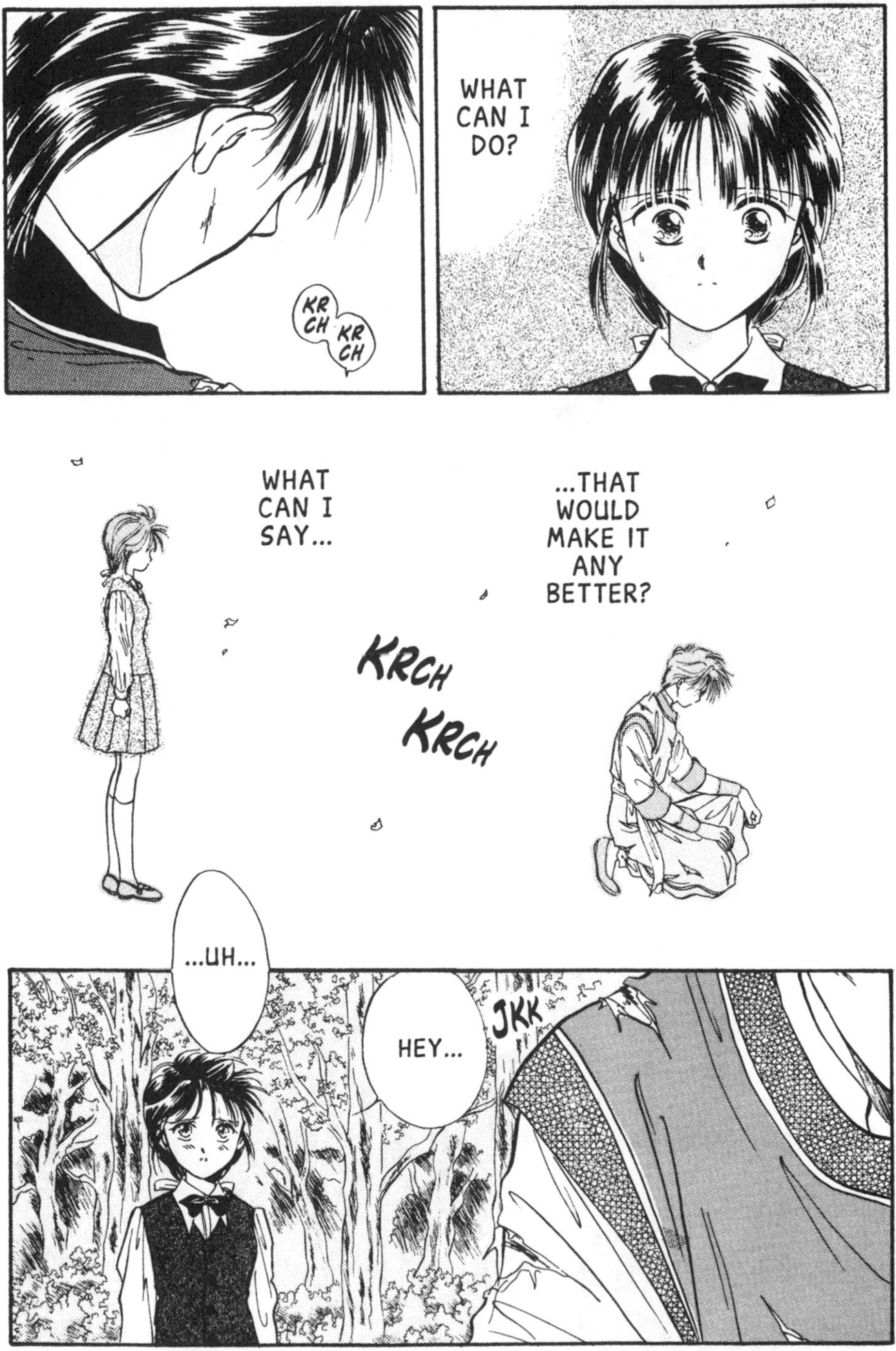
KRCH KRCH
WHAT CAN I DO?
WHAT CAN I SAY...
...THAT WOULD MAKE IT ANY BETTER?
KRCH KRCH
...UH...
HEY...
JKK

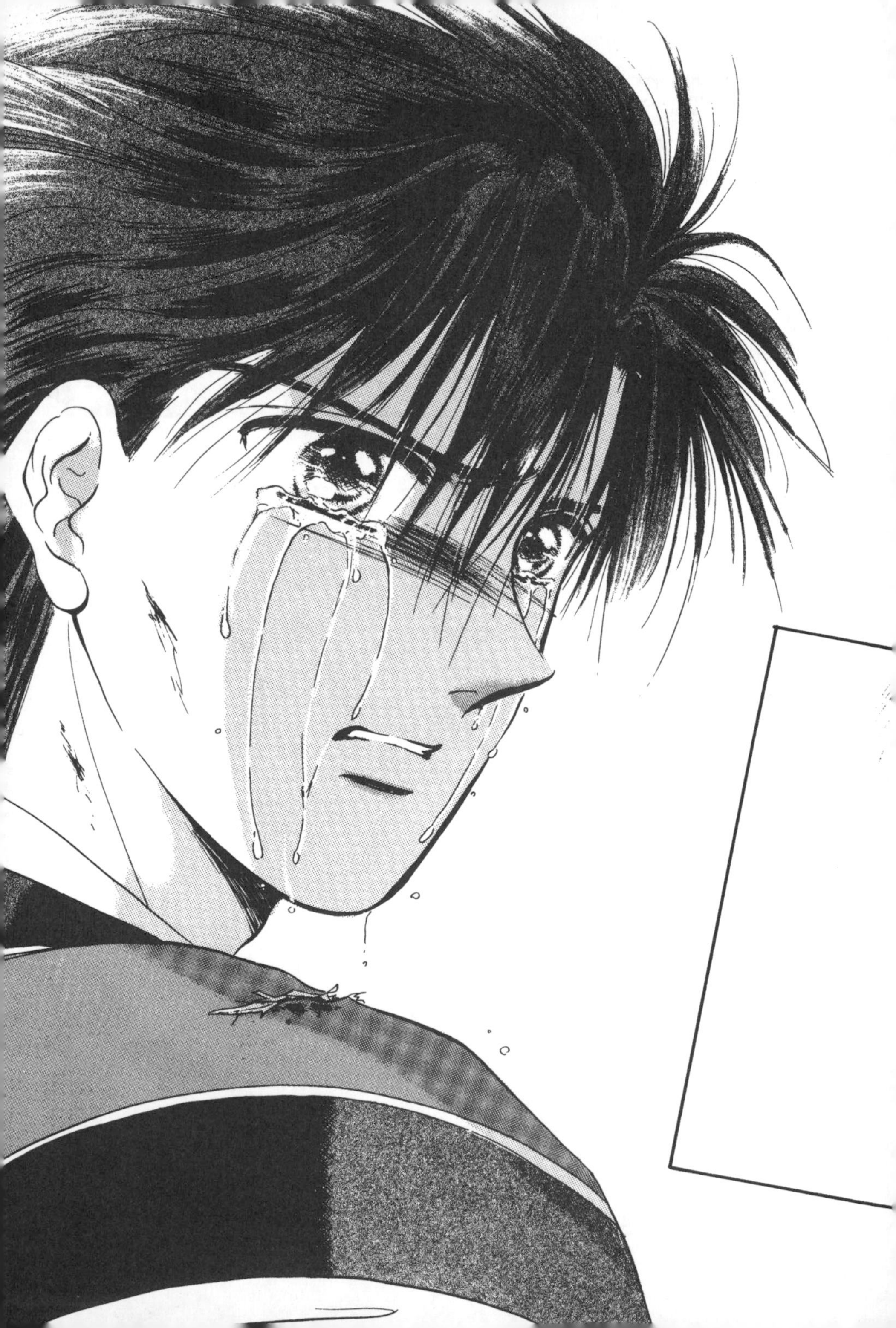

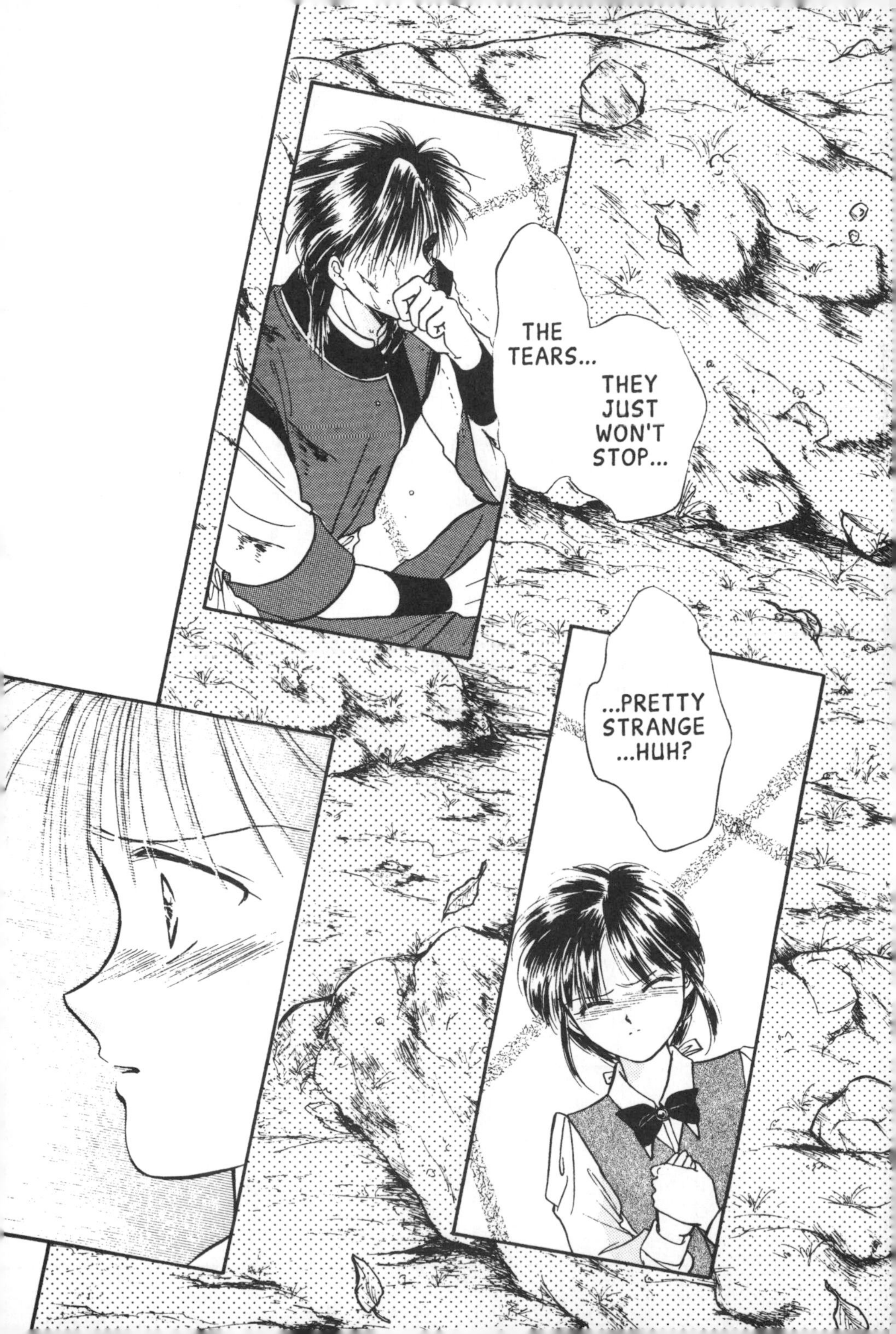
THE TEARS... THEY JUST WON'T STOP...
...PRETTY STRANGE ...HUH?

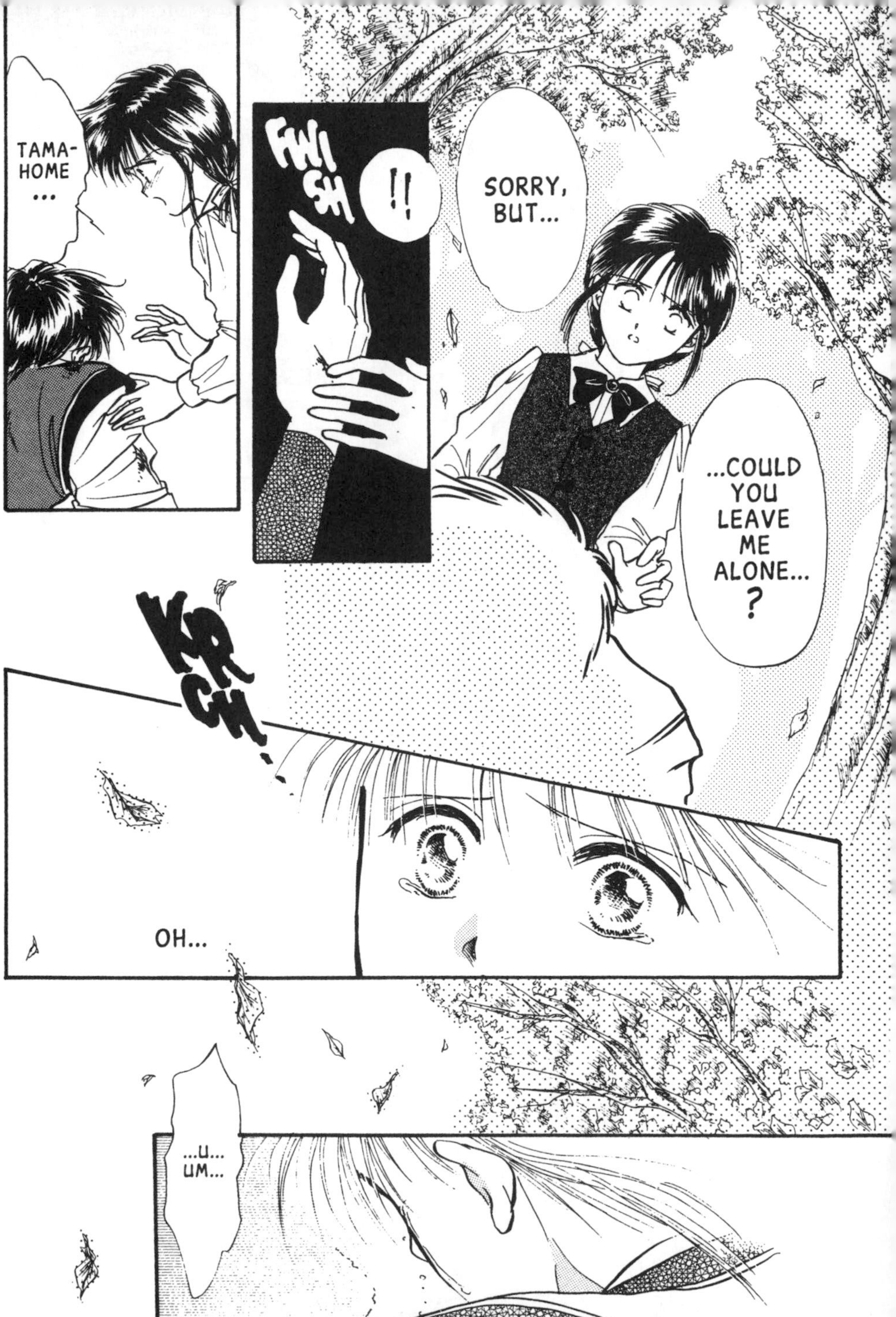
TAMA-HOME ...
FWISH
!!
SORRY, BUT...
...COULD YOU LEAVE ME ALONE...?
KRCH
OH...
...U... UM...

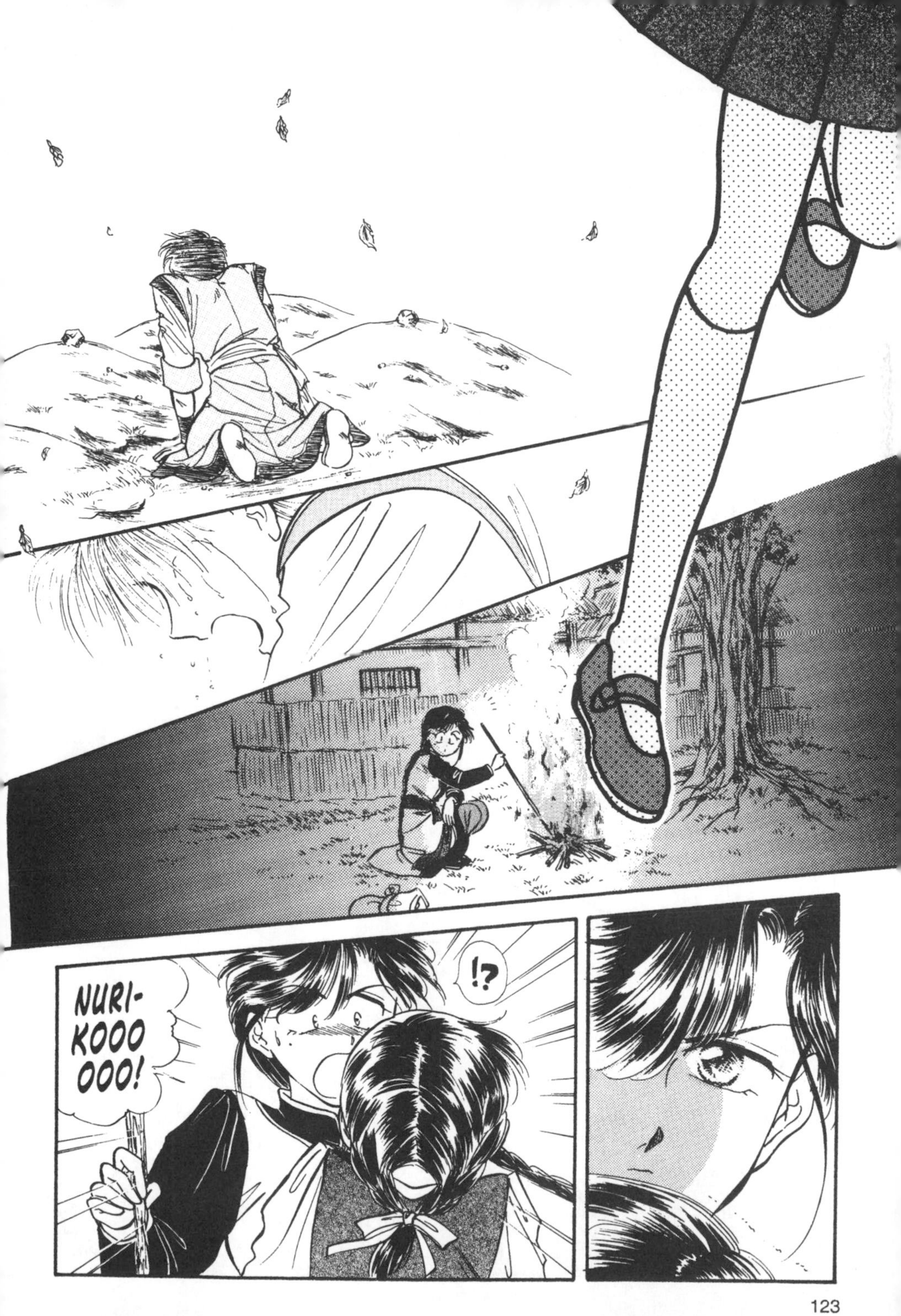
!?
NURI-
KOOO
OOO!

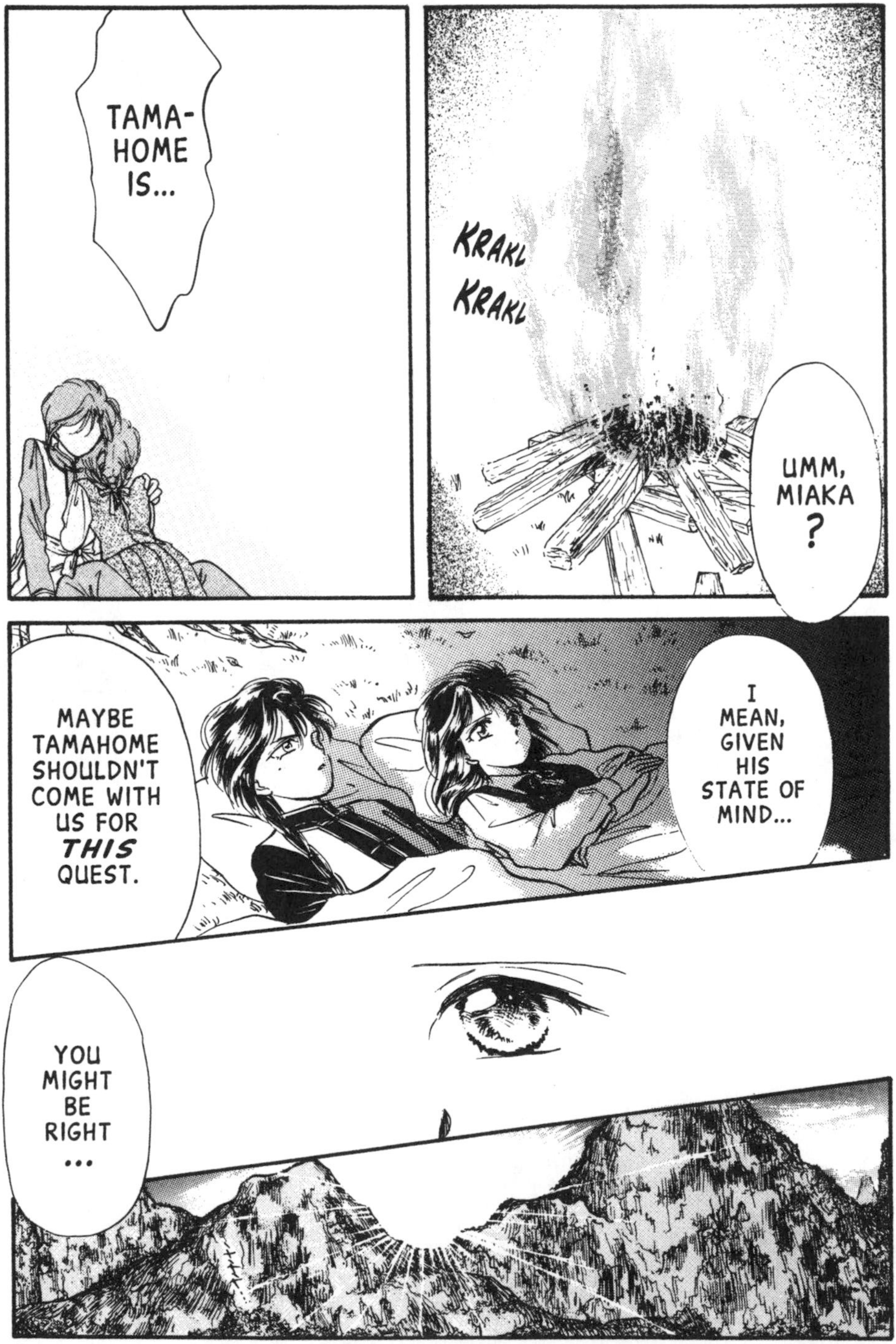
TAMA-HOME IS...
KRAKL
KRAKL
UMM, MIAKA ?
MAYBE TAMAHOME SHOULDN'T COME WITH US FOR *THIS* QUEST.
I MEAN, GIVEN HIS STATE OF MIND...
YOU MIGHT BE RIGHT ...

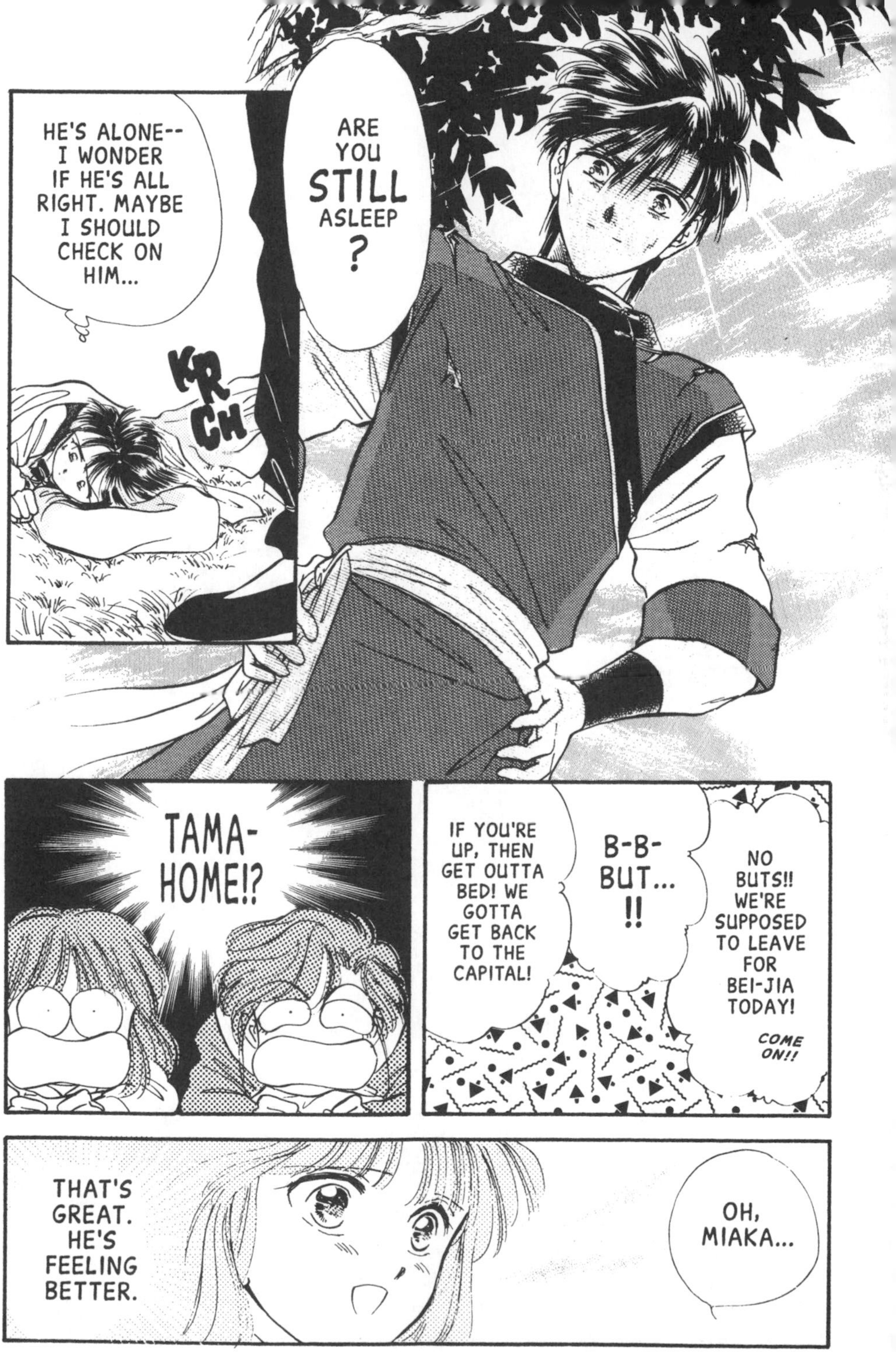
HE'S ALONE-- I WONDER IF HE'S ALL RIGHT. MAYBE I SHOULD CHECK ON HIM...
KRCH
ARE YOU STILL ASLEEP?
TAMA-HOME!?
IF YOU'RE UP, THEN GET OUTTA BED! WE GOTTA GET BACK TO THE CAPITAL!
B-B-BUT... !!
NO BUTS!! WE'RE SUPPOSED TO LEAVE FOR BEI-JIA TODAY!
COME ON!!
THAT'S GREAT. HE'S FEELING BETTER.
OH, MIAKA...

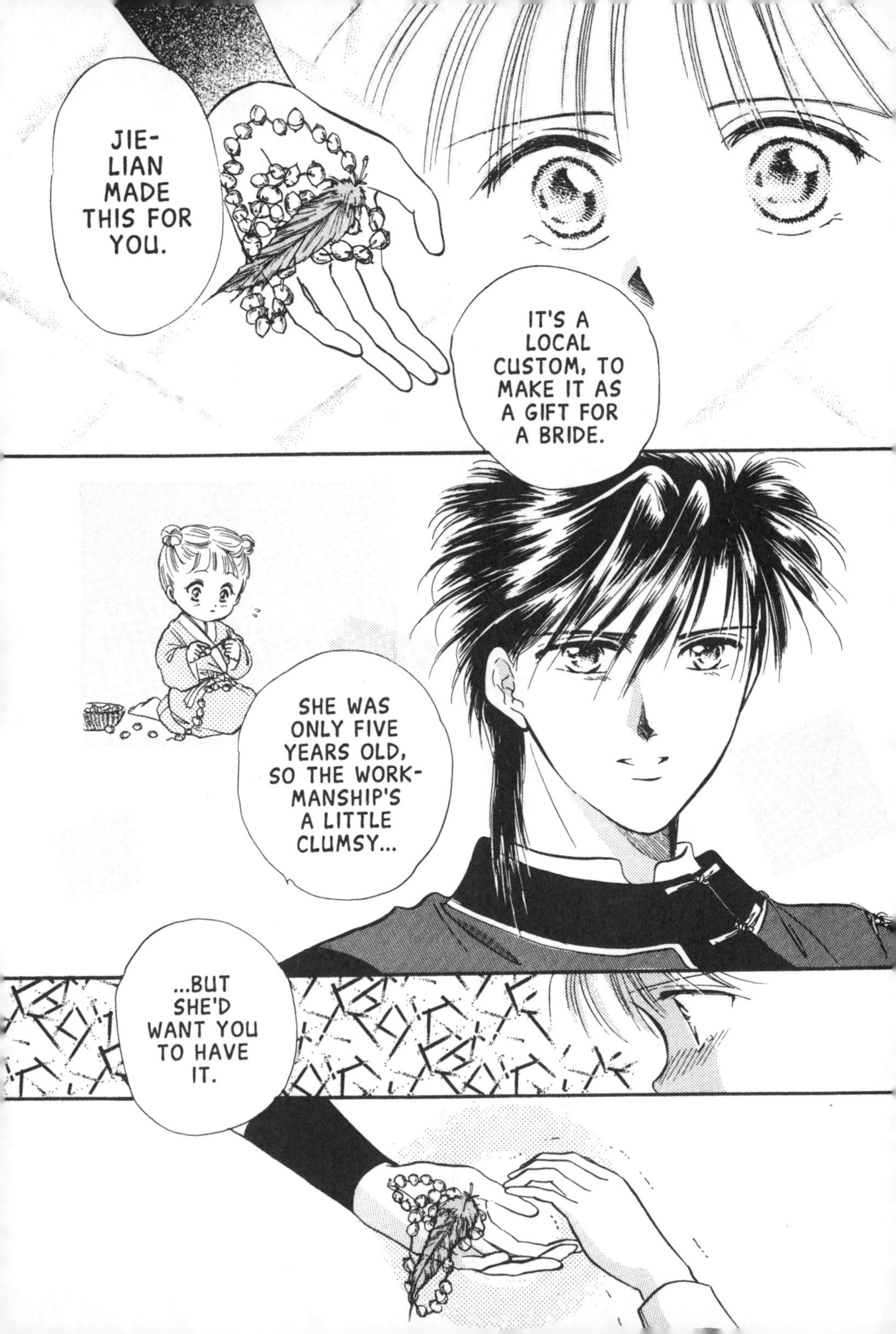
JIE-LIAN MADE THIS FOR YOU.
IT'S A LOCAL CUSTOM, TO MAKE IT AS A GIFT FOR A BRIDE.
SHE WAS ONLY FIVE YEARS OLD, SO THE WORK-MANSHIP'S A LITTLE CLUMSY...
...BUT SHE'D WANT YOU TO HAVE IT.

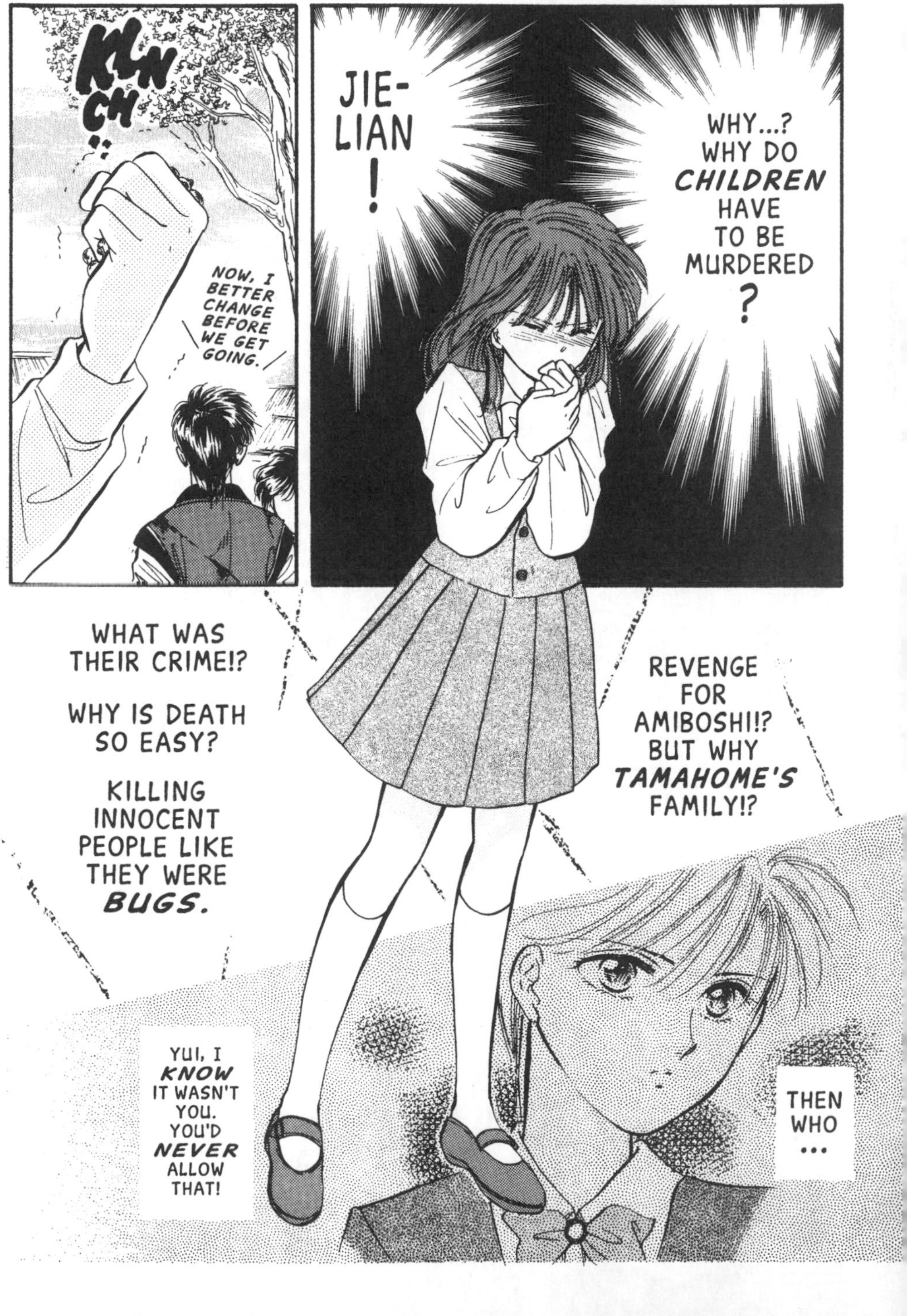
KLINCH
NOW, I BETTER CHANGE BEFORE WE GET GOING.
JIE-LIAN!
WHY...? WHY DO CHILDREN HAVE TO BE MURDERED?
WHAT WAS THEIR CRIME!?
WHY IS DEATH SO EASY?
KILLING INNOCENT PEOPLE LIKE THEY WERE BUGS.
REVENGE FOR AMIBOSHI!? BUT WHY TAMAHOME'S FAMILY!?
YUI, I KNOW IT WASN'T YOU. YOU'D NEVER ALLOW THAT!
THEN WHO...

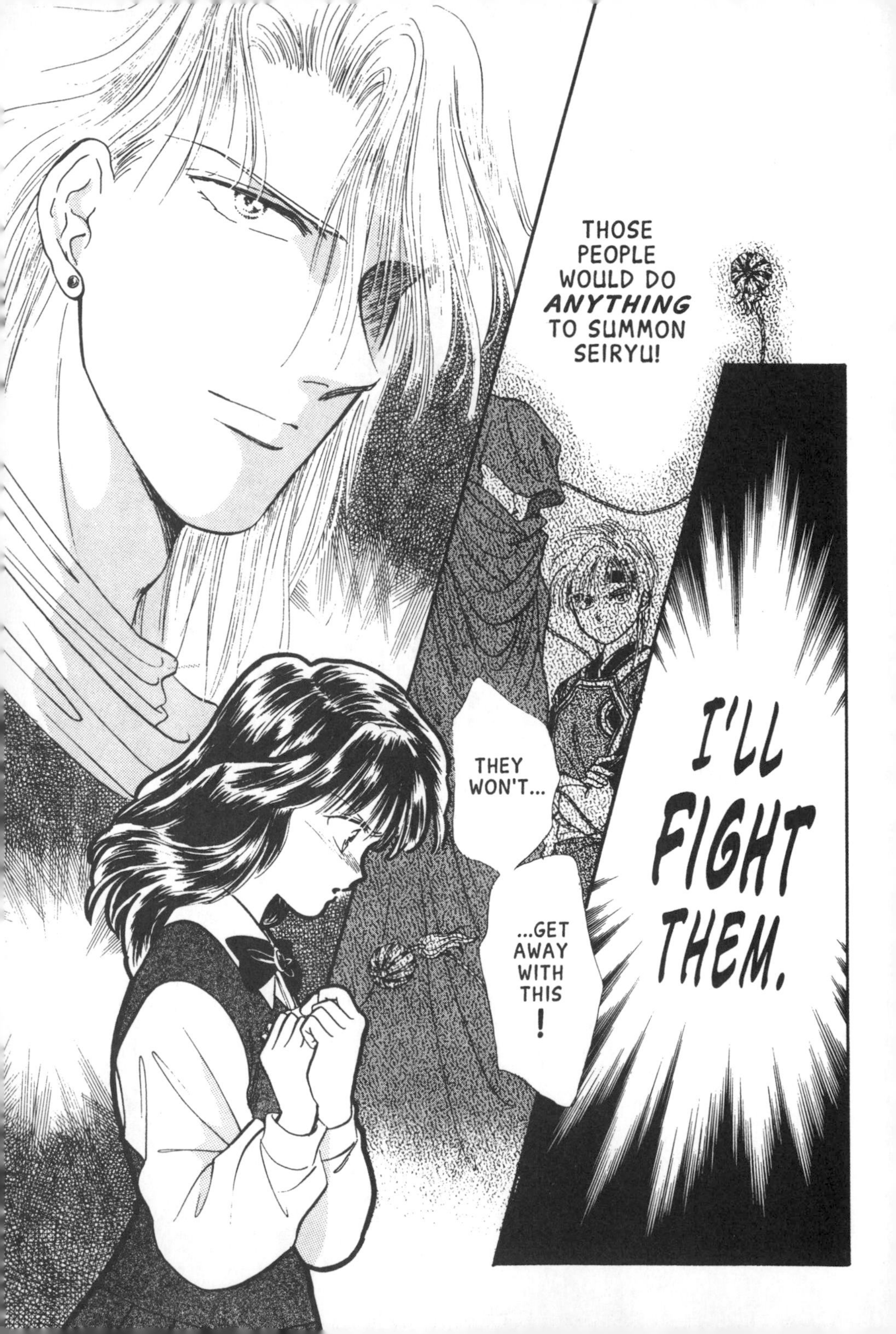
THOSE PEOPLE WOULD DO *ANYTHING* TO SUMMON SEIRYU!
THEY WON'T...
...GET AWAY WITH THIS!
I'LL FIGHT THEM.

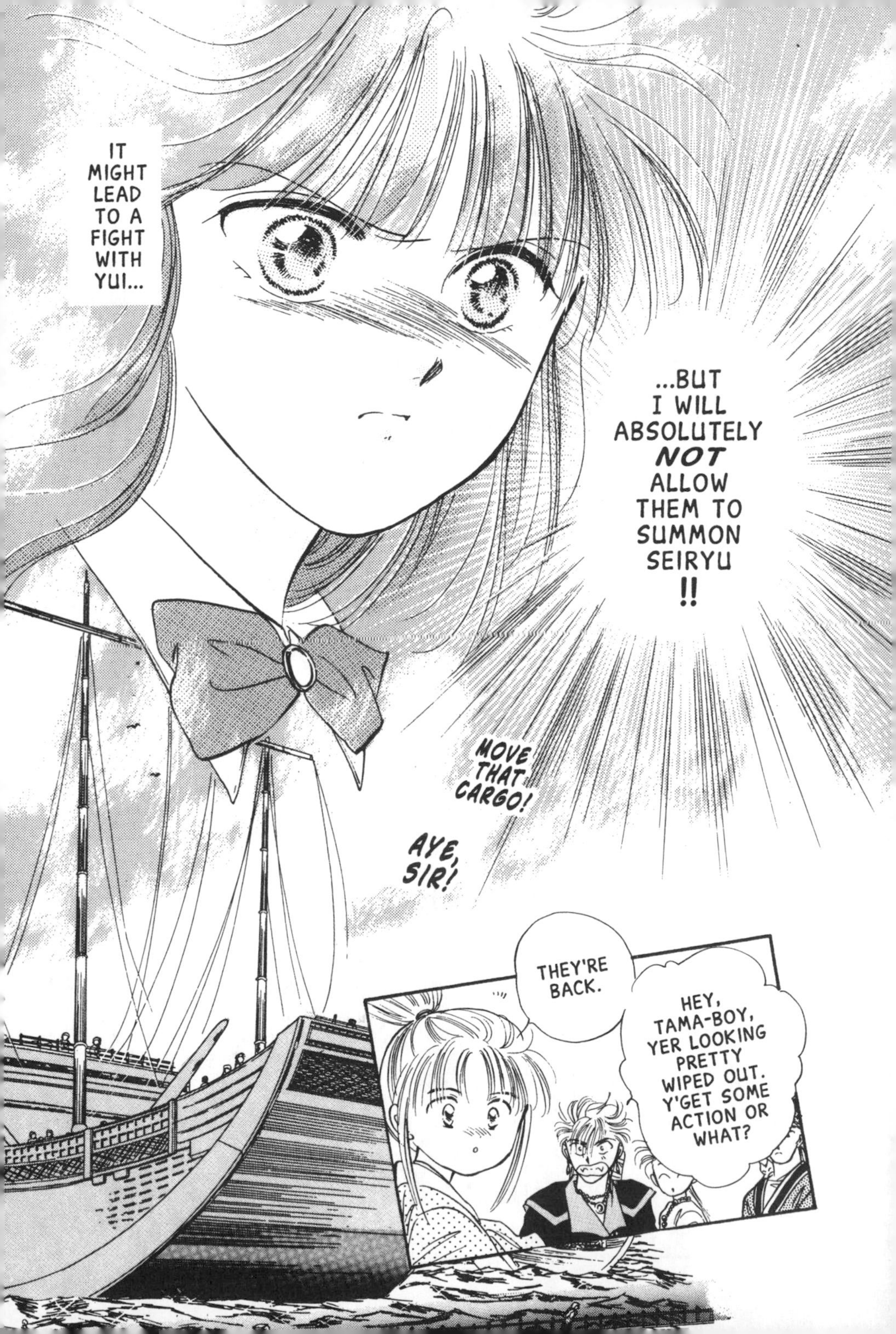
IT MIGHT LEAD TO A FIGHT WITH YUI...
...BUT I WILL ABSOLUTELY NOT ALLOW THEM TO SUMMON SEIRYU !!
MOVE THAT CARGO!
AYE, SIR!
THEY'RE BACK.
HEY, TAMA-BOY, YER LOOKING PRETTY WIPED OUT. Y'GET SOME ACTION OR WHAT?

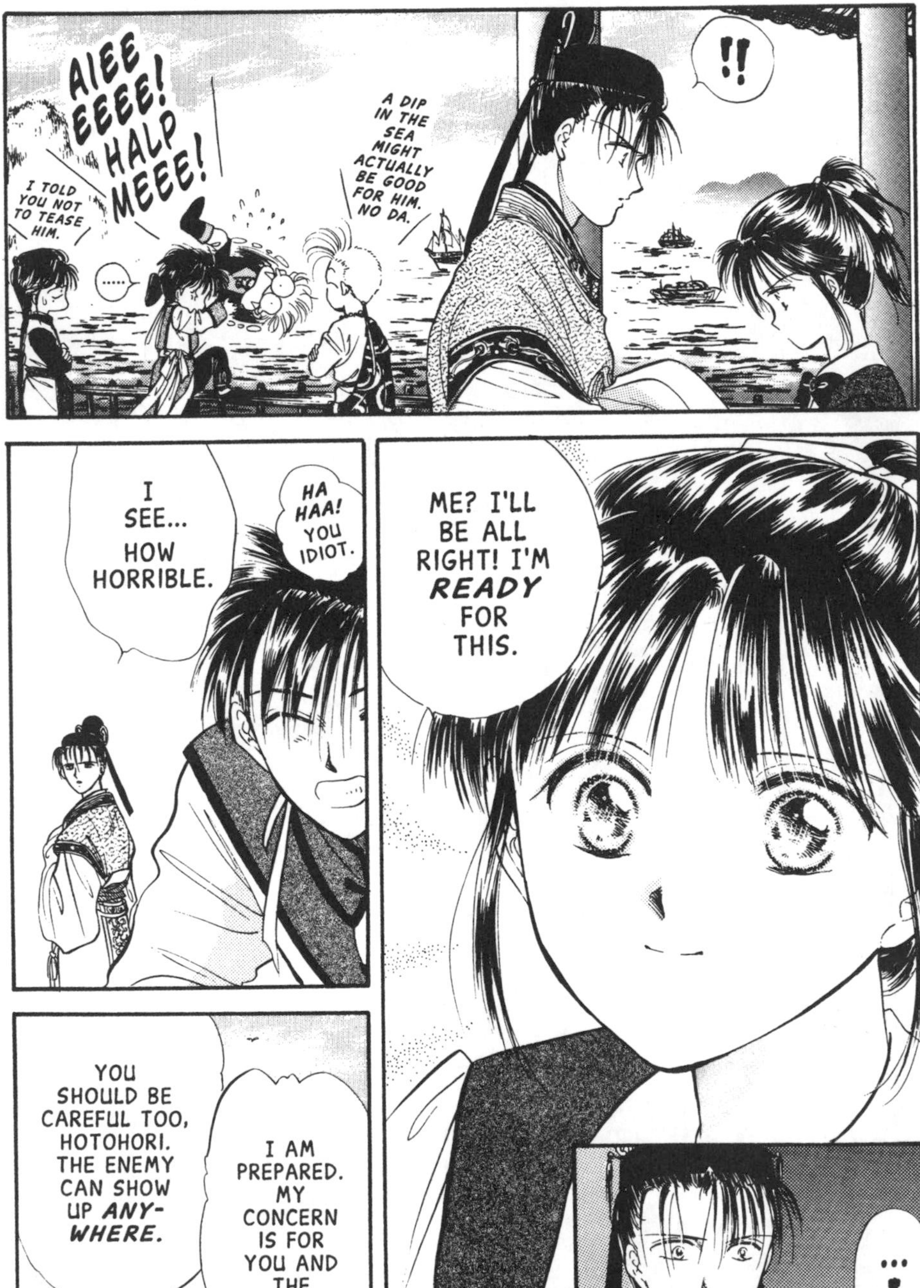
AIEE EEEE! HALP MEEE!
I TOLD YOU NOT TO TEASE HIM.
.....
A DIP IN THE SEA MIGHT ACTUALLY BE GOOD FOR HIM. NO DA.
!!
I SEE... HOW HORRIBLE.
HA HAA! YOU IDIOT.
YOU SHOULD BE CAREFUL TOO, HOTOHORI. THE ENEMY CAN SHOW UP ANY-WHERE.
I AM PREPARED. MY CONCERN IS FOR YOU AND THE OTHERS.
ME? I'LL BE ALL RIGHT! I'M READY FOR THIS.
...!

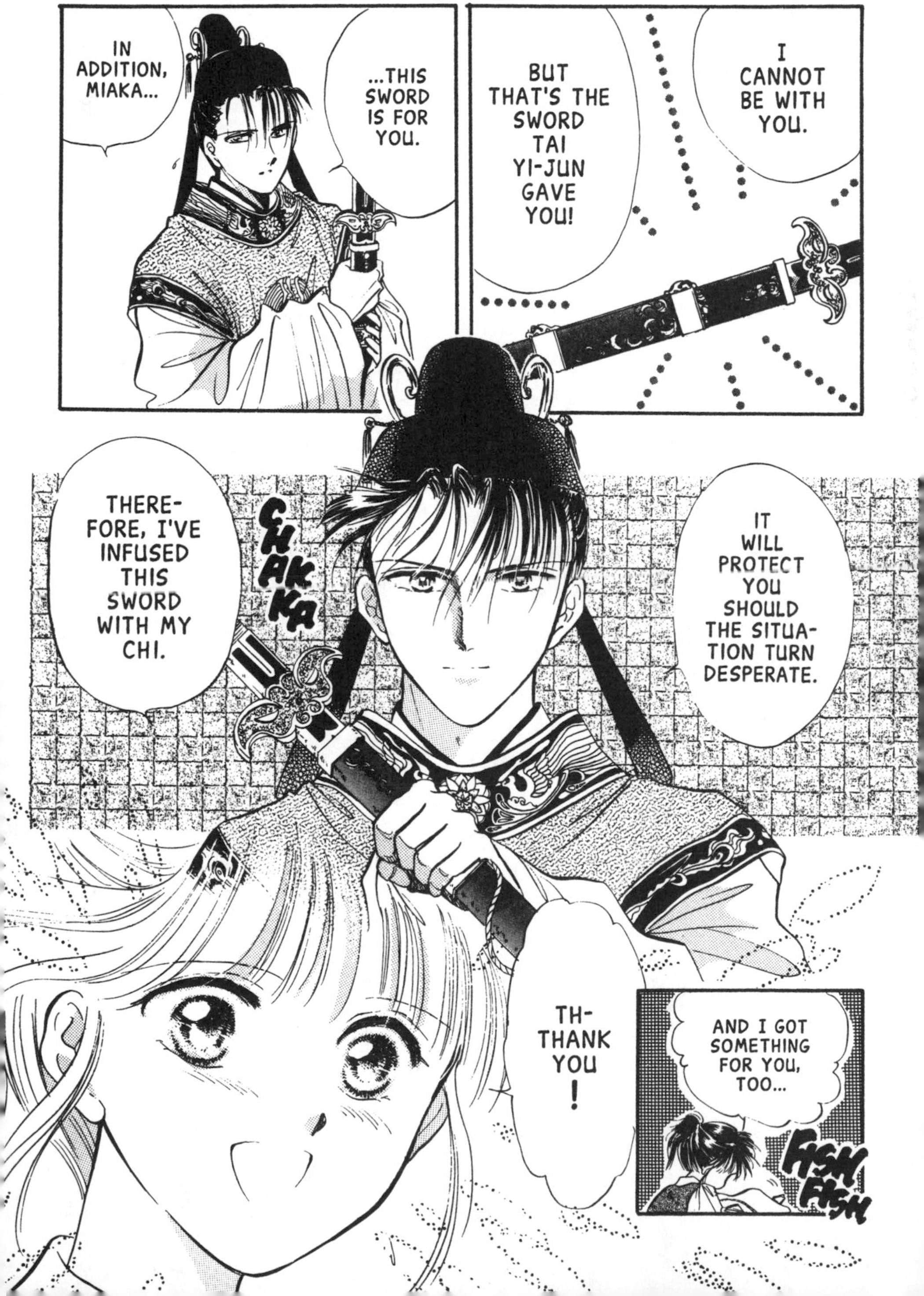
IN ADDITION, MIAKA...
...THIS SWORD IS FOR YOU.
BUT THAT'S THE SWORD TAI YI-JUN GAVE YOU!
I CANNOT BE WITH YOU.
THERE-FORE, I'VE INFUSED THIS SWORD WITH MY CHI.
CHAKA
IT WILL PROTECT YOU SHOULD THE SITUA-TION TURN DESPERATE.
TH-THANK YOU!
AND I GOT SOMETHING FOR YOU, TOO...
FISH FISH

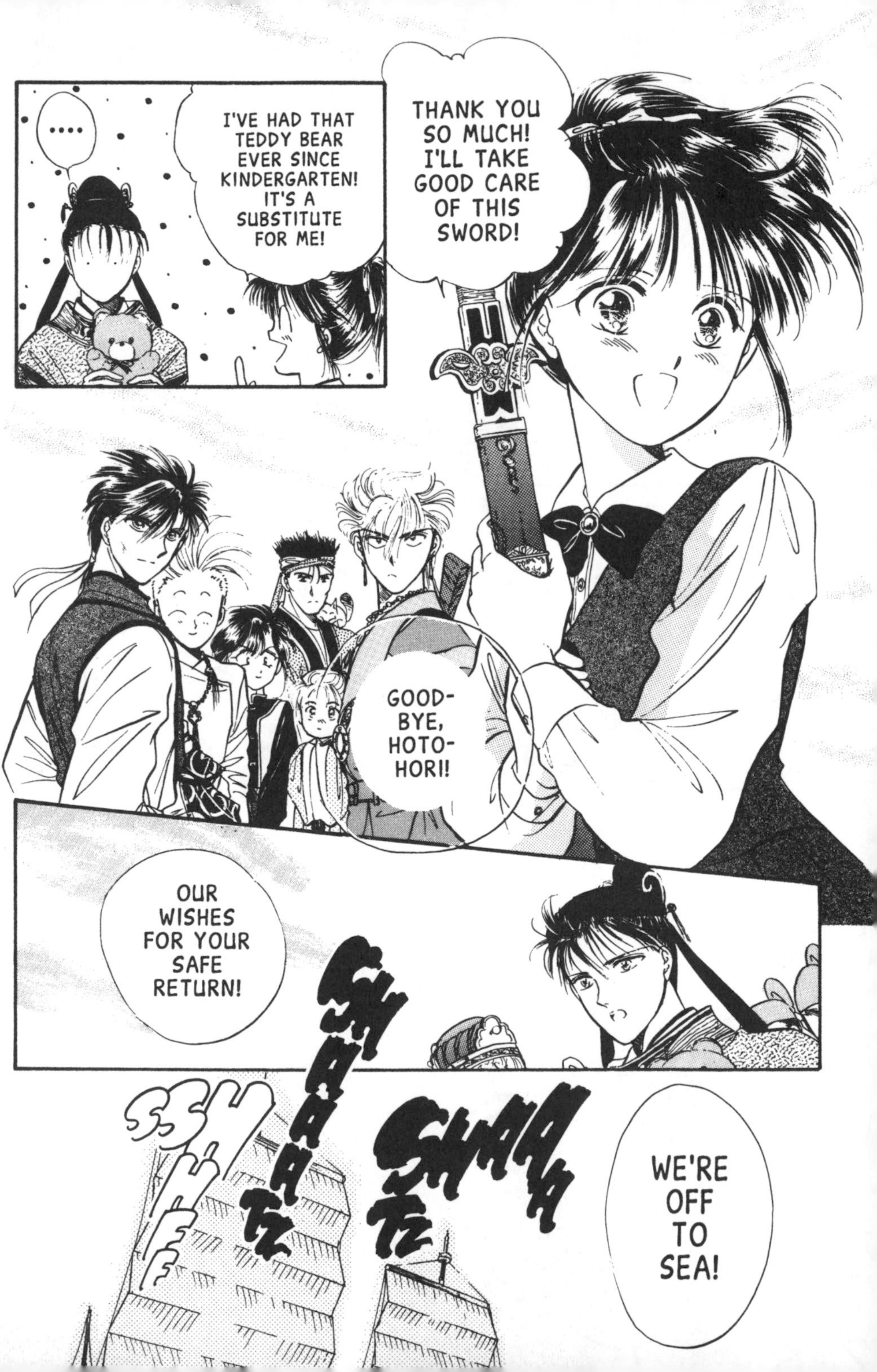
....
I'VE HAD THAT TEDDY BEAR EVER SINCE KINDERGARTEN! IT'S A SUBSTITUTE FOR ME!
THANK YOU SO MUCH! I'LL TAKE GOOD CARE OF THIS SWORD!
GOOD-BYE, HOTO-HORI!
OUR WISHES FOR YOUR SAFE RETURN!
WE'RE OFF TO SEA!

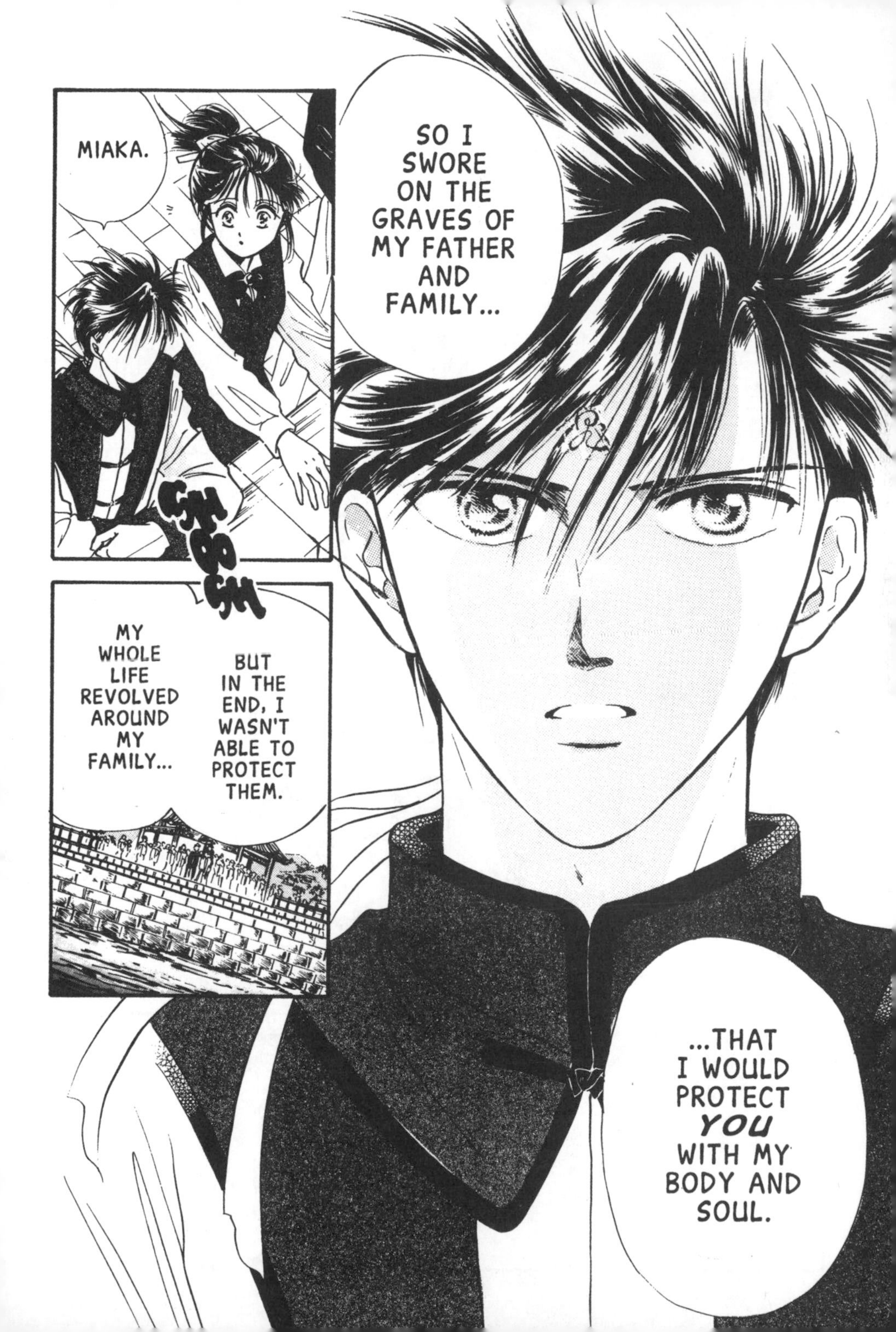
MIAKA.
MY WHOLE LIFE REVOLVED AROUND MY FAMILY...
BUT IN THE END, I WASN'T ABLE TO PROTECT THEM.
SO I SWORE ON THE GRAVES OF MY FATHER AND FAMILY...
...THAT I WOULD PROTECT *YOU* WITH MY BODY AND SOUL.

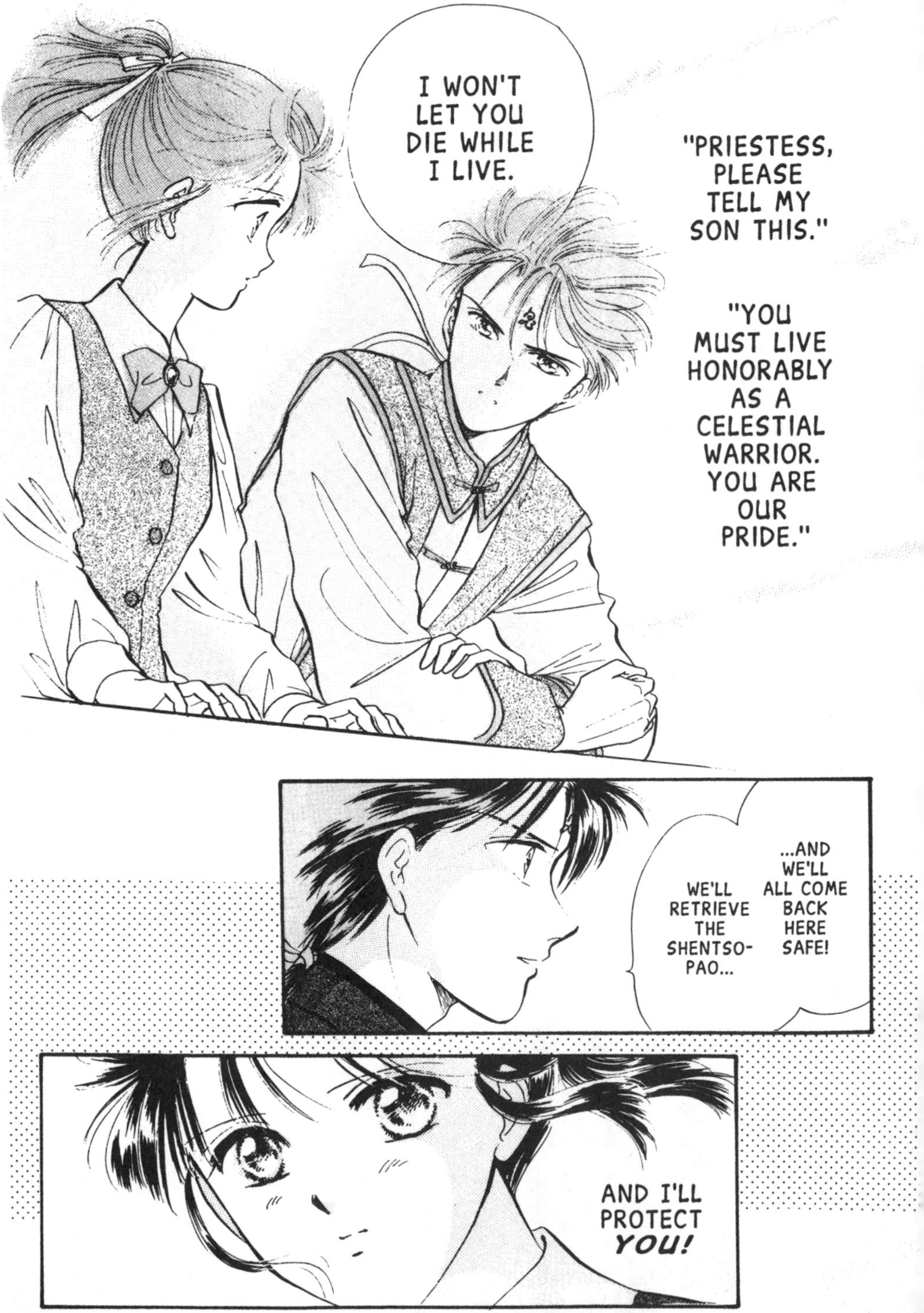
I WON'T LET YOU DIE WHILE I LIVE.
"PRIESTESS, PLEASE TELL MY SON THIS."
"YOU MUST LIVE HONORABLY AS A CELESTIAL WARRIOR. YOU ARE OUR PRIDE."
WE'LL RETRIEVE THE SHENTSO-PAO...
...AND WE'LL ALL COME BACK HERE SAFE!
AND I'LL PROTECT YOU!

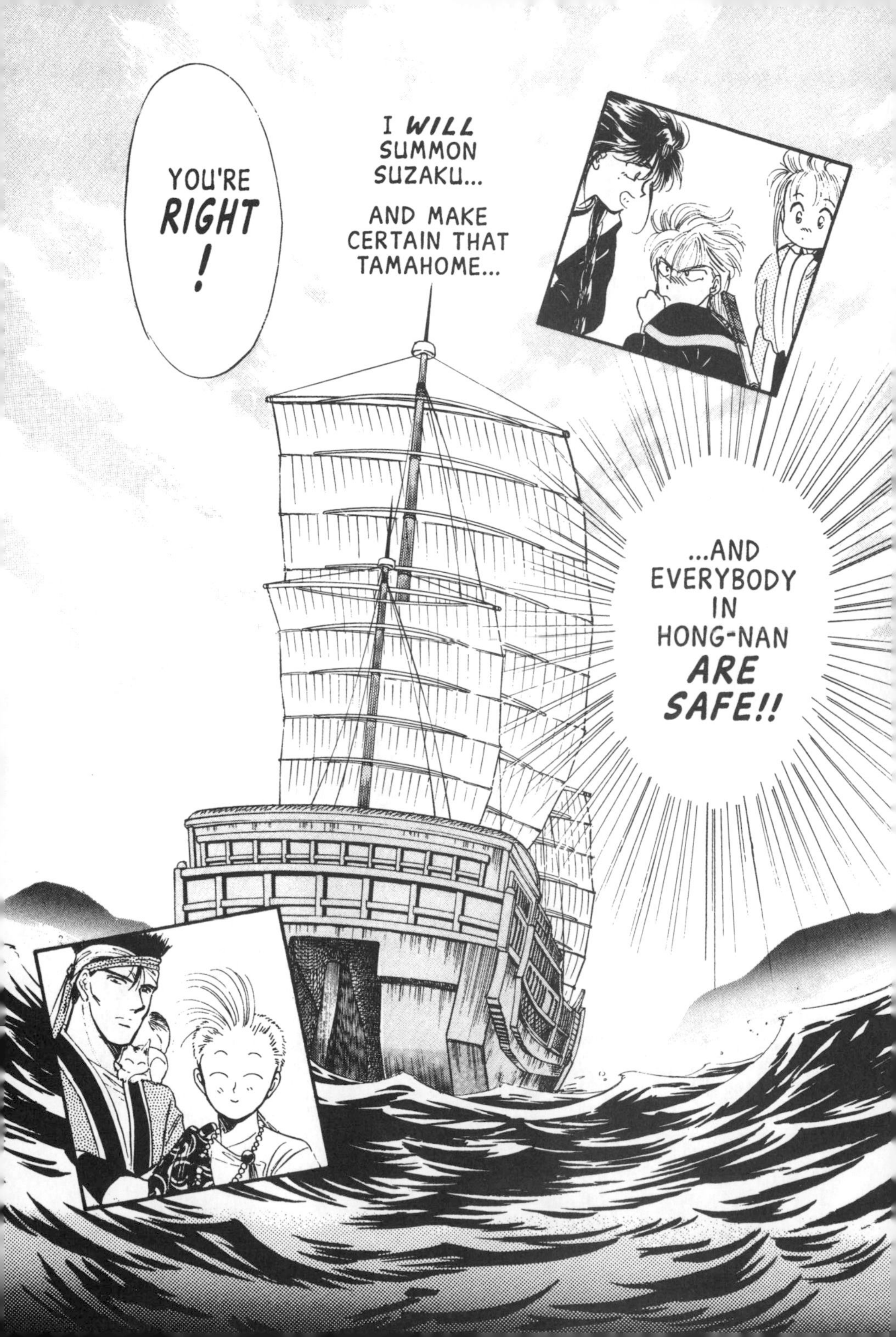
YOU'RE RIGHT!
I WILL SUMMON SUZAKU...
AND MAKE CERTAIN THAT TAMAHOME...
...AND EVERYBODY IN HONG-NAN ARE SAFE!!

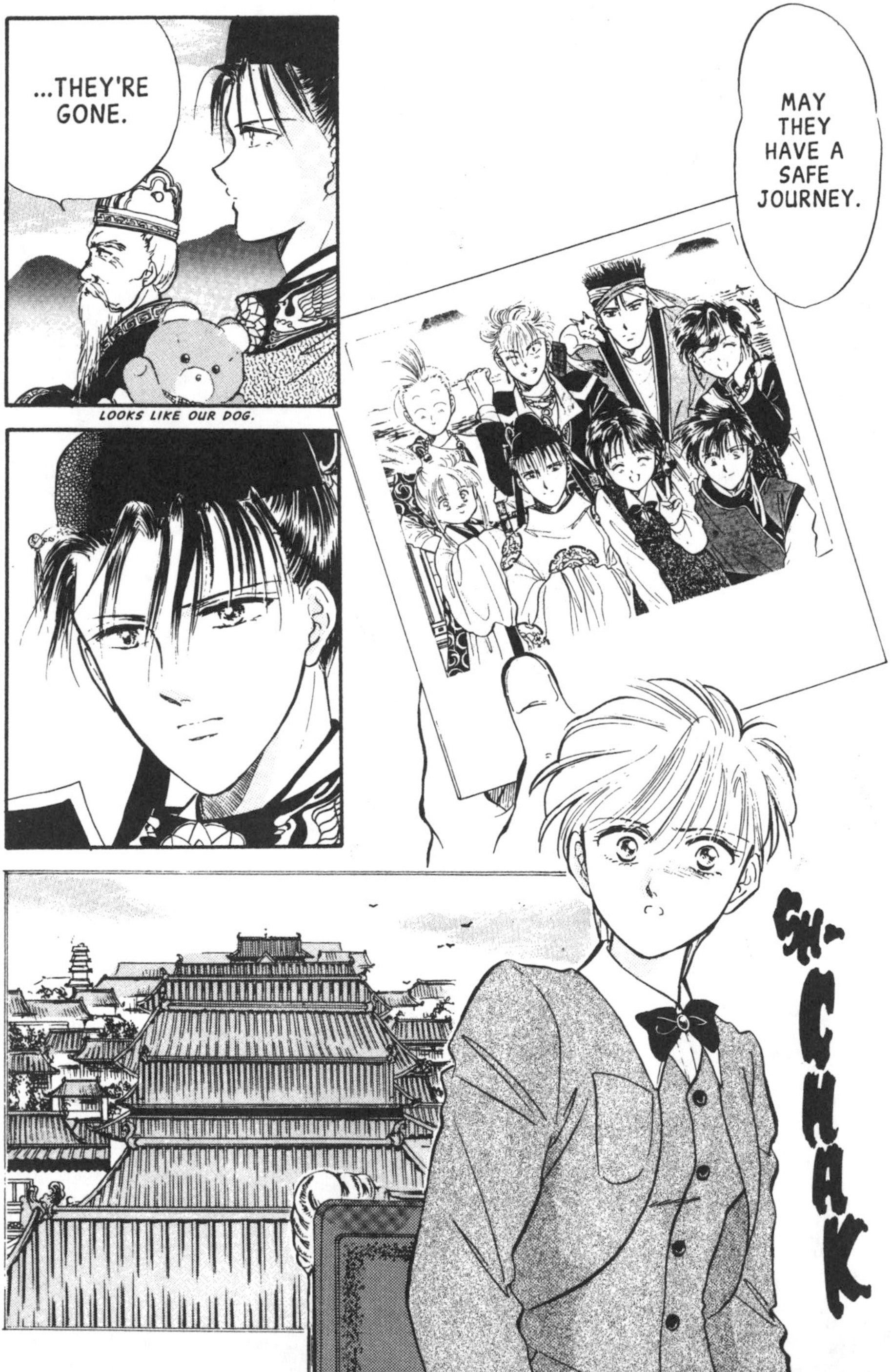
...THEY'RE GONE.
LOOKS LIKE OUR DOG.
MAY THEY HAVE A SAFE JOURNEY.
SH-CHAK

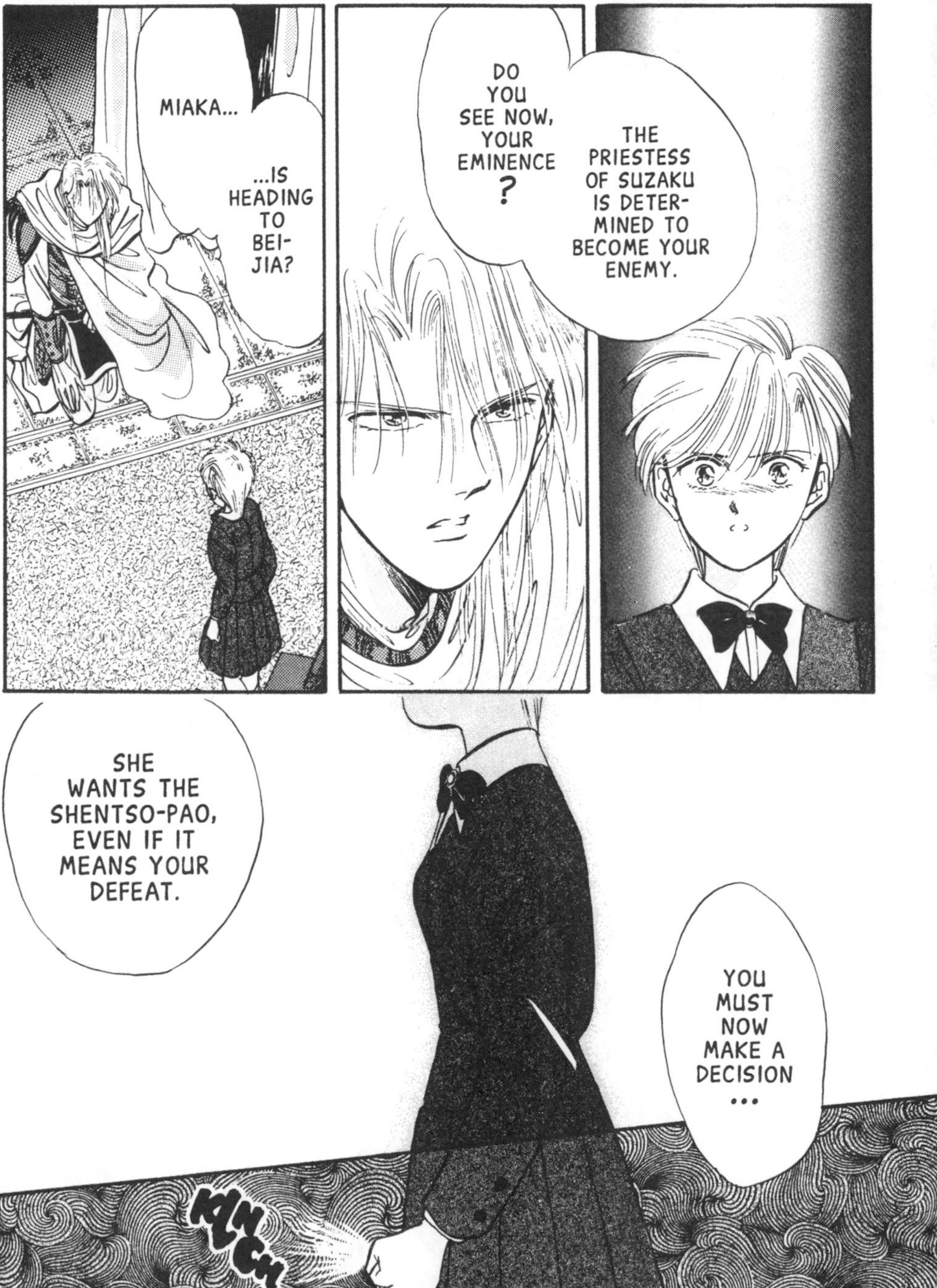
MIAKA...
...IS HEADING TO BEI-JIA?
DO YOU SEE NOW, YOUR EMINENCE?
THE PRIESTESS OF SUZAKU IS DETERMINED TO BECOME YOUR ENEMY.
SHE WANTS THE SHENTSO-PAO, EVEN IF IT MEANS YOUR DEFEAT.
YOU MUST NOW MAKE A DECISION...

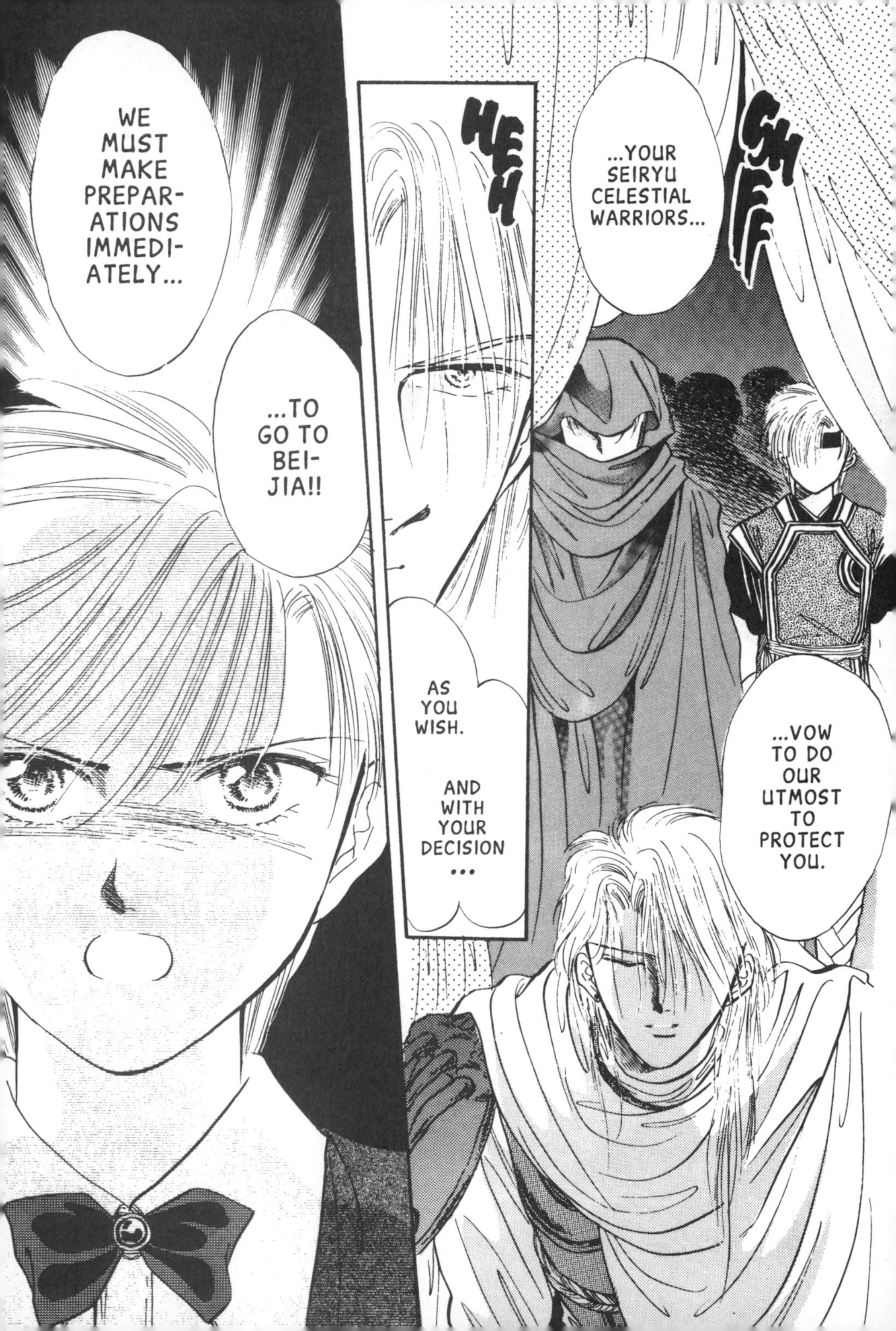
WE MUST MAKE PREPARATIONS IMMEDIATELY...
...TO GO TO BEIJIA!!
HEH
AS YOU WISH.
AND WITH YOUR DECISION...
GHFF
...YOUR SEIRYU CELESTIAL WARRIORS...
...VOW TO DO OUR UTMOST TO PROTECT YOU.

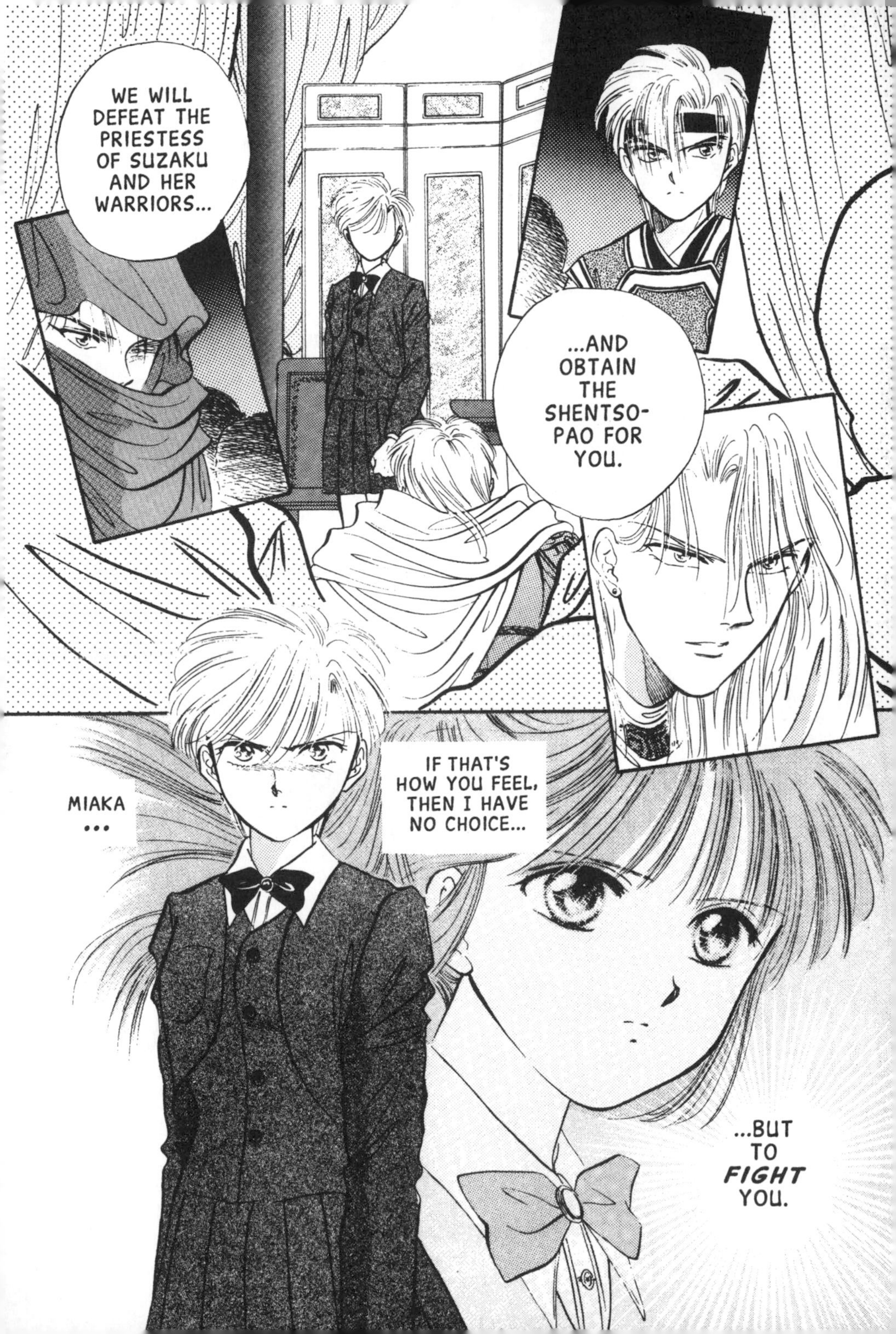
WE WILL DEFEAT THE PRIESTESS OF SUZAKU AND HER WARRIORS...
...AND OBTAIN THE SHENTSO-PAO FOR YOU.
MIAKA ...
IF THAT'S HOW YOU FEEL, THEN I HAVE NO CHOICE...
...BUT TO *FIGHT* YOU.

## CHAPTER FORTY-ONE

# THE MYSTERY OF THE UNIVERSE OF THE FOUR GODS

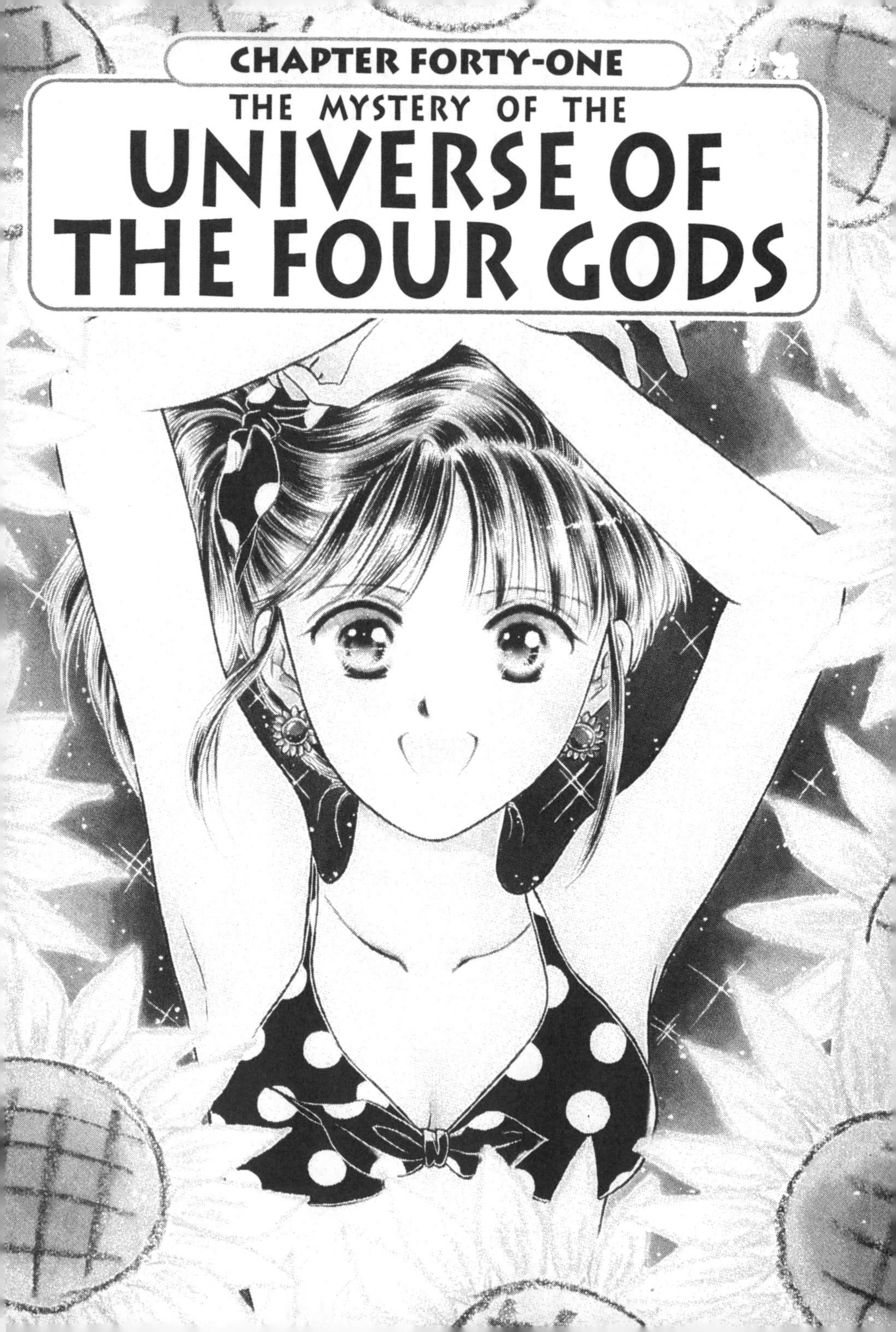

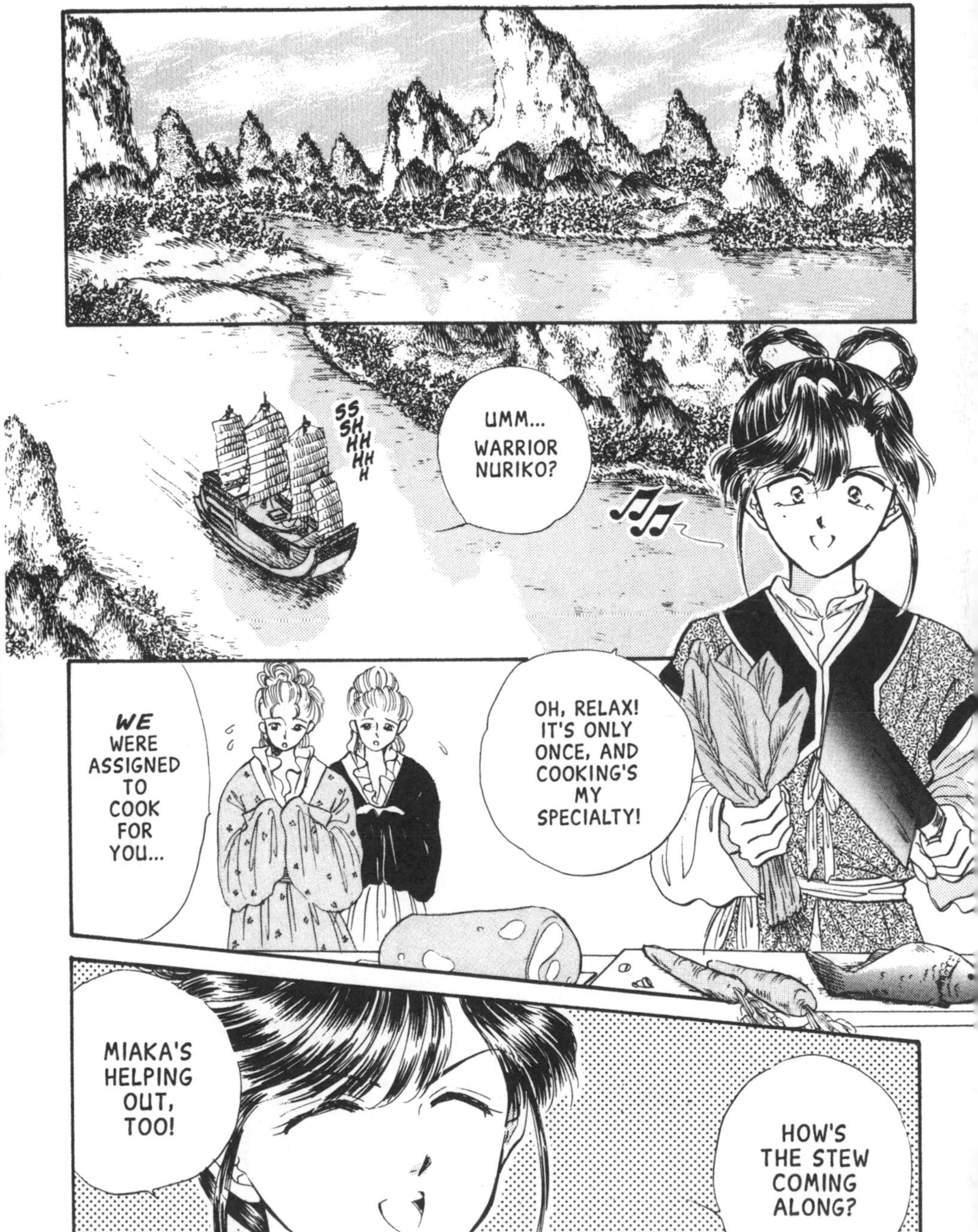

SS SH HH HH H
UMM... WARRIOR NURIKO?
WE WERE ASSIGNED TO COOK FOR YOU...
OH, RELAX! IT'S ONLY ONCE, AND COOKING'S MY SPECIALTY!
MIAKA'S HELPING OUT, TOO!
HOW'S THE STEW COMING ALONG?

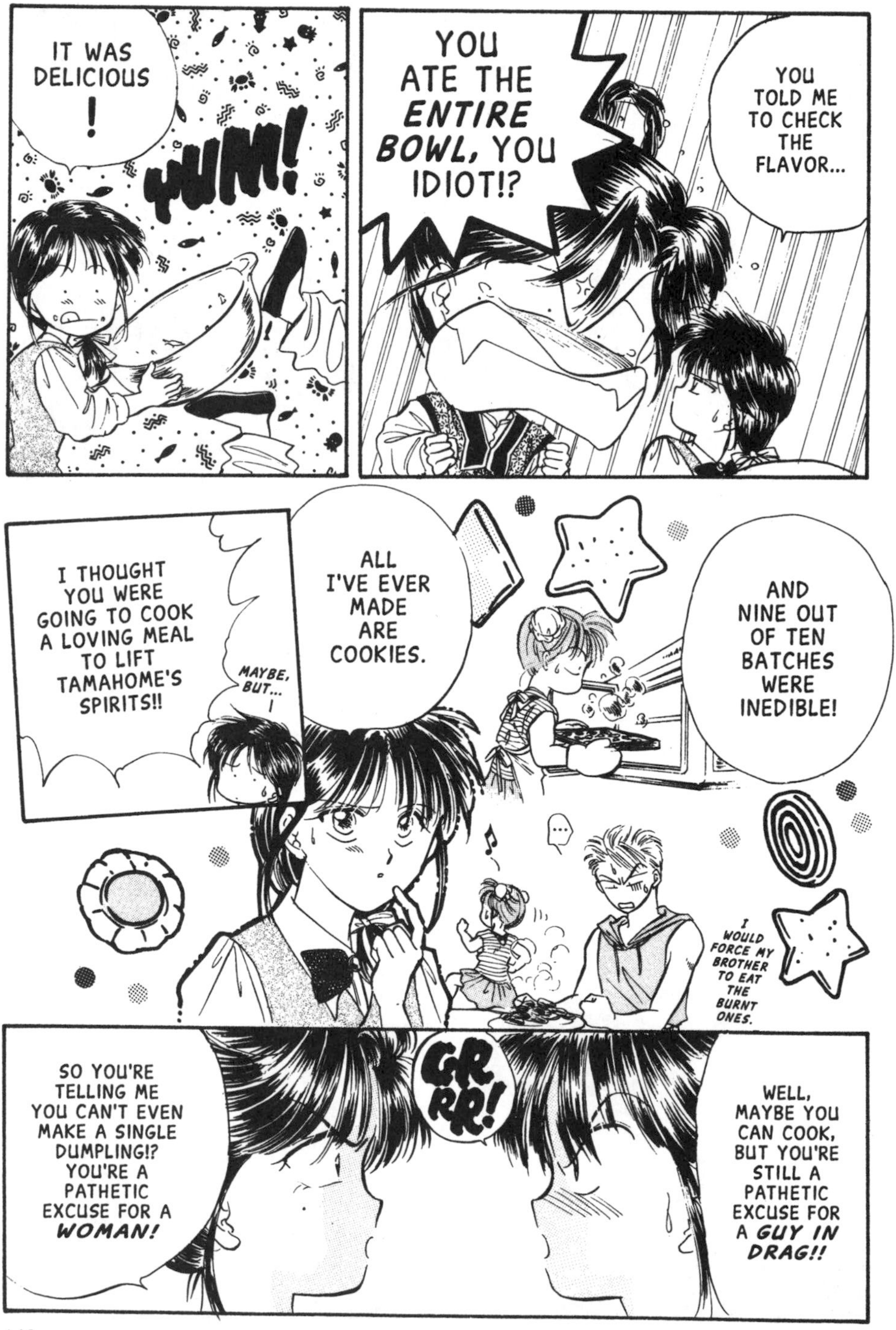
IT WAS DELICIOUS !
YUM!
YOU ATE THE ENTIRE BOWL, YOU IDIOT!?
YOU TOLD ME TO CHECK THE FLAVOR...
I THOUGHT YOU WERE GOING TO COOK A LOVING MEAL TO LIFT TAMAHOME'S SPIRITS!!
MAYBE, BUT... I
ALL I'VE EVER MADE ARE COOKIES.
AND NINE OUT OF TEN BATCHES WERE INEDIBLE!
...
I WOULD FORCE MY BROTHER TO EAT THE BURNT ONES.
SO YOU'RE TELLING ME YOU CAN'T EVEN MAKE A SINGLE DUMPLING!? YOU'RE A PATHETIC EXCUSE FOR A WOMAN!
GRRR!
WELL, MAYBE YOU CAN COOK, BUT YOU'RE STILL A PATHETIC EXCUSE FOR A GUY IN DRAG!!

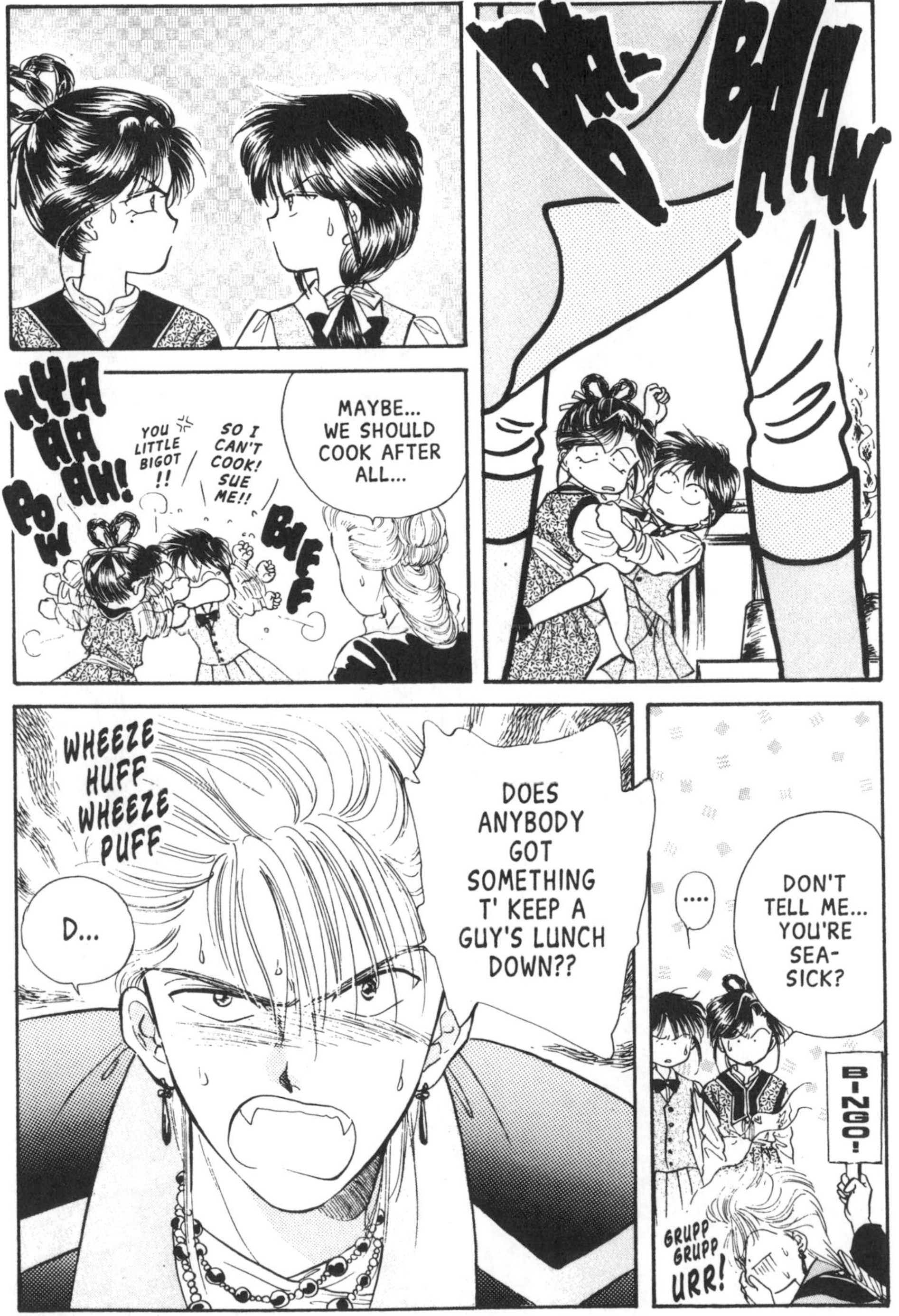
HYAAAAAH!
POW
YOU LITTLE BIGOT!!
SO I CAN'T COOK! SUE ME!!
MAYBE... WE SHOULD COOK AFTER ALL...
BIFF
BAAN
WHEEZE HUFF WHEEZE PUFF
D...
DOES ANYBODY GOT SOMETHING T' KEEP A GUY'S LUNCH DOWN??
....
DON'T TELL ME... YOU'RE SEA-SICK?
BINGO!
GRUPP GRUPP URR!

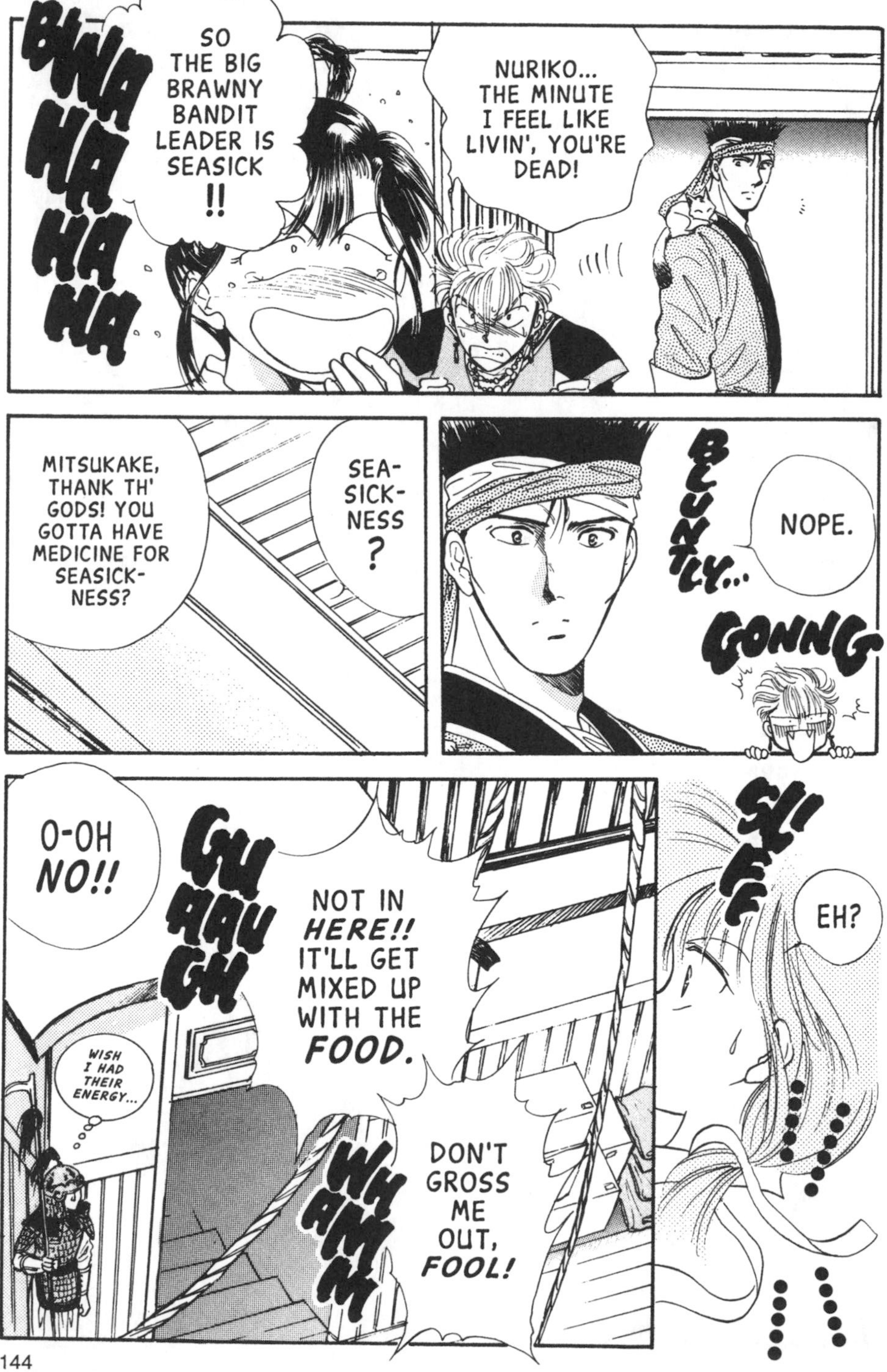

BWAHAHAHAHAHA
SO THE BIG BRAWNY BANDIT LEADER IS SEASICK !!
NURIKO... THE MINUTE I FEEL LIKE LIVIN', YOU'RE DEAD!
MITSUKAKE, THANK TH' GODS! YOU GOTTA HAVE MEDICINE FOR SEASICKNESS?
SEA-SICKNESS ?
BLUNTLY...
NOPE.
GONNG
O-OH NO!!
GUAAUGH
NOT IN HERE!! IT'LL GET MIXED UP WITH THE FOOD.
WISH I HAD THEIR ENERGY...
WHAMM
DON'T GROSS ME OUT, FOOL!
SNIFF
EH?
......

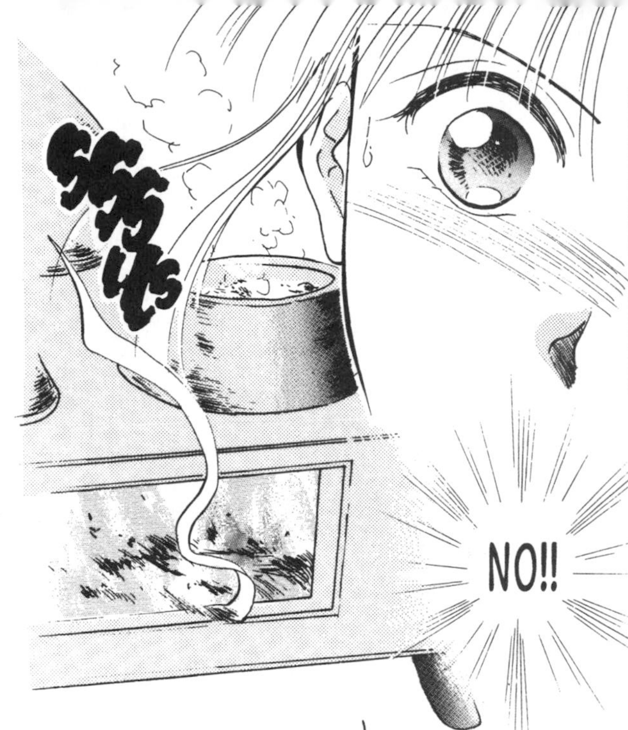
NO!!

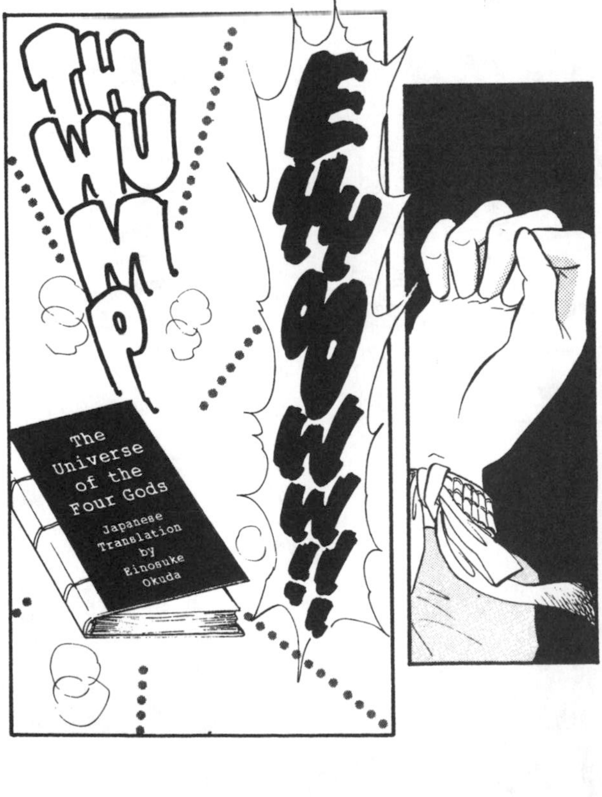
THWUMP
The Universe of the Four Gods
Japanese Translation by Einosuke Okuda

## Castaway

Because of the scary experience she had, I thought my dog would be too scared to go near the stairs. But soon enough she started climbing them again. Well, she did stop following everyone around, so I guess she learned something. I just wish she'd go to the bathroom properly. Please don't pee just to get attention!! And so my dog story comes to an end. Now, should I share another "Fushigi" story? Oh, we received a lot of complaints after the bonus pages weren't included in volume 5. It was simply because there were so many pages of art that the bonus pages and chapter-title pages wouldn't fit into the book (The number of pages for a graphic novel is limited.) If we added bonus pages, we would have had to cut manga pages, so we really had no choice but to leave them out. I'm so sorry! It's nice to know how important those pages are to you. In fact, the very reason I title each chapter was so the graphic novels would have room for bonus pages.
I've been receiving all sorts of questions, but a lot of them, I just can't answer. I think that if I had to answer them all, I wouldn't be able to find time to draw anymore! But many of your questions will be answered as the story unfolds, so please be patient and enjoy it! Your question will probably be answered in the future.
You'll see.

*It's constructed like a puzzle.*

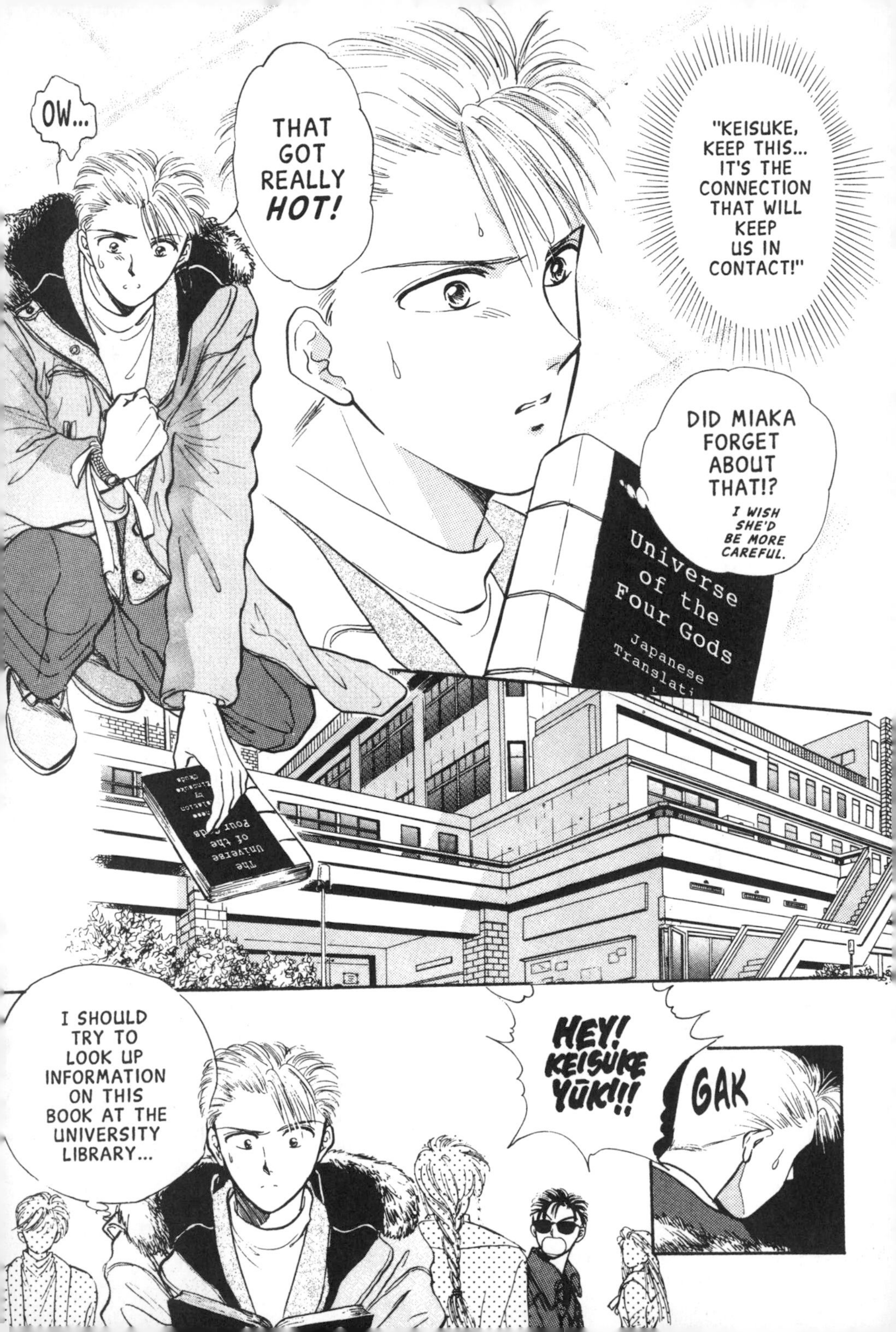
OW...
THAT GOT REALLY HOT!
"KEISUKE, KEEP THIS... IT'S THE CONNECTION THAT WILL KEEP US IN CONTACT!"
DID MIAKA FORGET ABOUT THAT!?
I WISH SHE'D BE MORE CAREFUL.
Universe of the Four Gods
Japanese Translati
I SHOULD TRY TO LOOK UP INFORMATION ON THIS BOOK AT THE UNIVERSITY LIBRARY...
HEY! KEISUKE YŪKI!!
GAK

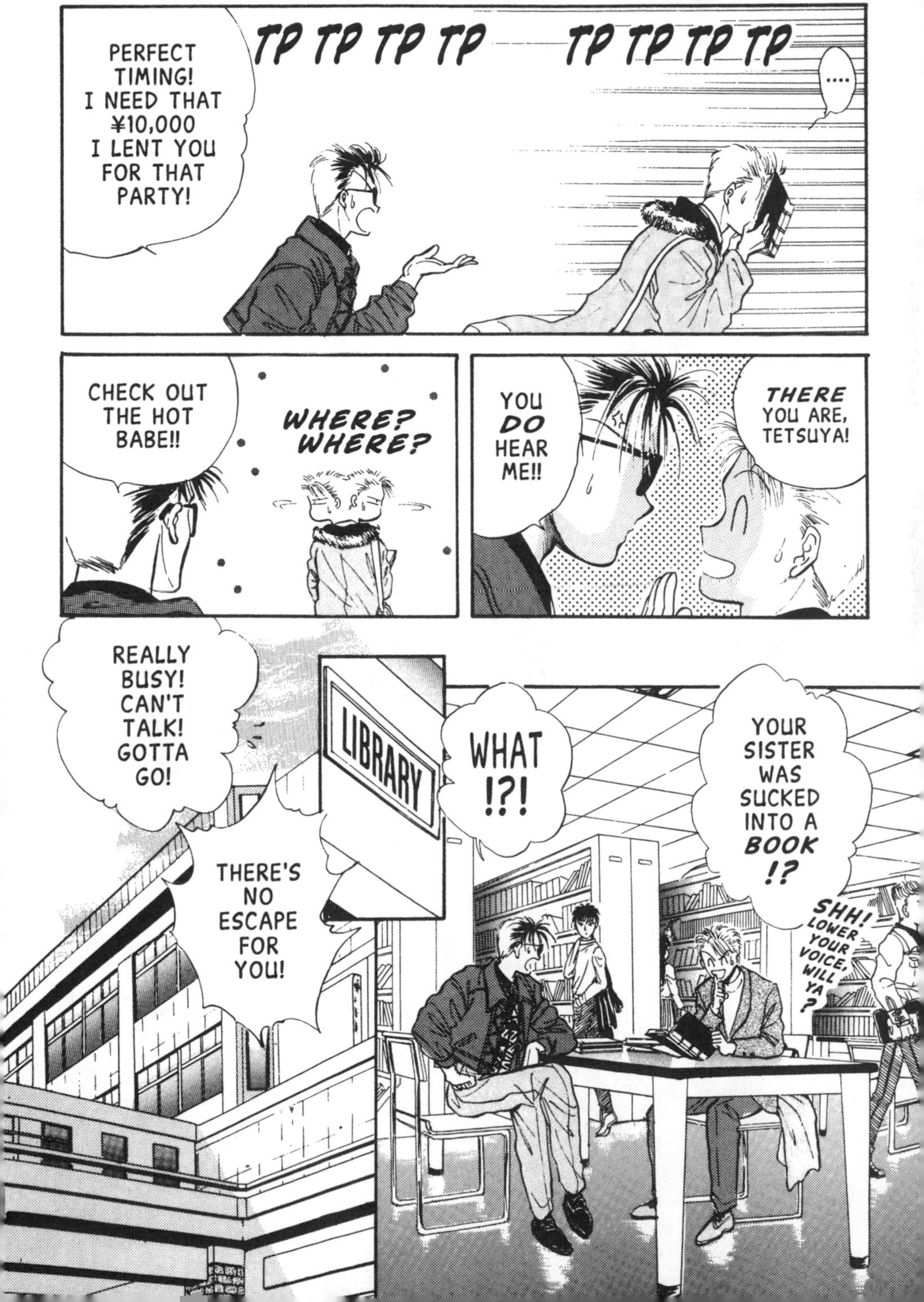
PERFECT TIMING! I NEED THAT ¥10,000 I LENT YOU FOR THAT PARTY!
TP TP TP TP
TP TP TP TP
....
CHECK OUT THE HOT BABE!!
WHERE? WHERE?
YOU DO HEAR ME!!
THERE YOU ARE, TETSUYA!
REALLY BUSY! CAN'T TALK! GOTTA GO!
LIBRARY
WHAT !?!
YOUR SISTER WAS SUCKED INTO A BOOK !?
THERE'S NO ESCAPE FOR YOU!
SHH! LOWER YOUR VOICE, WILL YA?

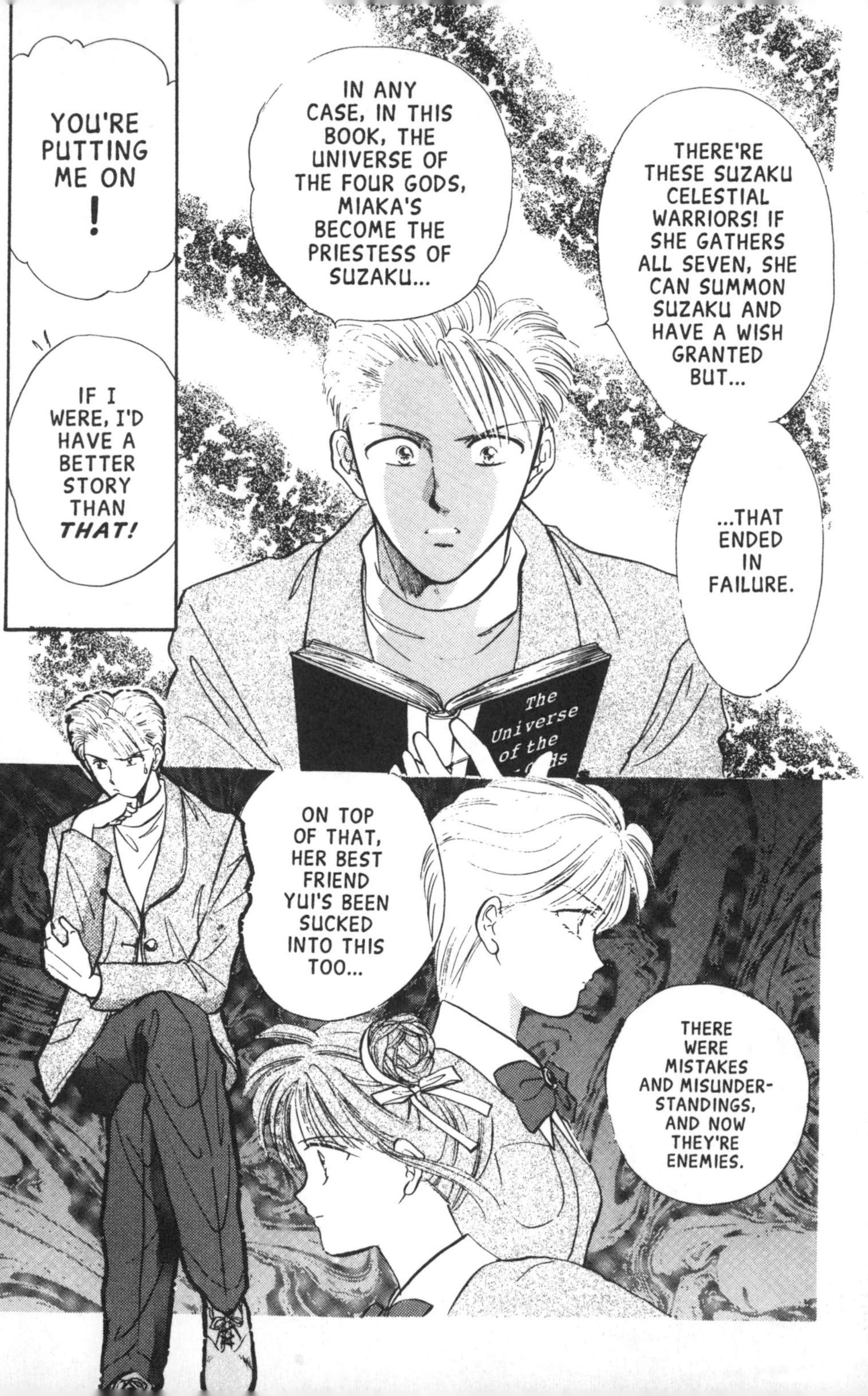
YOU'RE PUTTING ME ON !
IF I WERE, I'D HAVE A BETTER STORY THAN ***THAT!***
IN ANY CASE, IN THIS BOOK, THE UNIVERSE OF THE FOUR GODS, MIAKA'S BECOME THE PRIESTESS OF SUZAKU...
THERE'RE THESE SUZAKU CELESTIAL WARRIORS! IF SHE GATHERS ALL SEVEN, SHE CAN SUMMON SUZAKU AND HAVE A WISH GRANTED BUT...
...THAT ENDED IN FAILURE.
The Universe of the
ON TOP OF THAT, HER BEST FRIEND YUI'S BEEN SUCKED INTO THIS TOO...
THERE WERE MISTAKES AND MISUNDER-STANDINGS, AND NOW THEY'RE ENEMIES.

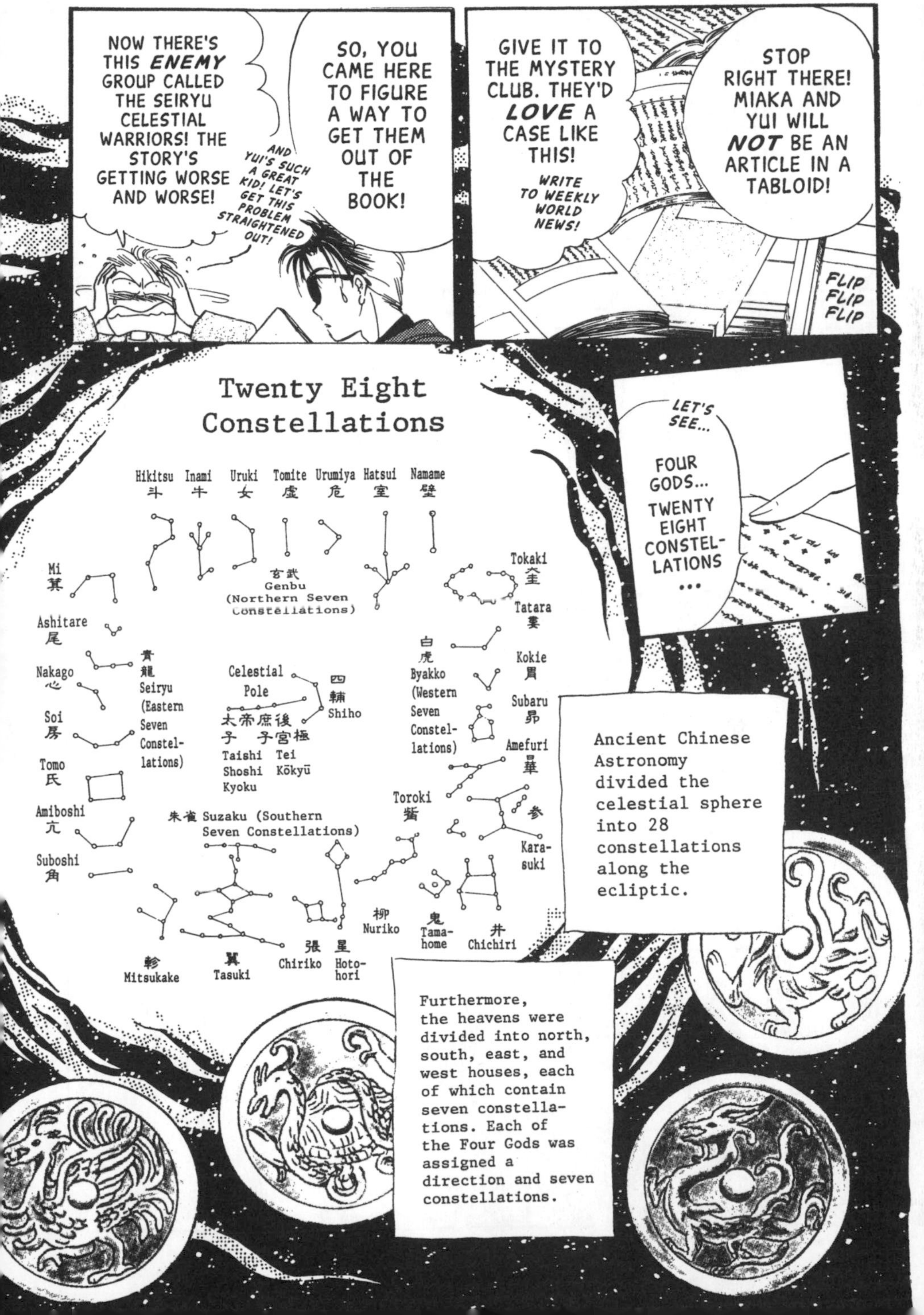
NOW THERE'S THIS ENEMY GROUP CALLED THE SEIRYU CELESTIAL WARRIORS! THE STORY'S GETTING WORSE AND WORSE!
AND YUI'S SUCH A GREAT KID! LET'S GET THIS PROBLEM STRAIGHTENED OUT!
SO, YOU CAME HERE TO FIGURE A WAY TO GET THEM OUT OF THE BOOK!
GIVE IT TO THE MYSTERY CLUB. THEY'D LOVE A CASE LIKE THIS!
WRITE TO WEEKLY WORLD NEWS!
STOP RIGHT THERE! MIAKA AND YUI WILL NOT BE AN ARTICLE IN A TABLOID!
FLIP FLIP FLIP
Twenty Eight Constellations
Hikitsu 斗
Inami 牛
Uruki 女
Tomite 虚
Urumiya 危
Hatsui 室
Namame 壁
玄武 Genbu (Northern Seven Constellations)
Mi 箕
Ashitare 尾
Nakago 心
Soi 房
Tomo 氐
Amiboshi 亢
Suboshi 角
青龍 Seiryu (Eastern Seven Constellations)
Celestial Pole
太子 帝 庶子 後宮 極
Taishi Tei Shoshi Kōkyū Kyoku
四輔 Shiho
白虎 Byakko (Western Seven Constellations)
Tokaki 奎
Tatara 婁
Kokie 胃
Subaru 昴
Amefuri 畢
Toroki 觜
参 Karasuki
朱雀 Suzaku (Southern Seven Constellations)
軫 Mitsukake
翼 Tasuki
張 Chiriko
星 Hotohori
柳 Nuriko
鬼 Tamahome
井 Chichiri
LET'S SEE...
FOUR GODS... TWENTY EIGHT CONSTELLATIONS...
Ancient Chinese Astronomy divided the celestial sphere into 28 constellations along the ecliptic.
Furthermore, the heavens were divided into north, south, east, and west houses, each of which contain seven constellations. Each of the Four Gods was assigned a direction and seven constellations.

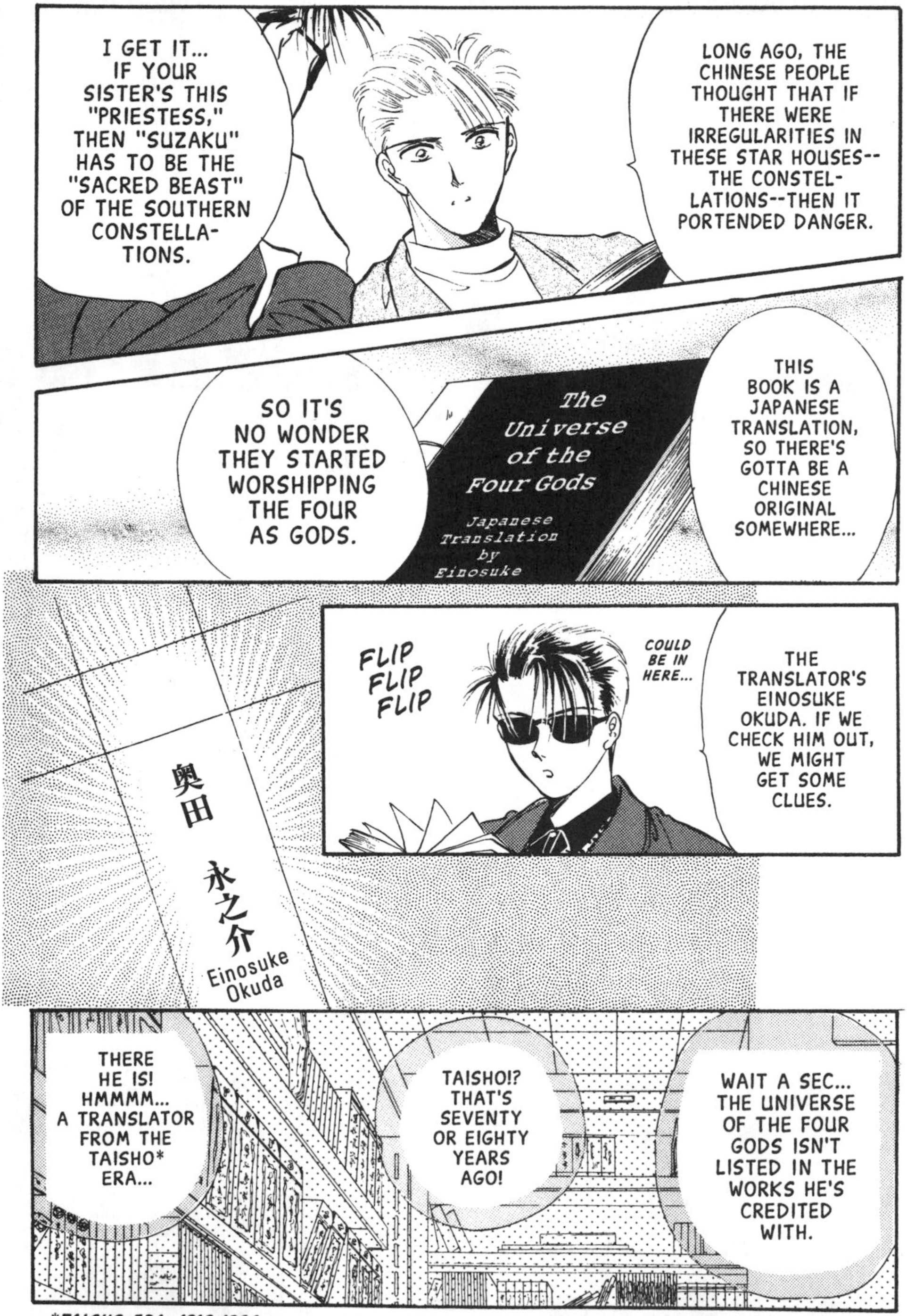
I GET IT... IF YOUR SISTER'S THIS "PRIESTESS," THEN "SUZAKU" HAS TO BE THE "SACRED BEAST" OF THE SOUTHERN CONSTELLATIONS.
LONG AGO, THE CHINESE PEOPLE THOUGHT THAT IF THERE WERE IRREGULARITIES IN THESE STAR HOUSES--THE CONSTELLATIONS--THEN IT PORTENDED DANGER.
SO IT'S NO WONDER THEY STARTED WORSHIPPING THE FOUR AS GODS.
The Universe of the Four Gods
Japanese Translation by Einosuke
THIS BOOK IS A JAPANESE TRANSLATION, SO THERE'S GOTTA BE A CHINESE ORIGINAL SOMEWHERE...
奥田 永之介
Einosuke Okuda
FLIP FLIP FLIP
COULD BE IN HERE...
THE TRANSLATOR'S EINOSUKE OKUDA. IF WE CHECK HIM OUT, WE MIGHT GET SOME CLUES.
THERE HE IS! HMMMM... A TRANSLATOR FROM THE TAISHO* ERA...
TAISHO!? THAT'S SEVENTY OR EIGHTY YEARS AGO!
WAIT A SEC... THE UNIVERSE OF THE FOUR GODS ISN'T LISTED IN THE WORKS HE'S CREDITED WITH.

*TAISHO ERA: 1912-1926.

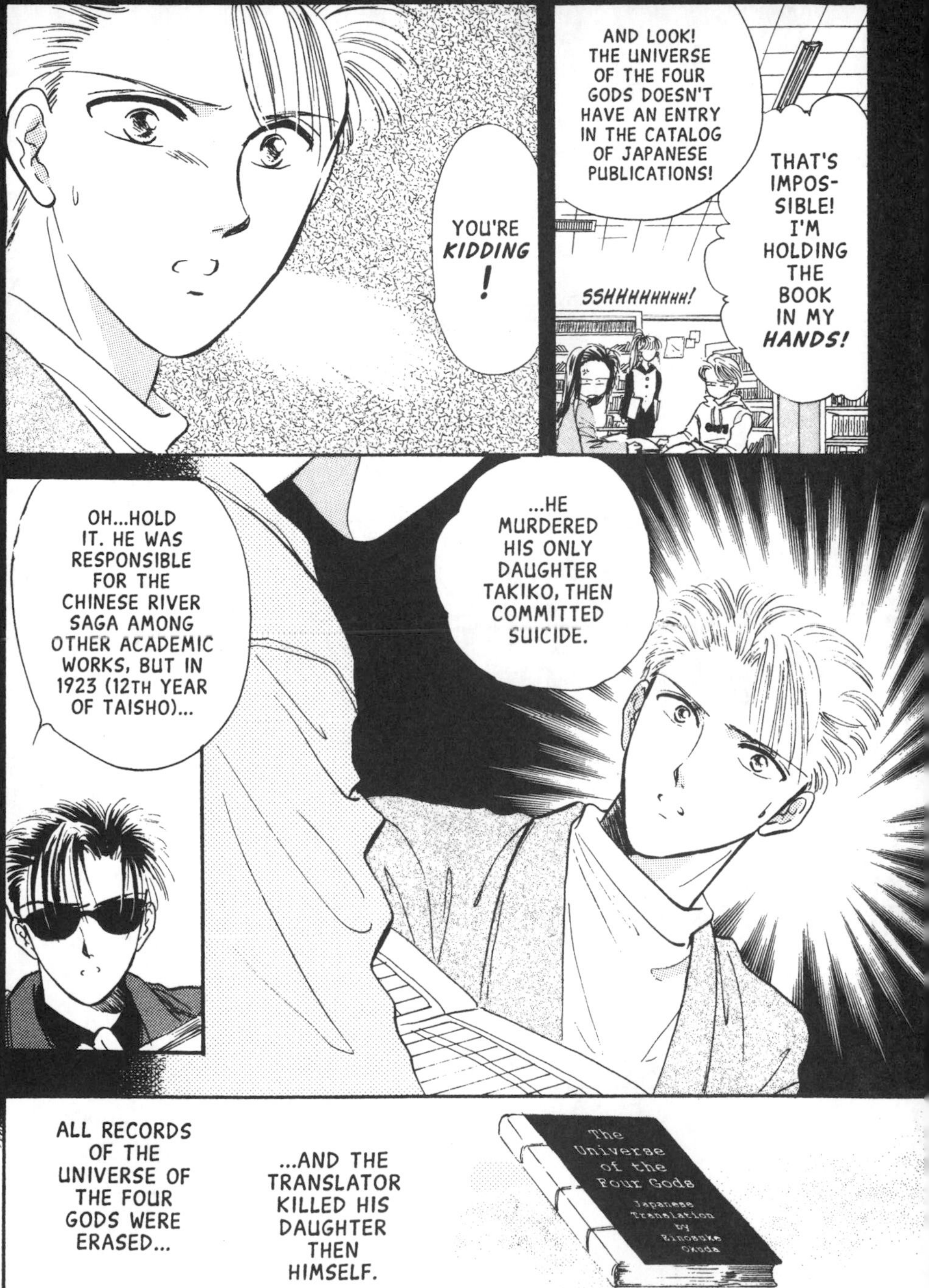
YOU'RE *KIDDING* !
AND LOOK! THE UNIVERSE OF THE FOUR GODS DOESN'T HAVE AN ENTRY IN THE CATALOG OF JAPANESE PUBLICATIONS!
THAT'S IMPOSSIBLE! I'M HOLDING THE BOOK IN MY *HANDS!*
SSHHHHHHHH!
OH...HOLD IT. HE WAS RESPONSIBLE FOR THE CHINESE RIVER SAGA AMONG OTHER ACADEMIC WORKS, BUT IN 1923 (12TH YEAR OF TAISHO)...
...HE MURDERED HIS ONLY DAUGHTER TAKIKO, THEN COMMITTED SUICIDE.
ALL RECORDS OF THE UNIVERSE OF THE FOUR GODS WERE ERASED...
...AND THE TRANSLATOR KILLED HIS DAUGHTER THEN HIMSELF.
The Universe of the Four Gods
Japanese Translation by Einosuke Okuda

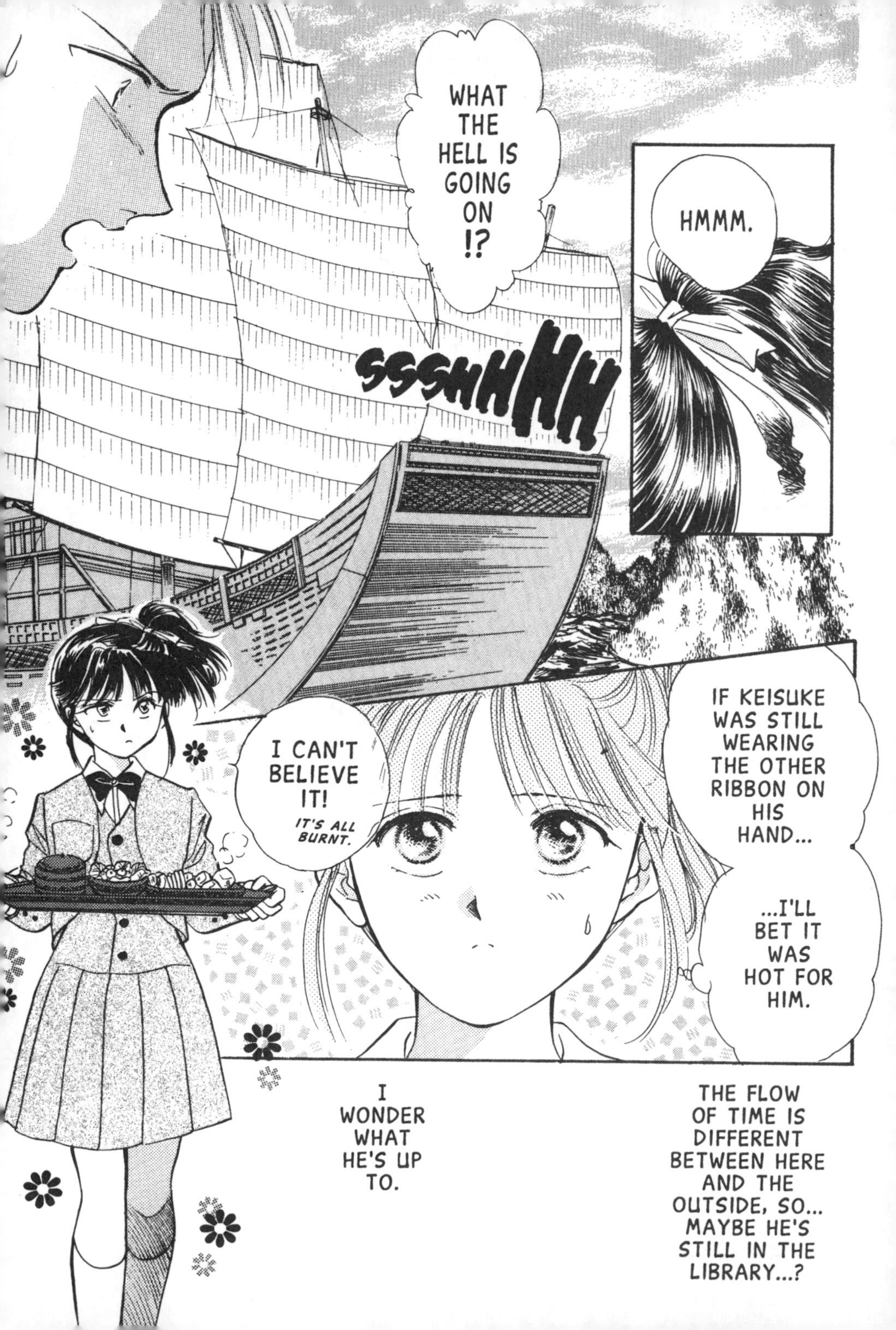
WHAT THE HELL IS GOING ON !?
SSSHHHHH
HMMM.
I CAN'T BELIEVE IT!
IT'S ALL BURNT.
IF KEISUKE WAS STILL WEARING THE OTHER RIBBON ON HIS HAND...
...I'LL BET IT WAS HOT FOR HIM.
I WONDER WHAT HE'S UP TO.
THE FLOW OF TIME IS DIFFERENT BETWEEN HERE AND THE OUTSIDE, SO... MAYBE HE'S STILL IN THE LIBRARY...?

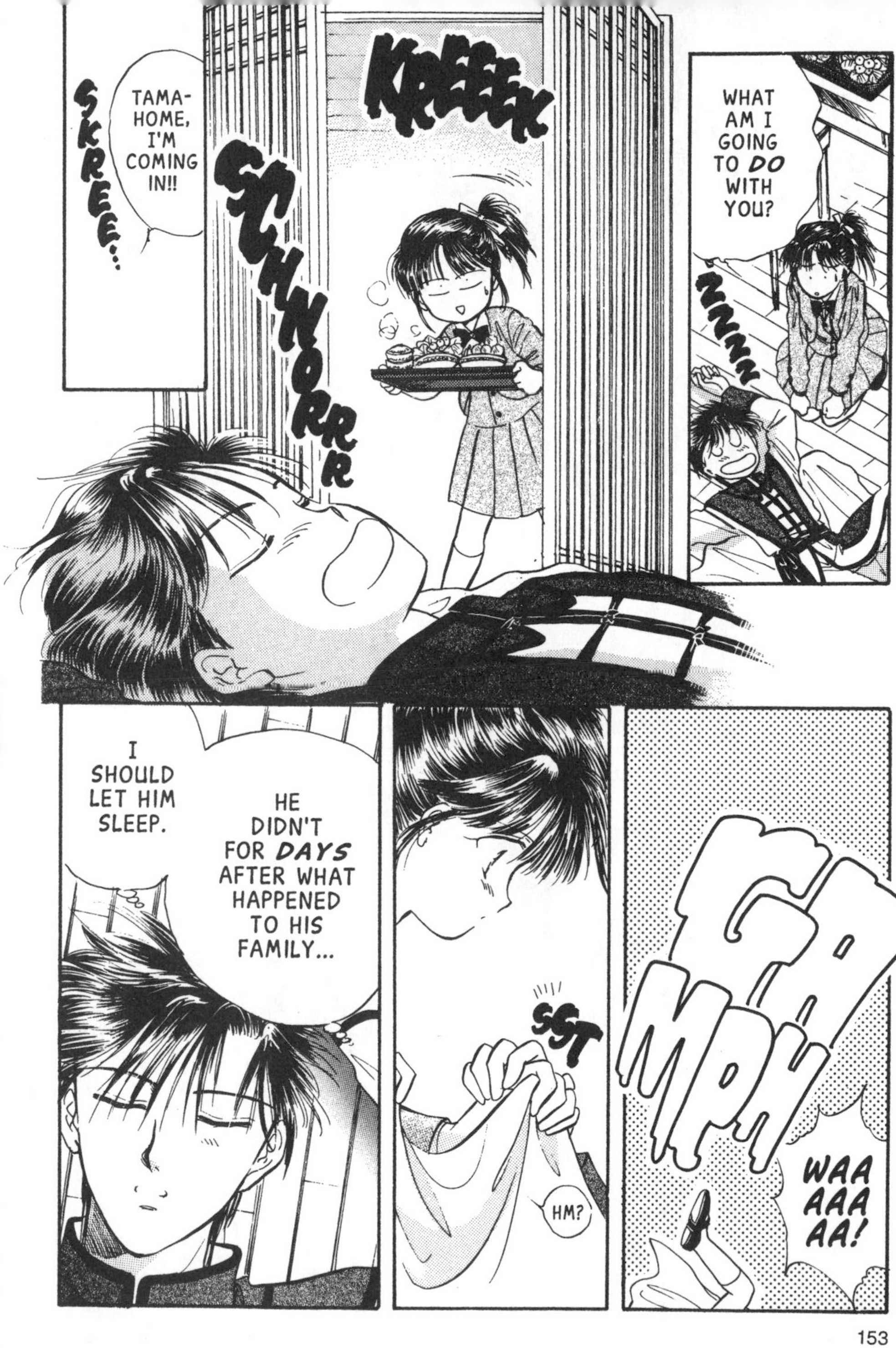
SKREE...
TAMA-HOME, I'M COMING IN!!
KREEEK
SCHNORRR
WHAT AM I GOING TO DO WITH YOU?
ZZZZZ
I SHOULD LET HIM SLEEP.
HE DIDN'T FOR DAYS AFTER WHAT HAPPENED TO HIS FAMILY...
SST
HM?
GAMPH
WAAAAAAAA!

FWUMP

T--TAMA-HOME!

L-LET *GO* OF ME!!

THE MAN IS *HOPELESS!*

YOU BETTER BE ASLEEP FOR REAL.

BUT SHE'S STILL HAPPY ABOUT IT.

HE'S NOT DOING IT ON PURPOSE, SO I CAN ALLOW IT THIS TIME...

IF THIS WERE THE *NORMAL* WORLD...

...AND TAMAHOME WAS A *NORMAL* HIGH-SCHOOL KID...

...WE COULD LOVE EACH OTHER WITHOUT RESTRICTIONS.

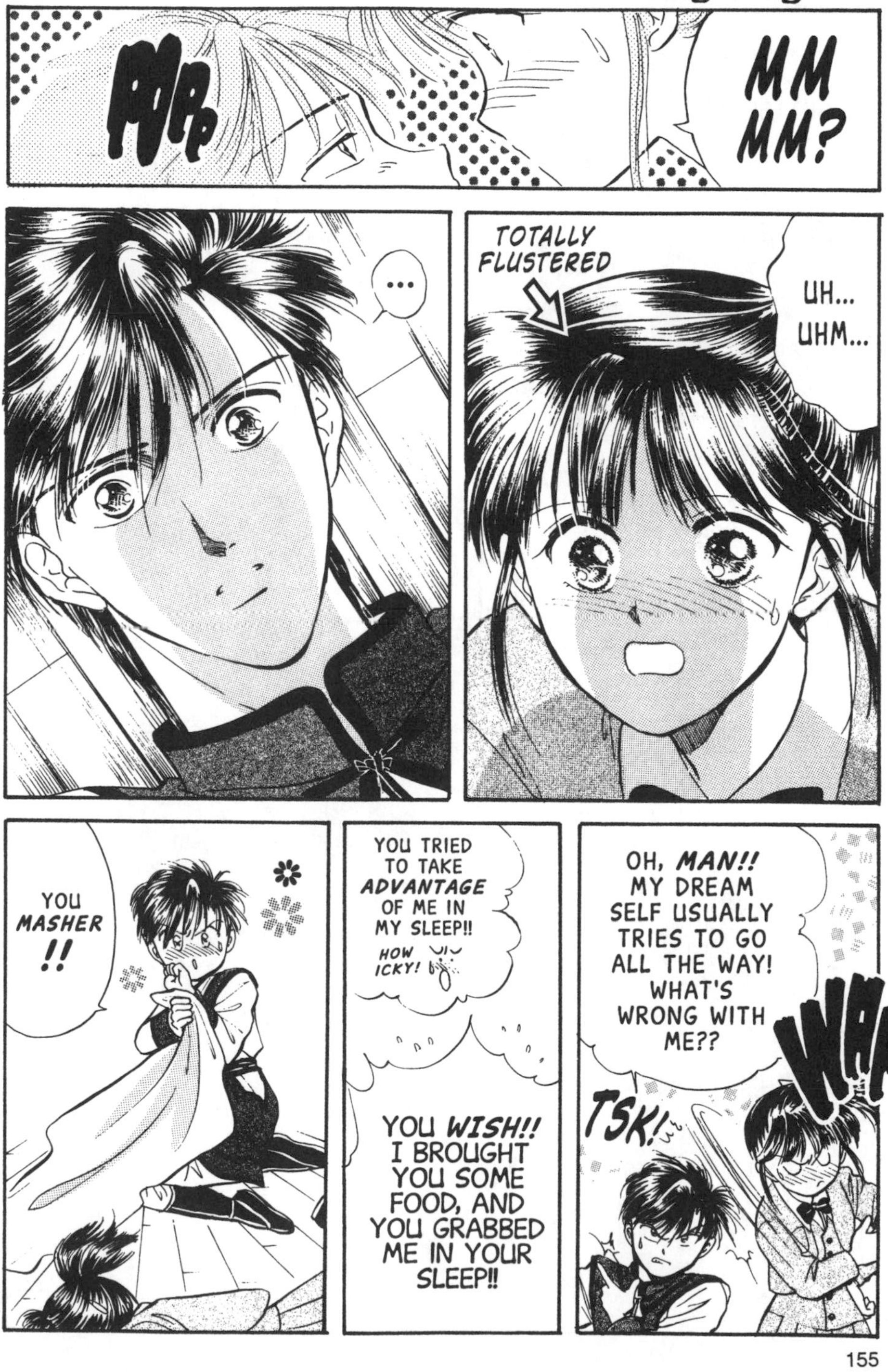
PPPPP
MM MM?
...
TOTALLY FLUSTERED
UH... UHM...
YOU MASHER !!
YOU TRIED TO TAKE ADVANTAGE OF ME IN MY SLEEP!!
HOW ICKY!
YOU WISH!! I BROUGHT YOU SOME FOOD, AND YOU GRABBED ME IN YOUR SLEEP!!
OH, MAN!! MY DREAM SELF USUALLY TRIES TO GO ALL THE WAY! WHAT'S WRONG WITH ME??
WAP
TSK!

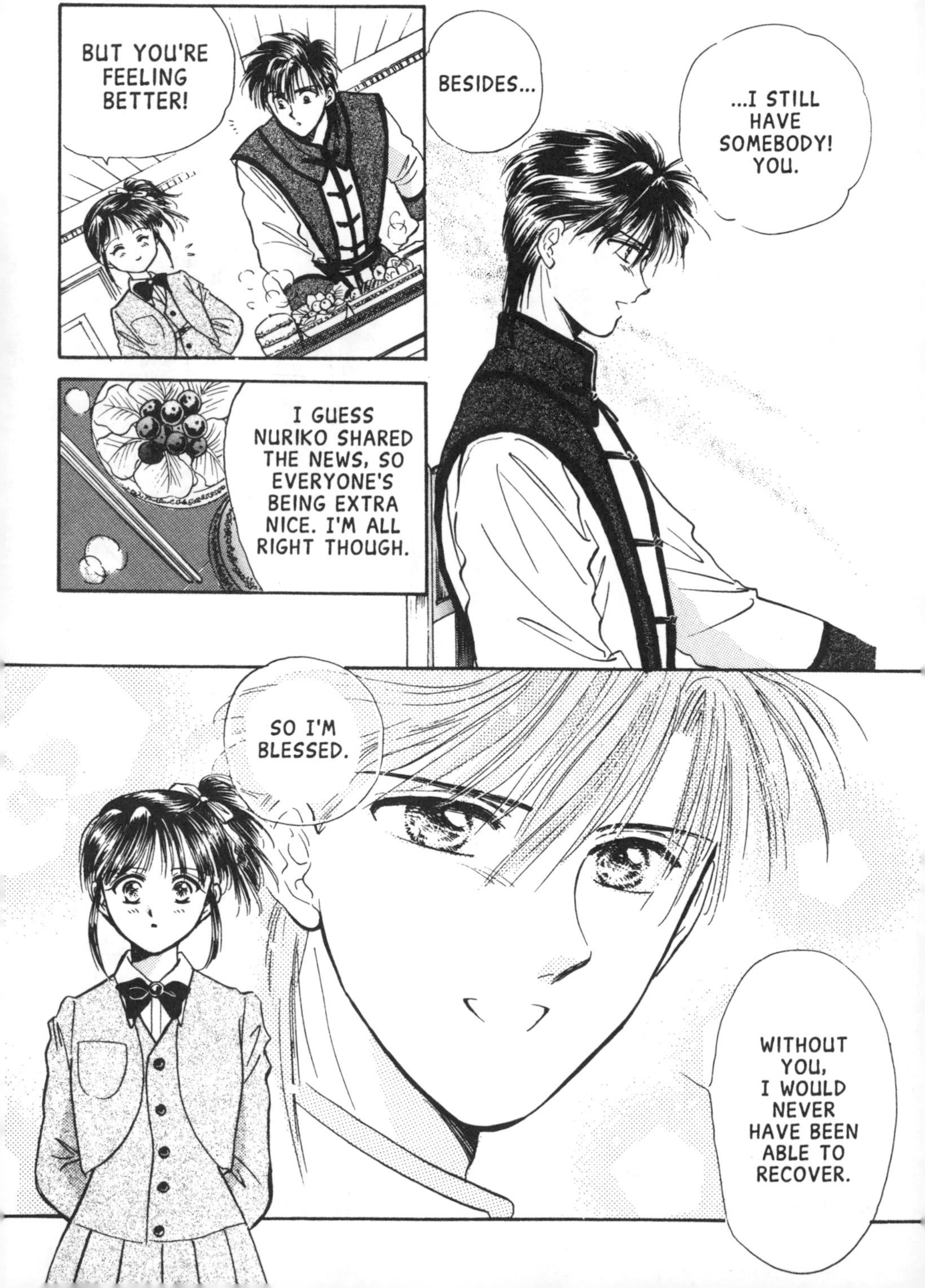
BUT YOU'RE FEELING BETTER!
I GUESS NURIKO SHARED THE NEWS, SO EVERYONE'S BEING EXTRA NICE. I'M ALL RIGHT THOUGH.
BESIDES...
...I STILL HAVE SOMEBODY! YOU.
SO I'M BLESSED.
WITHOUT YOU, I WOULD NEVER HAVE BEEN ABLE TO RECOVER.

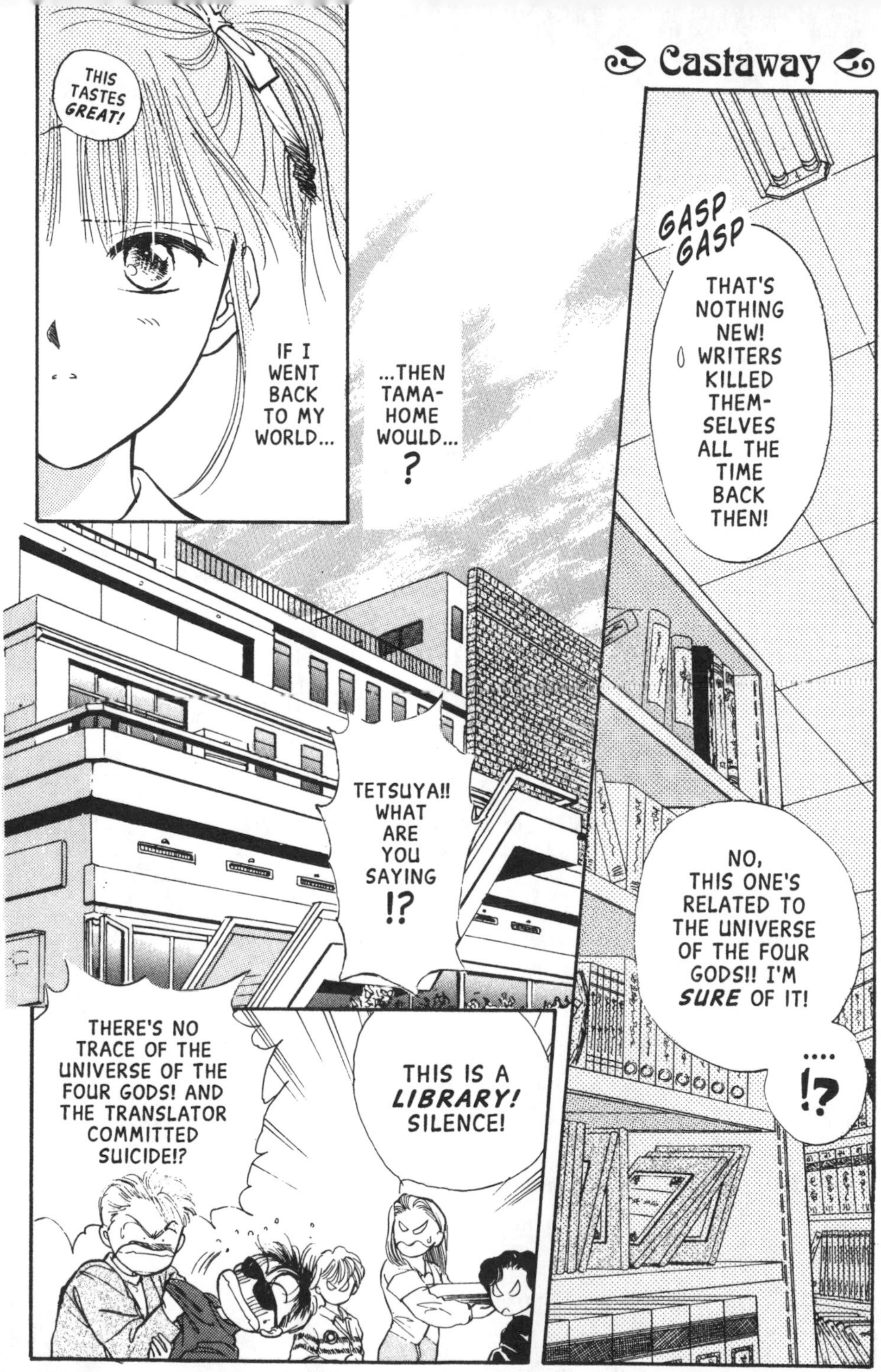
THIS TASTES GREAT!
IF I WENT BACK TO MY WORLD...
...THEN TAMA-HOME WOULD...
?
TETSUYA!! WHAT ARE YOU SAYING !?
THERE'S NO TRACE OF THE UNIVERSE OF THE FOUR GODS! AND THE TRANSLATOR COMMITTED SUICIDE!?
THIS IS A LIBRARY! SILENCE!
GASP GASP
THAT'S NOTHING NEW! WRITERS KILLED THEMSELVES ALL THE TIME BACK THEN!
NO, THIS ONE'S RELATED TO THE UNIVERSE OF THE FOUR GODS!! I'M SURE OF IT!
....
!?

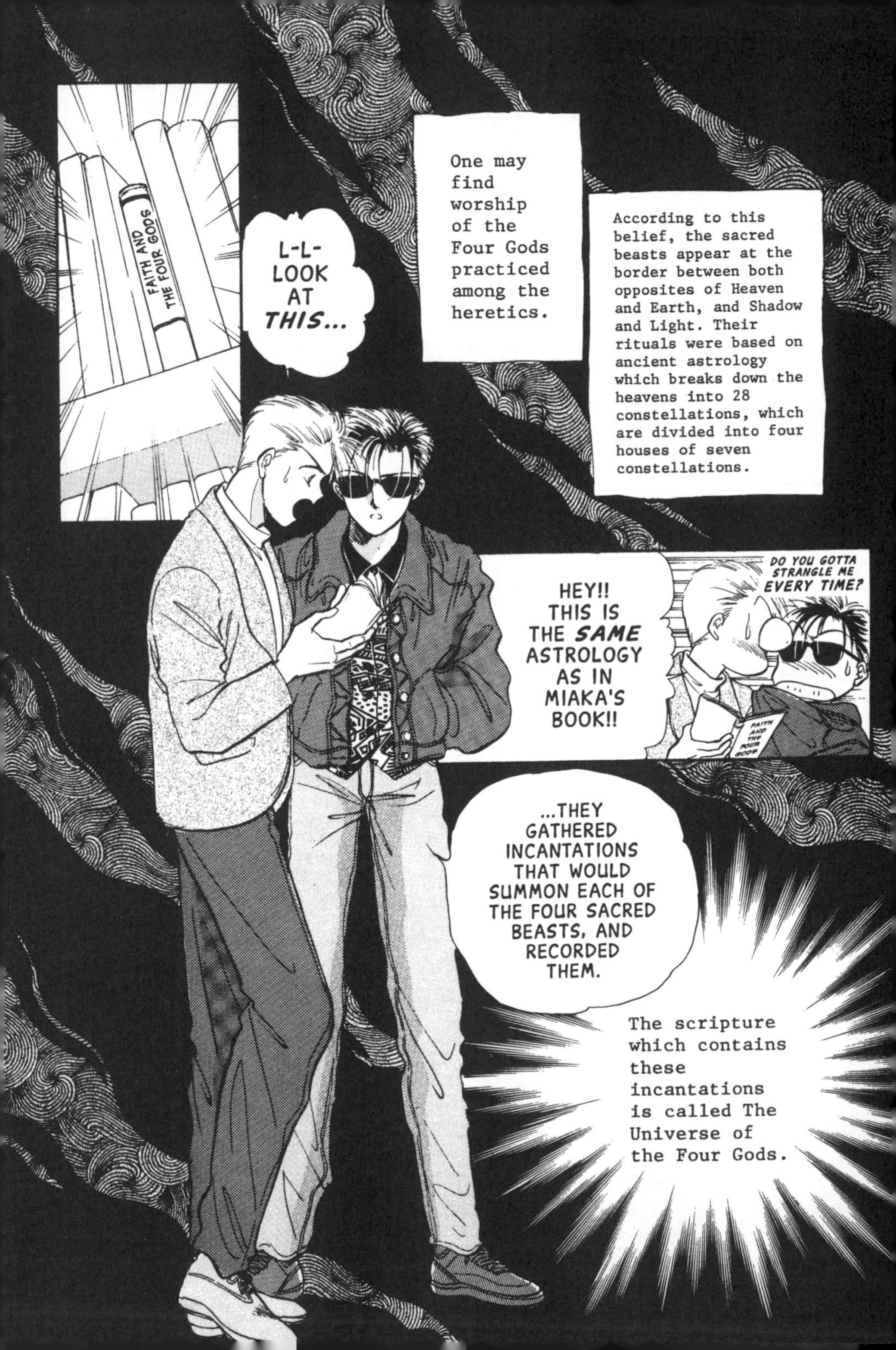
FAITH AND THE FOUR GODS
L-L-LOOK AT THIS...
One may find worship of the Four Gods practiced among the heretics.
According to this belief, the sacred beasts appear at the border between both opposites of Heaven and Earth, and Shadow and Light. Their rituals were based on ancient astrology which breaks down the heavens into 28 constellations, which are divided into four houses of seven constellations.
HEY!! THIS IS THE SAME ASTROLOGY AS IN MIAKA'S BOOK!!
DO YOU GOTTA STRANGLE ME EVERY TIME?
...THEY GATHERED INCANTATIONS THAT WOULD SUMMON EACH OF THE FOUR SACRED BEASTS, AND RECORDED THEM.
The scripture which contains these incantations is called The Universe of the Four Gods.

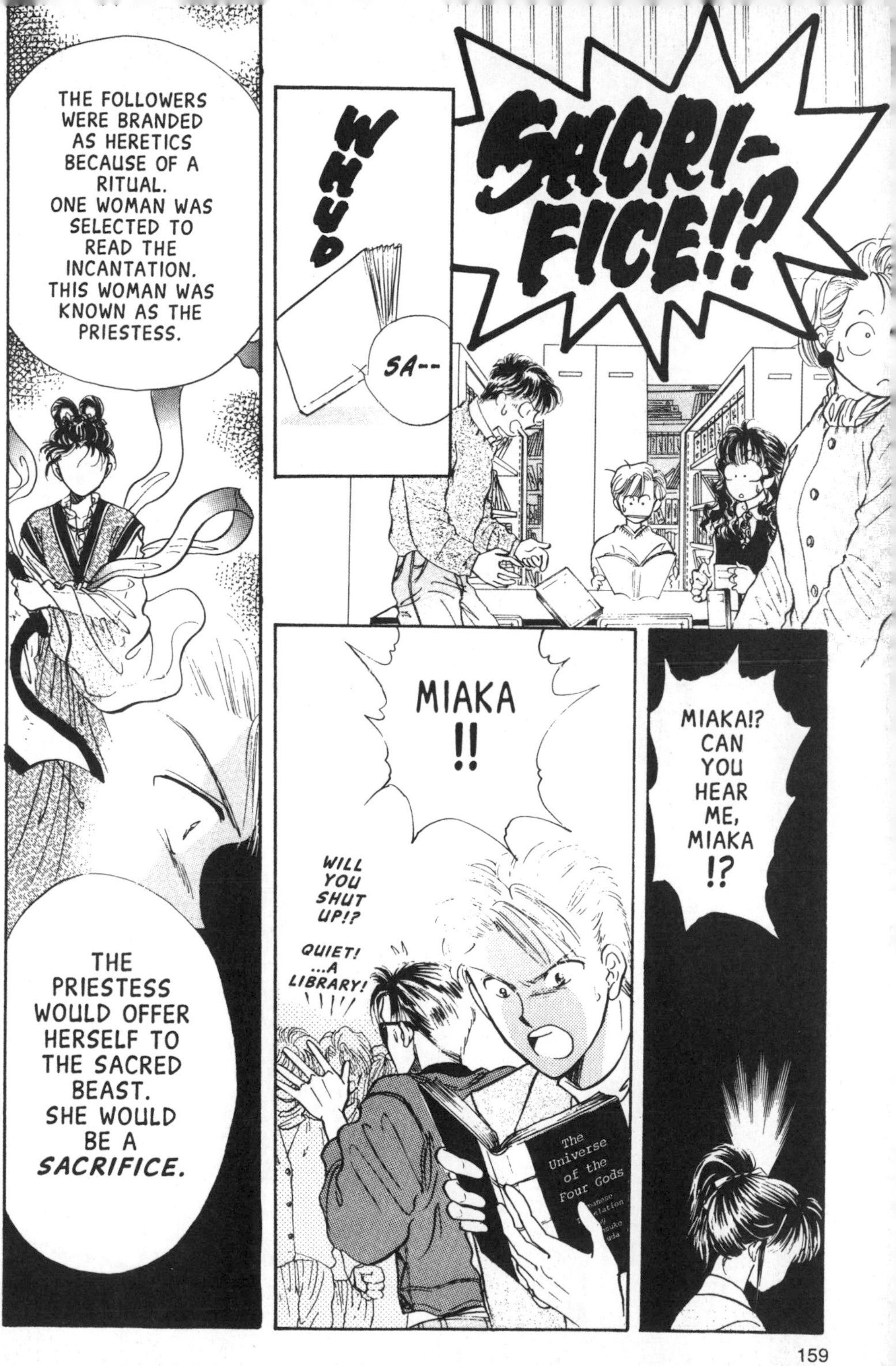
THE FOLLOWERS WERE BRANDED AS HERETICS BECAUSE OF A RITUAL. ONE WOMAN WAS SELECTED TO READ THE INCANTATION. THIS WOMAN WAS KNOWN AS THE PRIESTESS.
THE PRIESTESS WOULD OFFER HERSELF TO THE SACRED BEAST. SHE WOULD BE A *SACRIFICE.*
WHUD
SA--
SACRI-FICE!?
MIAKA !!
WILL YOU SHUT UP!?
QUIET! ...A LIBRARY!
The Universe of the Four Gods
MIAKA!? CAN YOU HEAR ME, MIAKA !?

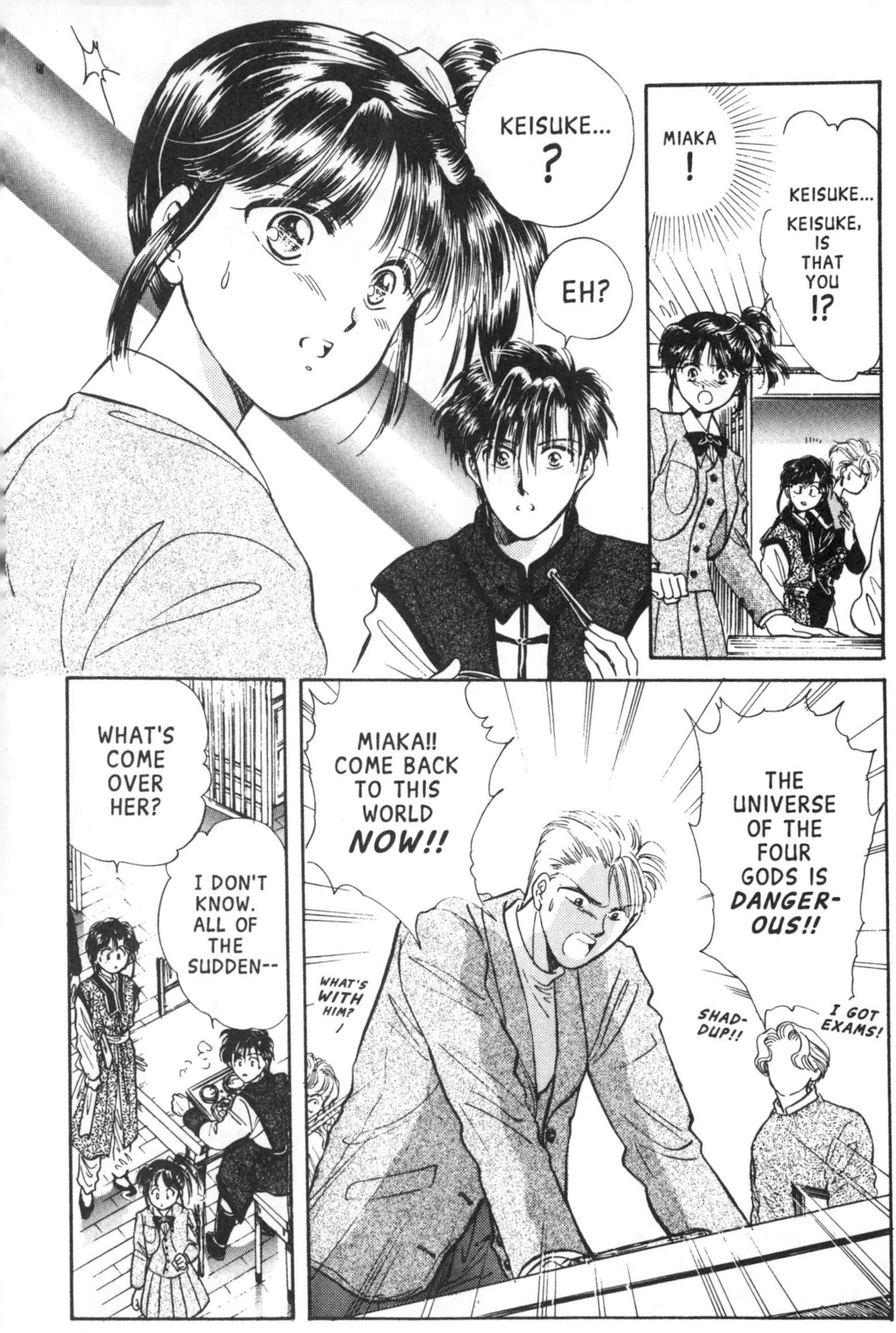
KEISUKE... ?
EH?
MIAKA !
KEISUKE... KEISUKE, IS THAT YOU !?
WHAT'S COME OVER HER?
I DON'T KNOW. ALL OF THE SUDDEN--
MIAKA!! COME BACK TO THIS WORLD NOW!!
THE UNIVERSE OF THE FOUR GODS IS DANGER-OUS!!
WHAT'S WITH HIM?
SHAD-DUP!!
I GOT EXAMS!

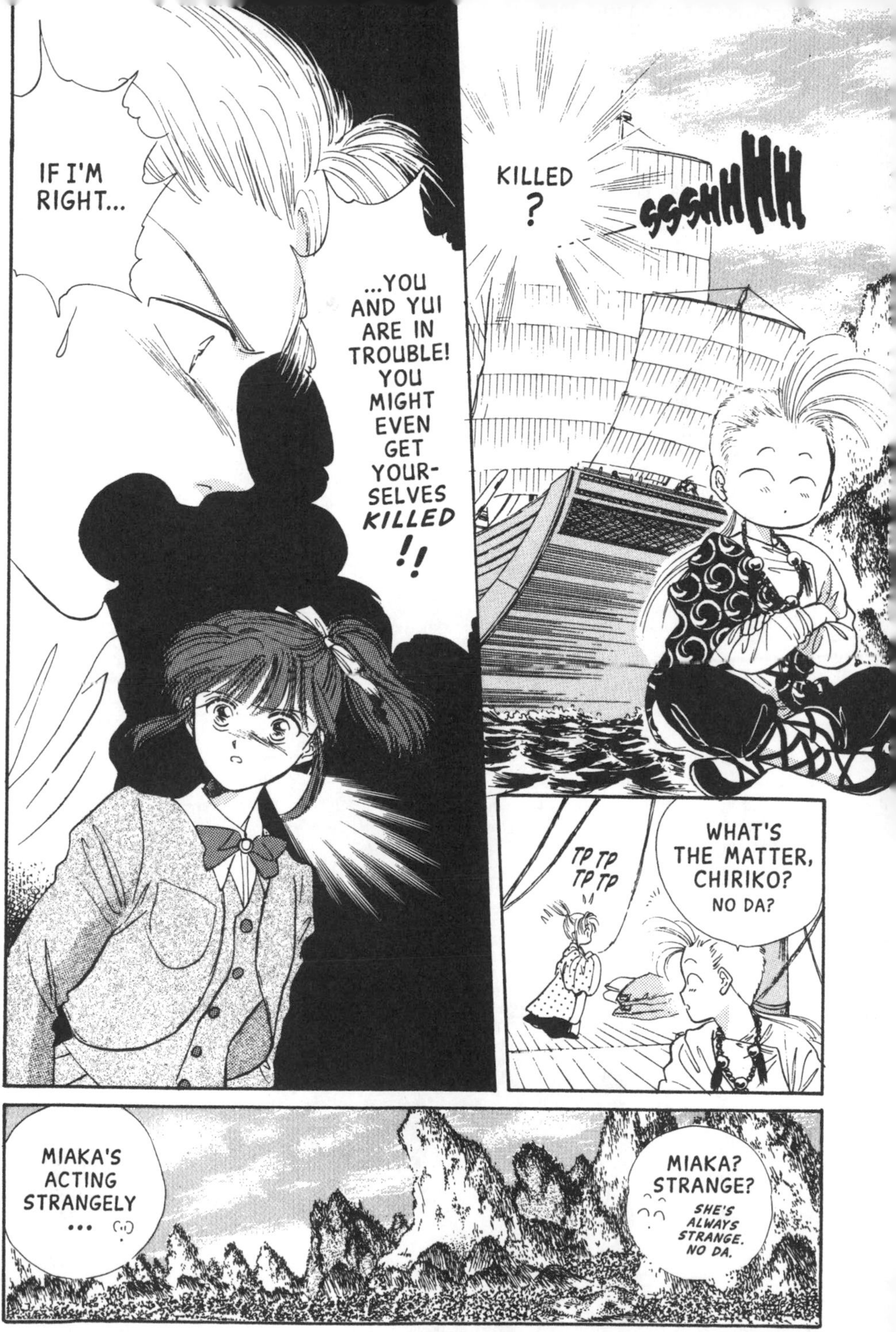
IF I'M RIGHT...
...YOU AND YUI ARE IN TROUBLE! YOU MIGHT EVEN GET YOUR-SELVES KILLED !!
KILLED ?
SSSHHHHH
TP TP TP TP
WHAT'S THE MATTER, CHIRIKO? NO DA?
MIAKA'S ACTING STRANGELY ...
MIAKA? STRANGE? SHE'S ALWAYS STRANGE. NO DA.

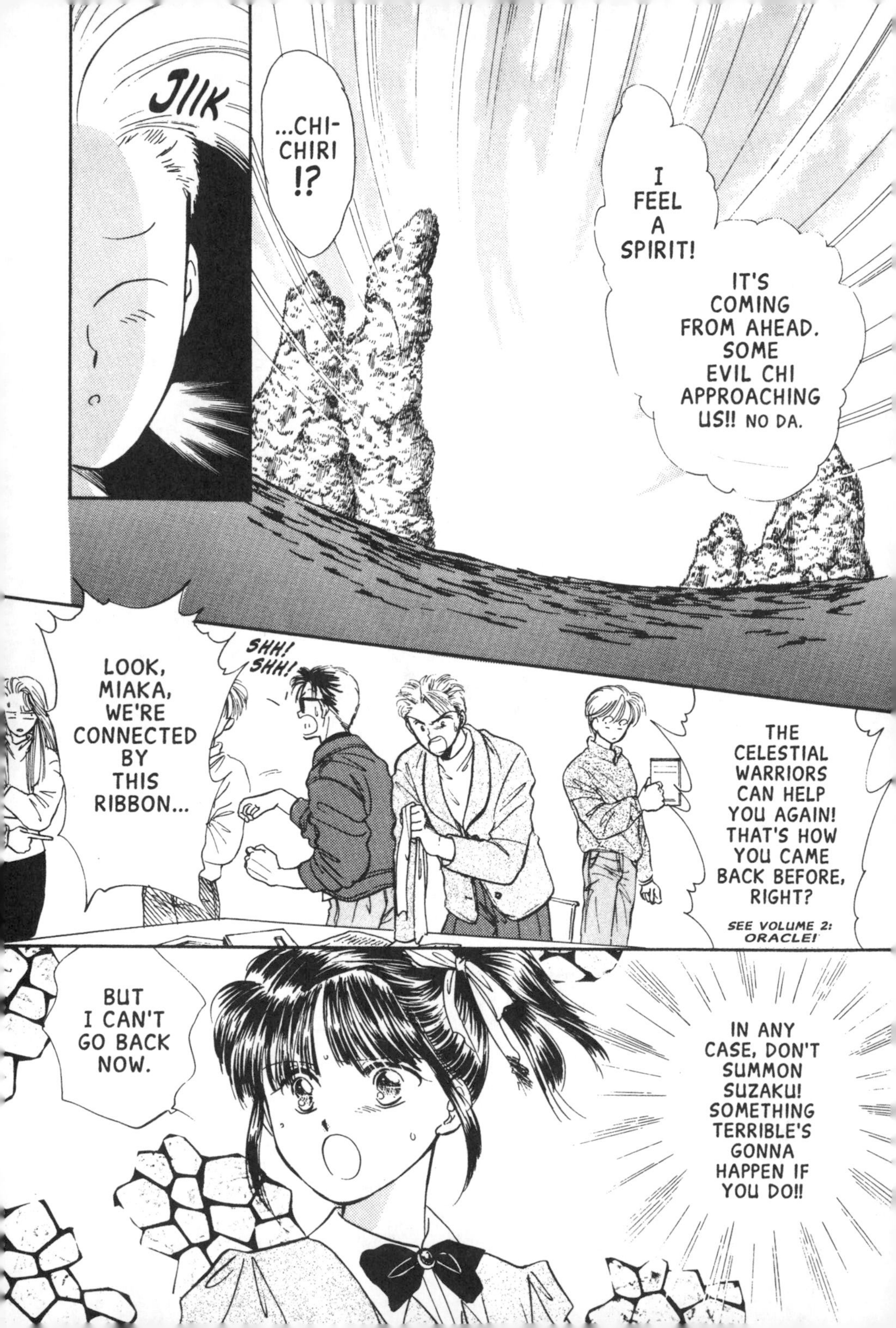

JIIK
...CHI-CHIRI !?
I FEEL A SPIRIT!
IT'S COMING FROM AHEAD. SOME EVIL CHI APPROACHING US!! NO DA.
LOOK, MIAKA, WE'RE CONNECTED BY THIS RIBBON...
SHH! SHH!
THE CELESTIAL WARRIORS CAN HELP YOU AGAIN! THAT'S HOW YOU CAME BACK BEFORE, RIGHT?
SEE VOLUME 2: ORACLE!
BUT I CAN'T GO BACK NOW.
IN ANY CASE, DON'T SUMMON SUZAKU! SOMETHING TERRIBLE'S GONNA HAPPEN IF YOU DO!!

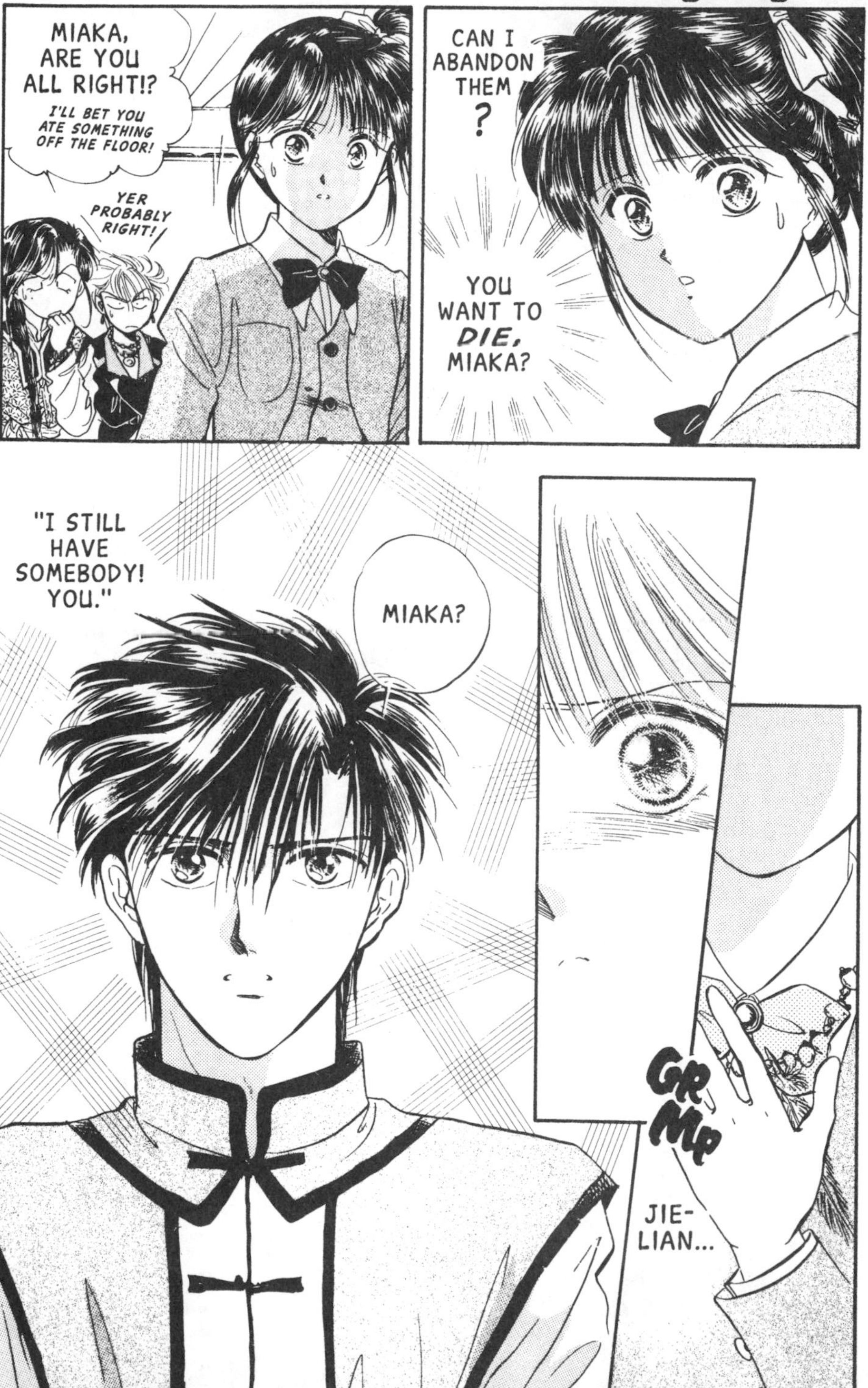
MIAKA, ARE YOU ALL RIGHT!?
I'LL BET YOU ATE SOMETHING OFF THE FLOOR!
YER PROBABLY RIGHT!
CAN I ABANDON THEM ?
YOU WANT TO DIE, MIAKA?
"I STILL HAVE SOMEBODY! YOU."
MIAKA?
GRMP
JIE-LIAN...

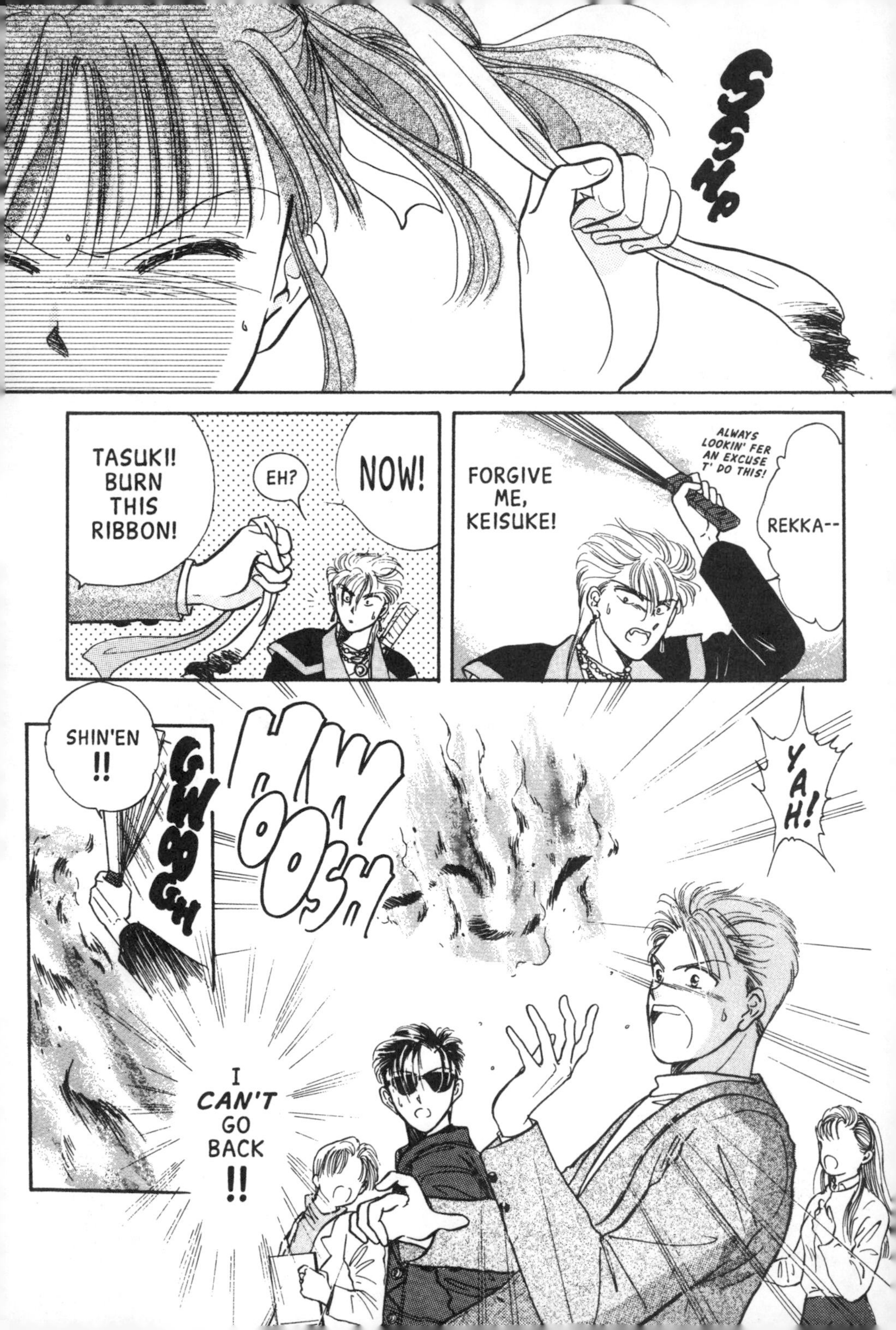
SSSHP
TASUKI! BURN THIS RIBBON!
EH?
NOW!
FORGIVE ME, KEISUKE!
ALWAYS LOOKIN' FER AN EXCUSE T' DO THIS!
REKKA--
SHIN'EN !!
GWOOOGH
HWOOOSH
YAH!
I CAN'T GO BACK !!

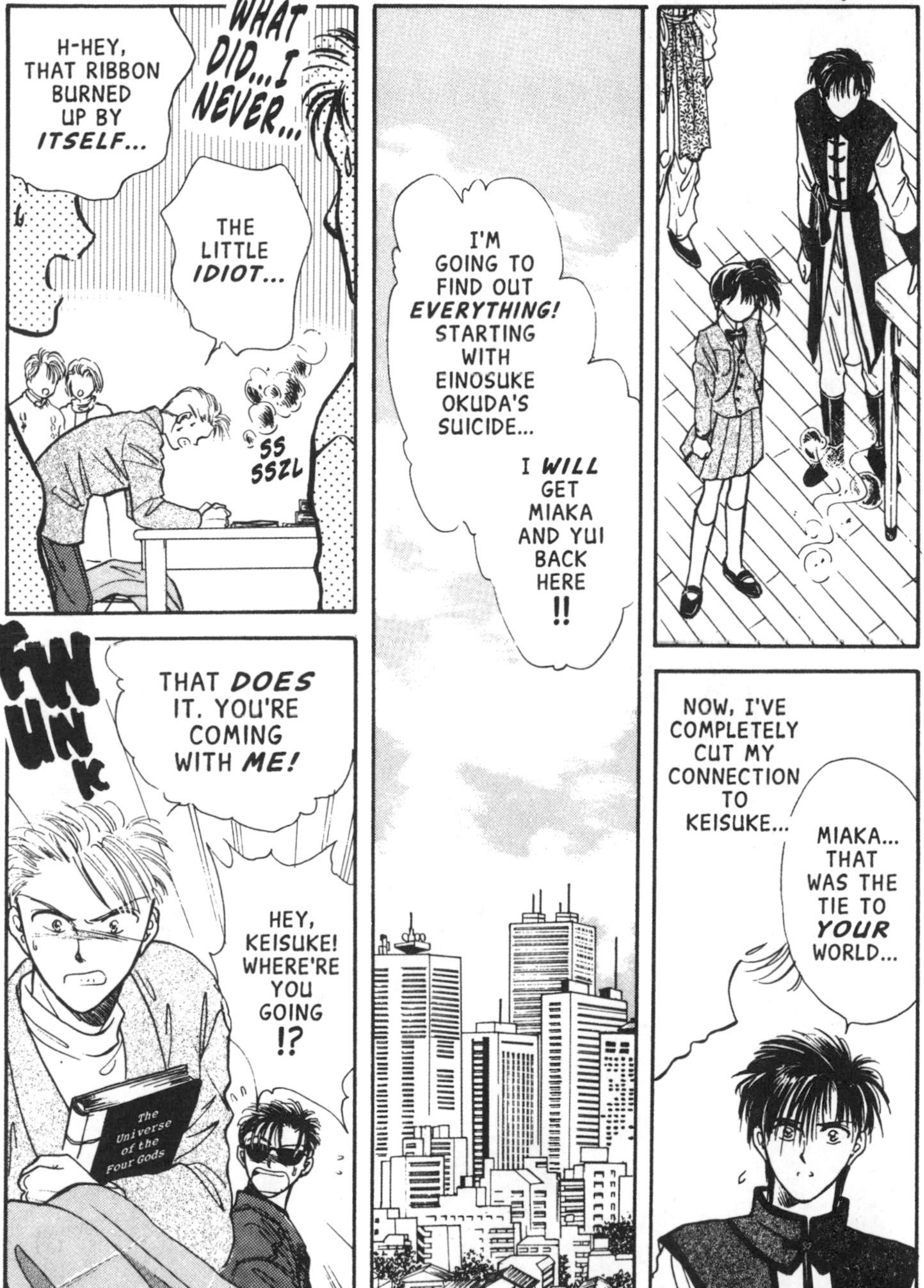
H-HEY, THAT RIBBON BURNED UP BY ITSELF...
WHAT DID...I NEVER...
THE LITTLE IDIOT...
SS SSZL
FWUNK
THAT DOES IT. YOU'RE COMING WITH ME!
HEY, KEISUKE! WHERE'RE YOU GOING !?
The Universe of the Four Gods
I'M GOING TO FIND OUT EVERYTHING! STARTING WITH EINOSUKE OKUDA'S SUICIDE...
I WILL GET MIAKA AND YUI BACK HERE !!
NOW, I'VE COMPLETELY CUT MY CONNECTION TO KEISUKE...
MIAKA... THAT WAS THE TIE TO YOUR WORLD...

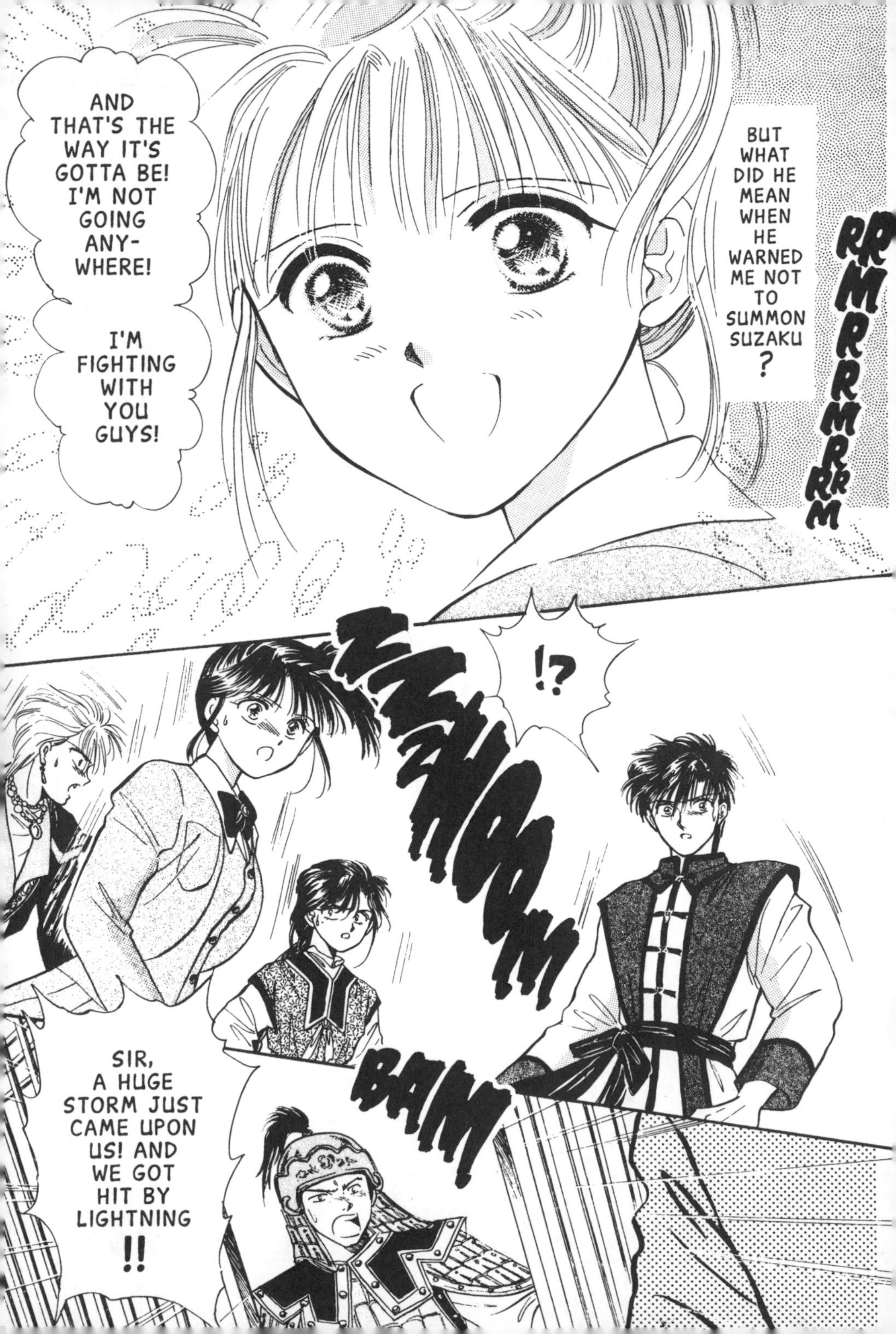
AND THAT'S THE WAY IT'S GOTTA BE! I'M NOT GOING ANY-WHERE!
I'M FIGHTING WITH YOU GUYS!
BUT WHAT DID HE MEAN WHEN HE WARNED ME NOT TO SUMMON SUZAKU?
RRMRRMRRRM
!?
BAM
SIR, A HUGE STORM JUST CAME UPON US! AND WE GOT HIT BY LIGHTNING!!

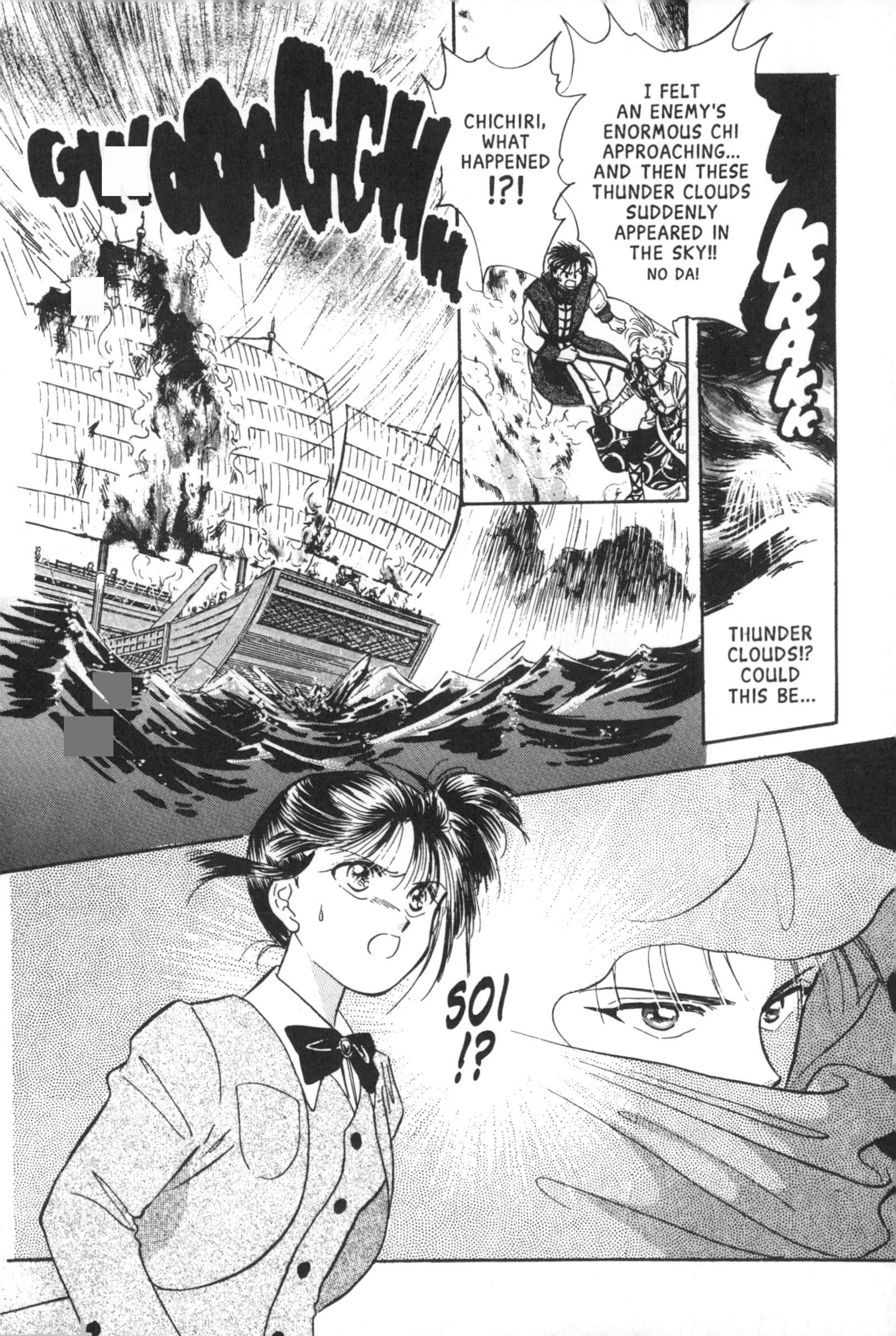
GHOOOGCH
CHICHIRI, WHAT HAPPENED !?!
I FELT AN ENEMY'S ENORMOUS CHI APPROACHING... AND THEN THESE THUNDER CLOUDS SUDDENLY APPEARED IN THE SKY!! NO DA!
THUNDER CLOUDS!? COULD THIS BE...
SOI !?

**CAUGHT IN THE POWERS OF THE FALSE CHIRIKO'S "SONG OF MASS MURDER," THE CELESTIAL WARRIORS SUFFER THEIR WORST NIGHTMARE!!**

# ふしぎ悪戯

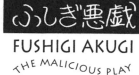

## FUSHIGI AKUGI

THE MALICIOUS PLAY

## NO. 7

Suggested by...a reader

I wanted to put in the reader's name, but by the time I was making up this page, my mom had filed the letter away, and I can't find it anymore!

I'M SO SORRY!!

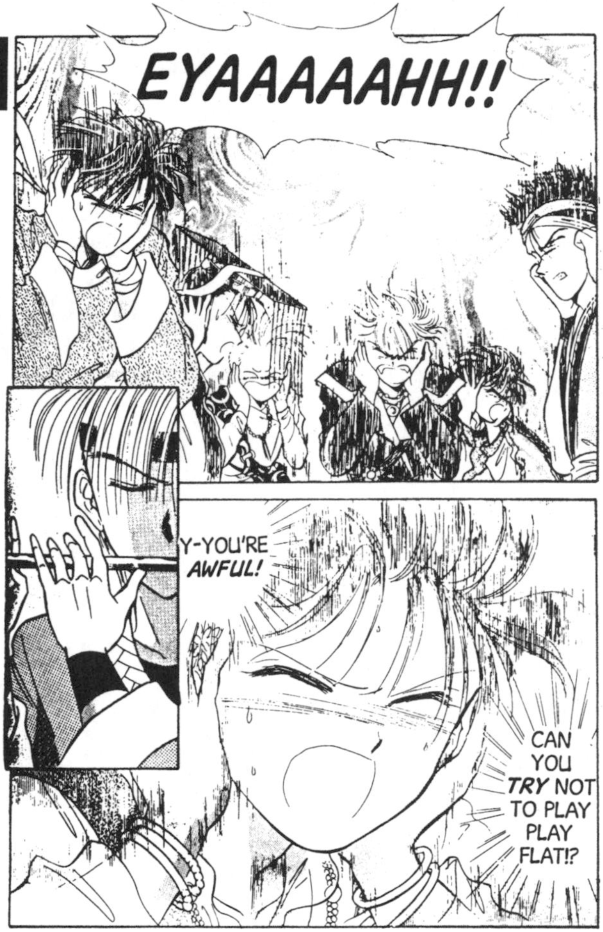
EYAAAAAAHH!!
Y-YOU'RE AWFUL!
CAN YOU TRY NOT TO PLAY PLAY FLAT!?

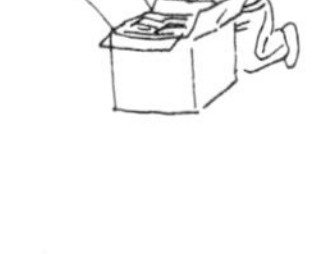
WHERE?
WHERE?
WHERE?

This seems like an obvious joke, but I only got two messages suggesting it. Still, it's really funny. One person's suggestion was much the same, but after the complaint, It's like they actually died from it.

There were several other really funny suggestions, but we'll leave them for later.

* Oh! I didn't get a chance to mention this in the chat sections, but thanks to everyone who bought the FY CD book! I hear the reviews were mostly favorable... I had no complaints with the voice actors. By the way, did you notice Tamahome's song, Kimi o Mamoritai ("I Want to Protect You")? At the end of the second verse, during the bridge, there were some words with digital effects over them. They are, "unmei" ("fate"), "densetsu" ("legend"), "kiseki no hito" ("miraculous one"), "shukumei" ("destiny"), and "seiza no sadame" ("fortune in the stars"). Probably! Oh, and of the seven images in the FY Calendar, six are originals that I still have to draw! Until next time!

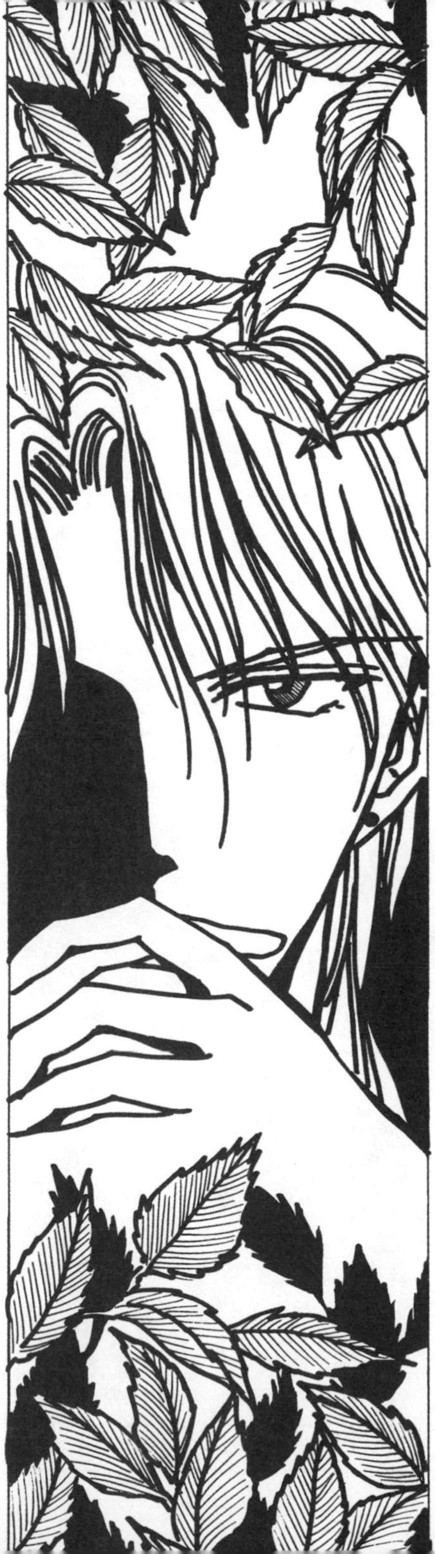

# CHAPTER FORTY-TWO

## REMINISCENCE OF THE FUTURE

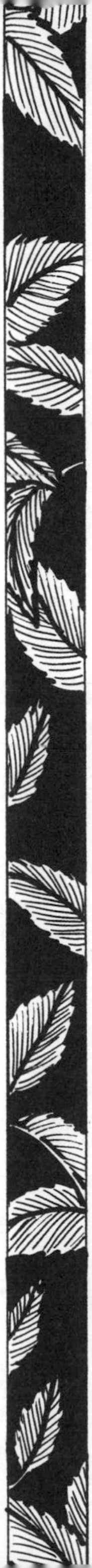

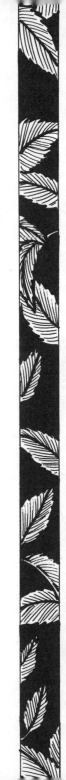

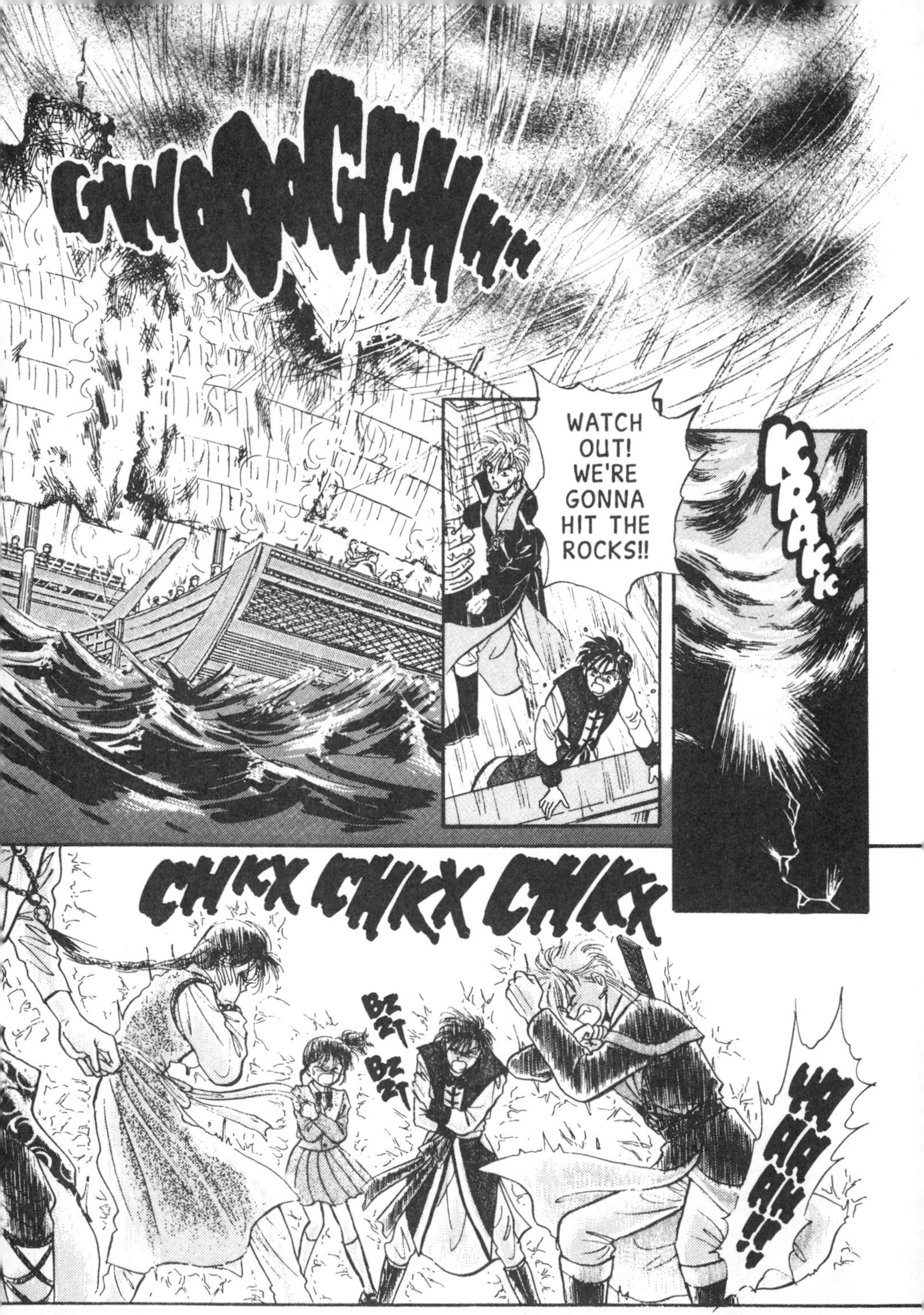
GWOOOGCHHH...
WATCH OUT! WE'RE GONNA HIT THE ROCKS!!
KRAKK
CHKX CHKX CHKX
BZZT BZZT
WAAAAH!!!

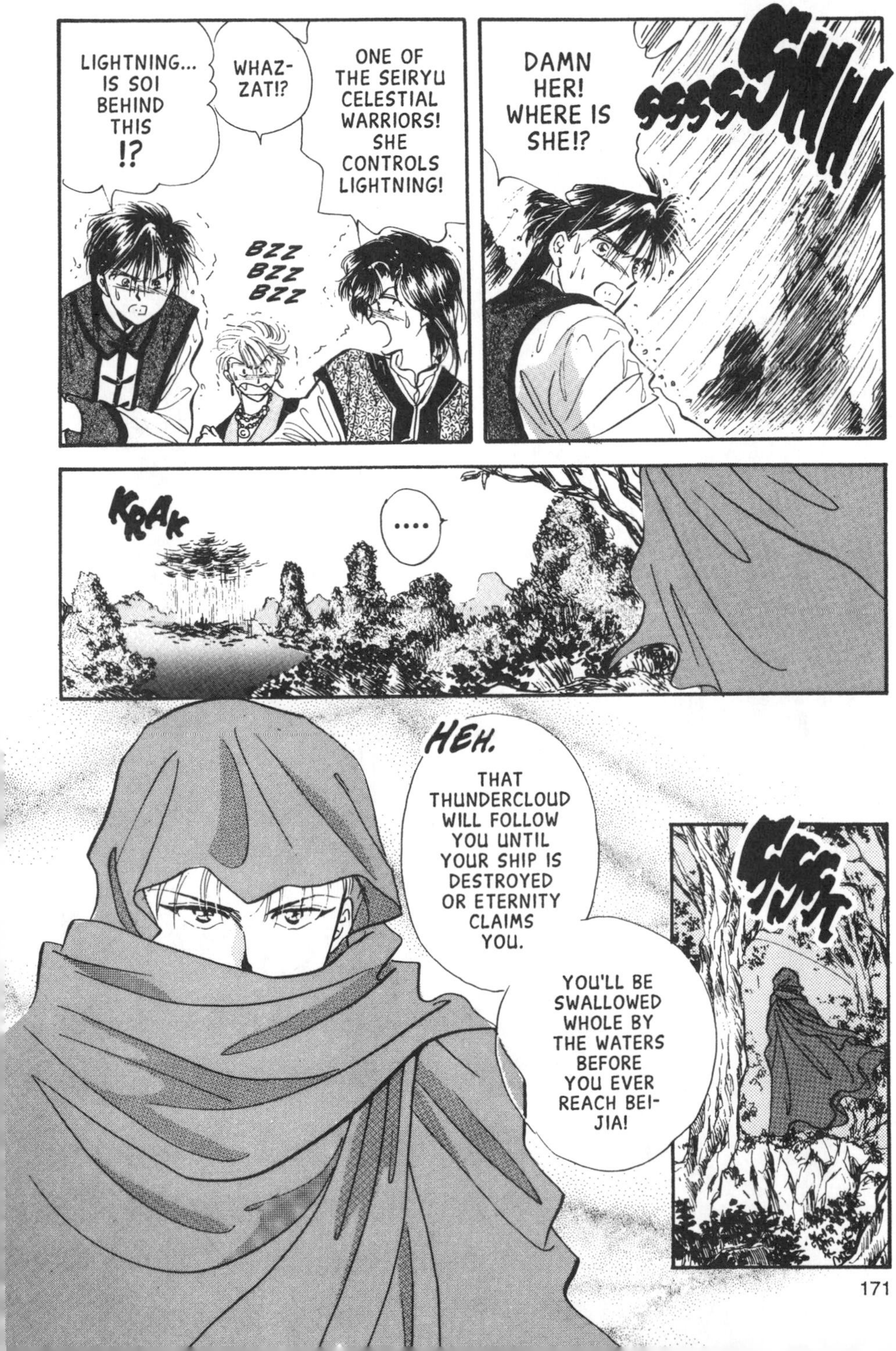
LIGHTNING... IS SOI BEHIND THIS !?
WHAZ-ZAT!?
ONE OF THE SEIRYU CELESTIAL WARRIORS! SHE CONTROLS LIGHTNING!
BZZ BZZ BZZ
DAMN HER! WHERE IS SHE!?
SSSSSSHH
KRAK
....
HEH.
THAT THUNDERCLOUD WILL FOLLOW YOU UNTIL YOUR SHIP IS DESTROYED OR ETERNITY CLAIMS YOU.
YOU'LL BE SWALLOWED WHOLE BY THE WATERS BEFORE YOU EVER REACH BEI-JIA!

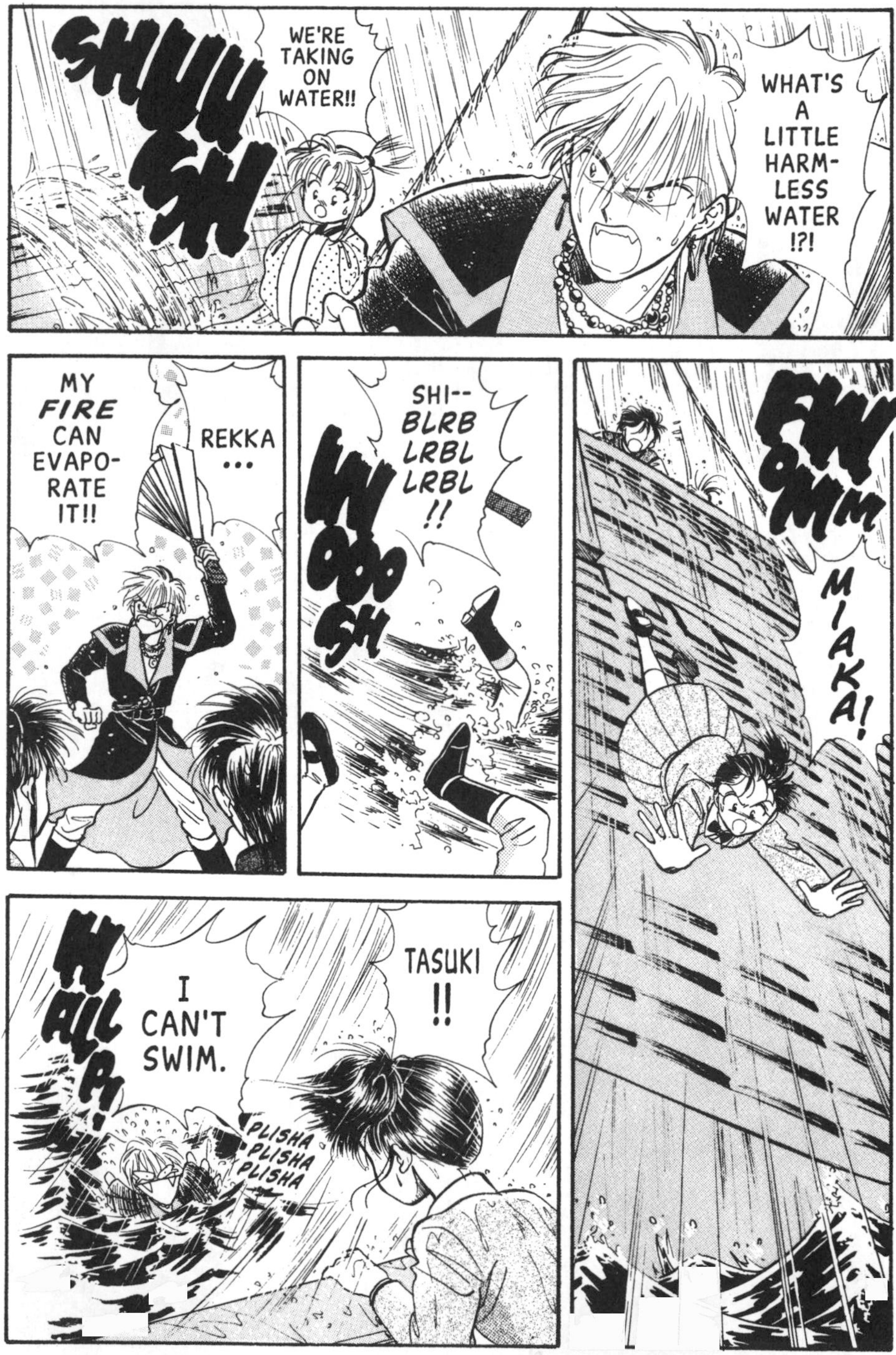
SHUUUSH
WE'RE TAKING ON WATER!!
WHAT'S A LITTLE HARMLESS WATER !?!
MY FIRE CAN EVAPORATE IT!!
REKKA...
SHI--BLRB LRBL LRBL !!
WHOOOSH
WHALP!
I CAN'T SWIM.
TASUKI !!
PLISHA PLISHA PLISHA
FWOMM
MIAKA!

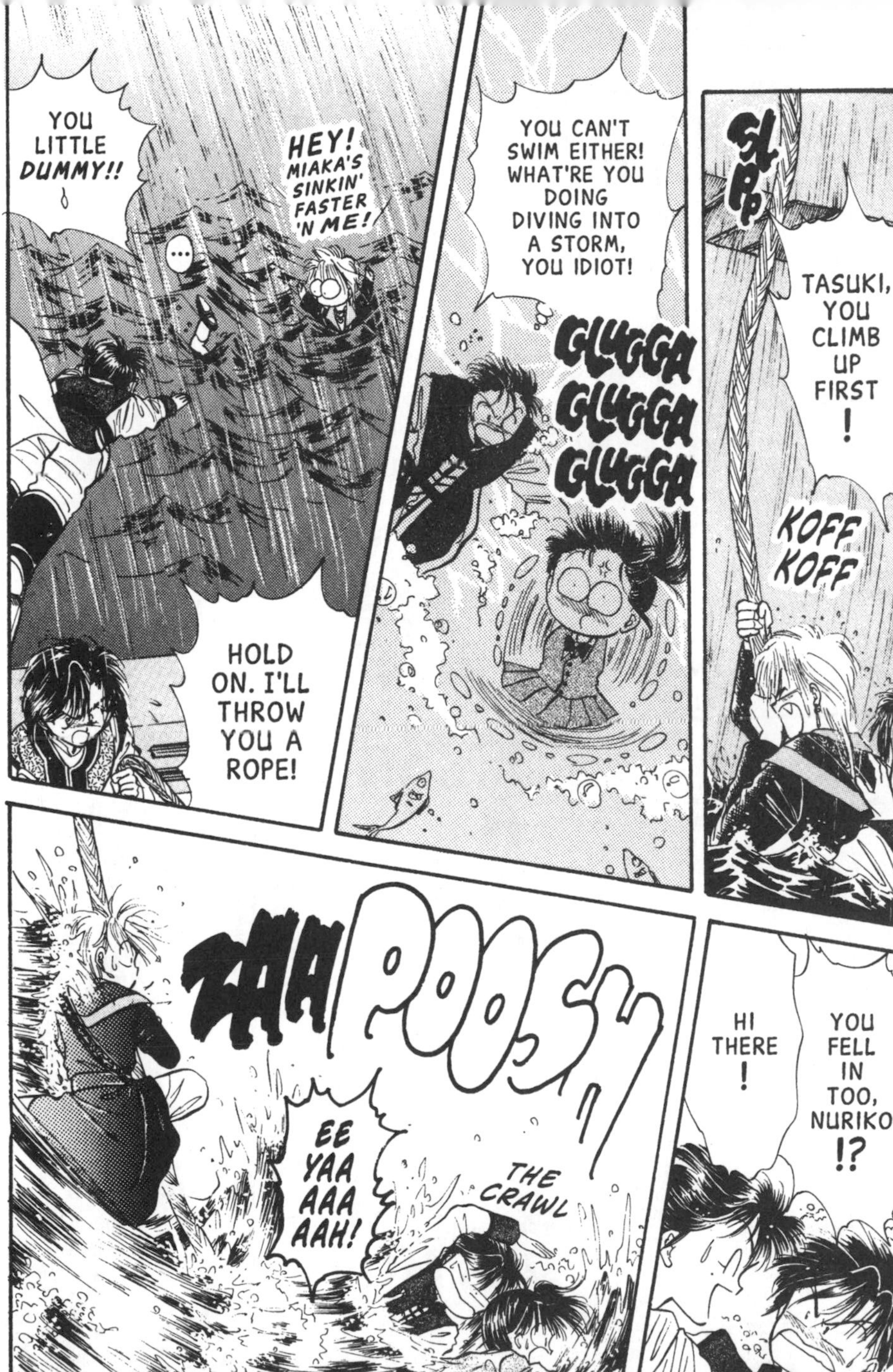

YOU LITTLE DUMMY!!
HEY! MIAKA'S SINKIN' FASTER 'N ME!
...
HOLD ON. I'LL THROW YOU A ROPE!
YOU CAN'T SWIM EITHER! WHAT'RE YOU DOING DIVING INTO A STORM, YOU IDIOT!
GLUGGA GLUGGA GLUGGA
SLIPP
TASUKI, YOU CLIMB UP FIRST!
KOFF KOFF
ZAA POOSH
EE YAAA AAA AAH!
THE CRAWL
HI THERE!
YOU FELL IN TOO, NURIKO!?

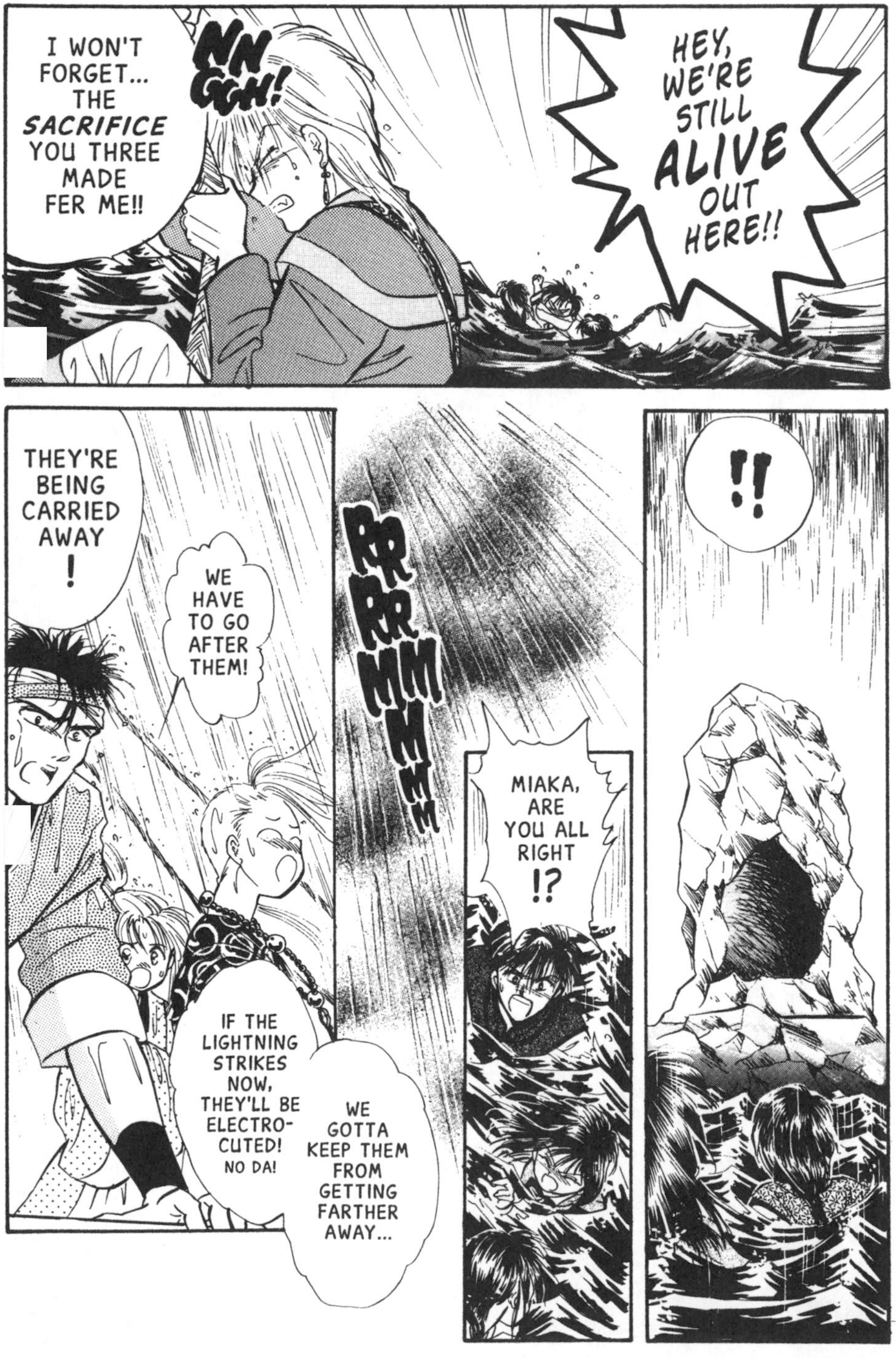
I WON'T FORGET... THE SACRIFICE YOU THREE MADE FER ME!!
NNGGH!
HEY, WE'RE STILL ALIVE OUT HERE!!
THEY'RE BEING CARRIED AWAY!
WE HAVE TO GO AFTER THEM!
IF THE LIGHTNING STRIKES NOW, THEY'LL BE ELECTRO-CUTED! NO DA!
WE GOTTA KEEP THEM FROM GETTING FARTHER AWAY...
RRRRMMMMM
MIAKA, ARE YOU ALL RIGHT!?
!!

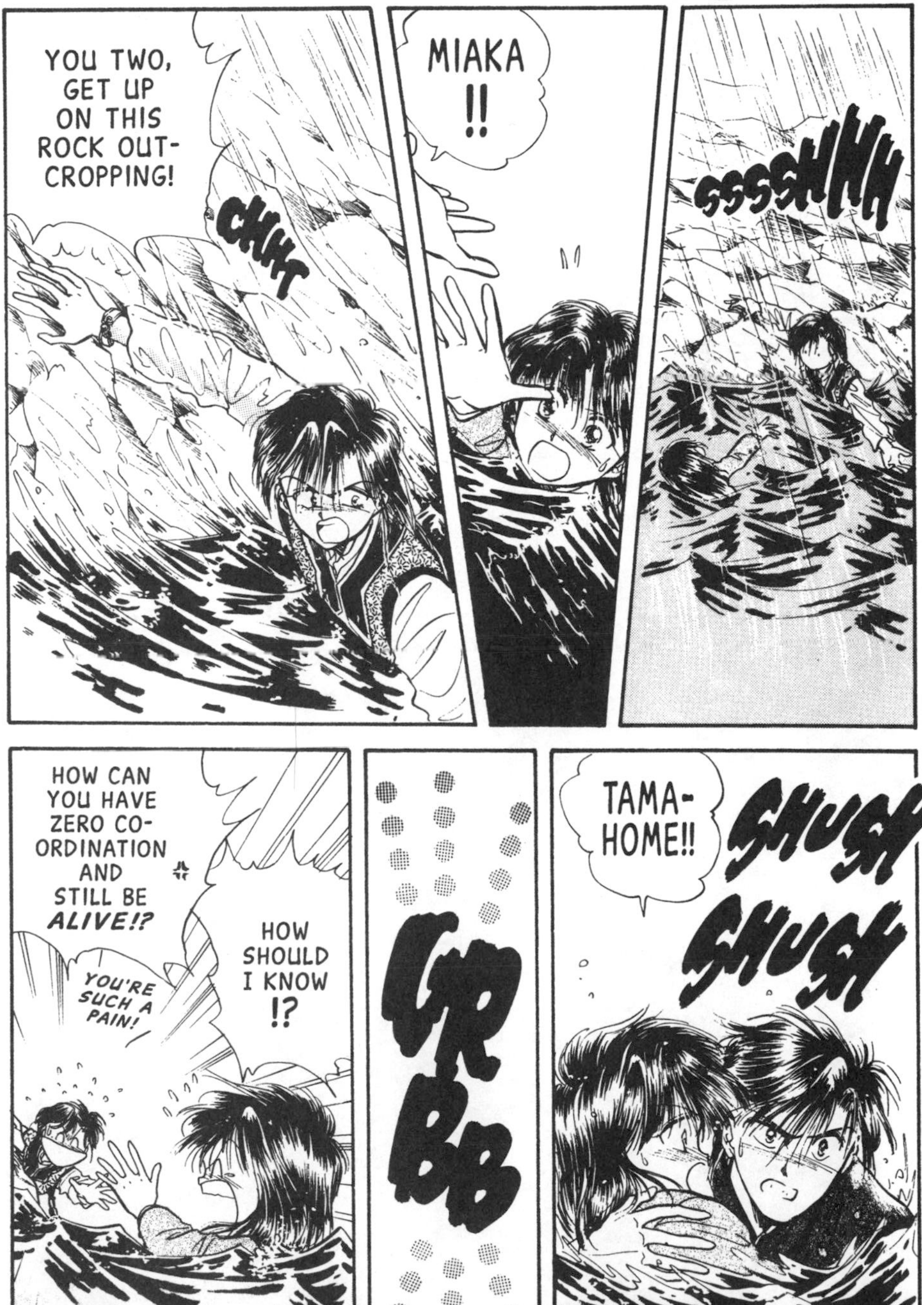
YOU TWO, GET UP ON THIS ROCK OUT-CROPPING!
CHHT
MIAKA !!
SSSSHHHH
HOW CAN YOU HAVE ZERO CO-ORDINATION AND STILL BE *ALIVE!?*
YOU'RE SUCH A PAIN!
HOW SHOULD I KNOW !?
GR BB
TAMA-HOME!!
SHUSH SHUSH

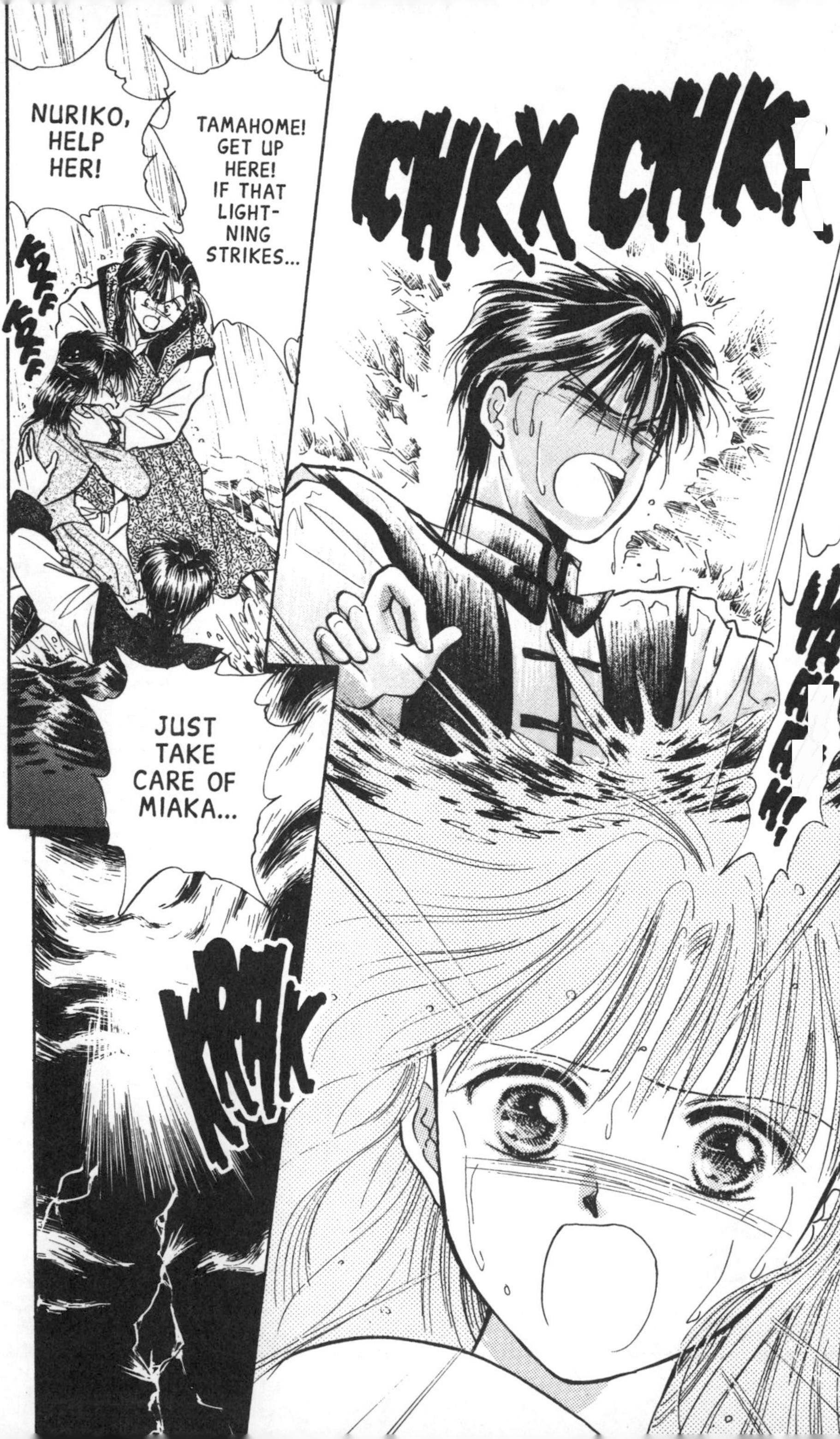
NURIKO, HELP HER!
TAMAHOME! GET UP HERE! IF THAT LIGHT-NING STRIKES...
KOFF KOFF
JUST TAKE CARE OF MIAKA...
WRAKK
CHKK CHKK
HAAAAAH!!

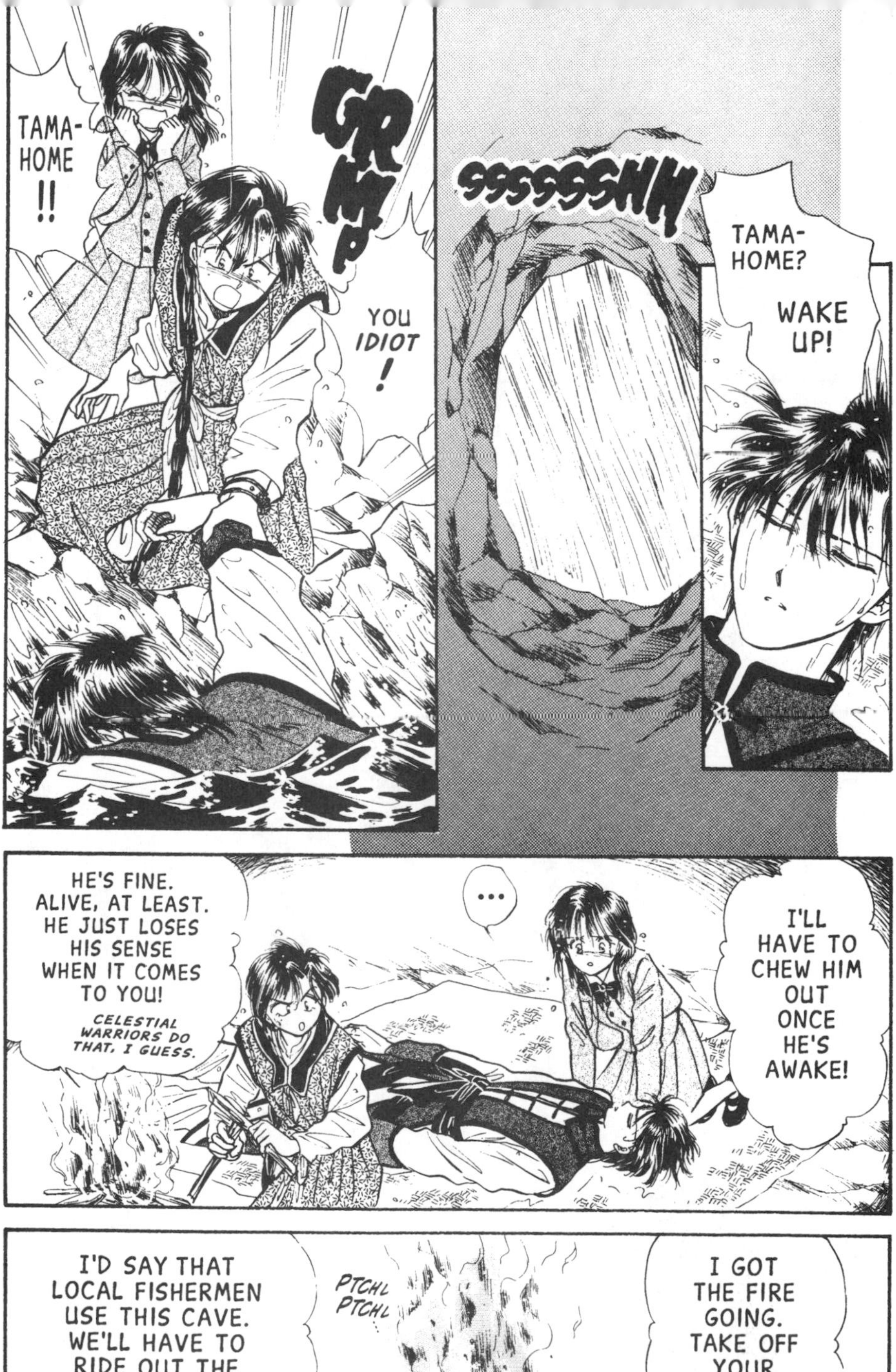
TAMA-HOME !!
GRMP
YOU IDIOT!
SSSSSSHH
TAMA-HOME?
WAKE UP!
HE'S FINE. ALIVE, AT LEAST. HE JUST LOSES HIS SENSE WHEN IT COMES TO YOU!
CELESTIAL WARRIORS DO THAT, I GUESS.
...
I'LL HAVE TO CHEW HIM OUT ONCE HE'S AWAKE!
I'D SAY THAT LOCAL FISHERMEN USE THIS CAVE. WE'LL HAVE TO RIDE OUT THE STORM HERE.
PTCHL PTCHL...
I GOT THE FIRE GOING. TAKE OFF YOUR CLOTHES.

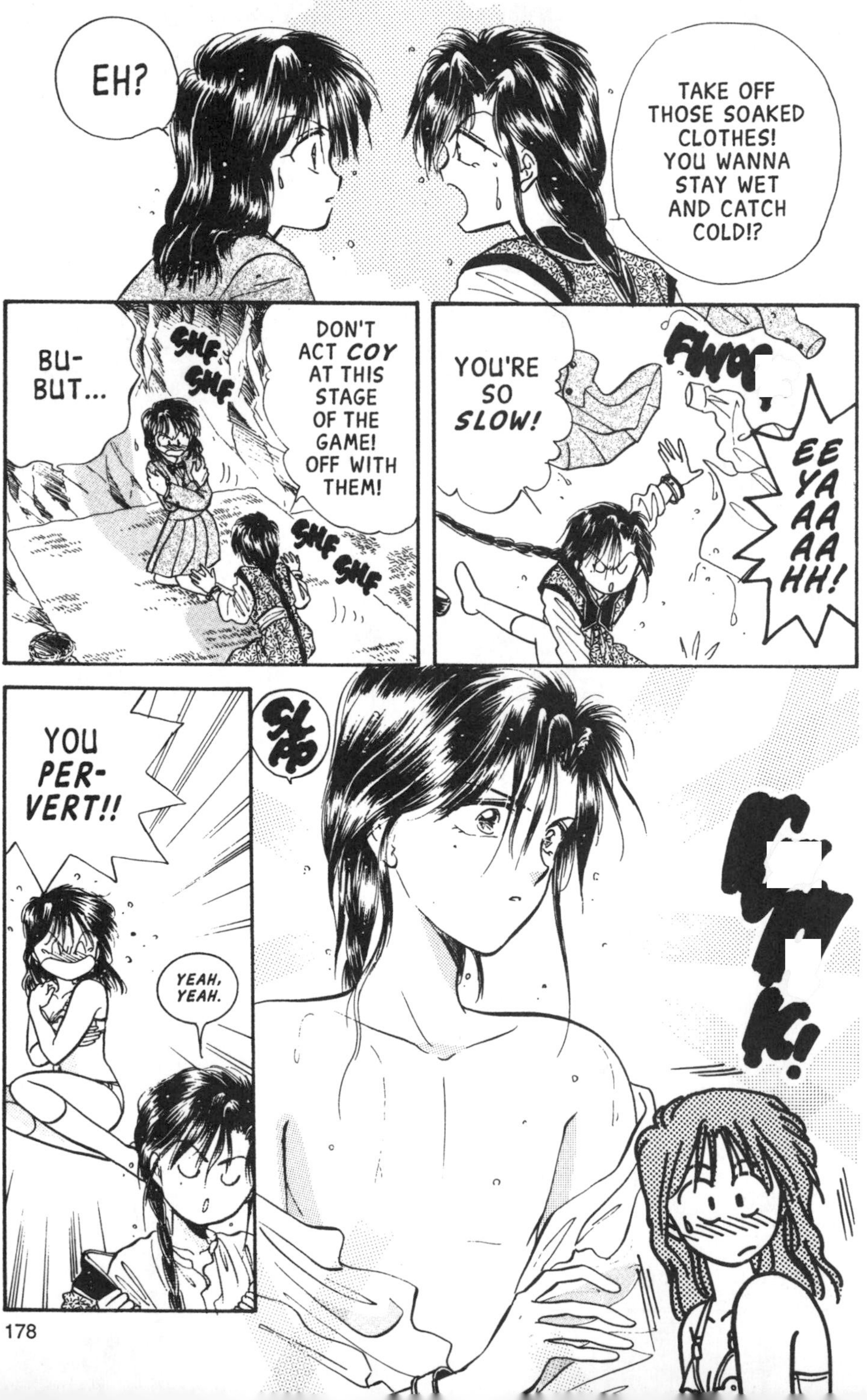
EH?
TAKE OFF THOSE SOAKED CLOTHES! YOU WANNA STAY WET AND CATCH COLD!?
BU- BUT...
SHF SHF
DON'T ACT *COY* AT THIS STAGE OF THE GAME! OFF WITH THEM!
SHF SHF
YOU'RE SO *SLOW!*
EEYAAAAAHH!
YOU *PERVERT!!*
YEAH, YEAH.
SLAP

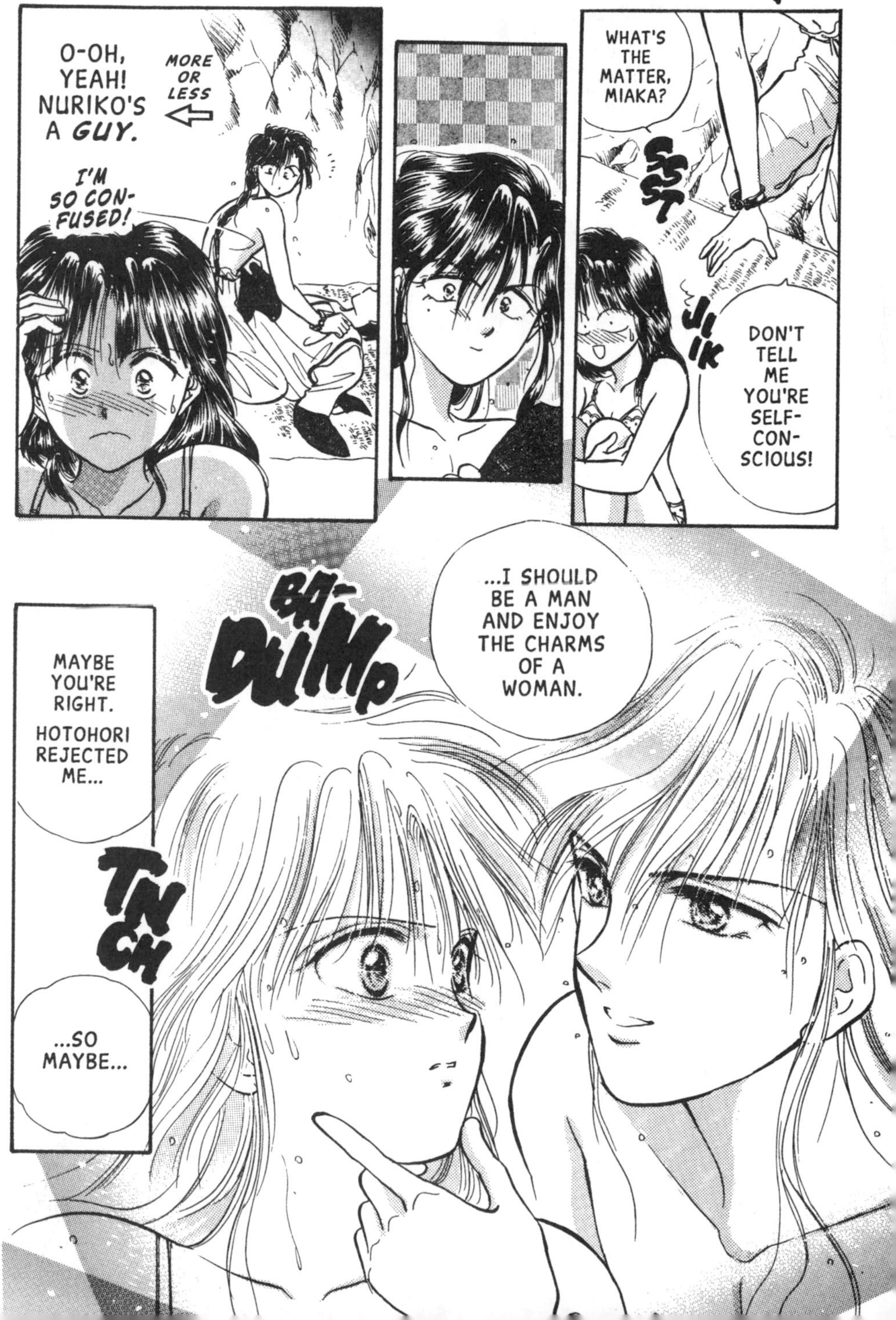
O-OH, YEAH! NURIKO'S A GUY.
MORE OR LESS
I'M SO CON-FUSED!
WHAT'S THE MATTER, MIAKA?
SSST
JIIK
DON'T TELL ME YOU'RE SELF-CONSCIOUS!
BA-DUMP
MAYBE YOU'RE RIGHT.
HOTOHORI REJECTED ME...
TNCH
...SO MAYBE...
...I SHOULD BE A MAN AND ENJOY THE CHARMS OF A WOMAN.

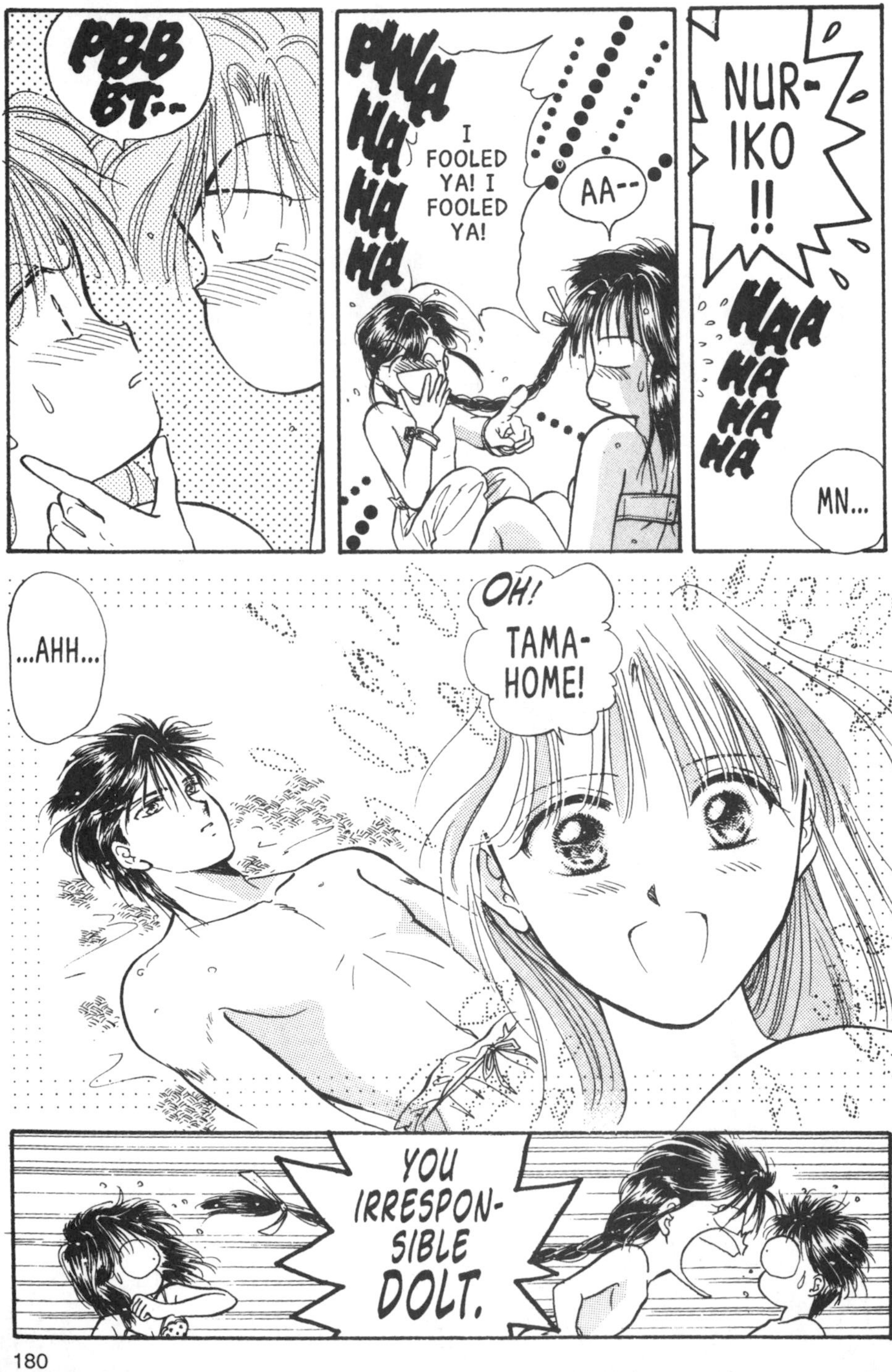
PBBBT--
PWAHAHAHAHAHA
I FOOLED YA! I FOOLED YA!
AA--
NUR-IKO!!
HAHAHAHAHA
MN...
...AHH...
OH! TAMA-HOME!
YOU IRRESPON-SIBLE DOLT.

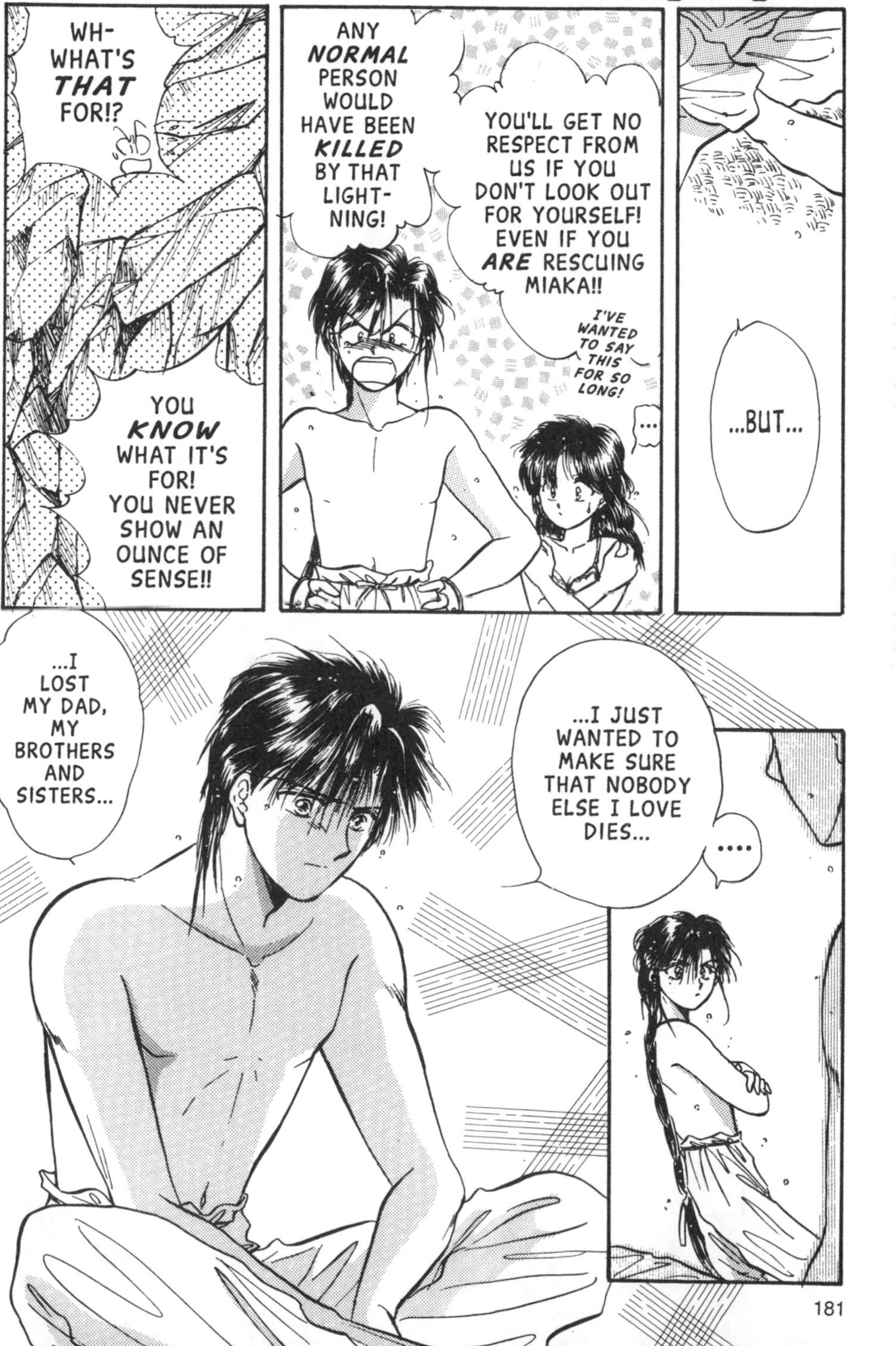
WH- WHAT'S THAT FOR!?
YOU KNOW WHAT IT'S FOR! YOU NEVER SHOW AN OUNCE OF SENSE!!
ANY NORMAL PERSON WOULD HAVE BEEN KILLED BY THAT LIGHT- NING!
YOU'LL GET NO RESPECT FROM US IF YOU DON'T LOOK OUT FOR YOURSELF! EVEN IF YOU ARE RESCUING MIAKA!!
I'VE WANTED TO SAY THIS FOR SO LONG!
...
...BUT...
...I LOST MY DAD, MY BROTHERS AND SISTERS...
...I JUST WANTED TO MAKE SURE THAT NOBODY ELSE I LOVE DIES...
....

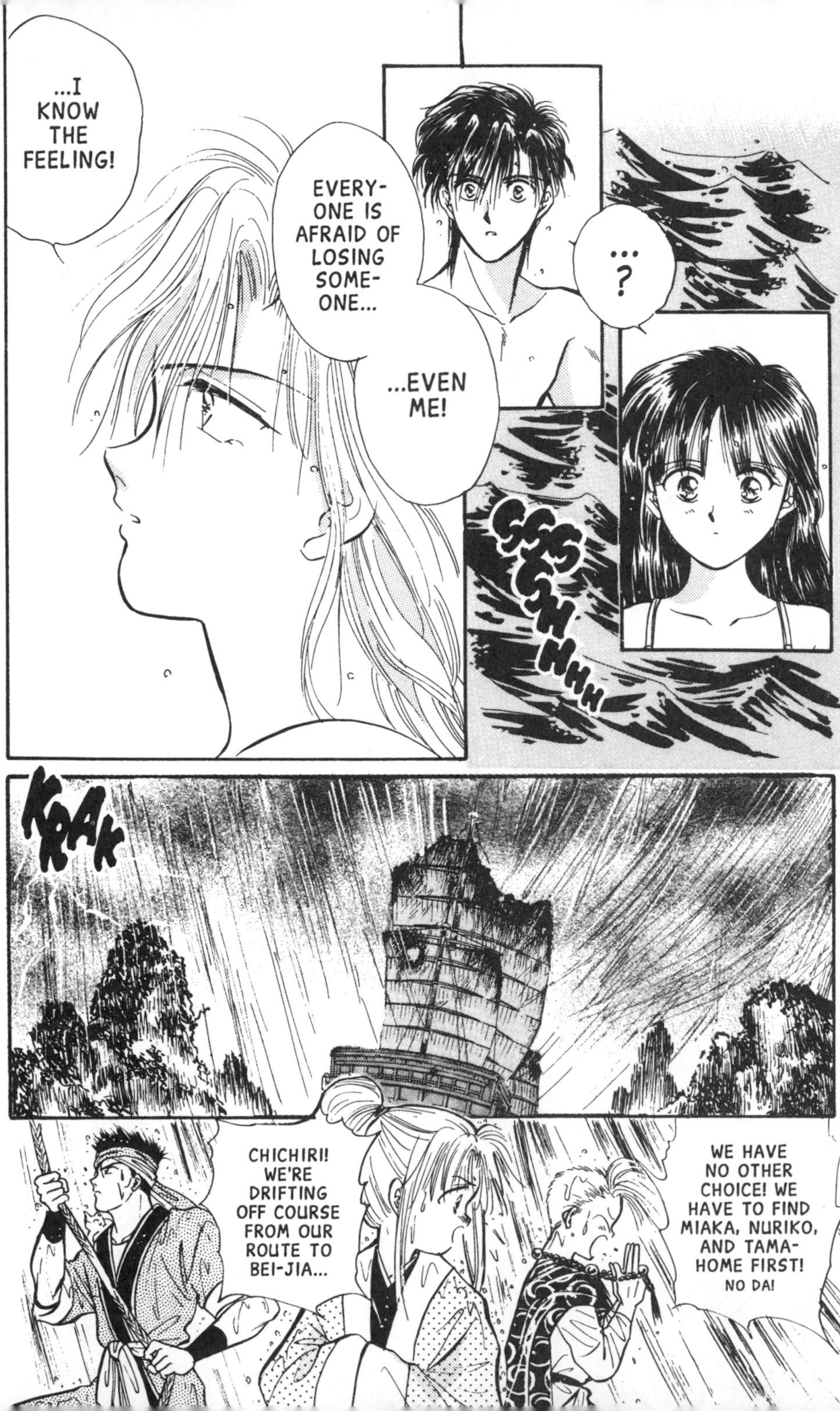
...I KNOW THE FEELING!
EVERY-ONE IS AFRAID OF LOSING SOME-ONE...
...EVEN ME!
...?
SSSHHHHH
KRAK
CHICHIRI! WE'RE DRIFTING OFF COURSE FROM OUR ROUTE TO BEI-JIA...
WE HAVE NO OTHER CHOICE! WE HAVE TO FIND MIAKA, NURIKO, AND TAMA-HOME FIRST! NO DA!

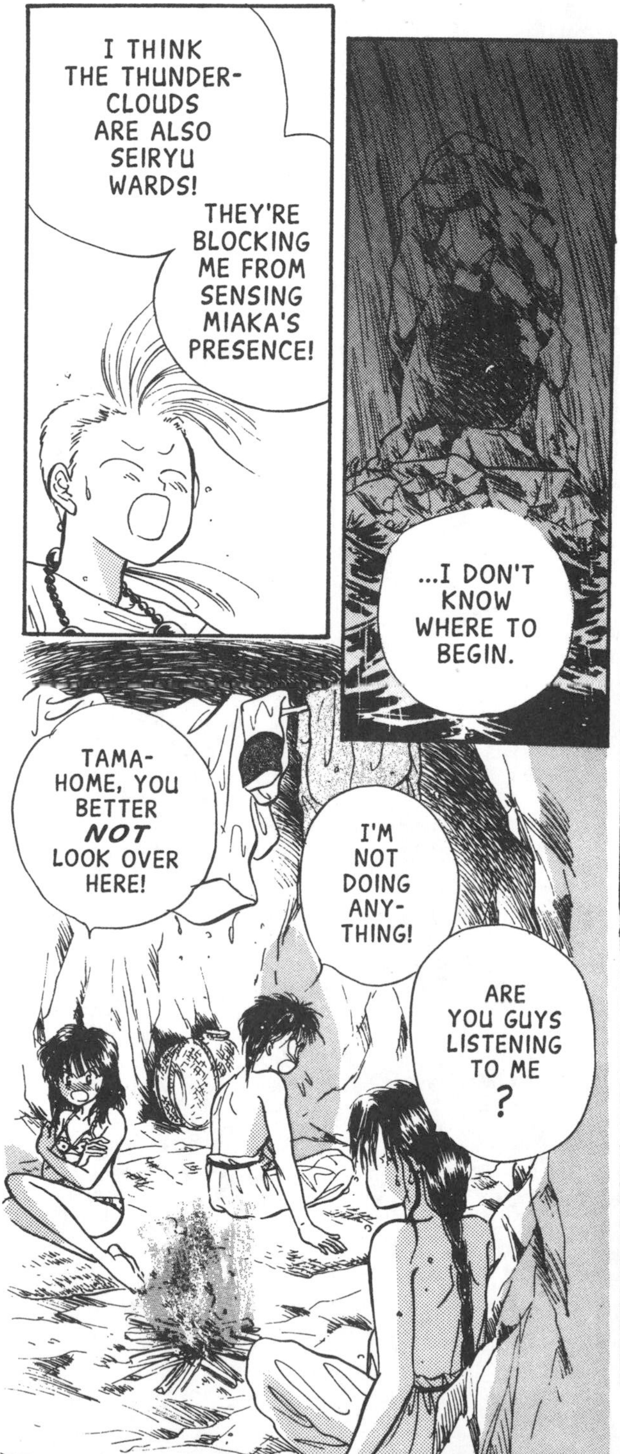
I THINK THE THUNDER-CLOUDS ARE ALSO SEIRYU WARDS!
THEY'RE BLOCKING ME FROM SENSING MIAKA'S PRESENCE!
...I DON'T KNOW WHERE TO BEGIN.
TAMA-HOME, YOU BETTER NOT LOOK OVER HERE!
I'M NOT DOING ANY-THING!
ARE YOU GUYS LISTENING TO ME?

## Castaway

I was given a dojinshi (fan-made comic) at a recent Fushigi Yūgi event. It was really entertaining (especially, the Nuriko story)! Thanks to Kobayashi in Chiba prefecture. A friend of mine went to the Comic Market (Comiket) and was totally shocked to see an appearance by "Yū Watase!" (It was someone else, apparently.) And I heard there was a dojinshi for B'z. Unlike other manga artists, I didn't launch my career with dojinshi, so I don't know that much about it (although my friends and assistants keep me informed). But I have to say the dojinshi shown to me have some really impressive artists. My friends and I did put together a book of original material right around the time I was first published, but I never really got that involved in the dojinshi scene... If any of you have my book, it's exremely rare. But whether you're a pro or amateur, the point is that you're drawing manga! And what matters most is that you enjoy what you're doing. *It's weird that I didn't know a thing about dojinshi or yaoi comics until I was 18. What was I doing?*

I also want to thank the people who shared their tricks for the game Street Fighter II! I was so crazy over it for a while. *I wasn't playing it right.*

See you all in volume 8!!

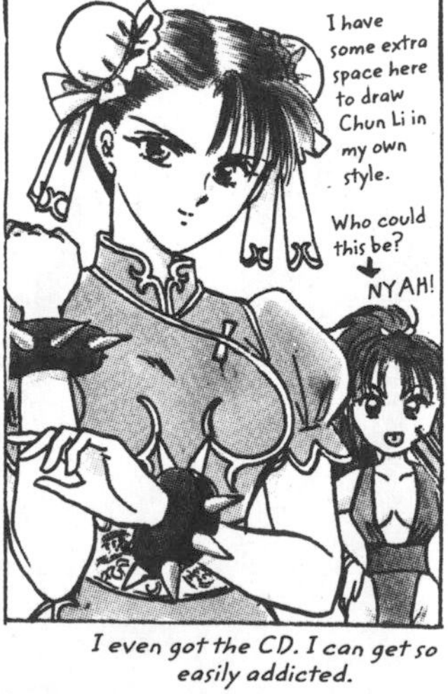
I have some extra space here to draw Chun Li in my own style.
Who could this be?
NYAH!

*I even got the CD. I can get so easily addicted.*

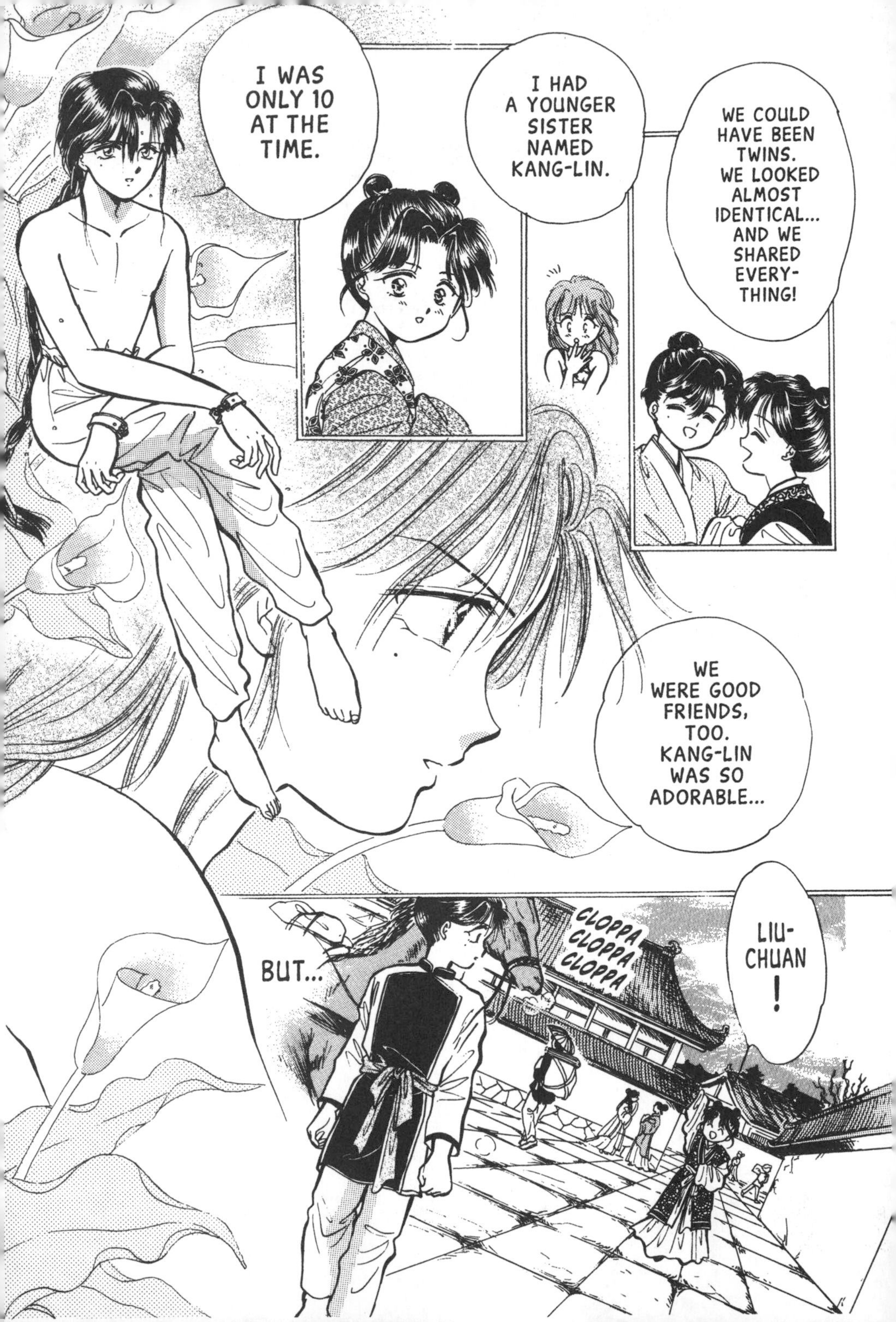
I WAS ONLY 10 AT THE TIME.
I HAD A YOUNGER SISTER NAMED KANG-LIN.
WE COULD HAVE BEEN TWINS. WE LOOKED ALMOST IDENTICAL... AND WE SHARED EVERY-THING!
WE WERE GOOD FRIENDS, TOO. KANG-LIN WAS SO ADORABLE...
BUT...
CLOPPA CLOPPA CLOPPA
LIU-CHUAN!

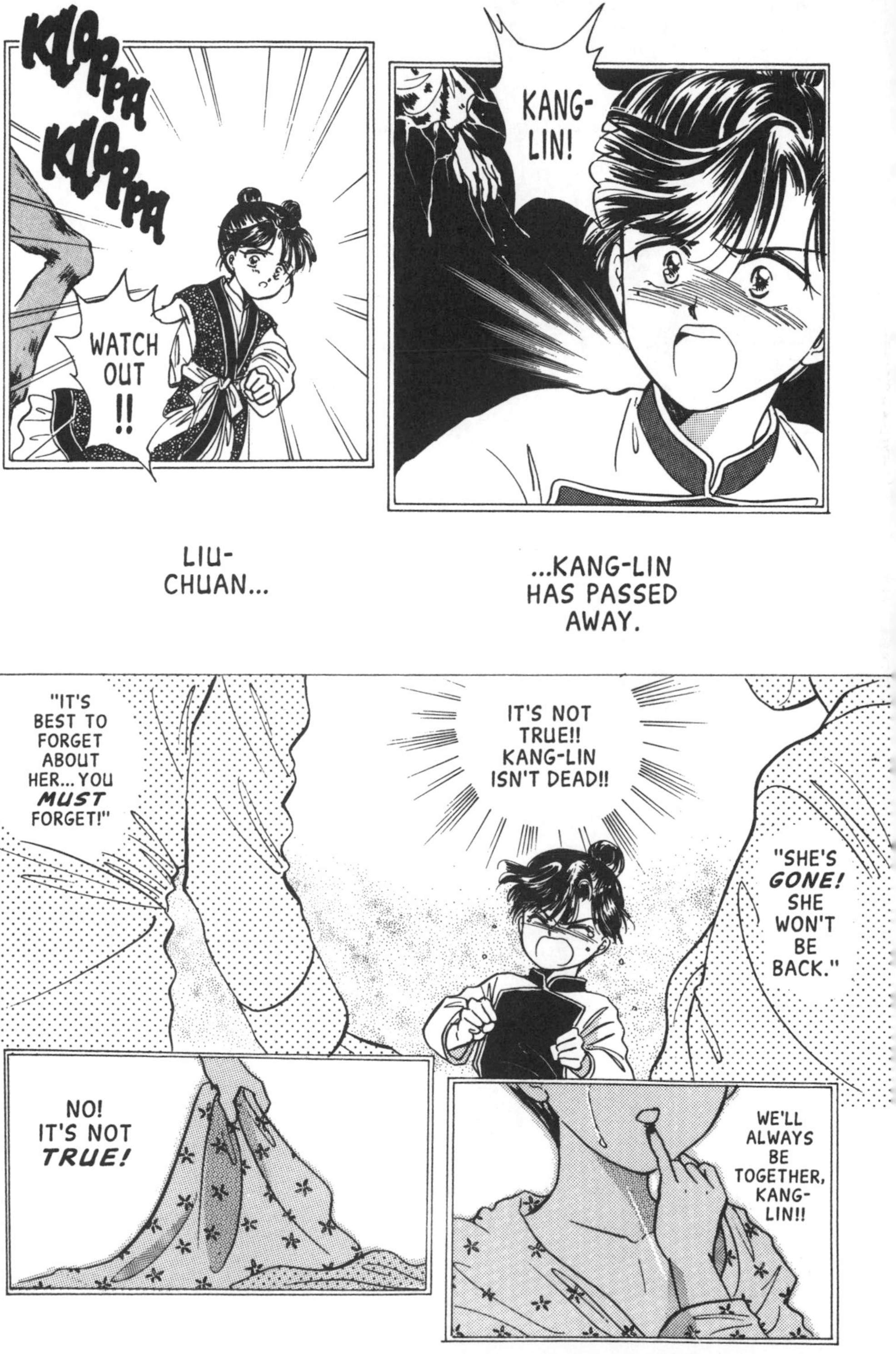
KLOPPA KLOPPA
WATCH OUT !!
KANG-LIN!
LIU-CHUAN...
...KANG-LIN HAS PASSED AWAY.
"IT'S BEST TO FORGET ABOUT HER... YOU *MUST* FORGET!"
IT'S NOT TRUE!! KANG-LIN ISN'T DEAD!!
"SHE'S *GONE!* SHE WON'T BE BACK."
NO! IT'S NOT *TRUE!*
WE'LL ALWAYS BE TOGETHER, KANG-LIN!!

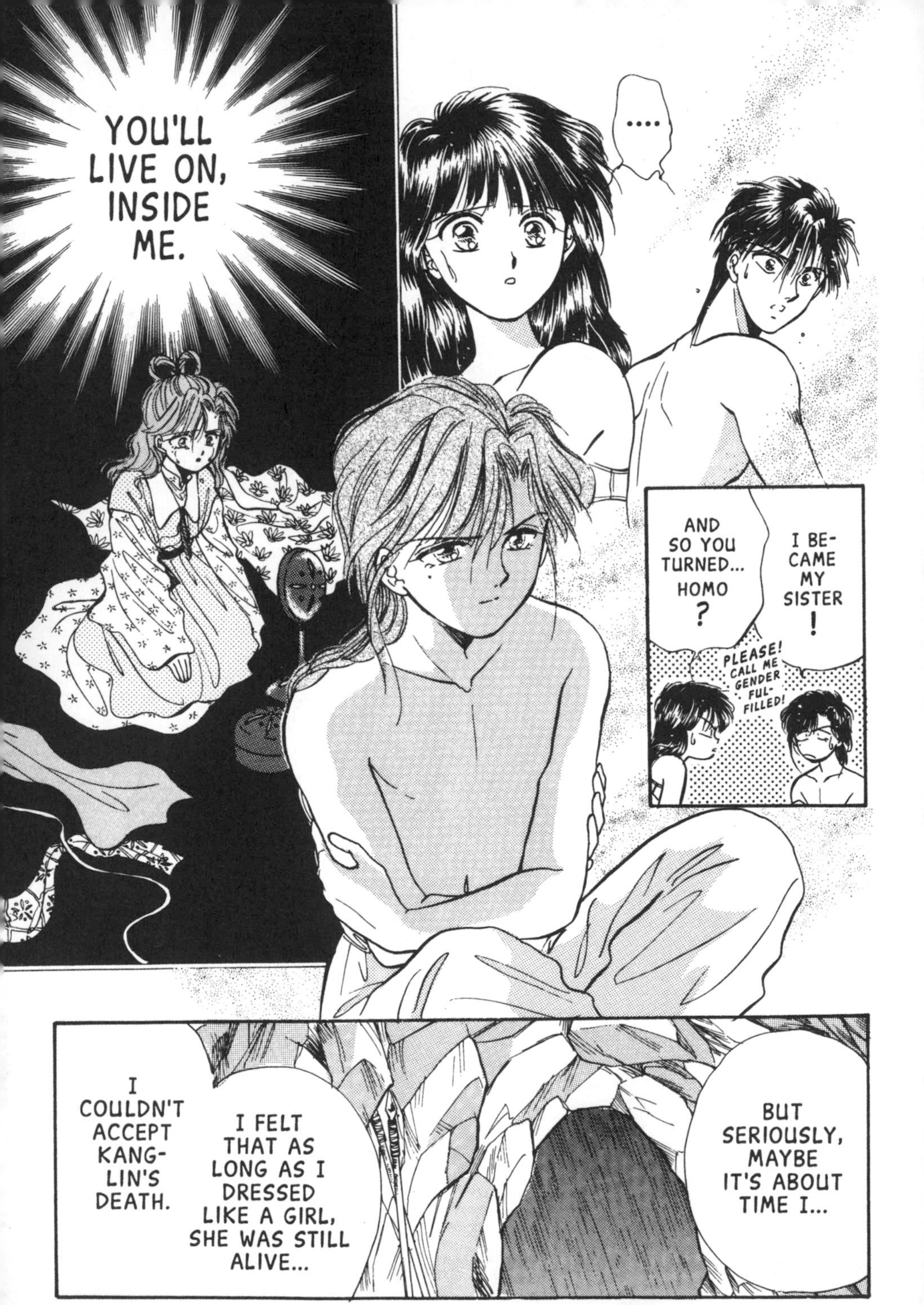
YOU'LL LIVE ON, INSIDE ME.
....
AND SO YOU TURNED... HOMO?
I BE-CAME MY SISTER!
PLEASE! CALL ME GENDER FUL-FILLED!
I COULDN'T ACCEPT KANG-LIN'S DEATH.
I FELT THAT AS LONG AS I DRESSED LIKE A GIRL, SHE WAS STILL ALIVE...
BUT SERIOUSLY, MAYBE IT'S ABOUT TIME I...

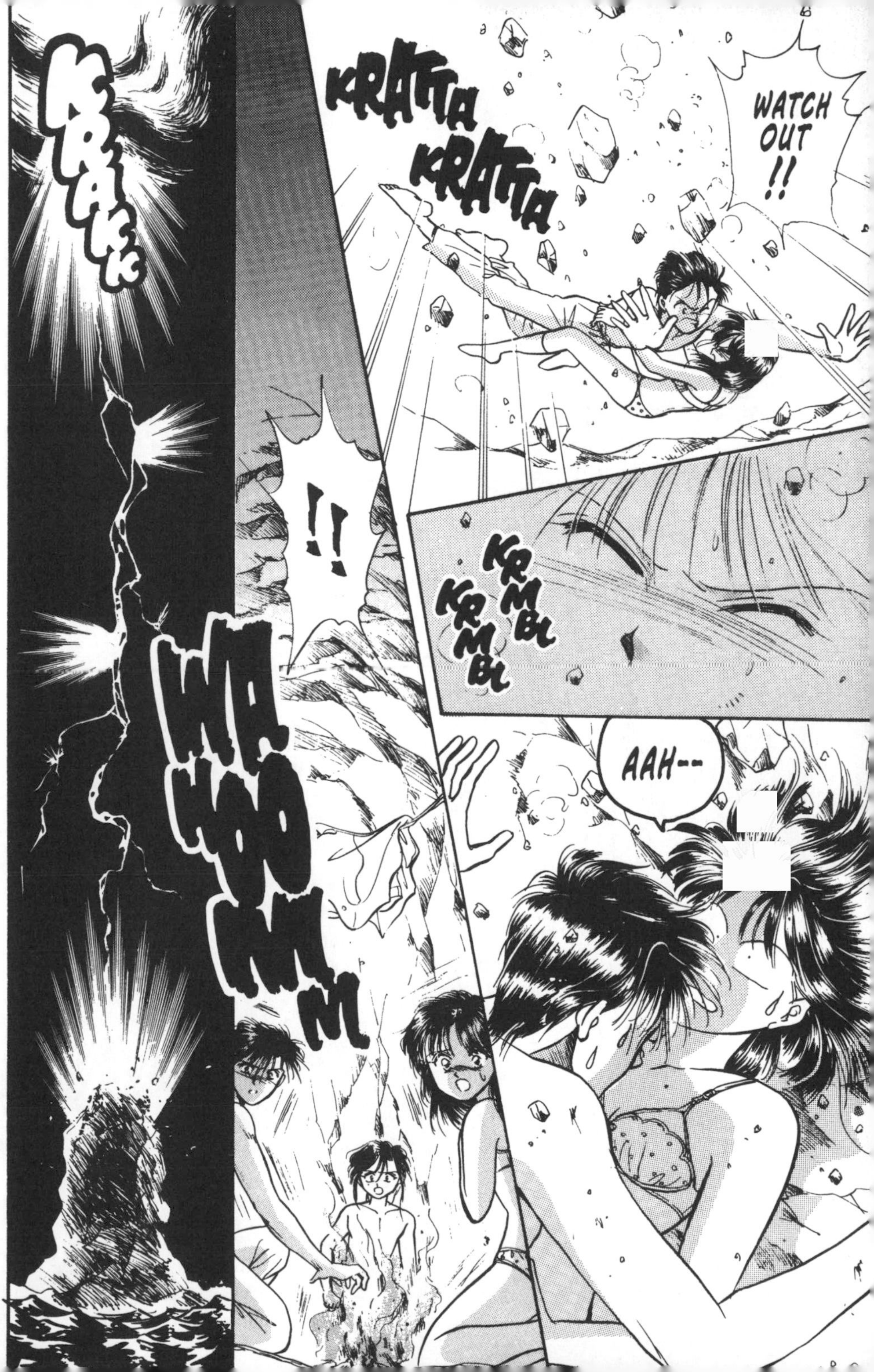
KRAACK
WHAWOOMM
!!
KRATTTA KRATTTA
WATCH OUT !!
KRMBL KRMBL
AAH--

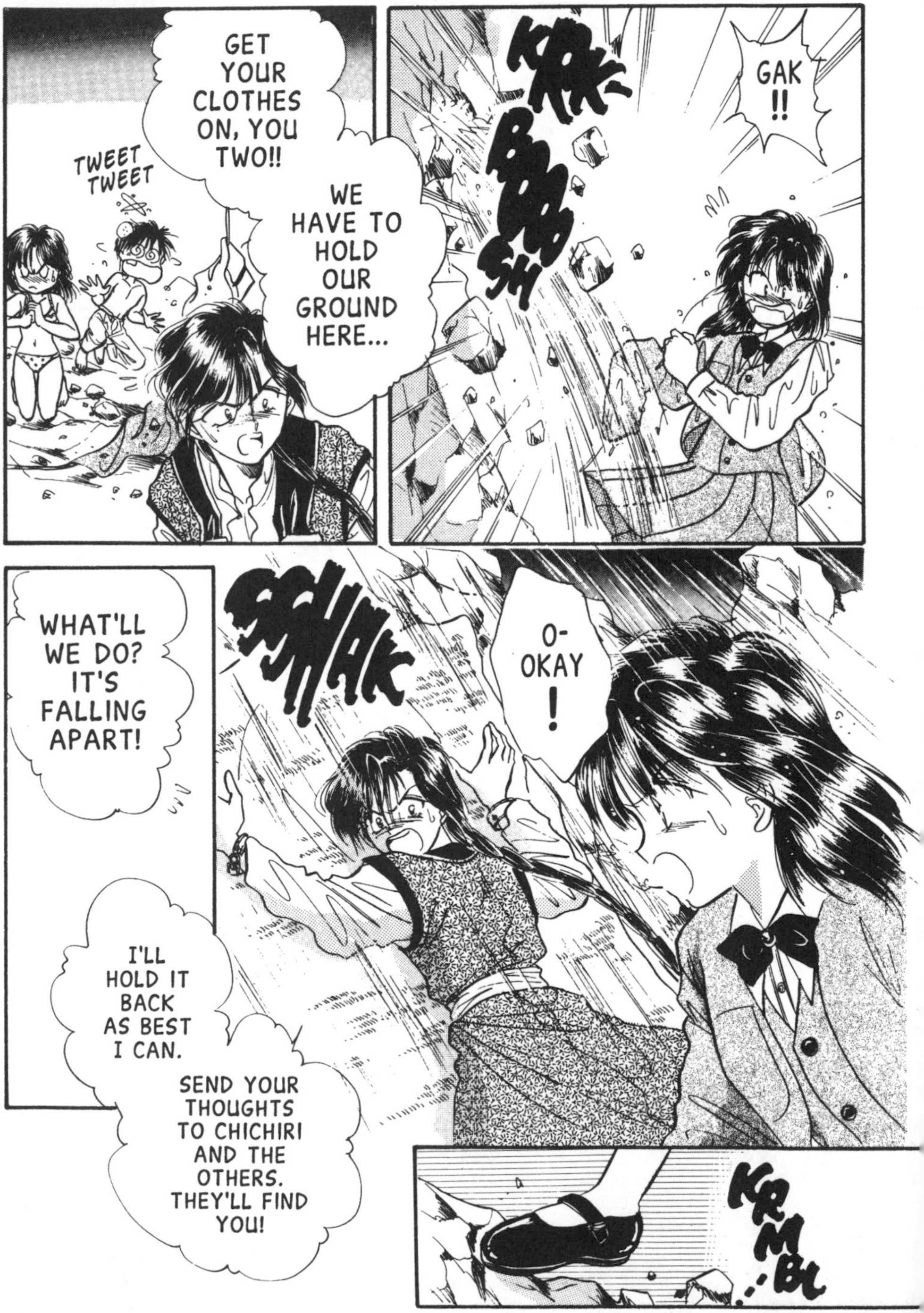
GET YOUR CLOTHES ON, YOU TWO!!
TWEET TWEET
WE HAVE TO HOLD OUR GROUND HERE...
GAK !!
WHAT'LL WE DO? IT'S FALLING APART!
O-OKAY !
I'LL HOLD IT BACK AS BEST I CAN.
SEND YOUR THOUGHTS TO CHICHIRI AND THE OTHERS. THEY'LL FIND YOU!

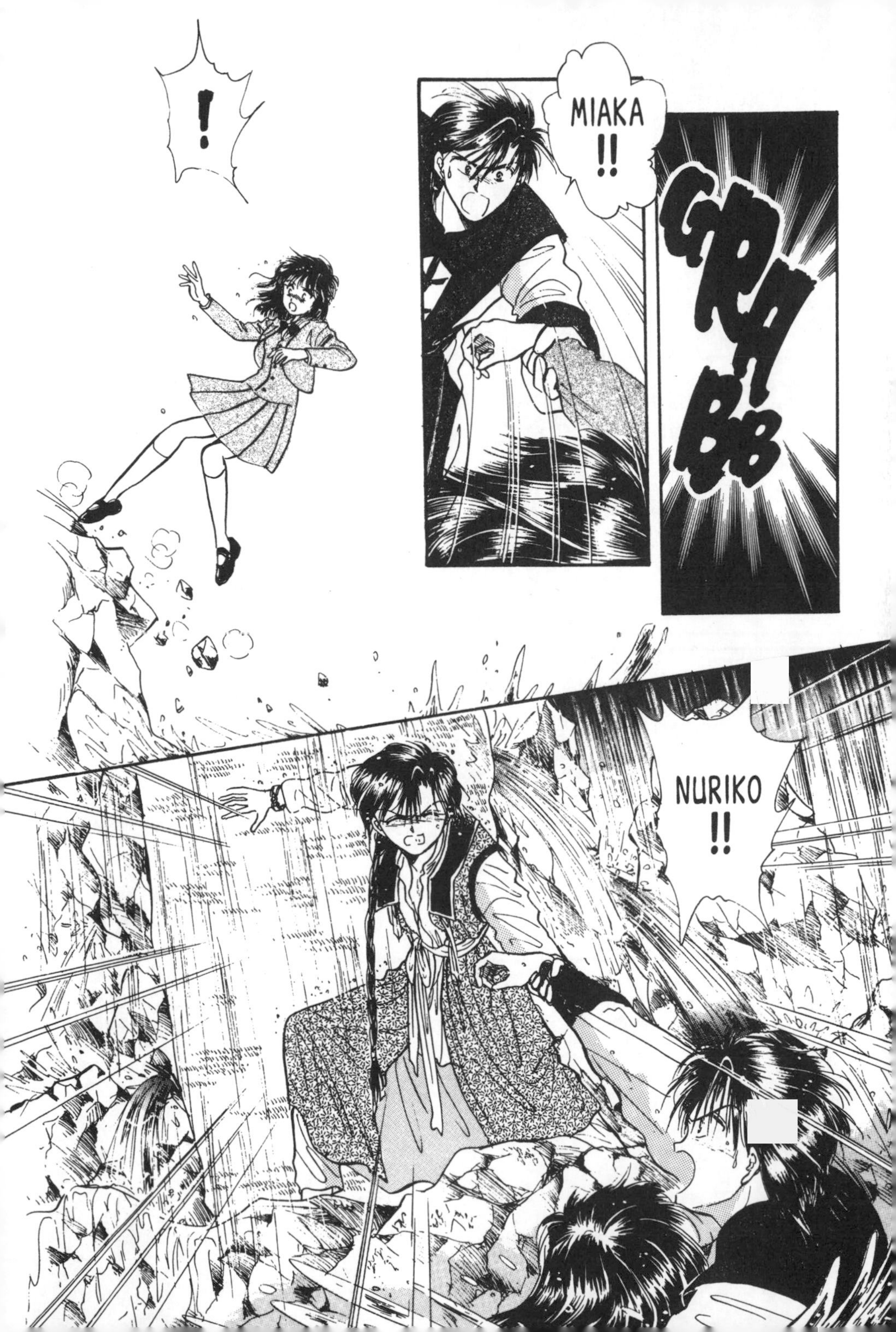
!
MIAKA !!
GRAB
NURIKO !!

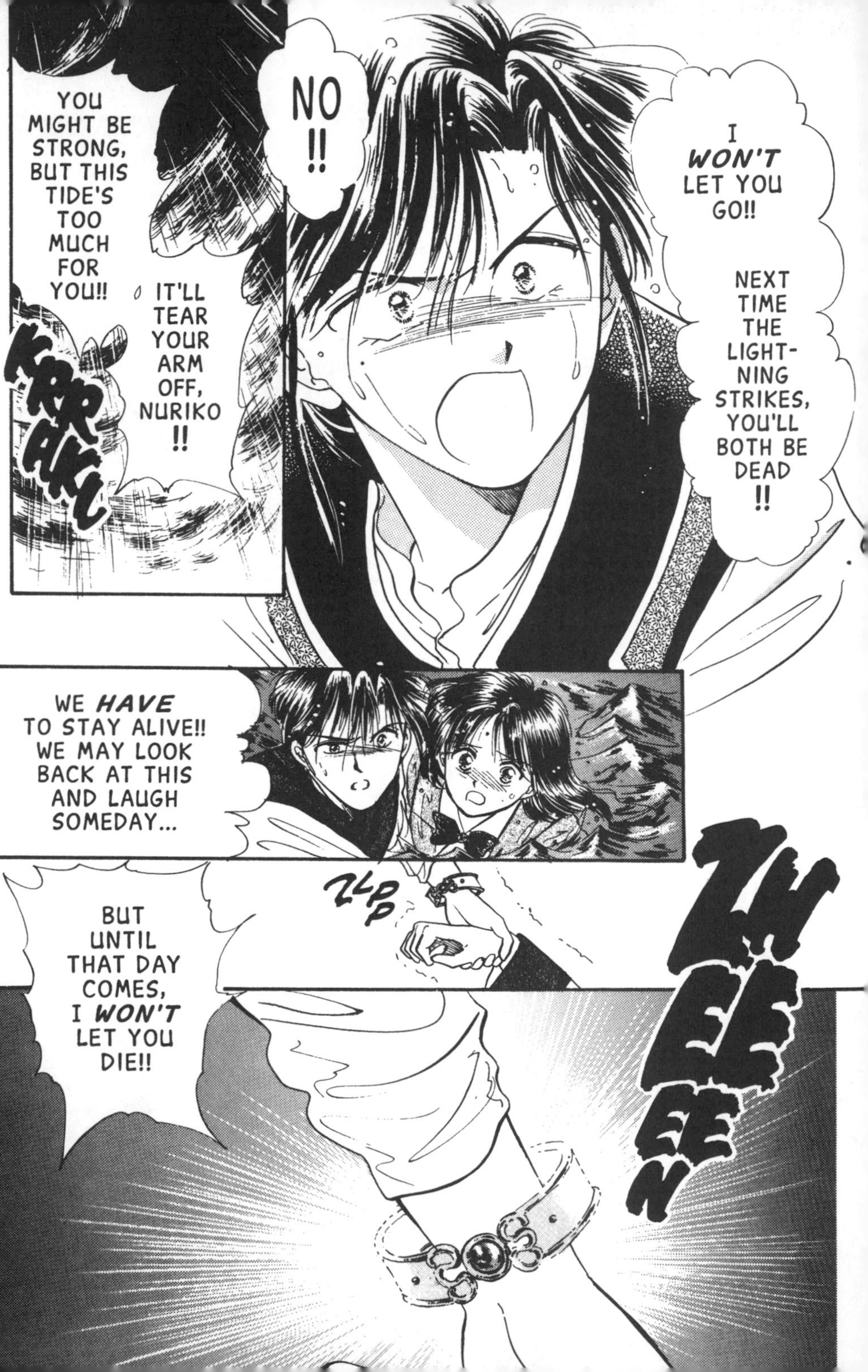

YOU MIGHT BE STRONG, BUT THIS TIDE'S TOO MUCH FOR YOU!!
IT'LL TEAR YOUR ARM OFF, NURIKO!!
NO!!
I *WON'T* LET YOU GO!!
NEXT TIME THE LIGHT-NING STRIKES, YOU'LL BOTH BE DEAD!!
WE *HAVE* TO STAY ALIVE!! WE MAY LOOK BACK AT THIS AND LAUGH SOMEDAY...
BUT UNTIL THAT DAY COMES, I *WON'T* LET YOU DIE!!

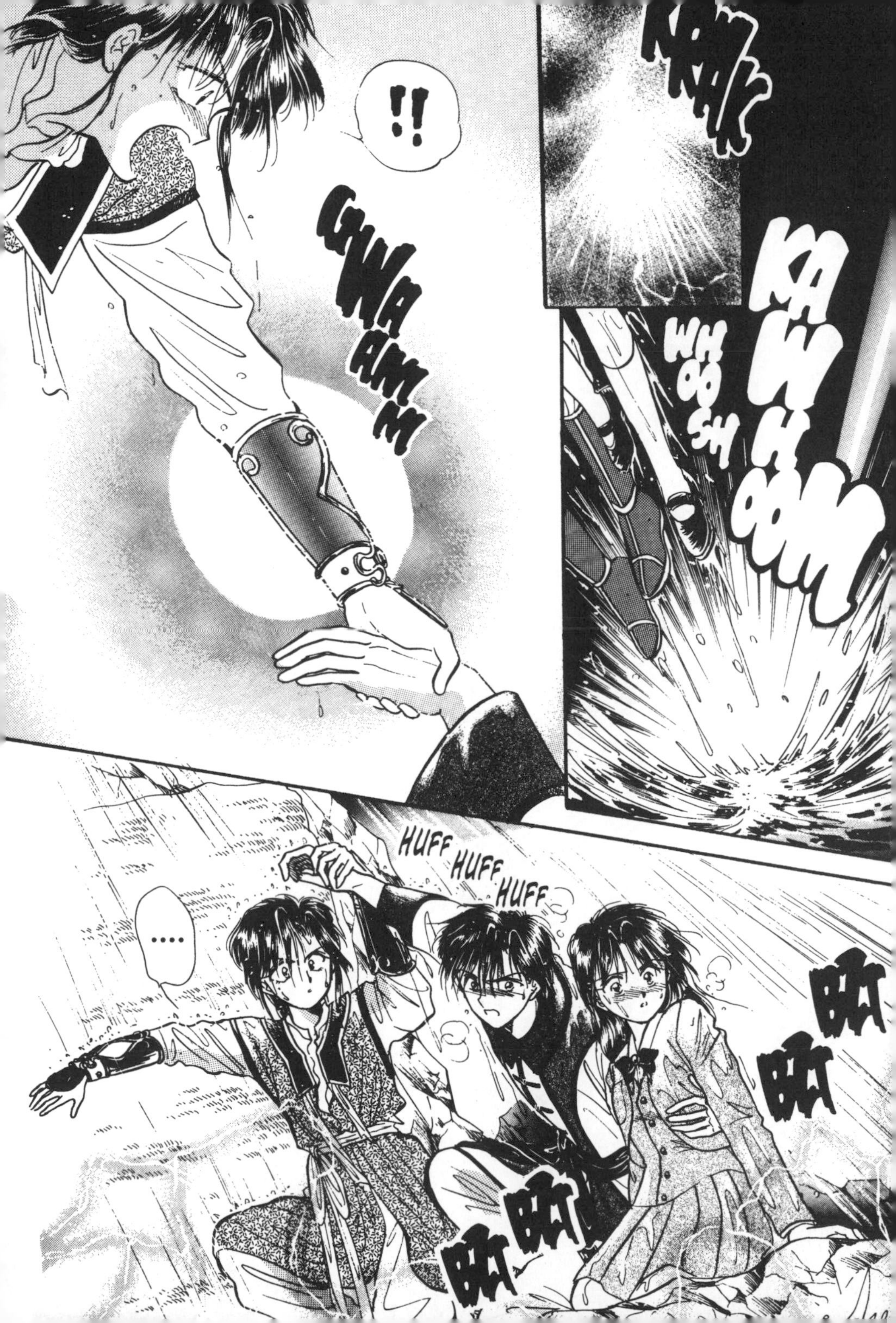
!!
GWAAMM
KRAK
WHOOSH
KAWHOOM
HUFF HUFF HUFF
....
BZZT BZZT
BZZT BZZT BZZT

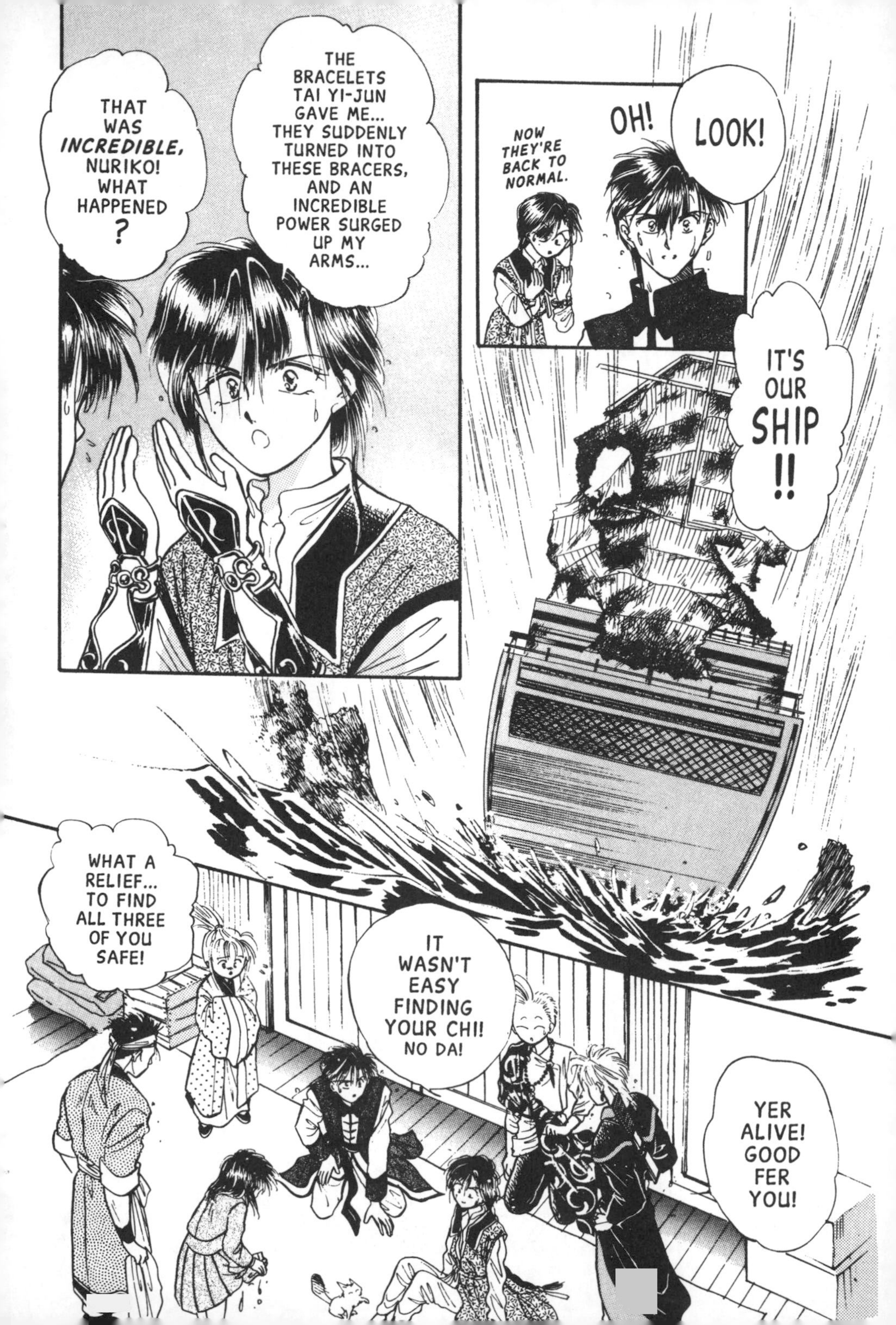
THAT WAS *INCREDIBLE,* NURIKO! WHAT HAPPENED ?
THE BRACELETS TAI YI-JUN GAVE ME... THEY SUDDENLY TURNED INTO THESE BRACERS, AND AN INCREDIBLE POWER SURGED UP MY ARMS...
NOW THEY'RE BACK TO NORMAL.
OH!
LOOK!
IT'S OUR SHIP !!
WHAT A RELIEF... TO FIND ALL THREE OF YOU SAFE!
IT WASN'T EASY FINDING YOUR CHI! NO DA!
YER ALIVE! GOOD FER YOU!

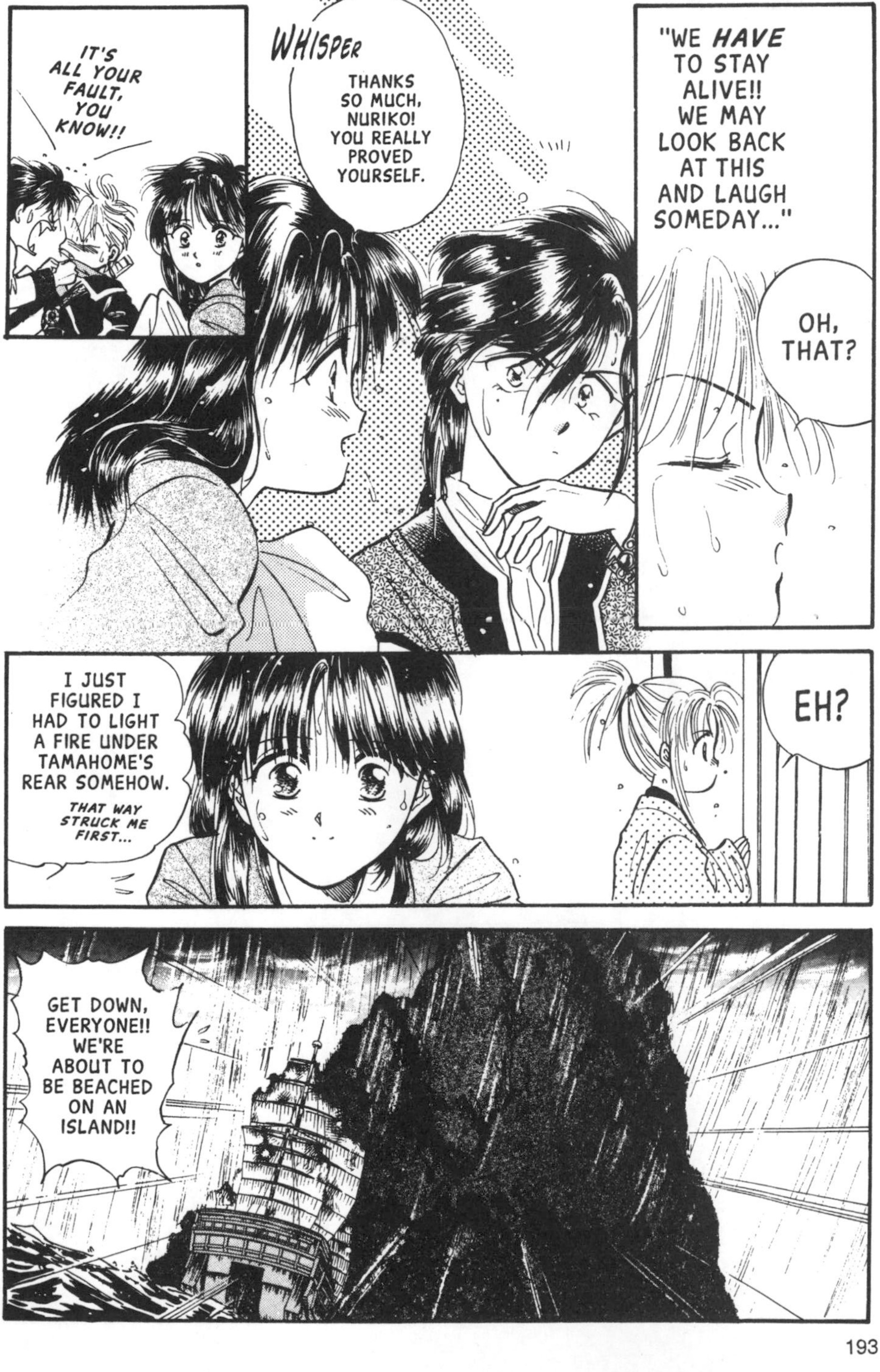
IT'S ALL YOUR FAULT, YOU KNOW!!
WHISPER
THANKS SO MUCH, NURIKO! YOU REALLY PROVED YOURSELF.
"WE *HAVE* TO STAY ALIVE!! WE MAY LOOK BACK AT THIS AND LAUGH SOMEDAY..."
OH, THAT?
I JUST FIGURED I HAD TO LIGHT A FIRE UNDER TAMAHOME'S REAR SOMEHOW.
THAT WAY STRUCK ME FIRST...
EH?
GET DOWN, EVERYONE!! WE'RE ABOUT TO BE BEACHED ON AN ISLAND!!

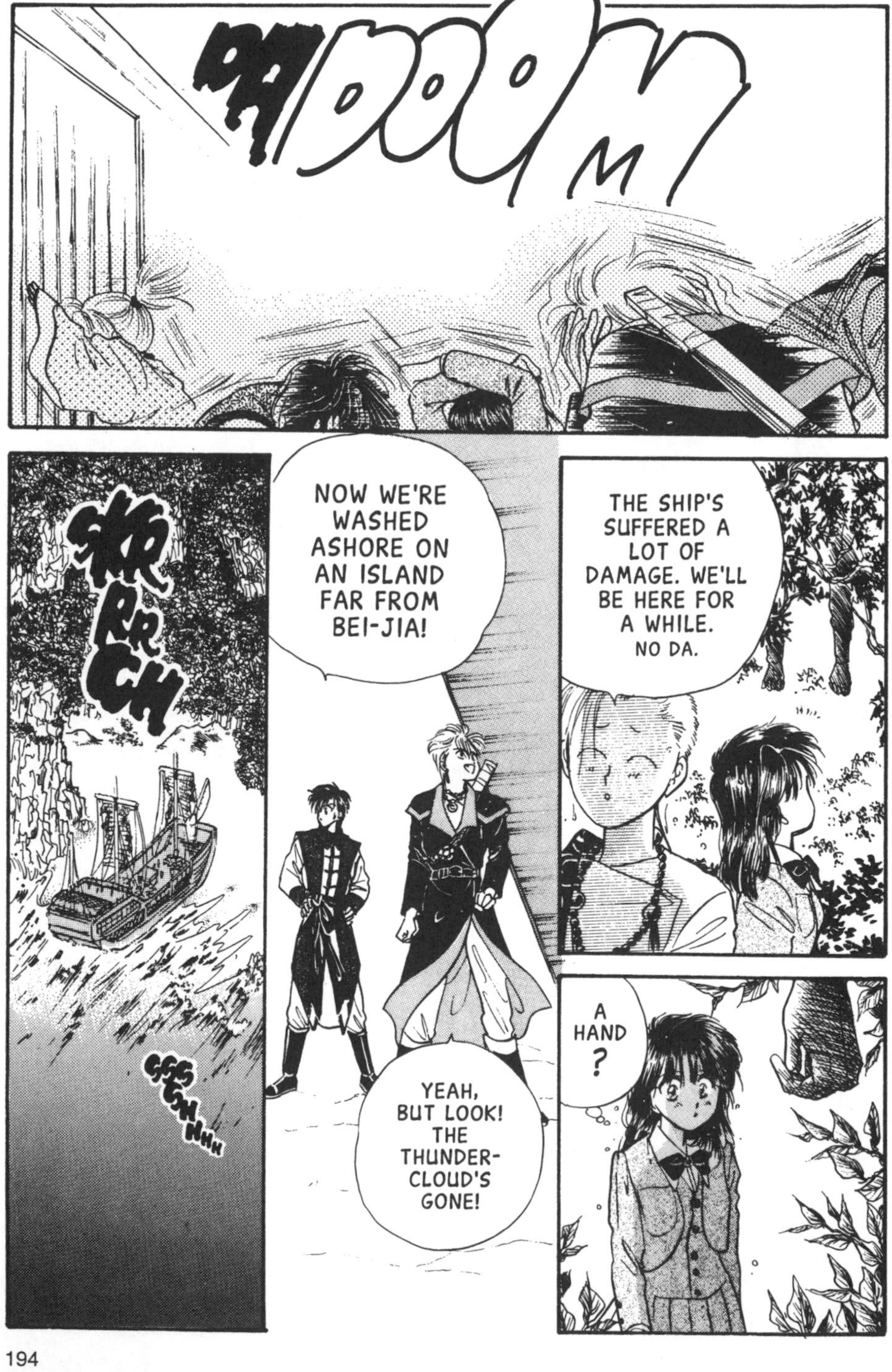
DADOOOMM
SKRRRCH
SSSSHHHH
NOW WE'RE WASHED ASHORE ON AN ISLAND FAR FROM BEI-JIA!
YEAH, BUT LOOK! THE THUNDER-CLOUD'S GONE!
THE SHIP'S SUFFERED A LOT OF DAMAGE. WE'LL BE HERE FOR A WHILE. NO DA.
A HAND?

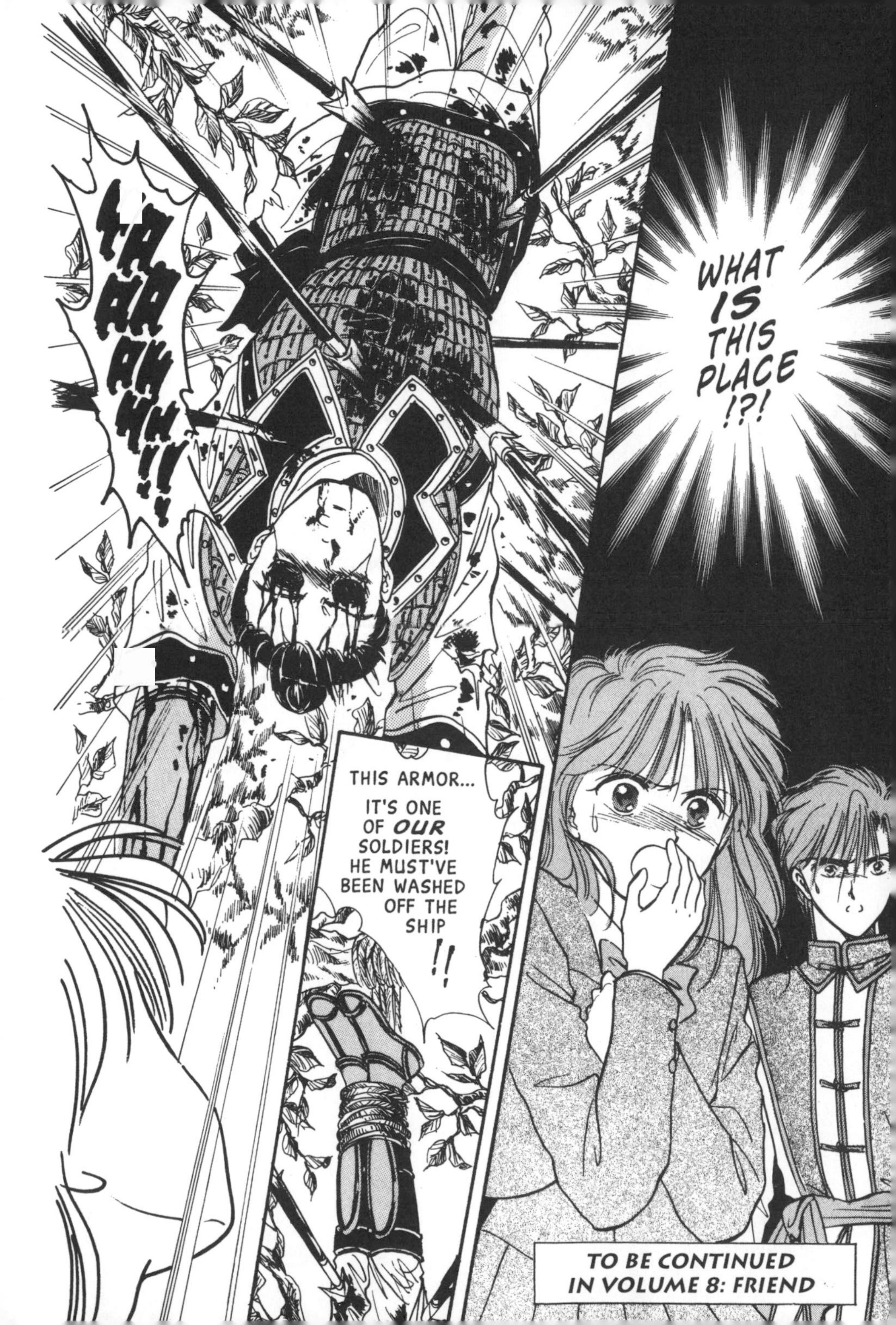
YAAAAAAHHH!!
THIS ARMOR... IT'S ONE OF *OUR* SOLDIERS! HE MUST'VE BEEN WASHED OFF THE SHIP!!
WHAT *IS* THIS PLACE!?!
TO BE CONTINUED IN VOLUME 8: FRIEND

# YÛ WATASE

Yû Watase was born on March 5 in a town near Osaka, and she was raised there before moving to Tokyo to follow the dream of creating manga. In the decade since her debut short story, PAJAMA DE OJAMA ("An Intrusion in Pajamas"), she has produced more than 50 compiled volumes of short stories and continuing series. Her latest series, ALICE 19TH, is currently running in the anthology magazine SHÔJO COMIC. Her long-running horror/romance story CERES: CELESTIAL LEGEND is now available in North America, published by Viz Communications. She loves science fiction, fantasy and comedy.

# MANGA FOR EVERYONE FROM ANIMERICA EXTRA

the anime fan's comic magazine

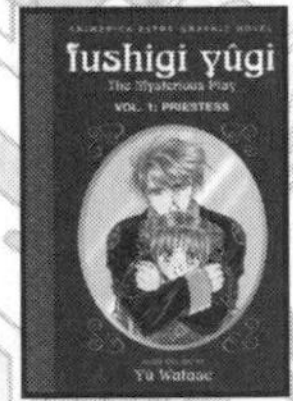
fushigi yûgi
The Mysterious Play
VOL. 1: PRIESTESS
Yû Watase

## FUSHIGI YÛGI

Stranded inside the pages of a magic book, schoolgirl Miaka becomes the Priestess of Suzaku, destined to save a kingdom and find true love!

*story & art by Yû Watase*
*192-200 pages each*

| VOLUME | PRICE | VOLUME | PRICE |
|---|---|---|---|
| Priestess | $15.95 | Rival | $15.95 |
| Oracle | $15.95 | Summoner | $15.95 |
| Disciple | $15.95 | Castaway | $15.95 |
| Bandit | $15.95 | Friend | *coming soon!* |

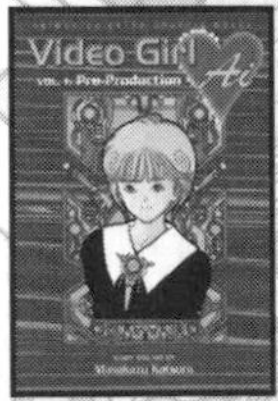
Video Girl Ai
vol. 1: Pre-Production

## VIDEO GIRL AI

When Ai emerged from Yota's VCR, she was supposed to be the girl of his dreams...but Yota will never trust video-box hype again!

*story & art by Masakazu Katsura*
*192-200 pages each*

| VOLUME | PRICE | VOLUME | PRICE |
|---|---|---|---|
| Preproduction | $15.95 | Off-Line | $15.95 |
| Mix Down | $15.95 | Spinoff | *coming soon!* |
| Recall | $15.95 | | |

## X/1999

In the city which is a blueprint for the Earth, the Seven Seals and Seven Harbingers fight for salvation or destruction...but the ultimate fate of the world rests on the young shoulders of super-psychic Kamui!

*story & art by CLAMP*
*184 pages each*

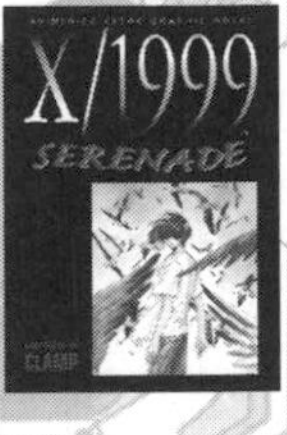
X/1999
SERENADE
CLAMP

| VOLUME | PRICE | VOLUME | PRICE |
|---|---|---|---|
| Prelude | $15.95 | Duet | $15.95 |
| Overture | $15.95 | Rhapsody | $15.95 |
| Sonata | $15.95 | Crescendo | $15.95 |
| Intermezzo | $15.95 | Requiem | *coming soon!* |
| Serenade | $15.95 | | |

## STEAM DETECTIVES

Start the engine! Stoke the fires! A young detective, a pretty nurse, and a giant robot fight crime in the Age of Steam!

*story & art by Kia Asamiya*
*192-208 pages each*

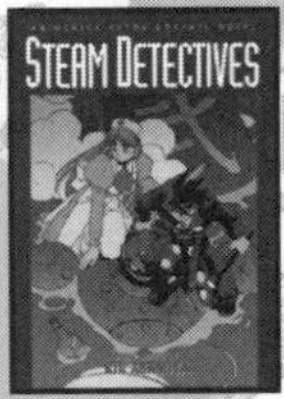
STEAM DETECTIVES

| VOLUME | PRICE | VOLUME | PRICE |
|---|---|---|---|
| 1 | $15.95 | 4 | $15.95 |
| 2 | $15.95 | 5 | $15.95 |
| 3 | $15.95 | 6 | *coming soon!* |

## SHORT PROGRAM

A collection of eight sensitive and surprising short stories from a master of manga storytelling.

*story & art by Mitsuru Adachi*
*256 pages*
*$16.95*

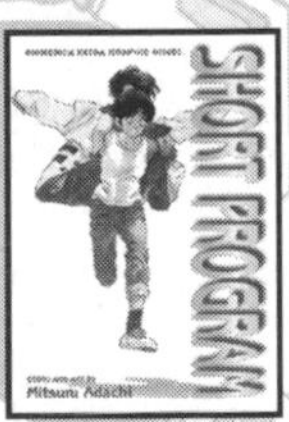
SHORT PROGRAM
Mitsuru Adachi

## MARIONETTE GENERATION

The odd love story of a befuddled artist, his cute-but-demanding assistant, and a living doll by one of Japan's most respected character designers.

*story & art by Haruhiko Mikimoto*
*184 pages each*

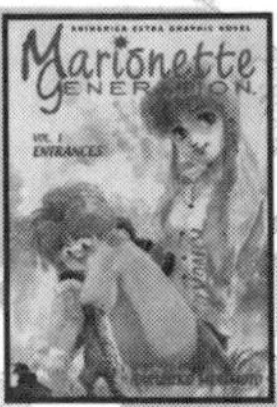
Marionette GENERATION
ENTRANCES

| VOLUME | PRICE | VOLUME | PRICE |
|---|---|---|---|
| Entrances | $15.95 | Manipulations | $14.95 |
| Pulling Strings | $14.95 | Improvisations | *coming soon!* |

## REVOLUTIONARY GIRL UTENA

Beautiful Utena has decided that being a princess is for wimps! She's going to duel all opponants and become a prince!

*manga by Chiho Saito*
*story by Be-Papas*
*200 pages each*

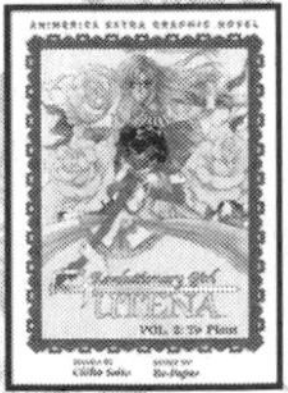
Revolutionary Girl UTENA

| VOLUME | PRICE | VOLUME | PRICE |
|---|---|---|---|
| To Till | $15.95 | To Sprout | *coming soon!* |
| To Plant | $14.95 | | |

## CHICAGO

Rei and and her handsome partner Uozumi search for clues to their would-be murderers while they rescue helpless hostages and kick kidnapper butt!

*story & art by Yumi Tamura*
*200 pages each*

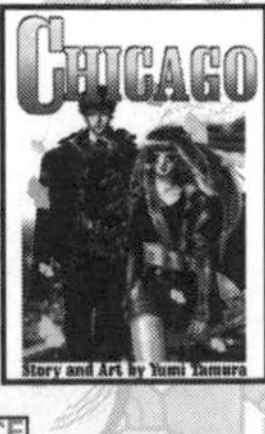
CHICAGO
Story and Art by Yumi Tamura

| VOLUME | PRICE |
|---|---|
| Book of Self | $15.95 |
| Book of Justice | *coming soon!* |

VIZ COMICS™

Viz Comics
P.O. Box 77010
San Francisco, CA 94107

store.viz.com
www.animerica-mag.com
www.viz.com